CLASSIC STORIES
OF
WORLD WAR II

Thunder Bay Press
An imprint of Printers Row Publishing Group
10350 Barnes Canyon Road, Suite 100, San Diego, CA 92121
www.thunderbaybooks.com

Copyright © Octopus Publishing Group Ltd 2018

All rights reserved. No part of this publication may be reproduced, distributed, or transmitted in any form or by any means, including photocopying, recording, or other electronic or mechanical methods, without the prior written permission of the publisher, except in the case of brief quotations embodied in critical reviews and certain other noncommercial uses permitted by copyright law.

Printers Row Publishing Group is a division of Readerlink Distribution Services, LLC. Thunder Bay Press is a registered trademark of Readerlink Distribution Services, LLC.

All notations of errors or omissions should be addressed to Thunder Bay Press, Editorial Department, at the above address. All other correspondence (author inquiries, permissions) concerning the content of this book should be addressed to Bounty Books, a division of Octopus Publishing Group Ltd, Carmelite House, 50 Victoria Embankment, London EC4Y 0DZ
www.octopusbooks.co.uk

Thunder Bay Press:
Publisher: Peter Norton
Associate Publisher: Ana Parker
Publishing/Editorial Team: April Farr, Kelly Larson, Kathryn Chipinka, Aaron Guzman
Editorial Team: JoAnn Padgett, Melinda Allman

Bounty Books:
Publisher: Lucy Pessell
Designer: Lisa Layton
Editor: Sarah Vaughan
Senior Production Manager: Peter Hunt

Acknowledgements for each story or excerpt can be found on page 256.

Library of Congress Cataloging-in-Publication Data is available upon request.

ISBN: 978-1-68412-422-0

Printed in China

22 21 20 19 18   1 2 3 4 5

CLASSIC STORIES
OF
WORLD WAR II

San Diego, California

Contents

A Perfect Morning
(from *The Young Lions*)

Irwin Shaw

The Platoon Lieutenant had been killed in the morning and Christian was in command when the order came to fall back. The Americans had not been pushing much and the battalion had been beautifully situated on a hill overlooking a battered village of two dozen houses in which three Italian families grimly continued to live.

"I have begun to understand how the Army operates," Christian heard a voice complain in the dark, as the platoon clanked along, scuffling in the dust. "A Colonel comes down and makes an examination. Then he goes back to Headquarters and reports. 'General,' he says, 'I am happy to report that the men have warm, dry quarters, in safe positions which can only be destroyed by direct hits. They have finally begun to get their food regularly, and the mail is delivered three times a week. The Americans understand that their position is impregnable and do not attempt any activity at all.' 'Ah, good,' says the General. 'We shall retreat.'"

Christian recognized the voice. Private Dehn, he noted down silently for future reference.

He marched dully, the Schmeisser on its sling already becoming a nagging burden on his shoulder. He was always tired these days, and the malaria headaches and chills kept coming back, too mildly to warrant hospitalization, but wearying and unsettling. Going back, his boots seemed to sound as he limped in the dust, going back, going back…

At least, he thought heavily, we don't have to worry about the planes in the dark. That pleasure would be reserved for later, when the sun came up. Probably back near Foggia, in a warm room, a young American lieutenant was sitting down to a breakfast of grapefruit juice, oatmeal, ham and eggs, and real coffee with cream, preparing to climb into his plane a little later and come skimming over the hills, his guns spitting at the black, scattered blur of men, crouched insecurely in shallow holes along the road, that would be Christian and the platoon.

As he plodded on, Christian hated the Americans. He hated them more for the ham and eggs and the real coffee than for the bullets and the planes. Cigarettes, too, he thought. Along with everything else, they have all the cigarettes they want. How could you beat a country that had all those cigarettes?

His tongue ached for the healing smoke of a cigarette. But he had only two cigarettes in his packet and he had rationed himself to one a day.

Christian thought of the faces of the American pilots he had seen, men who had been shot down behind the German lines and had waited to be taken, insolently smoking cigarettes, with arrogant smiles on their empty, untouched faces. Next time, he thought, next time I see one of them, I'm going to shoot him, no matter what the orders are.

Then he stumbled in a rut. He cried out as the pain knotted in his knee and hip.

"Are you all right, Sergeant?" asked the man behind him.

"Don't worry about me," Christian said. "Stay on the side of the road?"

He limped on, not thinking about anything any more, except the road in front of him.

The runner from the battalion was waiting at the bridge, as Christian had been told he would.

The platoon had been walking for two hours, and it was broad daylight by now. They had heard planes, on the other side of the small range of hills the platoon had been skirting, but they had not been attacked.

The runner was a corporal, who had hidden himself nervously in the ditch alongside the road. The ditch had six inches of water in it, but the Corporal had preferred safety to comfort, and he rose from the ditch muddy and wet. There was a squad of Pioneers on the other side of the bridge, waiting to mine it after Christian's platoon had gone through. It was not much of a bridge, and the ravine, which it crossed, was dry and smooth. Blowing the bridge wouldn't delay anyone more than a minute or two, but the Pioneers doggedly blew everything blowable, as though they were carrying out some ancient religious ritual.

"You're late," said the Corporal nervously. "I was afraid something had happened to you."

"Nothing has happened to us," said Christian shortly.

"Very well," said the Corporal. "It's only another three kilometres. The Captain is going to meet us, and he will show you where you are to dig in." He looked around nervously. The Corporal always looked like a man who expects to be shot by a sniper, caught in an open field by a strafing plane, exposed on a hill to a direct hit by an artillery shell. Looking at him, Christian was certain that the Corporal was going to be killed very shortly.

Christian gestured to the men and they started over the bridge behind the Corporal. Good, Christian thought dully, another three kilometres and then the Captain can start making decisions. The squad of Pioneers regarded them thoughtfully from their ditch, without love or malice.

Christian crossed the bridge and stopped. The men behind him halted automatically. Almost mechanically, without any conscious will on his part, his eye began to calculate certain distances, probable approaches, fields of fire.

"The Captain is waiting for us," said the Corporal, peering shiftily past the platoon, down the road on which later in the day the Americans would appear. "What are you stopping for?"

"Keep quiet," Christian said. He walked back across the bridge. He stood in the middle of the road, looking back. For a hundred metres the road went straight, then curved back round a hill, out of sight. Christian turned again and stared through the morning haze at the road and the hills before them. The road wound in mounting curves through the stony, sparsely shrubbed hills in that direction. Far off, eight hundred, a thousand metres away, on an almost cliff-like drop, there was an outcropping of boulders. Among those boulders, his mind registered automatically, it would be possible to set up a machine-gun and it would also be possible to sweep the bridge and its approach from there.

The Corporal was at his elbow. "I do not wish to annoy you, Sergeant," the Corporal said, his voice quivering, "but the Captain was specific. 'No delays, at all,' he said. 'I will not take any excuses.'"

"Keep quiet," said Christian.

The Corporal started to say something. Then he thought better of it. He swallowed and rubbed his mouth with his hand. He stood at the first stone of the bridge and stared unhappily towards the south.

Christian walked slowly down the side of the ravine to the dry stream-bed below. About ten metres back from the bridge, he noticed, his mind still working automatically, the slope leading down from the road was quite gentle, with no deep holes or boulders. Under the bridge the stream-bed was sandy and soft, with scattered worn stones and straggling undergrowth.

It could be done, Christian thought. It would be simple. He climbed slowly up to the road again. The platoon had cautiously got off the bridge by now and were standing at the edge of the road on the other side, ready to jump into the Pioneers' ditches at the sound of an aeroplane.

Like rabbits, Christian thought resentfully, we don't live like human beings at all.

The Corporal was jiggling nervously up and down at the entrance to the bridge. "All right, now, Sergeant?" he asked. "Can we start now?"

Christian ignored him. Once more he stared down the straight hundred metres towards the turn in the road. He half closed his eyes and he could almost imagine how the first American, flat on his belly, would peer around the bend to make sure nothing was waiting for him. Then the head would disappear. Then another head, probably a lieutenant's (the American Army seemed to have an unlimited number of lieutenants they were willing to throw away), would appear. Then, slowly, sticking to the side of the hill, peering nervously down at their feet for mines, the squad, or platoon, even the company would come around the bend, and approach the bridge.

Christian turned and looked again at the clump of boulders high up on the cliff-like side of the hill a thousand metres on the other side of the bridge. He was almost certain that from there, apart from being able to command the approach to the bridge and the bridge itself, he could observe the road to the south where it wound through the smaller hills they had just come through. He would be able to see the Americans for a considerable distance before they moved behind the hill from which they would have to emerge on the curve of the road that led up to the bridge.

He nodded his head slowly, as the plan, full-grown and thoroughly worked out, as though it had been fashioned by someone else and presented to him, arranged itself in his mind. He walked swiftly across the bridge. He went over to the Sergeant who was in command of the Pioneers.

The Pioneer Sergeant was looking at him inquisitively. "Do you intend to spend the winter on this bridge, Sergeant?" the Pioneer said.

"Have you put the charges under the bridge yet?" Christian asked.

"Everything's ready," said the Pioneer. "One minute after you're past we light the fuse. I don't know what you think you're doing, but I don't mind telling you you're making me nervous, parading up and down this way. The Americans may be along at any minute and then…"

"Have you a long fuse?" Christian asked. "One that would take, say, fifteen minutes to burn?"

"I have," said the Pioneer, "but that isn't what we're going to use. We have a one-minute fuse on the charges. Just long enough so that the man who sets them can get out of the way."

"Take it off," said Christian, "and put the long fuse on."

"Listen," said the Pioneer, "your job is to take these scarecrows back over my bridge. My job is to blow it up. I won't tell you what to do with your platoon, you don't tell me what to do with my bridge."

Christian stared silently at the Sergeant. He was a short man who miraculously had remained fat. He looked like the sort of fat man who also had a bad stomach, and his air was testy and superior. "I will also require ten of those mines," Christian said, with a gesture towards the mines piled haphazardly near the edge of the road.

"I am putting those mines in the road on the other side of the bridge," said the Pioneer.

"The Americans will come up with their detectors and pick them up one by one," said Christian.

"That's not my business," said the Pioneer sullenly. "I was told to put them in here and I am going to put them in here."

"I will stay here with my platoon," said Christian, "and make sure you don't put them in the road."

"Listen, Sergeant," said the Pioneer, his voice shivering in excitement, "this is no time for an argument. The Americans…"

"Pick those mines up," Christian said to the squad of Pioneers, "and follow me."

"See here," said the Pioneer in a high, pained voice, "I give orders to this squad, not you."

"Then tell them to pick up those mines and come with me," said Christian coldly, trying to sound as much like Lieutenant Hardenburg as possible. "I'm waiting," he said sharply.

The Pioneer was panting in anger and fear now, and he had caught the Corporal's habit of peering every few seconds towards the bend, to see if the Americans had appeared yet. "All right, all right," he said. "It doesn't mean anything to me. How many mines did you say you want?"

"Ten," said Christian.

"The trouble with this Army," grumbled the Pioneer, "is that there are too many people in it who think they know how to win the war all by themselves." But he snapped at his men to pick up the mines, and Christian led them down into the ravine and showed them where he wanted them placed. He made the men cover the holes carefully with brush and carry away in their helmets the sand they had dug up.

Even while he supervised the men down below, he noticed, with a grim smile, that the Pioneer Sergeant himself was attaching the long fuses to the small, innocent-looking charges of dynamite under the span of the bridge.

"All right," said the Pioneer gloomily, when Christian came up on the road again, the mines having been placed to his satisfaction, "the fuse is on. I do not know what you are trying to do, but I put it on to please you. Now, should I light it now?"

"Now," said Christian, "please get out of here."

"It is my duty," said the Pioneer pompously, "to blow up this bridge and I shall see personally that it is blown up."

"I do not want the fuse lighted," Christian said, quite pleasantly now, "until the Americans are almost here. If you wish personally to stay under the bridge until that time, I personally welcome you."

"This is not a time for jokes," said the Pioneer with dignity.

"Get out, get out," Christian shouted at the top of his voice, fiercely, menacingly, remembering with what good affect Hardenburg had used that trick. "I don't want to see you here one minute from now. Get back or you're going to get hurt!" He stood close to the Pioneer, towering ferociously above him, his hands twitching, as though he could barely restrain himself from knocking the Pioneer senseless where he stood.

The Pioneer backed away, his pudgy face paling under his helmet. "Strain," he said hoarsely. "No doubt you have been under an enormous strain in the line. No doubt you are not quite yourself."

"Fast!" said Christian.

The Pioneer turned hurriedly and strode back to where his squad was again assembled on the other side of the bridge. He spoke briefly, in a low voice, and the squad clambered up from the ditch. Without a backward glance they started down the road. Christian watched them for a moment, but did not smile, as he felt like doing, because that might ruin the healthful effect of the episode on his own men.

"Sergeant." It was the Corporal, the runner from battalion, again, his voice drier and higher than ever. "The Captain is waiting…"

Christian wheeled on the Corporal. He grabbed the man's collar and held him close to him. The man's eyes were yellow and glazed with fright.

"One more word from you," Christian shook him roughly, and the man's helmet clicked painfully down over his eyes, on to the bridge of his nose. "One more word and I will shoot you." He pushed him away.

"Dehn!" Christian called. A single figure slowly broke away from the platoon on the other side of the bridge and came towards Christian. "Come with me," said

Christian when Dehn had reached him. Christian half-slid, half-walked down the side of the ravine, carefully avoiding the small minefield he and the Pioneers had laid. He pointed to the long fuse that ran from the dynamite charge down the northern side of the arch.

"You will wait here," he said to the silent soldier standing beside him, "and when I give the signal, you will light that fuse."

Christian heard the deep intake of breath as Dehn looked at the fuse. "Where will you be, Sergeant?" he asked.

Christian pointed up the mountain to the outcropping of boulders about eight hundred metres away. "Up there. Those boulders below the point where the road turns. Can you see it?"

There was a long pause. "I can see it," Dehn whispered finally.

The boulders glittered, their colour washed out by distance, and sunlight, against the dry green of the cliff. "I will wave my coat," said Christian. "You will have to watch carefully. You will then set the fuse and make sure it is going. You will have plenty of time. Then get out on the road and run until the next turn. Then wait until you hear the explosion here. Then follow along the road until you reach us."

Dehn nodded dully. "I am to be all alone down here?" he asked.

"No," said Christian, "we will supply you with two ballet dancers and a guitar player."

Dehn did not smile.

"Is it clear now?" Christian asked.

"Yes, Sergeant," said Dehn.

"Good," Christian said. "If you set off the fuse before you see my coat, don't bother coming back."

Dehn did not answer. He was a large, slow-moving young man who had been a stevedore before the war, and Christian suspected that he had once belonged to the Communist party.

Christian took a last look at his arrangements under the bridge, and at Dehn standing stolidly, leaning against the curved, damp stone of the arch. Then he climbed up to the road again. Next time, Christian thought grimly, that soldier would be less free with criticism.

It took fifteen minutes, walking swiftly, to reach the clump of boulders overlooking the road. Christian was panting hoarsely by the time he got there. The men behind him marched doggedly, as though resigned to the fact that they were doomed to march, bent under their weight of iron, for the rest of their lives. There was no trouble about straggling, because it was plain to even the stupidest man in the platoon that if the Americans got to the bridge before the platoon turned away out of sight behind the boulders, the platoon would present a fair target, even at a great distance, to the pursuers.

Christian stopped, listening to his own harsh breathing, and peered down into the valley. The bridge was small, peaceful, and insignificant in the winding dust of the road. There was no movement to be seen anywhere, and the long miles of broken valley seemed deserted, forgotten, lost to human use.

Christian smiled as he saw that his guess had been right about the vantage point of the boulders. Through a cut in the hills it was possible to see a section of the road some distance from the bridge. The Americans would have to cross that before they disappeared momentarily from sight behind a spur of rock, around which they would then have to turn and appear again on the way to the bridge.

Even if they were going slowly and cautiously, it would not take them more than ten or twelve minutes to cover the distance, from the spot at which they would first come into sight, to the bridge itself.

"Heims," Christian said, "Richter. You stay with me. The rest of you go back with the Corporal." He turned to the Corporal. The Corporal now looked like a man who expects to be killed, but feels that there is a ten per cent chance he may postpone the moment of execution till tomorrow. "Tell the Captain," Christian said, "we will get back as soon as we can."

"Yes, Sergeant," the Corporal said, nervous and happy. He started walking, almost trotting, to the blessed safety of the turn in the road. Christian watched the platoon file by him, following the Corporal. The road was high on the side of the hill now. When they walked the men were outlined heroically and sadly against the shreds of cloud and wintry blue sky, and when they made their turns, one by one, in towards the hill, they seemed to step off into windy blue space. Heims and Richter were a machine-gun team. They were standing heavily, leaning against the roadside boulders, Heims holding the barrel and a box of ammunition, and Richter sweating under the base and more ammunition. They were dependable men, but, looking at them standing there, sweating in the cold, their faces cautious but non-committal, Christian felt suddenly that he would have preferred, at this moment, to have with him now the men of his old platoon, dead these long months in the African desert. He hadn't thought about his old platoon for a long time, but somehow, looking at the two machine-gunners, left behind on another hill this way, brought to mind the night more than a year before when the thirty-six men had thoughtfully and obediently dug the lonely holes which would a little later be their graves.

Somehow, looking at Heims and Richter, he felt that these men could not be depended upon to do their jobs as well. They belonged, by some slight, subtle deterioration in quality, to another army, an army whose youth had left it, an army that seemed, with all its experience, to have become more civilian, less willing to die. If he left the two men now, Christian thought, they would not stay at their posts for long. Christian shook his head. Ah, he thought, I am getting silly. They're probably fine. God knows what they think of me.

The two men leaned, thickly relaxed against the stones, their eyes warily on Christian, as though they were measuring him and trying to discover whether he was going to ask them to die this morning.

"Set it up here," Christian said, pointing to a level spot between two of the boulders, which made a rough "V" at their joining. Slowly but expertly the men set up the machine-gun.

When the gun was set up, Christian crouched down behind it and traversed it. He shifted it a little to the right and peered down the barrel. He adjusted the sight for the distance, allowing for the fact that they would be shooting downhill. Far below, caught on the fine iron line of the sight, the bridge lay in sunlight that changed momentarily to shadow as rags of cloud ghosted across the sky.

"Give them plenty of chance to bunch up near the bridge," Christian said. "They won't cross it fast, because they'll think it's mined. When I give you the signal to fire, aim at the men in the rear, not at the ones near the bridge. Do you understand?"

"The ones in the rear," Heims repeated. "Not the ones near the bridge." He moved the machine-gun slowly up and down on its rocker. He sucked reflectively at his teeth. "You want them to run forward, not back in the direction they are coming from…"

Christian nodded.

"They won't run across the bridge, because they are in the open there," said Heims thoughtfully. "They will run for the ravine, under the bridge, because they are out of the field of fire there."

Christian smiled. Perhaps he had been wrong about Heims, he thought, he certainly knew what he was doing here.

"Then they will run into the mines down there," said Heims flatly. "I see."

He and Richter nodded at each other. There was neither approval nor disapproval in their gesture. Christian took off his coat, so that he would be able to wave in it signal to Dehn, under the bridge, as soon as he saw the enemy. Then he sat on a stone behind Heims, who was sprawled out behind the gun. Richter knelt on one knee, waiting with a second belt of cartridges. Christian lifted the binoculars he had taken from the dead lieutenant the evening before. He fixed them on the break between the hills. He focused them carefully, noticing that they were good glasses.

There were two poplar trees, dark green and funereal, at the break in the road. They swayed glossily with the wind. It was cold on the exposed side of the hill, and Christian was sorry he had told Dehn he would wave his coat at him. He could have done with his coat now. A handkerchief would probably have been good enough. He could feel his skin contracting in the cold and he hunched inside his stiff clothes uncomfortably.

"Can we smoke, Sergeant?" Richter asked.

"No," said Christian, without lowering the glasses. Neither of the men said anything. Cigarettes, thought Christian, remembering, I'll bet he has a whole packet, two packets. If he gets killed or badly wounded in this, Christian thought, I must remember to look through his pockets.

They waited. The wind, sweeping up from the valley, circled weightily within Christian's ears and up his nostrils and inside his sinuses. His head began to ache, especially around the eyes. He was very sleepy. He felt that he had been sleepy for three years.

Heims stirred, as he lay outstretched, belly down, on the rock bed in front of Christian. Christian put down the glasses for a moment. The seat of Heims's trousers, blackened by mud, crudely patched, wide and shapeless, stared up at him. It is a sight, Christian thought foolishly, repressing a tendency to giggle, a sight completely lacking in beauty. The human form divine.

His forehead burned. The malaria. Not enough the English, not enough the French, the Poles, the Russians, the Americans, but the mosquitoes, too. Perhaps, he thought feverishly and cunningly, perhaps when this is over, I will have a real attack, one that cannot be denied, and they will have to send me back. He raised the glasses once more to his eyes, waiting for the chills to come, inviting the toxin in his blood to gain control.

Then he saw the small mud-coloured figures slowly plodding in front of the poplars. "Quiet," he said warningly, as though the Americans could hear Heims and the other man if they happened to speak.

The mud-coloured figures, looking like a platoon in any army, the fatigue of their movement visible even at this distance, passed in two lines, on each side of the road, across the binoculars' field of vision. Thirty-seven, thirty-eight, forty-two, forty-three, Christian counted. Then they were gone. The poplars waved as they had waved before, the road in front of them looked exactly the same as it had before. Christian put down the glasses. He felt wide-awake now, unexcited.

He stood up and waved his coat in large, deliberate circles. He could imagine the Americans moving in their cautious, slow way along the edge of the ridge, their eyes always nervously down on the ground, looking for mines.

A moment later he saw Dehn scramble swiftly out from beneath the bridge and run heavily up to the road. Dehn ran along the road, slowing down perceptibly as he tired, his boots kicking up minute puffs of dust. Then he reached a turn and he was out of sight. Now the fuse was set. It only remained for the enemy to behave in a normal, soldierly manner.

Christian put on his coat, grateful for the warmth. He plunged his hands in his pockets, feeling cozy and calm. The two men at the machine-gun lay absolutely still. Far off there was the drone of plane engines. High, to the south- west, Christian saw a formation of bombers moving slowly, small specks in the sky, moving north on a bombing mission. A pair of sparrows swept, chirping, across the face of the cliff, darting in a flicker of swift brown feathers across the sights of the gun.

Heims belched twice. "Excuse me," he said politely. They waited. Too long, Christian thought anxiously, they're taking too long. What are they doing back there? The bridge will go up before they get to the bend. Then the whole thing will be useless.

Heims belched again. "My stomach," he said aggrievedly to Richter.

Richter nodded, staring down at the magazine on the gun, as though he had heard about Heims's stomach for years.

Hardenburg, Christian thought, would have done this better. He wouldn't have gambled like this. He would have made more certain, one way or another. If the dynamite didn't go off, and the bridge wasn't blown, and they heard about it back at Division, and they questioned that miserable Sergeant in the Pioneers and he told them about Christian…Please, Christian prayed under his breath, come on, come on, come on…

Christian kept the glasses trained on the approach to the bridge. The glasses shook, and he knew that the chills were coming, although he did not feel them at that moment. There was a rushing, tiny noise, near him, and, involuntarily, he put the glasses down. A squirrel scurried up to the top of a rock ten feet away, then sat up and stared with beady, forest eyes at the three men. Another time, another place, Christian remembered, the bird strutting on the road through the woods outside Paris, before the French road-block, the overturned farm cart and the mattresses. The animal kingdom, curious for a moment about the war, then returning to its more important business.

Christian blinked and put the glasses to his eyes again. The enemy were out on the road now, walking slowly, crouched over, their rifles ready, every tense line shouting that their flesh inside their vulnerable clothing understood that they were targets.

The Americans were unbearably slow. They were taking infinitely small steps, stopping every five paces. The dashing, reckless young men of the New World. Christian had seen captured newsreels of them in training, leaping boldly through rolling surf from landing barges, flooding on to a beach like so many sprinters. They were not sprinting now. "Faster, faster," he found himself whispering, "faster…" What lies the American people must believe about their soldiers!

Heims belched. It was a rasping, ugly, old man's noise. Each man reacted to a war in his own way, and Heims's reaction was from the stomach. What lies the people at home believed about Heims and his comrades. *What were you doing when you won the Iron Cross? Mother, I was belching.* Only Heims and he and Richter knew what the truth was, only they and the forty-three men tenderly approaching the old stone of the bridge that had been put up by slow Italian labourers in the sunlight of 1840. They knew the truth, the machine-gunners and himself, and the forty-three men shuffling through the dust across the gun-sights eight hundred metres away, and they were more connected by that truth than to anyone else who wasn't there that morning. They knew of each other that their stomachs were contracting in sour spasms, and that all bridges are approached with timidity and a sense of doom…

Christian licked his lips. The last man was out from behind the bend now, and the officer in command, the inevitable childish Lieutenant, was waving to a man with the mine detector, who was moving regretfully up towards the head of the column. Slowly, foolishly, they were bunching, feeling a little safer closer together now, feeling that if they hadn't been shot yet they were going to get through this all right.

The man with the mine detector began to sweep the road twenty metres in front of the bridge. He worked slowly and very carefully, and as he worked, Christian could see the Lieutenant, standing in the middle of the road, put his binoculars to his eyes and begin to sweep the country all around him. Zeiss binoculars, no doubt, Christian's mind registered automatically, made in Germany. He could see the binoculars come up and almost fix on their boulders, as though some nervous, latent military sense in the young Lieutenant recognized instinctively that if there were any danger ahead of him, this would be the focus of it. Christian crouched a little lower; although he was certain that they were securely hidden. The binoculars passed over them, and then wavered back.

"Fire," Christian whispered. "Behind them. Behind them."

The machine-gun opened up. It made an insane, shocking noise as it broke the mountain stillness, and Christian couldn't help blinking again and again. Down on the road two of the men had fallen. The others were still standing there stupidly, looking down in surprise at the men on the ground. Three more men fell on the road. Then the others began to run down the slope towards the ravine and the protection of the bridge. They are sprinting now, Christian thought, where is the camera-man? Some were carrying and dragging the men who had been hit. They stumbled and rolled down the slope, their rifles thrown away, their arms and legs waving grotesquely. It was remote and disconnected, and Christian watched almost disinterestedly, as though he were watching the struggle of a beetle dragged down into a hole by ants.

Then the first mine went off. A helmet hurtled end over end, twenty metres straight up in the air, glinting dully in the sunlight, its straps whipping in its flight.

Heims stopped firing. Then the explosions came one on top of another, echoing and re-echoing along the walls of the hills. A large dirty cloud of dust and smoke bloomed from the bridge.

The noise of the explosions died slowly, as though the sound was moving heavily through the draws and along the ridges to collect in other places. The silence, when it came, seemed unnatural, dangerous. The two sparrows wheeled erratically, disturbed and scolding, across the gun. Down below, from beneath the arch of the bridge, a single figure came walking out, very slowly and gravely, like a doctor from a deathbed. The figure walked five or six metres, and then just as slowly sat down on a rock. Christian looked at the man through his glasses. The man's shirt had been blown off him, and his skin was pale and milky. He still had his rifle. While Christian watched, the man lifted his rifle, still with that lunatic deliberation and gravity. Why, thought Christian with surprise, he's aiming at us!

The sound of the rifle was empty and flat and the whistle of the bullets was surprisingly close over their heads. Christian grinned. "Finish him," he said.

Heims pressed the trigger of the machine-gun. Through his glasses, Christian could see the darting spurts of dust, flickering along a savage, swift line in an area around the man. He did not move. Slowly, with the unhurried care of a carpenter at his workbench, he was putting a new clip in his rifle. Heims swung the machine-gun, and the arc of dust splashes moved closer to the man, who still refused to notice them. He got the clip in his rifle and lifted it once more to his naked shoulder. There was something insane, disturbing, about the shirtless, white-skinned man, an ivory blob against the green and brown of the ravine, sitting comfortably on the stone with all his comrades dead around him, firing in the leisurely and deliberate way at the machine-gun he could not quite make out with his naked eye, paying no attention to the continuous, snapping bursts of bullets that would, in a moment or two, finally kill him.

"Hit him," Christian murmured irritably. "Come on, hit him."

Heims stopped firing for a moment. He squinted carefully and jiggled the gun.

It made a sharp, piercing squeak. The sound of the rifle came from the valley below, meaningless and undangerous, although again and again there was the whine of a bullet over Christian's head, or the plunk as it hit the hard-packed dirt below him.

Then Heims got the range and fired one short burst. The man put down his gun drunkenly. He stood up slowly and took two or three sober steps in the direction of the bridge. Then he lay down as though he were tired.

At that moment, the bridge went up. Chunks of stone spattered against the trees along the road, slicing white gashes in them and knocking branches off. It took a long time for the dust to settle, and when it did, Christian saw the lumpy, broken mud-coloured uniforms sticking out here and there, at odd angles from the debris. The half- naked American had disappeared under a small avalanche of earth and stones.

Christian sighed and put down his glasses. Amateurs, he thought, what are they doing in a war?

Heims sat up and twisted round. "Can we smoke now?" he asked. "Yes," said Christian, "you can smoke." He watched Heims take out a packet of cigarettes. Heims offered one to Richter, who took it silently. The machine-gunner did not offer a cigarette to Christian. The miserly bastard, thought Christian bitterly, and reached in and took out one of his two remaining cigarettes.

He held the cigarette in his mouth, tasting it, feeling its roundness for a long time before he lit it. Then, with a sigh, feeling, well, I've earned it, he lit the cigarette. He took a deep puff and held the smoke in his lungs as long as he could. It made him feel a little dizzy, but relaxed. I must write about this to Hardenburg, Christian thought, taking another pull at the cigarette, he'll be pleased; he wouldn't have been able to do better himself. He leaned back comfortably, taking a deep breath, smiling at the bright blue sky and the pretty little clouds racing overhead in the mountain wind, knowing that he would have at least ten minutes to rest before Dehn got there. What a pretty morning, he thought.

Then he felt the long, quivering shiver sliding down his body. Ah, he thought deliciously, the malaria, and this is going to be a real attack, they're bound to send me back. A perfect morning. He shivered again, then took another pull at his cigarette. Then he leaned back happily against the boulder at his back, waiting for Dehn to arrive, hoping Dehn would take his time climbing the slope.

Lunghua Camp
(from *Empire of the Sun*)

J. G. Ballard

Voices fretted along the murmuring wire, carried like stressed notes on the strings of a harp. Fifty feet from the perimeter fence, Jim lay in the deep grass beside the pheasant trap. He listened to the guards arguing with each other as they conducted their hourly patrol of the camp. Now that the American air attacks had become a daily event, the Japanese soldiers no longer slung their rifles over their shoulders. They clasped the long-barrelled weapons in both hands, and were so nervous that if they saw Jim outside the camp perimeter they would shoot at him without thinking.

Jim watched them through the netting of the pheasant trap. Only the previous day they had shot a Chinese coolie trying to steal into the camp. He recognized one of the guards as Private Kimura, a large-boned farmer's son who had grown almost as much as Jim in his years at the camp. The private's strong back had burst through his faded tunic, and only his ammunition webbing held the tattered garment together.

Before the war finally turned against the Japanese, Private Kimura often invited Jim to the bungalow he shared with three other guards and allowed him to wear his kendo armour. Jim could remember the elaborate ceremony as the Japanese soldiers dressed him in the metal and leather armour, and the ripe smell of Private Kimura's body that filled the helmet and shoulder guards. He remembered the burst of violence as Private Kimura attacked him with the two-handed sword, the whirlwind of blows that struck his helmet before he could fight back. His head had rung for days. Giving him his orders, Basie had been forced to shout until he woke the men's dormitory in E Block, and Dr Ransome had called Jim into the camp hospital and examined his ears.

Remembering those powerful arms, and the quickness of Private Kimura's eyes, Jim lay flat in the long grass behind the trap. For once he was glad that the trap had failed to net a bird. The two Japanese had stopped by the wire fence and were scanning the group of abandoned buildings that lay outside the north-west perimeter of Lunghua Camp. Beside them, just within the camp, was the derelict hulk of the assembly hall, the curved balcony of its upper circle open to the sky. The camp occupied the site of a teacher training college that had been bombed and overrun during the fighting around Lunghua Aerodrome in 1937. The damaged buildings nearest to the airfield had been excluded from the camp, and it was here, in the long grass quadrangles between the gutted residence halls, that Jim set his pheasant traps. After roll-call that morning he had slipped through the fence where it emerged from a bank of nettles surrounding a forgotten blockhouse on the airfield perimeter. Leaving his shoes on the blockhouse steps, he waded along a shallow canal, and then crawled through the deep grass between the ruined buildings.

The first of the traps was only a few feet from the perimeter fence, a distance that had seemed enormous to Jim when he first crept through the barbed wire. He had looked back at the secure world of the camp, at the barrack huts and water tower, at the guardhouse and dormitory blocks, almost afraid that he had been banished from them forever. Dr Ransome often called Jim a "free spirit," as he roved across the camp, hunting down some new idea in his head. But here, in the deep grass between the ruined buildings, he felt weighted by an unfamiliar gravity.

For once making the most of this inertia, Jim lay behind the trap. An aircraft was taking off from Lunghua Airfield, clearly silhouetted against the yellow facade of the apartment houses in the French Concession, but he ignored the plane. The soldier beside Private Kimura shouted to the children playing in the balcony of the assembly hall. Kimura was walking back to the wire. He scanned the surface of the canal and the clumps of wild sugar cane. The poor rations of the past year—the Japanese guards were almost as badly fed as their British and American prisoners—had drawn the last of the adolescent fat from Kimura's arms. After a recent attack of tuberculosis his strong face was puffy and coolie-like. Dr Ransome had repeatedly warned Jim never to wear Private Kimura's kendo armour. A fight between them would be less one-sided now, even though Jim was only fourteen. But for the rifle, he would have liked to challenge Kimura...

As if aware of the threat within the grass, Private Kimura called to his companion. He leaned his rifle against the pine fencing-post, stepped through the wire and stood in the deep nettles. Flies rose from the shallow canal and settled on his lips, but Kimura ignored them and stared at the strip of water that separated him from Jim and the pheasant traps.

Could he see Jim's footprints in the soft mud? Jim crawled away from the trap but the clear outline of his body lay in the crushed grass. Kimura was rolling his tattered sleeves, ready to wrestle with his quarry. Jim watched him stride through the nettles. He was certain that he could outrun Kimura, but not the bullet in the second soldier's rifle. How could he explain to Kimura that the pheasant traps had been Basie's idea? It was Basie who had insisted on the elaborate camouflage of leaves and twigs, and who made him climb through the wire twice a day, even though they had never seen a bird, let alone caught one. It was important to keep in with Basie, who had small but reliable sources of food. He could tell Kimura that Basie knew about the secret camp radio, but then the extra food would cease.

What most worried Jim was the thought that, if Kimura struck him, he would fight back. Few boys of his own age dared to touch Jim, and in the last year, since the rations had failed, few men. However, if he fought back against Kimura he would be dead.

He calmed himself, calculating the best moment to stand up and surrender. He would bow to Kimura, show no emotion and hope that the hundreds of hours he had spent hanging around the guardhouse—albeit at Basie's instigation—would count in his favour. He had once given English lessons to Kimura, but although they were clearly losing the war, the Japanese had not been interested in learning English.

Jim waited for Kimura to climb the bank towards him. The soldier stood in the centre of the canal, a bright black object gleaming in his hand. The creeks, ponds and disused wells within Lunghua Camp held an armoury of rusting weapons and unstable ammunition abandoned during the 1937 hostilities. Jim peered through the grass at the pointed cylinder, assuming that the tidal water in the canal had uncovered an old artillery shell or mortar bomb.

Kimura shouted to the second soldier waiting by the barbed wire. He brushed the flies from his face and spoke to the object, as if murmuring to a baby. He raised it behind his head, in the position taken by the Japanese soliders throwing a grenade. Jim waited for the explosion, and then realized that Private Kimura was holding a large fresh-water turtle. The creature's head emerged from its carapace, and Kimura began to laugh excitedly. His tubercular face resembled a small boy's, reminding Jim that Private Kimura had once been a child, as he himself had been before the war.

After crossing the parade ground, the Japanese soldiers disappeared among the lines of ragged washing between the barrack huts. Jim emerged from the damp cavern of the blockhouse. Wearing the leather golfing shoes given to him by Dr Ransome, he climbed through the wire. In his hand he carried Kimura's turtle. The ancient creature contained at least a pound of meat, and Basie, almost certainly, would know a special recipe for turtle. Jim could imagine Basie tempting it out of its shell with a live caterpillar, then skewering its head with his jack-knife…

In front of Jim was Lunghua Camp, his home and universe for the past three years, and the suffocating prison of nearly two thousand Allied nationals. The shabby barrack huts, the cement dormitory blocks, the worn parade ground and the guardhouse with its leaning watch-tower lay together under the June sun, a rendezvous for every fly and mosquito in the Yangtze basin. But once he stepped through the wire fence Jim felt the air steady around him. He ran along the cinder path, his tattered shirt flying from his bony shoulders like the tags of washing between the huts.

In his ceaseless journeys around the camp Jim had learned to recognize every stone and weed. A sun-bleached sign, crudely painted with the words "Regent Street," was nailed to a bamboo pole beside the pathway. Jim ignored it, as he did the similar signs enscribed "Piccadilly," "Knightsbridge" and "Petticoat Lane" which marked the main pathways within the camp. These relics of an imaginary London which many of the Shanghai-born British prisoners had never seen intrigued Jim but in some way annoyed him. With their constant talk about pre-war London, the older British families in the camp claimed a special exclusiveness. He remembered a line from one of the poems that Dr Ransome had made him memorize—"a foreign field that is for ever England…" But this was Lunghua, not England. Naming the sewage-stained paths between the rotting huts after a vaguely remembered London allowed too many of the British prisoners to shut out the reality of the camp, another excuse to sit back when they should have been helping Dr Ransome to clear the septic tanks. To their credit, in Jim's eyes, neither the Americans nor the Dutch and Belgians in the camp wasted their time on nostalgia. The years in Lunghua had not given Jim a high opinion of the British.

And yet the London street signs fascinated him, part of the magic of names that he had discovered in the camp. What, conceivably, were Lord's, the Serpentine, and the Trocadero? There were so few books or magazines that an unfamiliar brand name had all the mystery of a message from the stars. According to Basie, who was always right, the American fighters with the ventral radiators that strafed Lunghua Airfield were called "Mustangs," the name of a wild pony. Jim relished the name; to know that the planes were Mustangs was more important to him than the confirmation that Basie had his ear to the camp's secret radio. He hungered for names.

Jim stumbled on the worn path, unable to control the golf shoes. Too often these days he became light-headed. Dr Ransome had warned him not to run, but the American air attacks and the imminent prospect of the war's end made him too impatient to walk.

Trying to protect the turtle, he grazed his left knee. He limped across the cinder track and sat on the steps of the derelict drinking-water station. Here brackish water taken from the ponds in the camp had once been boiled by the prisoners. There was still a small supply of coal in the camp store-rooms, but the work gang of six Britons who stoked the fires had lost interest. Although Dr Ransome remonstrated with them, they preferred to suffer from chronic dysentery rather than make the effort of boiling the water.

While Jim nursed his knee the members of the gang sat outside the nearby barrack hut, watching the sky as if they expected the war to end within the next ten minutes. Jim recognized Mr Mulvaney, an accountant with the Shanghai Power Company who had often swum in the pool at Amherst Avenue. Beside him was the Reverend Pearce, a Methodist missionary whose Japanese-speaking wife openly collaborated with the guards, reporting to them each day on the prisoners' activities.

No one criticized Mrs Pearce for this, and in fact most of the prisoners in Lunghua were only too keen to collaborate. Jim vaguely disapproved, but agreed that it was probably sensible to do anything to survive. After three years in the camp the notion of patriotism meant nothing. The bravest prisoners—and collaboration was a risky matter—were those who bought their way into the favour of the Japanese and thereby helped their fellows with small supplies of food and bandages. Besides, there were few illicit activities to betray. No one in Lunghua would dream of trying to escape, and everyone rightly ratted on any fool about to step through the wire, for fear of the reprisals to come.

The water-workers scraped their clogs on the steps and stared into the sun, moving only to pick the ticks from between their ribs. Although emaciated, the process of starvation had somehow stopped a skin's depth from the skeleton below. Jim envied Mr Mulvaney and the Reverend Pearce—he himself was still growing. The arithmetic that Dr Ransome had taught him made it all too clear that the food supplied to the camp was shrinking at a faster rate than that at which the prisoners were dying.

In the centre of the parade ground a group of twelve-year-old boys were playing marbles on the baked earth. Seeing the turtle, they ran towards Jim. Each of them controlled a dragonfly tied to a length of cotton. The blue flames flicked to and fro above their heads.

"Jim! Can we touch it?"

"What is it?"

"Did Private Kimura give it to you?"

Jim smiled benignly. "It's a bomb." He held out the turtle and generously allowed everyone to inspect it. Despite the gap in years, several of the boys had been close friends in the days after his arrival in Lunghua, when he had needed every ally he could find. But he had outgrown them and made other friends—Dr Ransome, Basie and the American seamen in E Block, with their ancient pre-war copies of the *Reader's Digest* and *Popular Mechanics* that he devoured. Now and then, as if recapturing his lost childhood, Jim re-entered the world of boyish games and would play tops and marbles and hopscotch.

"Is it dead? It's moving!"

"It's bleeding!"

A smear of blood from Jim's knee gave the turtle's head a piratical flourish.

"Jim, you killed it!"

The largest of the boys, Richard Pearce, reached out to touch the reptile, but Jim tucked it under his arm. He disliked and slightly feared Richard Pearce, who was almost as big as himself. He envied Richard the extra Japanese rations which his mother fed to him. As well as the food, the Pearces had a small library of confiscated books, which they guarded jealously.

"It's a blood bond," Jim explained grandly. By rights turtles belonged to the sea, to the open river visible a mile to the west of the camp, that broad tributary of the Yangtze down which he had once dreamed of sailing with his parents to the safety of a world without war.

"Watch out…" He waved Richard aside. "I've trained it to attack!"

The boys backed away from him. There were times when Jim's humour made them uneasy. Although he tried to stop himself, Jim resented their clothes—hand-me-downs stitched together by their mothers, but far superior to his own rags. More than this, he resented that they had mothers and fathers at all. During the past year Jim had gradually realized that he could no longer remember what his parents looked like. Their veiled figures still entered his dreams, but he had forgotten their faces.

THE CUBICLE

"Young Jim…!"

An almost naked man wearing clogs and ragged shorts shouted to him from the steps of G Block. In his hands he held the shafts of a wooden cart with iron wheels. Although the cart carried no load, its handles had almost wrenched the man's arms from their sockets. He spoke to the English women sitting on the concrete steps in their faded cotton frocks. As he gestured to them his shoulder blades seemed to be working themselves loose from his back, about to fly across the barbed wire.

"I'm here, Mr Maxted!" Jim pushed Richard Pearce aside and ran along the cinder path to the dormitory block. Seeing the empty food cart, it occurred to him that he might have missed the daily meal. The fear of being without food for even a single day was so intense that he was ready to attack Mr Maxted.

"Come on, Jim. Without you it won't taste the same." Mr Maxted glanced at Jim's golf shoes, these nailed brogues that had a life of their own and propelled his scarecrow figure on his ceaseless rounds of the camp. To the women he remarked: "Our Jim's spending all his time at the 19th hole."

"I promised, Mr Maxted. I'm always ready..." Jim had to stop as he reached the entrance to G Block. He worked his lungs until the dizziness left his head, and ran forward again. Turtle in hand, he raced up the steps into the foyer and swerved between two old men stranded like ghosts in the middle of a conversation they had forgotten.

On either side of the corridor was a series of small rooms, each furnished with four wooden bunks. After the first winter in the camp, when many of the children in the uninsulated barracks had died, families with children were moved into the residence halls of the former training college. Although unheated, the rooms with their cement walls remained above freezing point.

Jim shared his room with a young English couple, Mr and Mrs Vincent, and their six-year-old son. He had lived within inches of the Vincents for two and a half years, but their existences could not have been more separate. On the day of Jim's arrival Mrs Vincent had hung an old bedspread around his nominal quarter of the room. She and her husband—a broker on the Shanghai Stock Exchange— never ceased to resent Jim's presence, and over the years they had strengthened his cubicle, stringing together a worn shawl, a petticoat and the lid of a cardboard box, so that it resembled one of the miniature shanties that seemed to erect themselves spontaneously around the beggars of Shanghai.

Not content with walling Jim into his small world, the Vincents had repeatedly tried to encroach upon it, moving the nails and string from which the bedspread hung. Jim had defended himself, first by bending the nails until, to the Vincents's horror, the entire structure collapsed one night as they were undressing, and then by calibrating the wall with a ruler and pencil. The Vincents promptly retaliated by superimposing their own system of marks.

All this Jim took in his stride. For some reason he still liked Mrs Vincent, a handsome if frayed blonde, although her nerves were always stretched and she had never made the slightest attempt to care for him. He knew that if he starved to death in his bunk she would find some polite reason for doing nothing to help him. During the first year in Lunghua the few single children were neglected, unless they were prepared to let themselves be used as servants. Jim alone had refused, and had never fetched and carried for Mr Vincent.

Mrs Vincent was sitting on her straw mattress when he burst into the room, her pale hands folded on her lap like a forgotten pair of gloves. She stared at the whitewashed wall above her son's bunk, as if watching an invisible film projected on to a screen. Jim worried that Mrs Vincent spent too much of her time watching these films. As he peered at her through the cracks in his cubicle he tried to guess what she saw—a home-made cine film, perhaps, of herself in England before she was married, sitting on one of those sunlit lawns that seemed to cover the entire country. Jim assumed that it was those lawns that had provided the emergency airfields for the Battle of Britain. As he was aware from his observations in Shanghai, the Germans were not too keen on sunlit lawns. Was this why they had lost the Battle of Britain? Many of his ideas were hopelessly confused in a way that even Dr Ransome was too tired to disentangle.

"You're late, Jim," Mrs Vincent told him disapprovingly, her eyes on his golf shoes. Like everyone else, she was unable to cope with their intimidating presence. Already Jim felt that the shoes gave him a special authority. "The whole of G Block has been waiting for you."

"I've been with Basie, hearing the latest war news. Mrs Vincent, what's the 19th hole?"

"You shouldn't work for Basie. The things those Americans ask you to do… I've told you that we come first."

"G Block comes first, Mrs Vincent." Jim meant it. He ducked under the flap into his cubicle. Catching his breath, he lay on the bunk with the turtle inside his shirt. The reptile preferred its own company, and Jim turned his attention to his new shoes. With their polished toecaps and bright studs, they were an intact piece of the pre-war world that he could stare at for hours, like Mrs Vincent and her films. Laughing to himself, Jim lay back as the hot sunlight shone through the wall of the cubicle, outlining the curious stains on the old bedspread. Looking at them, he visualized the scenes of air-battles and armadas, the sinking of the Petrel, and even the garden at Amherst Avenue.

"Jim, kitchen time…!" he heard someone call from the steps below the window. But Jim rested on his bunk. It was a long haul to the kitchens, and there was no point in being early. The Japanese had celebrated VE Day in their own way, by cutting the already meagre rations in half. The first arrivals often received less than the later ones, when the cooks realized how many of the prisoners had died or were too ill to collect their rations.

Besides, there was no obligation on Jim to help with the food cart nor, for that matter, on Mr Maxted. But as Jim had noticed, those who were prepared to help their fellow prisoners tended to do so, and this did nothing to stop those too lazy to work from endlessly complaining. The British were especially good at complaining, something the Dutch and Americans never did. Soon Jim reflected with a certain grim pleasure, they would be too sick even to complain.

He gazed at his shoes, consciously imitating the childlike smile on Private Kimura's lips. The wooden bunk filled the cubicle, but Jim was at his happiest in this miniature universe. On the walls he had pinned several pages from an old *Life* magazine that Basie had given to him. There were photographs of Battle of Britain pilots sitting in armchairs beside their Spitfires, of a crashed Heinkel bomber, of St Paul's floating like a battleship on a sea of fire. Next to them was a full-page colour advertisement for a Packard motorcar, as beautiful in Jim's eyes as the Mustang fighters, which strafed Lunghua Airfield.

Did the Americans bring out a new-model Mustang every year or every month? Perhaps there would be an air raid that afternoon, when he could check the latest design modifications to the Mustangs and Superfortresses. Jim looked forward to the air raids.

Besides the Packard was a small section that Jim had cut from a larger photograph of a crowd outside the gates of Buckingham Palace in 1940. The blurred images of a man and a woman standing arm-in-arm reminded Jim of his parents. This unknown English couple, perhaps dead in an air raid, had almost become his mother and father. Jim knew that they were complete strangers, but he kept the pretence alive, so that in turn he could keep alive the lost memory of his parents. The world before the war, his childhood in Amherst Avenue, his class at the Cathedral School, belonged to that invisible film which Mrs Vincent watched from her bunk.

Jim allowed the turtle to crawl across his straw mat. If he carried it around with him Private Kimura or one of the guards might guess that he had left the camp. Now that the war was ending the Japanese guards were convinced that the British and American prisoners were constantly trying to escape—the last notion, in fact, to cross their minds. In 1943 a few Britishers had escaped, hoping to be sheltered by neutral friends in Shanghai, but had soon been discovered by the army of informers. Several groups of Americans had set out in the summer of 1944 for Chungking, the Nationalist Chinese capital nine hundred miles to the west. All had been betrayed by Chinese villagers terrified of reprisals, handed over to the Japanese and executed. From then on escape attempts ceased altogether. By June 1945, the landscape around Lunghua was so hostile, roamed by bandits, starving villagers and deserters from the puppet armies, that the camp and its Japanese guards offered the only security.

With his finger Jim stroked the turtle's ancient head. It seemed a pity to cook it—Jim envied the reptile its massive shell, a private fortress against the world. From below his bunk he pulled out a wooden box, which Dr Ransome had helped him to nail together. Inside were his possessions—a Japanese cap badge given to him by Private Kimura; three steel-bossed fighting tops; a chess set and a copy of *Kennedy's Latin Primer* on indefinite loan from Dr Ransome; his Cathedral School blazer, a carefully folded memory of his younger self; and the pair of clogs he had worn for the past three years.

Jim placed the turtle in the box and covered it with the blazer. As he raised the flap of his cubicle Mrs Vincent watched his every move. She treated him like her Number Two Coolie, and he was well aware that he tolerated this for reasons he barely understood. Like all the men and older boys in G Block, Jim was attracted to Mrs Vincent, but her real appeal for Jim lay elsewhere. Her long hours staring at the whitewash, and her detachment even from her own son— she fed the dysentery-ridden boy and changed his clothes without looking at him for minutes at a time—suggested to Jim that she remained forever above the camp, beyond the world of guards and hunger and American air attacks to which he himself was passionately committed. He wanted to touch her, less out of adolescent lust than simple curiosity.

"You can use my bunk, Mrs Vincent, if you want to sleep."

As Jim reached to her shoulder she pushed his hand away. Her distracted eyes could come to a remarkably sharp focus.

"Mr Maxted is still waiting, Jim. Perhaps it's time you went back to the huts."

"Not the huts, Mrs Vincent," he pretended to groan. Not the huts, he repeated fiercely to himself as he left the room. The huts were cold, and if the war lasted beyond the winter of 1945 many more people would die in those freezing barracks. However, for Mrs Vincent perhaps he would go back to the huts...

THE UNIVERSITY OF LIFE

All over the camp there sounded the scraping of iron wheels. In the windows of the barrack huts, on the steps of the dormitory blocks, the prisoners were sitting up, roused for a few minutes by the memory of food.

Jim left the foyer of G Block, and found Mr Maxted still holding the wooden handles of the food cart. Having made the effort twenty minutes earlier to lift the handles, he had exhausted his powers of decision. The former architect and entrepreneur, who had represented so much that Jim most admired about Shanghai, had been sadly drained by his years in Lunghua. After arriving at the camp Jim had been glad to find him there, but by now he realized how much Mr Maxted had changed. His eyes forever watched the cigarette butts thrown down by the Japanese guards, but only Jim was quick enough to retrieve them. Jim chafed at this, but he supported Mr Maxted out of nostalgia for his childhood dream of growing up one day to be like him.

The Studebaker and the afternoon girls in the gambling casinos had prepared Mr Maxted poorly for the world of the camp. As Jim took the wooden handles he wondered how long the architect would have stood on the sewage-stained path. Perhaps all day, watched until he dropped by the same group of British prisoners who sat on the steps without once offering to help. Half-naked in their ragged clothes, they stared at the parade ground, uninterested even in a Japanese fighter that flew overhead. Several of the married couples held their mess-plates, already forming a queue, a reflex response to Jim's arrival.

"At last..."

"...that boy..."

"...running wild."

These mutters drew an amiable smile from Mr Maxted. "Jim you're going to be blackballed by the country club. Never mind."

"I don't mind." When Mr Maxted stumbled Jim held his arm. "Are you all right, Mr Maxted?"

Jim waved to the men sitting on the step, but no one moved. Mr Maxted steadied himself. "Let's go, Jim. Some work and some watch, and that's all there is to it."

For the past year there had been a third member of the team, Mr Carey, the owner of the Buick agency in Nanking Road. But six weeks earlier he had died of malaria, and by then the Japanese had cut the food ration to a point where only two of them were needed to push the cart.

Propelled by his new shoes, Jim sped along the cinder path. The iron wheels struck sparks from the flinty stones. Mr Maxted held his shoulder, panting to keep up.

"Slow down, Jim. You'll get there before the war ends."

"When will the war end, Mr Maxted?"

"Jim…is it going to end? Another year, 1946. You tell me, you listen to Basie's radio."

"I haven't heard the radio, Mr Maxted," Jim answered truthfully. Basie was far too canny to admit a Britisher into the secret circle of listeners. "I know the Japanese surrendered at Okinawa. I hope the war ends soon."

"Not too soon, Jim. Our problem might begin then. Are you still giving English lessons to Private Kimura?"

"He isn't interested in learning English," Jim had to admit. "I think the war's really ended for Private Kimura."

"Will the war really end for you, Jim? You'll see your mother and father again."

"Well…" Jim preferred not to talk about his parents, even with Mr Maxted. The two of them had formed a long-standing partnership, though Mr Maxted did little to help Jim and rarely referred to his son Patrick or to their visits to the Shanghai clubs and bars. Mr Maxted was no longer the dapper figure who fell into swimming-pools. What worried Jim was that his mother and father might also have changed. Soon after arriving in Lunghua he heard that his parents were interned in a camp near Soochow, but the Japanese refused to consider the notion of a transfer.

They crossed the parade ground and approached the camp kitchens behind the guardhouse. Some twenty food carts and their teams were drawn up beside the serving hatch, jostling together like a crowd of rickshaws and their coolies. As Jim had estimated, he and Mr Maxted would take their place halfway down the queue. Late-comers clattered along the cinder paths, watched by hundreds of emaciated prisoners. One day during the previous week there had been no food, as a reprisal for a Superfortress raid that had devastated Tokyo, and the prisoners had continued to stare at the kitchens until late afternoon. The silence had unsettled Jim, reminding him of the beggars outside the house in Amherst Avenue. Without thinking, he had removed his shoes and hidden them among the graves in the hospital cemetery.

Jim and Mr Maxted took their places in the queue. Outside the guardhouse a work party of British and Belgian prisoners were strengthening the fence. Two of the prisoners unwound a coil of barbed wire, which the others cut and nailed to the fencing posts. Several of the Japanese soldiers were working shoulder to shoulder with their prisoners, ragged uniforms barely distinguishable from the faded khaki of the inmates.

The object of this activity was a group of thirty Chinese camped outside the gates. Destitute peasants and villagers, soldiers from the puppet armikes and abandoned children, they sat in the open road, staring at the barbed-wire gates being strengthened against them. The first of these impoverished people had appeared three months earlier. At night some of the more desperate would climb through the wire, only to be caught by the internees' patrols. Those who survived in the guardhouse till dawn were taken down to the river by the Japanese and clubbed to death on the bank.

As they moved forward to the serving hatch Jim watched the Chinese. Although it was summer the peasants still wore their quilted winter clothes. Needless to say, none of the Chinese was ever admitted to Lunghua Camp, let alone fed. Yet still they came, attracted to this one place in the desolate land where there was food. Worryingly for Jim, they stayed until they died. Mr Maxted was right when he said that with the conclusion of the war the prisoners' real problems would not end, but begin.

Jim worried about Dr Ransome and Mrs Vincent, and the rest of his fellow-prisoners. How would they survive, without the Japanese to look after them? He worried especially for Mr Maxted, whose tired repertory of jokes about the country club meant nothing in the real world. But at least Mr Maxted was trying to keep the camp going, and it was the integrity of the camp on which they depended.

During 1943, when the war was still moving in Japan's favour, the prisoners had worked together. The entertainments committee, of which Mr Maxted had been chairman, organized a nightly programme of lectures and concert parties. This was the happiest year of Jim's life. Tired of his cramped cubicle and Mrs Vincent's nail-tapping aloofness, he spent every evening listening to lectures on an endless variety of topics: the construction of the pyramids, the history of the world land-speed record, the life of a district commissioner in Uganda (the lecturer, a retired Indian Army officer, claimed to have named after himself a lake the size of Wales, which amazed Jim), the infantry weapons of the Great War, the management of the Shanghai Tramways Company, and a score of others.

Sitting in the front row of the assembly hall, Jim devoured these lectures, many of which he attended two or three times. He helped to copy the parts for the Lunghua Players' productions of *Macbeth* and *Twelfth Night*, he moved scenery for *The Pirates of Penzance* and *Trial by Jury*. For most of 1944 there was a camp school run by the missionaries, which Jim found tedious by comparison with the evening lectures. But he deferred to Basie and Dr Ransome. Both agreed that he should never miss a class, if only, Jim suspected, to give themselves a break from his restless energy.

But by the winter of 1944 all this had ended. After the American fighter attacks on Lunghua Airfield, and the first bombing raids on the Shanghai dockyards, the Japanese enforced an evening curfew. The supply of electric current to the camp was switched off for good, and the prisoners retreated to their bunks. The already modest food ration was cut to a single meal each day. American submarines blockaded the Yangtze estuary, and the huge Japanese armies in China began to fall back to the coast, barely able to feed themselves.

The prospect of their defeat, and the imminent assault on the Japanese home islands, made Jim more and more nervous. He ate every scrap of food he could find, aware of the rising numbers of deaths from beri beri and malaria. Jim admired the Mustangs and Superfortresses, but sometimes he wished that the Americans would return to Hawaii and content themselves with raising their battleships at Pearl Harbor. Then Lunghua Camp would once again be the happy place that he had known in 1943.

* * *

When Jim and Mr Maxted returned with the rations to G Block the prisoners were waiting silently with their plates and mess-tins. They stood on the steps, the bare-chested men with knobbed shoulders and birdcage ribs, their faded wives in shabby frocks, watching without expression as if about to be presented with a corpse. At the head of the queue were Mrs Pearce and her son, followed by the missionary couples who spent all day hunting for food.

Hundreds of flies hovered in the steam that rose from the metal pails of cracked wheat and sweet potatoes. As he heaved on the wooden handles Jim winced with pain, not from the strain of pulling the cart, but from the heat of the stolen sweet potato inside his shirt. As long as he remained doubled up no one would see the potato, and he put on a pantomime of grimaces and groans.

"Oh, no…oh, my God…"

"Worthy of the Lunghua Players, Jim." Mr Maxted had watched him remove the potato from the pail as they left the kitchens, but he never objected. Crouching forward, Jim abandoned the cart to the missionaries. He ran up the steps, past the Vincents, who stood plates in hand—it never occurred to them, nor to Jim, that they should bring his plate with them. He dived through the curtain into his cubicle and dropped the steaming potato under his mat, hoping that the damp straw would smother the vapour. He seized his plate, and darted back to the foyer to take his place at the head of the queue. Mr Maxted had already served the Reverend and Mrs Pearce, but Jim shouldered aside their son. He held out his plate and received a ladle of boiled wheat and a second sweet potato which he had pointed out to Mr Maxted within moments of leaving the kitchens.

Returning to his bunk, Jim relaxed for the first time. He drew the curtain and lay back, the warm plate like a piece of the sun against his chest. He felt drowsy, but at the same time light-headed with hunger. He rallied himself with the thought that there might be an American air raid that afternoon—who did he want to win? The question was important.

Jim cupped his hands over the sweet potato. He was almost too hungry to enjoy the grey pith, but he gazed at the photograph of the man and woman outside Buckingham Palace, hoping that his parents, wherever they were, also had an extra potato.

When the Vincents returned with their rations Jim sat up and folded back the curtain so that he could examine their plates. He liked to watch Mrs Vincent eating her meals. Keeping a close eye on her, Jim studied the cracked wheat. The starchy grains were white and swollen, indistinguishable from the weevils that infested these warehouse sweepings. In the early years of the camp everyone pushed the weevils to one side, or flicked them through the nearest window, but now Jim carefully husbanded them. Often there was more than a hundred insects in three rows around the rim of Jim's plate, though recently even their number was in decline. "Eat the weevils," Dr Ransome had told him, and he did so, although everyone else washed them away. But there was protein in them, a fact that Mr Maxted seemed to find depressing when Jim informed him of it.

After counting the eighty-seven weevils—their numbers, Jim calculated, were falling less steeply than the ration—he stirred them into the cracked wheat, an animal feed grown in northern China, and swallowed the six spoonfuls. Giving himself a breather, he waited for Mrs Vincent to begin her sweet potato.

"Must you, Jim?" Mr Vincent asked. No taller than Jim, the stockbroker and former amateur jockey sat on his bunk beside his ailing son. With his black hair and lined yellow face like a squeezed lemon, he reminded Jim of Basie, but Mr Vincent had never come to terms with Lunghua. "You'll miss this camp when the war's over. I wonder how you'll take to school in England."

"It might be a bit strange," Jim admitted, finishing the last of the weevils. He felt sensitive about his ragged clothes and his determined efforts to stay alive. He wiped his plate clean with his finger, and remembered a favourite phrase of Basie's. "All the same, Mr Vincent, the best teacher is the university of life."

Mrs Vincent lowered her spoon. "Jim, could we finish our meal? We've heard your views on the university of life."

"Right. But we should eat the weevils, Mrs Vincent."

"I know, Jim. Dr Ransome told you so."

"He said we need the protein."

"Dr Ransome is right. We should all eat the weevils." Hoping to brighten the conversation, Jim asked: "Mrs Vincent, do you believe in vitamins?" Mrs Vincent stared at her plate. She spoke with true despair.

"Strange child..."

The rebuff began to bother Jim. Everything about this distant woman with her thinning blond hair intrigued him, although in many ways he distrusted her. Six months earlier, when Dr Ransome thought that Jim had contracted pneumonia, she had done nothing to look after him, and Dr Ransome was forced to come in every day and wash Jim himself. Yet the previous evening she had helped him with his Latin homework, matter-of-factly pointing out the distinction between gerunds and gerundives.

Jim waited until she began her sweet potato. After confirming that his own potato was the largest of the four in the room, and deciding not to save any for the turtle under his bunk, he broke the skin and swiftly devoured the warm pulp. When the last morsel had gone he lay back and lowered the curtain. Alone now— the Vincents, although only a few feet away from him, might as well have been on another planet—Jim pondered the jobs ahead of him that day. First, there was the second potato to be smuggled from the room. There were his Latin homework for Dr Ransome, errands to be run for Basie and Private Kimura, and then the afternoon air raid—all in all, a full programme until the evening curfew, when he would probably roam the G Block corridors with his chess set, ready to take on all comers.

The *Kennedy Primer* in hand, Jim stepped from his cubicle. The second potato bulged in his trouser pocket, but for several months the presence of Mrs Vincent had sometimes given him an unexpected erection, and he relied on the confusion to make his escape.

His spoon halfway to his mouth, Mr Vincent stared at the bulge with an expression of deep gloom. His wife gazed in her level fashion at Jim, who side-stepped quickly from the room. Glad as always to be free of the Vincents, he skipped down the corridor to the external door below the fire-escape, and vaulted over the children squatting on one step. As the warm air ruffled the ragged strips of his shirt he ran off into the familiar and reassuring world of the camp.

The Big Day
(from *From Here to Eternity*)

James Jones

Milt Warden did not really get up early the morning of the big day. He just had not been to bed.

He had gone around to the Blue Chancre, after Karen had gone home at 9:30, on a vague hunch that Prewitt might be there. Karen had asked him about him again and they had discussed him a long time. Prewitt hadn't been there, but he ran into Old Pete and the Chief; Pete was helping the Chief to celebrate his last night in town before going back into his garrison headquarters at Choy's. They had already made their bomb run on the whorehouse and dropped their load on Mrs Kipfer's New Congress. After Charlie Chan closed up the Blue Chancre, the four of them had sat out in the back room and played stud poker for a penny a chip while drinking Charlie's bar whiskey.

It was always a dull game; Charlie could not play poker for peanuts; but he always let them have the whiskey at regular wholesale prices and if they complained loud enough he would even go in on it and pay a full share, although he drank very little. So they were always willing to suffer his poker playing. They would always overplay a hand to him now and then to keep him from finding out how lousy he was.

When they had drunk as much as they could hold without passing out, it was so late the Schofield cabs had stopped running. They had hired a city cab to take them back because there was nowhere else to go at 6:30 on Sunday morning.

Besides, Stark always had hotcakes-and-eggs and fresh milk on Sundays. There is nothing as good for a hangover as a big meal of hotcakes-and-eggs and fresh milk just before going to bed.

They were too late to eat early chow in the kitchen, and the chow line was already moving slowly past the two griddles. Happily drunkenly undismayed, the three of them bucked the line amid the ripple of curses from the privates, and carried their plates in to eat at the First-Three-Graders' table at the head of the room.

It was almost like a family party. All the platoon sergeants were there, and Stark was there in his sweated undershirt after getting the cooks started, and Malleaux the supply sergeant. Even Baldy Dhom was there, having been run out by his wife for getting drunk last night at the NCO Club. All of this in itself did not happen often, and today being Sunday nobody was less than half tight and since there had been a big shindig dance at the Officers' Club last night none of the officers had shown up, so that they did not have to be polite.

The conversation was mostly about Mrs Kipfer's. That was where Pete and the Chief had wound up last night, and most of the others had gone there. Mrs Kipfer had just got in a shipment of four new beaves, to help take care of the influx of draftees that was raising Company strengths all over Schofield. One was a shy dark-haired little thing who was apparently appearing professionally for the first time, and who showed promise of someday stepping into Lorene's shoes when Lorene went back home. Her name was Jeanette and she was variously recommended back and forth across the table.

At least one officer was always required to eat the men's food in the messhall, either Lt Ross, or Chicken Culpepper, or else one of the three new ROTC boys the Company had been issued during the last week; the five of them passed the detail around them; but whichever one got it, it was still always the same and put a damper over the noncoms' table. But today it was just like a big family party. Minus the mother-in-law.

Stark was the only one, outside of Warden and Baldy, who had not been around to Mrs Kipfer's last night. But he was drunk, too. Stark had picked himself off a shackjob down at the Wailupe Naval Radio Station while they had had the CP out at Hanauma Bay. Some of them had seen her, and she was a hot-looking, wild, I'll-go-as-far-as-you-will wahine, but Stark would not talk about her. So he did not enter the conversation much at the table; but he listened. He had not spoken to Warden since the night at Hickam Field except in the line of duty, and at the table he ignored Warden and Warden ignored him.

It was a typical Sunday morning breakfast for the first weekend after payday. At least a third of the Company was not home. Another third was still in bed asleep. But the last third more than made up for the absences in the loudness of their drunken laughter and horseplay and the clashing of cutlery and halfpint milk bottles.

Warden was just going back for seconds on both hotcakes and eggs, with that voracious appetite he always had when he was drunk, when this blast shuddered by under the floor and rattled the cups on the tables and then rolled on off across the quad like a high wave at sea in a storm.

He stopped in the doorway of the KP room and looked back at the messhall. He remembered the picture the rest of his life. It had become very quiet and everybody had stopped eating and looked up at each other.

"Must bed doin some dynamitin down to Wheeler Field," somebody said tentatively.

"I heard they was clearin some ground for a new fighter strip," somebody else agreed.

That seemed to satisfy everybody. They went back to their eating.

Warden heard a laugh ring out above the hungry gnashings of cutlery on china, as he turned back into the KP room. The tail of the chow line was still moving past the two griddles, and he made a mental note to go behind the cooks' serving table when he bucked the line this time, so as not to make it so obvious.

That was when the second blast came. He could hear it a long way off coming toward them under the ground; then it was there before he could move, rattling the cups and plates in the KP sinks and the rinsing racks; then it was gone and he

33

could hear it going away northeast toward the 21st Infantry's football field. Both the KPs were looking at him.

He reached out to put his plate on the nearest flat surface, holding it carefully in both hands so it would not get broken while he congratulated himself on his presence of mind, and then turned back to the messhall, the KPs still watching him.

As there was nothing under the plate, it fell on the floor and crashed in the silence, but nobody heard it because the third groundswell of blast had already reached the PX and was just about to them. It passed under, rattling everything, just as he got back to the NCOs' table.

"This is it," somebody said quite simply.

Warden found that his eyes and Stark's eyes were looking into each other. There was nothing on Stark's face, except the slack relaxed peaceful look of drunkenness, and Warden felt there must not be anything on his either. He pulled his mouth up and showed his teeth in a grin, and Stark's face pulled up his mouth in an identical grin. Their eyes were still looking into each other.

Warden grabbed his coffee cup in one hand and his halfpint of milk in the other and ran out through the messhall screen door onto the porch. The far door, into the dayroom, was already so crowded he could not have pushed through. He ran down the porch and turned into the corridor that ran through to the street and beat them all outside but for one or two. When he stopped and looked back he saw Pete Karelsen and Chief Choate and Stark were all right behind him. Chief Choate had his plate of hotcakes-and-eggs in his left hand and his fork in the other. He took a big bite. Warden turned back and swallowed some coffee.

Down the street over the trees a big column of black smoke was mushrooming up into the sky. The men behind were crowding out the door and pushing those in front out into the street. Almost everybody had brought his bottle of milk to keep from getting it stolen, and a few had brought their coffee too. From the middle of the street Warden could not see any more than he had seen from the edge, just the same big column of black smoke mushrooming up into the sky from down around Wheeler Field. He took a drink of his coffee and pulled the cap off his milk bottle.

"Gimme some of that coffee," Stark said in a dead voice behind him, and held up his own cup. "Mine was empty."

He turned around to hand him the cup and when he turned back a big tall thin red-headed boy who had not been there before was running down the street toward them, his red hair flapping in his self-induced breeze, and his knees coming up to his chin with every step. He looked like he was about to fall over backwards.

"Whats up, Red?" Warden hollered at him. "Whats happening? Wait a minute! Whats going on?"

The red-headed boy went on running down the street concentratedly, his eyes glaring whitely at them.

"The Japs is bombing Wheeler Field!" he hollered over his shoulder.

"The Japs is bombing Wheeler Field! I seen the red circles on the wings!"

He went on running down the middle of the street, and quite suddenly right behind him came a big roaring, getting bigger and bigger; behind the roaring came an airplane, leaping out suddenly over the trees.

Warden, along with the rest of them, watched it coming with his milk bottle still at his lips and the twin red flashes winking out from the nose. It came over and down and up and away and was gone, and the stones in the asphalt pavement at his feet popped up in a long curving line that led up the curb and puffs of dust came up from the grass and a line of cement popped out of the wall to the roof, then back down the wall to the grass and off out across the street again in a big S-shaped curve.

With a belated reflex, the crowd of men swept back in a wave toward the door, after the plane was already gone, and then swept right back out again pushing the ones in front into the street again.

Above the street between the trees Warden could see other planes down near the smoke column. They flashed silver like mirrors. Some of them began suddenly to grow larger. His shin hurt from where a stone out of the pavement had popped him.

"All right, you stupid f—!" he bellowed. "Get back inside! You want to get your ass shot of?"

Down the street the red-haired boy lay sprawled out floppy-haired, wild-eyed, and silent, in the middle of the pavement. The etched line on the asphalt ran up to him and continued on on the other side of him and then stopped.

"See that?" Warden bawled. "This aint jawbone, this is for record. Thems real bullets that guy was usin."

The crowd moved reluctantly back toward the dayroom door. But one man ran to the wall and started probing with his pocketknife in one of the holes and came out with a bullet. It was a .50 caliber. Then another man ran out in the street and picked up something which turned out to be three open-end metal links. The middle one still had a .50 caliber casing in it. The general movement toward the dayroom stopped.

"Say! Thats pretty clever," somebody said. "Our planes is still usin web machinegun belts that they got to carry back home!" The two men started showing their finds to the men around them. A couple of other men ran out into the street hurriedly.

"This'll make me a good souvenir," the man with the bullet said contentedly. "A bullet from a Jap plane on the day the war started."

"Give me back my goddam coffee!" Warden hollered at Stark. "And help me shoo these dumb bastards back inside!"

"What you want me to do?" Chief Choate asked. He was still holding his plate and fork and chewing excitedly on a big bite.

"Help me get em inside," Warden hollered.

Another plane, on which they could clearly see the red discs, came skidding over the trees firing and saved him the trouble. The two men hunting for metal links in the street sprinted breathlessly. The crowd moved back in a wave to the door, and stayed there. The plane flashed past, the helmeted head with the square goggles over the slant eyes and the long scarf rippling out behind it and the grin on the face as he waved, all clearly visible for the space of a wink, like a traveltalk slide flashed on and then off of a screen.

Warden, Stark, Pete and the Chief descended on them as the crowd started to wave outward again, blocking them off and forcing the whole bunch back inside the dayroom.

The crowd milled indignantly in the small dayroom, everybody talking excitedly. Stark posted himself huskily in the doorway with Pete and the Chief flanking him. Warden gulped off the rest of his coffee and set the cup on the magazine rack and pushed his way down to the other end and climbed up on the pingpong table.

"All right, all right, you men. Quiet down. Quiet down. It's only a war. Aint you ever been in a war before?"

The word war had the proper effect. They began to yell at each other to shut up and listen.

"I want every man to go upstairs to his bunk and stay there," Warden said. "Each man report to his squad leader. Squad leaders keep your men together at their bunks until you get orders what to do."

The earth shudders rolling up from Wheeler Field were already commonplace now. Above it, they heard another plane go roaring machinegun rattling over.

"The CQ will unlock the rifle racks and every man get his rifle and hang onto it. *But stay inside at your bunks.* This aint no manoeuvres. You go runnin around outside you'll get your ass shot off. And you cant do no good anyway. You want to be heroes, you'll get plenty chances later; from now on. You'll probly have Japs right in your laps, by time we get down to beach positions.

"Stay off the porches. *Stay inside.* I'm making each squad leader responsible to keep his men *inside.* If you have to use a rifle butt to do it, thats okay too."

There was a mutter of indignant protest.

"You heard me!" Warden hollered. "You men want souvenirs; buy them off the widows of the men who went out after them. If I catch anybody runnin around outside, I'll personally beat his head in, and then see he gets a goddam general court martial."

There was another indignant mutter of protest.

"What if the f—bomb us?" somebody hollered.

"If you hear a bomb coming, you're free to take off for the brush," Warden said. "But not unless you do. I don't think they will. If they was going to bomb us, they would of started with it already. They probly concentratin all their bombs on the Air Corps and Pearl Harbor."

There was another indignant chorus.

"Yeah," somebody hollered, "but what if they aint?"

"Then you're shit out of luck," Warden said. "If they *do* start to bomb, get everybody outside—on the side *away* from the quad—not *into* the quad and disperse; *away* from the big buildings."

"That wont do us no good if they've already laid one on the roof," somebody yelled.

"All right," Warden hollered, "can the chatter. Lets move. We're wasting time. Squad leaders get these men upstairs. BAR men, platoon leaders and first-three-graders report to me here."

With the corporals and buck sergeants haranguing them, the troops gradually began to sift out through the corridor to the porch stairs. Outside another plane went over. Then another, and another. Then what sounded like three planes together. The platoon leaders and guides and BAR men pushed their way down to the pingpong table that Warden jumped down off of.

"What you want me to do, First?" Stark said; his face still had the same expression of blank, flat refusal—like a stomach flatly refusing food—that he had had in the messhall; "what about the kitchen force? I'm pretty drunk, but I can still shoot a BAR."

"I want you to get your ass in the kitchen with every man you got and start packing up," Warden said, looking at him. He rubbed his hand hard over his own face. "We'll be movin out for the beach as soon as this tapers off a little, and I want that kitchen all packed and ready to roll. Full field. Stoves and all. While you're doin that, make a big pot of coffee on the big stove. Use the biggest #18 pot you got."

"Right," Stark said, and took off for the door into the messhall.

"Wait!" Warden hollered. "On second thought, make two pots. The two biggest you got. We're going to need it."

"Right," Stark said, and went on. His voice was not blank, his voice was crisp. It was just his face, that was blank.

"The rest of you guys," Warden said.

Seeing their faces, he broke off and rubbed his own face again. It didn't do any good. As soon as he stopped rubbing it settled right back into it, like a campaign hat that had been blocked a certain way.

"I want the BAR men to report to the supply room right now and get their weapons and all the loaded clips they can find and go up on the roof. When you see a Jap plane, shoot at it. Dont worry about wasting ammo. Remember to take a big lead. Thats all. Get moving."

"The rest of you guys," Warden said, as the BAR men moved away at a run. "The rest of you guys. The first thing. The main thing. Every platoon leader is responsible to me personally to see that all of his men stay inside, except the BAR men up on the roof. A rifleman's about as much good against a low flying pursuit ship as a boy scout with a sling-shot. And we're going to need every man we can muster when we get down to beach positions. I dont want none of them wasted here, by runnin outside to shoot rifles at airplanes. Or by goin souvenir huntin. The men stay inside. Got it?"

There was a chorus of hurried vacant nods. Most of the heads were on one side, listening to the planes going over and over in ones twos and threes.

It looked peculiar to see them all nodding on one side like that. Warden found himself wanting to laugh excitedly.

"The BARs will be up on the roof," he said. "They can do all the shooting that we can supply ammo for. Anybody else will just be getting in the way."

"What about my MGs Milt?" Pete Karelsen asked him.

The easy coolness in old Pete's voice shocked Warden to a full stop. Drunk or not, Pete seemed to be the only one who sounded relaxed, and Warden remembered his two years in France.

"Whatever you think, Pete," he said.

"I'll take one. They couldnt load belts fast enough to handle more than one. I'll take Mikeovitch and Grenelli up with me to handle it."

"Can you get the muzzle up high enough on those ground tripods?"

"We'll put the tripod over a chimney," Pete said. "And then hold her down by the legs."

"Whatever you think, Pete," Warden said, thinking momentarily how wonderful it was to be able to say that.

"Come on, you two," Pete said, almost boredly, to his two section leaders. "We'll take Grenelli's because we worked on it last."

"Remember," Warden said to the rest of them as Pete left with his two machinegunners. "The men stay inside. I dont care how you handle it. Thats up to you. I'm going to be up on the roof with a BAR. If you want to get in on the fun, go yourself. Thats where I'm going to be. But make damn sure your men are going to stay inside, off the porches, before you go up."

"Like hell!" Liddell Henderson said. "You aint goin to catch this Texan up on no roof. Ah'll stay down with ma men."

"Okay," Warden said, jabbing a finger at him. "Then you are hereby placed in charge of the loading detail. Get ten or twelve men, as many as you can get in the supplyroom, and put them to loading BAR clips and MG belts. We're going to need all the ammo we can get. Anybody else dont want to go up?"

"I'll stay down with Liddell," Champ Wilson said.

"Then you're second-in-command of the loading detail," Warden said. "All right, lets go. If anybody's got a bottle laying around, bring it up with you. I'm bringing mine."

When they got out to the porch, they found a knot of men arguing violently with S/Sgt Malleaux in front of the supplyroom.

"I dont give a damn," Malleaux said. "Thats my orders. I cant issue any live ammo without a signed order from an officer."

"But there aint no goddamned officers, you jerk!" somebody protested angrily.

"Then there aint no live ammo," Malleaux said.

"The officers may not get here till noon!"

"I'm sorry, fellows," Malleaux said. "Thats my orders. Lt Ross give them to me himself. No signed order, no ammo."

"What the f—hell is all this?" Warden said.

"He wont let us have any ammo, Top," a man said.

"He's got it locked up and the keys in his pocket," another one said. "Gimme them keys," Warden said.

"Thats my orders, Sergeant," Malleaux said, shaking his head. "I got to have a signed order from an officer before I can issue any live ammo to an enlisted man."

Pete Karelsen came out of the kitchen and across the porch wiping his mouth off with the back of his hand. From the screendoor Stark disappeared inside putting a pint bottle back into his hip pocket under his apron.

"What the hells the matter?" Pete asked his two machinegunners happily.

"He wont give us no ammo, Pete," Grenelli said indignantly.

"Well for—Jesus Christ!" Pete said disgustedly.

"Thats my orders, Sergeant," Malleaux said irrefragably.

From the southeast corner of the quad a plane came over firing, the tracers leading irrevocably in under the porch and up the wall as he flashed over, and the knot of men dived for the stairway.

"F—your orders!" Warden bawled. "Gimme them goddam keys!"

Malleaux put his hand in his pocket protectively. "I cant do that, Sergeant. I got my orders from Lt Ross himself."

"Okay," Warden said happily, "Chief, bust the door down." To Malleaux he said, "Get the hell out of the way."

Choate, and Mikeovitch and Grenelli the two machinegunners, got back for a run at the door, the Chief's big bulk towering over the two lightly built machinegunners.

Malleaux stepped in front of the door. "You cant get by with this, Sergeant," he told Warden.

"Go ahead," Warden grinned happily at the Chief. "Bust it down. He'll get out of the way." Across the quad, there were already two men up on top of the Headquarters Building.

Chief Choate and the two machinegunners launched themselves at the supply room door like three blocking backs bearing down on an end. Malleaux stepped out of the way. The door rattled ponderously.

"This is your responsibility, Sergeant" Malleaux said to Warden. "I did my best."

"Okay," Warden said. "I'll see you get a medal."

"Remember I warned you, Sergeant," Malleaux said.

"Get the f—out of my way," Warden said.

It took three tries to break the wood screws loose enough to let the Yale night lock come open. Warden was the first one in. The two machinegunners were right behind him, Mikeovitch burrowing into a stack of empty belt boxes looking for full ones while Grenelli got his gun lovingly out of the MG rack. There were men up on both the 3rd and 1st Battalion roofs by now, to meet the planes as they came winging back, on first one then the other of the cross legs of their long figure 8.

Warden grabbed a BAR from the rack and passed it out with a full bag of clips. Somebody grabbed it and took off for the roof, and somebody else stepped up to receive one. Warden passed out three of them from the rack, each with a full bag of clips, before he realized what he was doing.

"To hell with this noise," he said to Grenelli who was unstrapping his tripod on his way out the door. "I could stand here and hand these out all day and never get up on the roof."

He grabbed a BAR and clip bag for himself and pushed out the door, making a mental note to eat Malleaux's ass out. There were a dozen bags of full clips in there, left over from the BAR practice firing in August. They should have been unloaded and greased months ago.

Outside, he stopped beside Henderson. Pete, Grenelli and Mikeovitch were already rounding the stair landing out of sight with the MG and eight belt boxes.

"Get your ass in there and start passing them out," Warden told Henderson, "and start loading clips. And belts. Have Wilson go up and get a detail of men. Soons you get a batch loaded send a couple men up with them. Put three men on belts, the rest on BAR clips."

"Yes, Sir," Henderson said nervously.

Warden took off for the stairs. On the way up he stopped off at his room to get the full bottle that he kept in his footlocker for emergencies.

In the squadroom men were sitting on their bunks with their helmets on holding their empty rifles in black despair. They looked up hopefully and called to him as he passed.

"What gives, Sarge?" "Whats the deal, First?" "Are we going up on the roofs now?" "Where the hells the ammunition, Top?" "These guns aint worth nothing without no ammunition." "Hell of a note to sit on your bunk with an empty rifle and no ammunition while they blow your guts out." "Are we soljers? or boy-scouts?"

Other men, the ones who had slept through breakfast and were now getting up tousle-headed and wide-eyed, stopped dressing and looked up hopefully to see what he'd say.

"Get into field uniforms," Warden said, realizing he had to say something. "Start rolling full field packs," he told them ruthlessly in an iron voice. "We're moving out in fifteen minutes. Full field equipment."

Several men threw their rifles on their beds disgustedly.

"Then what the hell're you doin with a BAR?" somebody hollered.

"Field uniforms," Warden said pitilessly, and went on across the squadroom. "Full field equipment. Squad leaders, get them moving."

Disgustedly, the squad leaders began to harangue them to work.

In the far doorway onto the outside porch Warden stopped. In the corner under an empty bunk that had three extra mattresses piled on it, S/Sgt Turp Thornhill from Mississippi lay on the cement floor in his underwear with his helmet on hugging his empty rifle.

"You'll catch a cold, Turp," Warden said.

"Dont go out there, First Sergeant!" Turp pleaded. "You'll be killed! They shootin it up! You'll be dead! You'll not be alive any more! Dont go out there!"

"You better put your pants on," Warden said.

In his room on the porch splinters of broken glass lay all over Warden's floor, and a line of bullet holes was stitched across the top of his foot-locker and up the side of Pete's locker and across its top. Under Pete's locker was a puddle and the smell of whiskey fumes was strong in the air. Cursing savagely, Warden unlocked his footlocker and flung back the lid. A book in the tray had a slanting hole drilled right through its center. His plastic razor box was smashed and the steel safety razor bent almost double. Savagely he jerked the tray out and threw it on the floor. In the bottom of the locker two 30 caliber bullets were nestled in the padding of rolled socks and stacked underwear, one on either side of the brown quart bottle. The bottle was safe.

Warden dropped the two bullets into his pocket and got the unbroken bottle out tenderly and looked in his wall locker to make sure his record-player and records were safe. Then he hit the floor in the broken glass, holding the bottle carefully and under him, as another plane went over going east over the quad.

As he beat it back out through the squadroom the men were beginning bitterly to roll full field packs. All except Turp Thornhill, who was still under the bunk and four mattresses in his helmet and underwear; and Private Ike Galovitch, who was lying on top his bunk with his rifle along his side and his head under his pillow.

On the empty second floor, from which men were hurriedly carrying their full field equipment downstairs to roll into packs, at the south end of the porch by the latrine Readall Treadwell was going up the ladder in the latrine-supplies closet to the roof hatch carrying a BAR and grinning from ear to ear.

"First time in my goodam life," he yelled down; "I'm really goin to git to shoot a BAR, by god. I wount never of believe it."

He disappeared through the hatch and Warden followed him on up, and out into the open. Across G Company's section of roof most of G Company's first-three graders were waiting to meet the enemy from behind one of the four chimneys, or else down on their knees in one of the corners, the BAR forearms propped on the crotch-high wall, or a chimney top, their muzzles looking eagerly into the sky, and their bottles of whisky sitting beside them close up against the wall. Reedy Treadwell, who did not have a bottle, was just dropping down happily beside Chief Choate, who did. Two of the first-three-graders had hopped across the wall onto F Company's roof and were standing behind two of their chimneys. A knot of first-three-graders from F Co. were just coming up through their own hatch. They crossed the roof and began to argue violently with the two first-three-graders from G Co., demanding their chimneys. All down the 2nd Battalion roof, and on the 1st and 3rd Battalion roofs, first-three-graders were coming up through the hatches eagerly with BARS, rifles, pistols, and here and there a single MG. There were a few buck sergeants visible among them, but the only privates visible anywhere were Readall Treadwell and the two other BAR men from G CO.

"Throw your empty clips down into the Gompny Yard," Warden hollered as he moved down the roof. "Pass it along. Throw your empty clips down in the Gompny Yard. The loading detail will pick em up. Thrown your empty—"

A "V" of three planes came winging over from the southeast firing full blast, and the waiting shooters cheered happily like a mob of hobos about to sit down to their first meal in years. All the artillery on all the roofs cut loose in a deafening roar and the earth stopped. The argument on F Co.'s roof also stopped, while both sides all dived behind the same chimney. Warden turned without thinking, standing in his tracks, and fired from the shoulder without a rest, the bottle clutched tightly between his knees.

The big BAR punched his shoulder in a series of lightning left jabs. On his right Pete Karelsen was happily firing the little air-cooled 30 caliber from behind the chimney while Mikeovitch and Grenelli hung grimly onto the bucking legs of the tripod laid over the chimney, bouncing like two balls on two strings.

The planes sliced on over, unscathed, winging on down to come back up the other leg of the big figure 8. Everybody cheered again anyway, as the firing stopped.

"Holymarymotherofgod," Chief Choate boomed in his star basso that always took the break-line of the Regimental song uncontested. "I aint had so much fun since granmaw got her tit caught in the wringer."

"Shit!" old Pete said disgustedly in a low voice behind Warden. "He was on too much of an angle. Led him too far."

Warden lowered his BAR, his belly and throat tightening with a desire to let loose a high hoarse senseless yell of pure glee. This is *my* outfit. These are *my* boys. He got his bottle from between his knees and took a drink that was not a drink but an expression of feeling. The whiskey burned his throat savagely, joyously.

"Hey, Milt!" Pete called him. "You can come over here with us if you want. We got enough room for you and the bottle."

"Be right with you!" Warden roared. Gradually his ears had become aware of a bugle blowing somewhere insistently, the same call over and over. He stepped to the inside edge of the roof and looked down over the wall.

In the corner of the quad at the megaphone, among all the men running back and forth, the guard bugler was blowing The Charge.

"What the f—are *you* doing," Warden bellowed.

The bugler stopped and looked up and shrugged sheepishly. "You got me," he yelled back. "Colonel's orders." He went on blowing.

"Here they come, Pete!" Grenelli hollered. "Here comes one!" His voice went off up into falsetto excitedly.

It was a single, coming in from the northeast on the down leg of the 8. The voice of every gun on the roofs rose to challenge his passage, blending together in one deafening roar like the call of a lynch mob. Down below, the running men melted away and the bugler stopped blowing and ran back under the E Company porch.

Warden screwed the cap back on his bottle and ran crouching over to Pete's chimney and swung around to fire, again with no rest. His burst curved off in tracer smoke lines well behind the swift-sliding ship that was up, over, and then gone. Got to take more lead.

"Wouldnt you know it?" Pete said tragically. "Shot clear behind that one."

"Here, Mike," he said. "Move back a little and make room for the 1st/Sgt so he can fire off the corner for a rest. You can set the bottle down right here, Milt. Here," he said, "I'll take it for you."

"Have a drink first," Warden said happily.

"Okay." Pete wiped his soot-rimmed mouth with the back of his sleeve. There were soot flecks on his teeth when he grinned. "Did you see what they done to our room?"

"I seen what they done to your locker," Warden said.

From down below came the voice of the bugle blowing The Charge again.

"Listen to that stupid bastard," Warden said. "Colonel Delbert's orders."

"I dint think the Colonel's be up this early," Pete said.

"Old Jake must of served his first hitch in the Cavalry," Warden said.

"Say, listen," Grenelli said, "listen, Pete. When you going to let me take it a while?"

"Pretty soon," Pete said, "pretty soon."

"Throw your empty clips down in the Compny Yard, you guys!" Warden yelled around the roof. "Throw your empty clips down in the Compny Yard. Pass it along, you guys."

Down along the roof men yelled at each other to throw the empties down into the yard and went right on piling them up beside them. "God damn it!" Warden roared, and moved out from behind the chimney. He walked down along behind them like a quarterback bolstering up his linemen. "Throw them clips down, goddam you Frank. Throw your clips down, Teddy."

"Come on, Pete," Grenelli said behind him. "Let me take it a while now, will you?"

"I got first on it," Mikeovitch said.

"Like hell!" Grenelli said. "Its my gun aint it?"

"Shut up," Pete said. "Both of you. You'll both get your chance. Pretty soon."

Warden was behind the Chief and Reedy Treadwell on the inside edge when the next ones came in, a double flying in an echelon from the northeast like the single, and he dropped down beside them. Down below the bugler stopped blowing and ran back in under the E Company porch again.

Straight across from Warden on the roof of the Headquarters Building there were only two men up. One of them he recognized as M/Sgt Big John Deterling, the enlisted football coach. Big John had a .30 caliber water-cooled with no tripod, holding it cradled in his left arm and firing it with his right. When he fired a burst, the recoil staggered him all over the roof.

The winking noseguns of the incoming planes cut two foot-wide swathes raising dust across the quad and up the wall and over the D Co. Roof like a wagon road through a pasture. Warden couldnt fire at them from laughing at Big John Deterling on the Headquarters roof. This time Big John came very near to falling down and spraying the roof. The other man up over there had wisely put the chimney between him and Big John, instead of between him and the planes.

"Look at that son of a bitch," Warden said, when he could stop laughing.

Down below the loading detail dived out to pick up the clips in the lull, and the bugler ran back to the megaphone.

"I been watching him," Chief grinned. "The son of a bitch is drunk as a coot. He was down to Mrs Kipfer's last night when me and Pete was there."

"I hope his wife dont find out," Warden said.

"He ought to have a medal," Chief said still laughing.

"He probly will," Warden grinned.

As it turned out, later, he did. M/Sgt John L. Deterling; the Silver Star; for unexampled heroism in action.

Another "V" of three flashed sliding in from the southeast and Warden turned and ran back to Pete's chimney as everybody opened up with a joyous roar. Firing with the BAR forearm resting on his hand on the chimney corner, he watched his tracers get lost in the cloud of tracers around the lead plane spraying the nose, spraying the cockpit, and on back into the tail assembly. The plane shivered like a man trying to get out from under a cold shower and the pilot jumped in his seat twice like a man tied to a hot stove. They saw him throw up his arms helplessly in a useless try to ward it off, to stop it pouring in on him. There was a prolonged cheer. A hundred yards beyond the quad, with all of them watching it now in anticipatory silence, the little Zero began to fall off on one wing and slid down a long hill of air onto one of the goalposts of the 19th Infantry football field. It crashed into flames. A vast happy college-yell cheer went up from the quad and helmets were thrown into the air and backs were slapped as if our side had just made a touchdown against Notre Dame.

Then, as another "V" of three came in from the northeast, there was a wild scramble for helmets.

"You got him, Pete!" Grenelli yelled, bobbing around on the bucking tripod leg, "you got him!"

"Got him hell," Pete said without stopping firing. "Nobody'll ever know who got that guy."

"Hey, Milt!"

In the lull, Chief Choate was yelling at him from the roof edge.

"Hey, Milt! Somebody's yellin for you down below."

"Coming up!" Warden bawled. Behind him as he ran, Grenelli was pleading:

"Come on, Pete. Let me take it for a while now. You got one already."

"In a minute," Pete said. "In a minute. I just want to try one more."

Looking down over the wall, Warden saw Lt Ross standing in the yard looking up angrily, large bags under his eyes, a field cap on his uncombed head, his pants still unbuttoned, and his shoes untied and his belt unbuckled. He started buttoning his pants without looking down.

"What the hell are you doing up there, Sergeant?" he yelled. "Why arent you down here taking care of the Company? We're going to move out for the beach in less than an hour. Its probably alive with Japs already."

"Its all taken care of," Warden yelled down. "The men are rolling full field packs right now in the squadroom."

"But we've got to get the kitchen and supply ready to move, too, goddam it," Lt Ross yelled up.

"The kitchen is bein packed," Warden yelled down. "I gave Stark the orders and he's doing it now. Should be all ready in fifteen minutes."

"But the supply—" Lt Ross started to yell up.

"They're loading clips and belts for us," Warden yelled down. "All they got to do is carry the water-cooled MGs for the beach out to the trucks and throw in Leva's old field repair kit and they are ready to go.

"And," he yelled, "they makin coffee and sandwiches in the kitchen. Everything's all taken care of. Whynt you get a BAR and come on up?"

"There arent any left," Lt Ross yelled up angrily.

"Then get the hell under cover." Warden yelled down as he looked up. "Here they come."

Lt Ross dived under the porch for the supplyroom as another single came blasting in from the southeast and the roaring umbrella of fire rose from the roofs to engulf it. It seemed impossible that he could fly right through it and come out untouched. But he did. Right behind him, but flying due north along Waianae Avenue and the Hq Building, came another plane; and the umbrella swung that way without even letting go of its triggers.

The plane's gastank exploded immediately into flames that engulfed the whole cockpit and the plane veered off down on the right wing, still going at top speed. As the belly and left under-wing came up into view, the blue circle with the white star in it showed plainly in the bright sunlight. Then it was gone, off down through some trees that sheered off the wings, and the fuselage, still going at top speed, exploded into some unlucky married officer's house quarters with everyone watching it.

"That was one of ours!" Reedy Treadwell said in a small still voice. "That was an American plane!"

"Tough," Warden said, without stopping firing at the new double coming in from the northeast. "The son of a bitch dint have no business there."

After the Jap double had flashed past, unscathed, Warden turned back and made another circuit up and down the roof, his eyes screwed up into that strained look of having been slapped in the face that he sometimes got, and that made a man not want to look at him.

"Be careful, you guys," he said. Up the roof. Down the roof. "That last one was one of ours. Try and be careful. Try and get a look at them before you shoot. Them stupid bastards from Wheeler liable to fly right over here. So try and be careful after this." Up the roof. Down the roof. The same strained squint was in his voice as was in his eyes.

"Sergeant Warden!" Lt Ross roared up from down below. "God damn it! Sergeant *Warden*."

He ran back to the roof edge. "What now?"

"I want you down here, god damn it!" Lt Ross yelled up. He had his belt buckled and his shoes tied now and was smoothing back his hair with his fingers under his cap. "I want you to help me get this orderly room ready to move out! You have no business up there! Come down!"

"Goddamn it, I'm busy!" Warden yelled. "Get Rosenberry. Theres a goddamn war on, Lieutenant."

"I've just come from Col. Delbert," Lt Ross yelled up. "And he has given orders we're to move out as soon as this aerial attack is over."

"G Company's ready to move now," Warden yelled down. "And I'm busy. Tell that goddam Henderson to send up some clips and belts."

Lt Ross ran back under the porch and then ran back out again. This time he had a helmet on.

"I told him," he yelled up.

"And tell Stark to send us up some coffee."

"God *damn* it." Lt Ross raged up at him. "What is this? a Company picnic? Come down here, Sergeant! I want you! Thats an order! Come down here immediately! You hear me? Thats an order! All Company Commanders have orders from Col. Delbert personally to get ready to move out within the hour!"

"Whats that?" Warden yelled. "I cant hear you."

"I said, we're moving out within the hour."

"What?" Warden yelled. "What? Look out," he yelled; "here they come again!"

Lt Ross dove for the supplyroom and the two ammo carriers ducked their heads back down through the hatch.

Warden ran crouching back to Pete's chimney and rested his BAR on the corner and fired a burst at the "V" of three that flashed past.

"Get that goddam ammo up here!" he roared at them in the hatchway.

"Milt!" Chief Choate yelled. "Milt Warden! They want you downstairs."

"You cant find me," Warden yelled. "I've gone someplace else."

Chief nodded and relayed it down over the edge. "I cant find him, Lootenant. He's gone off someplace else." He listened dutifully down over the edge and then turned back to Warden. "Lt Ross says tell you we're moving out within the hour," he yelled.

"You cant find me," Warden yelled.

"Here they come!" Grenelli yelled from the tripod.

They did not move out within the hour. It was almost another hour before the attack was all over. And they did not move out until early afternoon three and a half hours after the attack was over. G Company was ready, but it was the only company in the Regiment that was.

Warden stayed up on the roof, by one subterfuge or another, until the attack was over. Lt Ross, it turned out, stayed down in the supplyroom and helped load ammunition. The Regimental fire umbrella claimed one more positive, and two possibles that might have been hit by the 27th and already going down when they passed over the quad. Stark himself, personally, with two of the KPs, brought them up coffee once, and then still later brought up coffee and sandwiches. In gratitude for which, Pete Karelsen let him take the MG for a while.

After it was all over, and the dead silence which no sound seemed able to penetrate reigned, they all smoked a last cigarette up on the roof and then, dirty-faced, red-eyed, tired happy and let-down, they trooped down reluctantly into the new pandemonium that was just beginning below and went to roll their full field packs. Nobody had even been scratched. But they could not seem to get outside of the ear-ringing dead silence. Even the pandemonium of moving out could not penetrate it.

Warden, instead of rolling his pack, went straight to the orderly room. In the three and a half hours before they finally left he was in the orderly room all the time, getting it packed up. Lt Ross, whose Company was the only one that was ready ahead of time, had already forgotten to be angry and came in and helped him. So did Rosenberry. Warden had plenty of time and to spare, to pack the orderly room. But he did not have any time left to roll his full field pack or change into a field uniform. Or, if he did, he forgot it.

The result of this was that he had to sleep in the popcorn vendor's wagon at Hanauma Bay without blankets for five days before he could get back up to Schofield to get his stuff, and he would have welcomed even a woolen OD field-uniform shirt. He did not see how the hell he could have possibly have forgotten that.

One by one, each company's consignment of trucks lined up before its barracks in a double file and settled down to wait. One by one, the platoons of troops filed out into their company yards and sat down on their packs holding their rifles and looked at the waiting trucks. The Regiment moved as a unit.

No two companies were going to the same place. And when they got there each company would be a separate unit on its own. But one company, that was ready, did not leave out by itself for its beach position ahead of the other companies that were not ready. The Regiment moved as a unit.

Everywhere trucks. Everywhere troops sitting on their packs. The quad filled up with trucks until even the Colonel's jeep could not worm through between them. The yards filled up with troops until even the Colonel's adjutants and messengers could not work through them. There was much swearing and sweaty disgust. The Regiment moved as a unit.

And in the G Co. orderly room, Warden chortled to himself smugly, as he worked. Once, when Lt Ross had gone to the supply room, Maylon Stark stuck his head in at the door. "The kitchen truck's loaded and ready to roll."

"Right," Warden said, without looking up.

"I want you to know I think you done a hell of a swell job," Stark said reluctantly strangledly. "It'll be two hours, anyway, before any other kitchen in this outfit is ready; and some of them probly have to stay behind to get loaded and come down later."

"You done a good job yourself," Warden said, still not looking up.

"It wasnt me," Stark said. "It was you. And I just want you to know I think you done a hell of a job."

"Okay," Warden said, "thanks," and went on working without looking up.

He rode down in the jeep at the head of the Company's convoy with Lt Ross, Weary Russell driving. There was terrific traffic. The roads were alive with trucks and taxis as far as the eye could see, bumper to bumper. The trucks were taking them down, to beach positions; the taxis were taking them up, to Schofield, where their outfits would already be gone. Recons and jeeps slithered in and out among the long lines of trucks, but the big two-and-a-halfs could only lumber on, a few feet at a time, stopping when the truck in front of them stopped in back of the truck in front of him, waiting to move on until the truck in front of them moved on a little in back of the truck in front of him.

The trucks had been stripped of their tarps and one man with his BAR or machinegun mounted over the cab rode standing on the truckbed wall. Helmeted heads were poked above the naked ribs watching the sky like visitors inspecting the dinosaur's skeleton in the Smithsonian Institute.

In the jeep, riding up and down haranguing on the road shoulder alongside the Company's column, Warden saw them all, a lot of times. Their faces were changed and they did not look the same any more. It was somewhat the same look as Stark had had in the messhall, only the drunkenness was evaporating out of it leaving only the hard set of the dry plaster. Out here on the highway, lost among hundreds of other outfits, the idea was not only clearer but bigger, much bigger, than back at your home barracks in your own quad. Chief Choate, riding with a BAR up, looked down at him from above his truck cab and Warden looked back.

They had all left everything behind, civilian clothes, garrison shoes and uniforms, campaign hat collections, insignia collections, photograph albums, private papers. To hell with all that. This was war. We wont need that. They brought nothing but the skeletal field living equipment, and the only man who packed in anything comfortable to bring with him was Pete Karelsen. Pete had been in France. Gradually, foot by foot, the trucks moved on down toward Honolulu and whatever waited on the beaches. Up till now it had been a day off, it had been fun.

Pearl Harbor, when they passed it, was a shambles. Wheeler Field had been bad, but Pearl Harbor numbed the brain. Pearl Harbor made a queasiness in the testicles. Wheeler Field was set back quite a ways from the road, but parts of Pearl Harbor were right on the highway. Up till then it had been a big lark, a picnic; they had fired from the roofs and been fired at from the planes and the cooks had served them coffee and sandwiches and the supply detail had brought them up ammo and they had got two or three planes and only one man in the whole Regiment had been hit (with a .50 caliber in the fleshy part of his calf, didnt even hit a bone, he walked up to the dispensary by himself), and he was getting himself a big Purple Heart. Almost everybody had had a bottle and they all had been half-drunk anyway when it started and it had all been a sort of super-range-season with live targets to shoot at. The most exciting kind: Men. But now the bottles were fast wearing off and there was no immediate prospect of getting any more and there were no live targets to shoot at. Now they were thinking. Why, it might be months—even years—before they could get hold of a bottle again! This was a big war.

As the trucks passed through the new Married NCO Quarters that had been added onto Pearl Harbor recently, women and children and an occasional old man standing in the yards cheered them. The troops rode on through in silence, staring at them dully.

Going through the back streets of town, all along the route, men, women and children stood on porches, fences, cartops, and roofs and cheered them roundly. They waved Winnie Churchill's "V"-for-Victory sign at them, and held their thumbs up in the air. Young girls threw them kisses. Mothers of young girls, with tears in their eyes, urged their daughters to throw them more kisses.

The troops, looking wistfully at all this ripe young stuff running around loose that they could not get into, and remembering the old days when civilian girls were not allowed—and did not desire—to speak to soldiers on the street in broad daylight let alone at night in a bar, gave them back the old one-finger salute of the clenched fist stabbing the stiff middle finger into the air. They returned Winnie Churchill's "V"-for-Victory sign with an even older one of their own, in which the fist is clenched and the middle finger and thumb are extended and pinched repeatedly together.

The ecstatic civilians, who did not know that this last was the Old Army sign for the female, or that the fist meant "F—you!" cheered them even more roundly and the troops, for the first time since they'd left Schofield, grinned a little bit at each other, slyly, and redoubled with their saluting.

From Waikiki on east, the trucks in the Company's convoy began to peel off to deliver the various three- and four-man details each with its noncom to their various beach positions. By the time they reached the rise up over the Kioko Head saddle where the road turned off down to the CP at Haunauma Bay, there were only four trucks left. The two for Position 28 at Makapuu Head, one for the CP personnel and Position 27, and the kitchen truck. The first two, the CP truck and the kitchen truck, pulled off onto the side road and stopped and the last two bound for Makapuu went on, then, past them. They had all had their big day with the civilians, which most of them had waited from two to five years for, and now they were preparing to pay for it.

Among the troops in the trucks there was a certain high fervor of defense and patriotism that exploded into a weak feeble cheer in the heavy perpetual wind, as they passed Lt Ross and The Warden who had climbed out of the jeep on the road-shoulder to watch them go past. A few fists were shaken in the air up between the bare truck ribs and Friday Clark, current-rifleman and ex-apprentice-Company-bugler, shook a wildly promising two-finger "V"-for-Victory sign at Lt Ross from over the tailgate of the last truck as they pulled on away.

This general patriotic enthusiasm lasted about three days.

Lt Ross, standing beside his jeep to watch his men go off to possible maiming and death, certainly off to a war that would last a long time, looked at Friday sadly and without acknowledgment from across a great gulf of years, pity, and superior knowledge, his eyes set in a powerful emotion, a look of great age and fearful responsibility on his face.

1st/Sgt Warden, standing beside his Company Commander and watching his face, wanted to boot his Company Commander hard in the ass.

It was perhaps the stringing of the barbed wire, more than anything else, that ate into the patriotism of the troops in the next few days. The men who had acquired the new unknown disease of aching veins in their arm joints from the building of these positions now found it coming back on them doubly powerfully from putting up barbed wire to protect these positions. So that even when they were not pulling guard at night, they couldn't sleep anyway. The stringing of the barbed wire, after the first day, was an even more powerful astringent to the patriotism than their getting crummy with no prospect of a shower, or their getting itchy with beard and no prospect of a shave, or their having to sleep on the rocks with nothing but a single shelterhalf and two blankets over them when it rained.

Actually, this war that had started out so well Sunday morning and given them such high hopes of the future, was turning out to be nothing more than an extended maneuvre. With the single difference that this showed no prospect of ending.

It was five days before things were organized enough to allow the sending of a detail back to Schofield for the rest of their stuff, that they had not thought they'd need, and the Company's quota of pyramidal tents. But even these didnt do the men at Makapuu any good since out there there werent any trees to set them up under.

Warden, armed with the request list of each man which altogether covered an entire pad of legal-size scratch paper, led the detail of three trucks. Pete Karelsen, who was the only man in the Company who had been anywhere near comfortable in the five days, was his second-in-command. They pulled into the quad with their three trucks to find another outfit already moved into the barracks and the footlockers and wall lockers of G Company thoroughly rifled. Their lists were useless. Pete Karelsen, again, had been practically the only man in the Company who had bothered to lock either his footlocker or wall locker that Sunday morning. But even Pete's extra set of false teeth, which had been out on the table, were gone.

And, of course, none of the new tenants they talked to knew a damn thing about it.

Warden's records and player were gone, also his $120 Brooks Bros. suit, saddle-stitched Forstmann jacket, and the white dinner jacket and tux pants he had bought but never worn yet, together with all of his uniforms. Also, the brand new $260 electric guitar, still less than half paid for, that Andy and Friday had bought while Prew was in the Stockade, was gone too, speaker jackplug and all.

If it had not been for 1st/Sgt Dedrick of A Company, who was about his size and had remembered to lock his wall locker, he would not have even been able to scare up two whole field uniforms. Just about the only thing that had been left untouched were the folded pyramidal tents in the supply room.

By the end of the seventh day, when they had got the tents back downtown and distributed out to the positions and set up ready to occupy, every man on the Company roster—including the two men serving time in the Stockade who had been released with the rest of the prisoners—had shown up and reported for duty. With the single exception of Prewitt.

The Landing on Kuralei
(from *Tales of the South Pacific*)

James A. Michener

We would have captured Kuralei according to plan if it had not been for Lt Col Kenjuro Hyaichi. An honor graduate from California Tech, he was a likely choice for the job the Japs gave him.

As soon as our bombers started to soften up Konora, where we built the airstrip, the Jap commander on Kuralei gave Hyaichi his instructions: "Imagine that you are an American admiral. You are going to invade this island. What would you do?"

Hyaichi climbed into a plane and had the pilot take him up 12,000 feet. Below him Kuralei was like a big cashew nut. The inside bend faced north, and in its arms were two fine sandy bays. They were the likely places to land. You could see that even from the air. But there was a small promontory protruding due south from the outside bend. From the air Hyaichi studied that promontory with great care. "Maybe they know we have the two bays fortified. Maybe they will try that promontory."

The colonel had his pilot drop to three thousand feet and then to five hundred. He flew far out to sea in the direction from which our search planes came. He roared in six times to see if he could see what an American pilot, scared and in a hurry, would think he saw.

Then he studied the island from a small boat. Had it photographed from all altitudes and angles. He studied the photographs for many days. He had two Jap spies shipped in one night from Truk. They crept ashore at various points. "What did you see?" he asked them. "Did you think the bay was defended? What about that promontory?"

He had two trained observers flown over from Palau. They had never seen Kuralei before. When their plane started to descend, they were blindfolded. "The bays?" Hyaichi asked. "And that promontory? Did you think there was sand in the two small beaches there? Did you see the cliffs?"

Jap intelligence officers brought the colonel sixty-page and seventy-page reports of interrogations of American prisoners. They showed him detailed studies of every American landing from Guadalcanal to Konora. They had a complete book on Admiral Kester, an analysis of each action the admiral had ever commanded. At the end of his study Lt Col Hyaichi ruled out the possibility of our landing at the promontory. "It couldn't be done," he said. "That coral shelf sticking out two hundred yards would stop anything they have."

But before the colonel submitted his recommendations that all available Jap power be concentrated at the northern bays, a workman in Detroit had a beer.

After his beer this workman talked with a shoe salesman from St Louis, who told a brother-in-law, who passed the word on to a man heading for Texas, where the news was relayed to Mexico and thence to Tokyo and Kuralei that "General Motors is building a boat that can climb over the damnedest stuff you ever saw."

Lt Col Hyaichi tore up his notes. He told his superiors: "The Americans will land on either side of the promontory." "How can they?" he was asked. "They have new weapons," he replied. "Amphibious tanks with treads for crossing coral." Almost a year before, Admiral Nimitz had decided that when we hit Kuralei we would not land at the two bays. "We will hit the promontory. We will surprise them."

Fortunately for us, Lt Col Hyaichi's superiors were able to ignore his conclusions. It would be folly, they said, to move defenses from the natural northern landing spots. All they would agree to was that Hyaichi might take whatever material he could find and set up secondary defenses at the promontory. How well he did his job you will see.

At 0527 our first amphibs hit the coral shelf which protruded underwater from the shore. It was high tide, and they half rode, half crawled toward land. They had reached a point twenty feet from the beach, when all hell ripped loose. Lt Col Hyaichi's fixed guns blasted our amphibs right out of the water. Our men died in the air before they fell back into the shallow water on the coral shelf. At low tide their bodies would be found, gently wallowing in still pools of water. A few men reached shore. They walked the last twenty feet through a haze of bullets.

At 0536 our second wave reached the imaginary line twenty feet from shore. The Jap five-inch guns ripped loose. Of nine craft going in, five were sunk. Of the three hundred men in those five amphibs, more than one hundred were killed outright. Another hundred died wading to shore. But some reached shore. They formed a company, the first on Kuralei. It was now dawn. The LSC-108 had nosed in toward the coral reef to report the landings. We sent word to the flagship. Admiral Kester started to sweat at his wrists. "Call off all landing attempts for eighteen minutes," he said.

At 0544 our ships laid down a gigantic barrage. How had they missed those five-inch guns before? How had anything lived through our previous bombardment? Many Japs didn't. But those hiding in Lt Col Hyaichi's special pillboxes did. And they lived through this bombardment, too.

On the small beach to the west of the promontory 118 men huddled together as the shells ripped overhead. Our code for this beach was Green, for the one to the east, Red. The lone walkie-talkie on Green Beach got the orders: "Wait till the bombardment ends. Proceed to the first line of coconut trees." Before the Signalman could answer, one of our short shells landed among the men. The survivors reformed, but they had no walkie-talkie.

At 0602 the third wave of amphibs set out for the beach. The vast bombardment rode over their heads until they were onto the coral shelf. Then a shattering silence followed. It was full morning. The sun was rising. Our amphibs waddled over the coral. At the fatal twenty-foot line some Japs opened up on the amphibs. Three were destroyed. But eight got through and deposited their men ashore. Jap machine gunners and snipers tied into tall trees took a heavy toll. But our men formed and set out for the first line of coconut trees.

They were halfway to the jagged stumps when the japs opened fire from carefully dug trenches behind the trees. Our men tried to outfight the bullets but could not. They retreated to the beach. The coconut grove was lined with fixed positions, a trench behind each row of trees.

As our men withdrew they watched a hapless amphib broach to on the coral. It hung suspended, turning slowly. A Jap shell hit it full in the middle. It rose in the air. Bodies danced violently against the rising sun and fell back dead upon the coral. "Them poor guys," the Marines on the beach said.

At 0631 American planes appeared. F6F's. They strafed the first trench until no man but a Jap could live. They bombed. They ripped Green Beach for twelve minutes. Then the next wave of amphibs went in. The first two craft broached to and were blown to shreds of steaming metal. "How can those Japs live?" the man at my side said. In the next wave four more amphibs were sunk.

So at 0710 the big ships opened up again. They fired for twenty-eight minutes this time, concentrating their shells about sixty yards inland from the first row of coconut stumps. When they stopped, our men tried again. This time they reached the trees, but were again repulsed. Almost four hundred men were ashore now. They formed in tight circles along the edge of the beach.

At 0748 we heard the news from Red Beach, on the other side of the promontory. "Repulsed four times. First men now safely ashore!" Four times! we said to ourselves. Why, that's worse than here! It couldn't be! Yet it was, and when the tide started going out on Red Beach, the Japs pushed our men back onto the coral.

This was fantastic! When you looked at Alligator back in Noumea you knew it was going to be tough. But not like this! There were nine rows of coconut trees. Then a cacao grove. The edge of that grove was Line Albany. We had to reach the cacaos by night. We knew that an immense blockhouse of sod and stone and concrete and coconut trees would have to be reduced there before night. We were expected to start storming the blockhouse by 1045. That was the schedule.

At 1400 our men were still hudddled on the beach. Kester would not withdraw them. I don't think they would have come back had he ordered them to do so. They hung on, tried to cut westward but were stopped by the cliffs, tried to cut eastward but were stopped by fixed guns on the promontory.

At 1422 Admiral Kester put into operation his alternative plan. While slim beachheads were maintained at Red and Green all available shock troops were ordered to hit the rugged western side of the promontory. We did not know if landing craft could get ashore. All we knew was that if they could land, and if they could establish a beach, and if they could cut a path for men and tanks down through the promontory, we might flank each of the present beachheads and have a chance of reaching the cacaos by dark.

At 1425 we got our orders. "LCS-108. All hands to Objective 66." The men winked at one another. They climbed into the landing barges. The man whose wife had a baby girl. The young boy who slept through his leave in Frisco. They went into the barges. The sun was starting to sink westward as they set out for the shore.

Lt Col Hyaichi's men waited. Then two fixed guns whose sole purpose was to wait for such a landing fired. Shells ripped through the barges. One with men from 108 turned in the air and crushed its men to death. They flung their arms outward and tried to fly free, but the barge caught them all. A few swam out from under. They could not touch bottom, so they swam for the shore, as they had been trained to do. Snipers shot at them. Of the few, a few reached shore. One man shook himself like a dog and started into the jungle. Another made it and cried out to a friend. "Red Beach! Green Beach! Sonova Beach!" You can see that in the official reports. "At 1430 elements from LCS-108 and the transport Julius Kennedy started operations at Sonova Beach."

The hidden guns on the promontory continued firing. Kester sent eight F6F's after them. They dived the emplacements and silenced one of the guns. I remember one F6F that seemed to hang for minutes over a Jap gun, pouring lead. It was uncanny. Then the plane exploded! It burst into a violent puff of red and black. Its pieces were strewn over a wide area, but they hurt no one. They were too small.

At 1448 a rear-admiral reported to Kester, "Men securely ashore at Objective 66." The admiral diverted all available barges there. Sonova Beach was invaded. Barges and men turned in the air and died alike with hot steel in their guts, but the promontory was invaded. Not all our planes nor all our ships could silence those damned Jap gunners, but Sonova Beach, that strip of bleeding coral, it was invaded.

At 1502 Admiral Kester sent four tanks ashore at Sonova with orders to penetrate the promontory and to support whichever beach seemed most promising. Two hundred men went along with axes and shovels. I watched the lumbering tanks crawl ashore and hit their first banyan trees. There was a crunching sound. I could hear it above the battle. The tanks disappeared among the trees.

At 1514 came the Japs' only airborne attack that day. About thirty bombers accompanied by forty fighters swept in from Truk. They tried for our heavy ships. The fleet threw up a wilderness of flak. Every ship in the task force opened up with its five-inchers, Bofors, Oerlikons, three-inchers and .50 calibers. The air was heavy with lead. Some Jap planes spun into the sea. I watched a bomber spouting flames along her port wing. She dived to put them out. But a second shell hit her amidships. The plane exploded and fell into the ocean in four pieces. The engine, badly afire, hit the water at an angle and ricocheted five times before it sank in hissing rage.

One of our transports was destroyed by a Jap bomb. It burst into lurid flame as it went down. Near by, a Jap plane plunged into the sea. Then, far aloft an F6F came screaming down in a mortal dive. "Jump!" a thousand voices urged. But the pilot never did. The plane crashed into the sea right behind the Jap bomber and burned.

A Jap fighter, driven low, dived at the 108 and began to strafe. I heard dull spats of lead, the firing of our own guns, and a cry. The Jap flashed past, unscathed. Men on the 108 cursed. The young skipper looked ashen with rage and hurried aft to see who had been hit.

The Japs were being driven off. As a last gesture a fighter dived into the bridge of one of our destroyers. There were four explosions. The superstructure was blown away with three dozen men and four officers. Two other fighters tried the same trick. One zoomed over the deck of a cruiser and bounced three times into a boiling sea. The other came down in a screaming vertical spin and crashed deep into the water not far from where I stood. There were underwater explosions and a violent geyser spurting high in the air.

Our planes harried the remaining Japs to death, far out at sea. Our pilots, their fuel exhausted, went into the sea themselves. Some died horribly of thirst, days later. Others were picked up almost immediately and had chicken for dinner.

While the Jap suicide planes were crashing into the midst of the fleet, a Jap shore battery opened up and hit an ammunition ship. It disintegrated in a terrible, gasping sound. Almost before the last fragments of that ship had fallen into the water, our big guns found the shore battery and destroyed it.

Meanwhile power had been building up on Green Beach. At 1544, with the sun dropping lower toward the ocean, they tried the first row of coconut trees again. They were driven back. This time, however, not quite to the coral. They held onto some good positions fifteen or twenty yards inland.

At 1557 Admiral Kester pulled them back onto the coral. For the last time that day. He sent the planes in to rout out that first trench. This time with noses almost in the coconut stumps, our fliers roared up and down the trenches. They kept their powerful .50's aimed at the narrow slits like a woman guiding a sewing machine along a predetermined line. But the 50's stitched death.

At 1607 the planes withdrew. At a signal, every man on that beach, every one, rose and dashed for the first trench. The Japs knew they were coming, and met them with an enfilading fire. But the Green Beach boys piled on. Some fell wounded. Others died standing up and took a ghostly step toward the trench. Some dropped from fright and lay like dead men. But most went on, grunting as they met the Japs with bayonets. There was a muddled fight in the trench. Then things were quiet. Some Americans started crawling back to pick up their wounded. That meant our side had won.

Japs from the second trench tried to lead a charge against the exhausted Americans. But some foolhardy gunners from a cruiser laid down a pinpoint barrage of heavy shells. Just beyond the first trench. It was dangerous, but it worked. The Japs were blown into small pieces. Our men had time to reorganize. They were no longer on coral. They were inland. On Kuralei's earth.

At 1618 Admiral Kester made his decision. Green Beach was our main chance. To hell with Red. Hang on, Red! But everything we had was thrown at Green. It was our main chance. "Any word from the tanks?" "Beating down the peninsula, sir." It was no use banging the table. If the tanks could get through, they would.

At 1629 about a hundred amphibs sped for Green Beach. They were accompanied by a tremendous barrage that raked the western end of the beach toward the cliffs. Thirty planes strafed the Jap part of the promontory. A man beside me started yelling frantically. A Jap gun, hidden somewhere in that wreckage, was raking our amphibs. "Get that gun!" he shouted. "It's right over there!" He jumped up and down and had to urinate against the bulkhead. "Get that gun!" Two amphibs were destroyed by the gun. But more than ninety made the beach. Now, no matter how many Japs counterattacked, we had a chance to hold the first trench.

"A tank!" our lookout shouted. I looked, but saw none. Then, yes! There was a tank! But it was a Jap tank. Three of them! The Jap general had finally conceded Lt Col Hyaichi's point. He was rushing all moveable gear to the promontory. And our own tanks were still bogged down in the jungle.

"LCS-108! Beach yourself and use rockets!" The order came from the flagship. With crisp command the young skipper got up as much speed as possible. He drove his small craft as near the battle lines as the sea would take it. We braced ourselves and soon felt a grinding shock as we hit coral. We were beached, and our bow was pointed at the Jap tanks.

Our first round of rockets went off with a low swish and headed for the tanks. "Too high!" the skipper groaned. The barrage shot into the cacao trees. The Jap tanks bore down on our men in the first ditch. Our next round of rockets gave a long hisss. The first tank exploded loudly and blocked the way of the second Jap.

At this moment a Jap five-incher hit the 108. We heeled over to port. The men at the rocket-launching ramps raised their sights and let go with another volley. The second tank exploded. Japs climbed out of the manhole. Two of them dived into the cacaos. Two others were hit by rifle fire and hung head downward across the burning tank.

The third Jap tank stopped firing at our men in the first trench and started lobbing shells at LCS-108. Two hit us, and we lay far over on the coral. The same foolhardy gunners on the cruiser again ignored our men in the first trench. Accurately they plastered the third tank. We breathed deeply. The Japs probably had more tanks coming, but the first three were taken care of.

Our skipper surveyed his ship. It was lost. It would either be hauled off the reef and sunk or left there to rot. He felt strange. His first command! What kind of war was this? You bring a ship all the way from Norfolk to stop two tanks. On land. You purposely run your ship on a coral reef. It's crazy. He damned himself when he thought of that Jap plane flashing by. It had killed two of his men.

Not one of our bullets hit that plane. It all happened so fast. "So fast!" he muttered. "This is a hell of a war!"

At 1655 the Marines in trench one, fortified by new strength from the amphibs, unpredictably dashed from the far western end of their trench and overwhelmed the Japs in the opposite part of trench two. Then ensued a terrible, hidden battle as the Marines stolidly swept down the Jap trench. We could see arms swinging above the trench, and bayonets. Finally, the men in the eastern end of trench one could stand the suspense no longer. Against the bitterest kind of enemy fire, they rushed past the second row of coconut stumps and joined their comrades. Not one Jap survived that brutal, silent, hidden struggle. Trench two was ours.

At 1659 more than a thousand Jap reinforcements arrived in the area. Not yet certain that we had committed all our strength to Green Beach, about half the Japs were sent to Red. Lt Col Hyaichi, tight-lipped and sweating, properly evaluated our plan. He begged his commanding officer to leave only a token force at Red Beach and to throw every ounce of man and steel against Green. This was done. But as the reserves moved through the coconut grove, the skipper of the LCS-108 poured five rounds of rockets right into their middle. Results passed belief. Our men in trench two stared in frank astonishment at what the rockets accomplished. Then, shouting, they swamped the third Jap trench before it could be reinforced.

At 1722, when the sun was beginning to eat into the treetops of Kuralei, our tanks broke loose along the shore of the promontory. Sixty sweating footslogging axmen dragged themselves after the tanks. But ahead lay an unsurmountable barrier of rock. The commanding officer of the tanks appraised the situation correctly. He led his ménage back into the jungle. The japs also foresaw what would happen next. They moved tank destroyers up. Ship fire destroyed them. We heard firing in the jungle.

At 1740 our position looked very uncertain. We were still six rows from Line Albany. And the Japs had their blockhouse right at the edge of the cacaos. Our chances of attaining a reasonably safe position seemed slight when a fine shout went up. One of our tanks had broken through! Alone, it dashed right for the heart of the Jap position. Two enemy tanks, hidden up to now, swept out from coconut emplacements and engaged our tank. Bracketed by shells from each side, our tank exploded. Not one man escaped.

But we soon forgot the first tank. For slowly crawling out of the jungle came the other three. Their treads were damaged. But they struggled on. When the gloating Jap tanks saw them coming, they hesitated. Then, perceiving the damage we had suffered, the Japs charged. Our tanks stood fast and fired fast. The Japs were ripped up and down. One quit the fight. Its occupants fled. The other came on to its doom. Converging fire from our three tanks caught it. Still it came. Then, with a fiery gasp, it burned up. Its crew did not even try to escape.

At 1742 eleven more of our tanks landed on Sonova Beach. You would have thought their day was just beginning. But the sun was on their tails as they grunted into the jungle like wild pigs hunting food.

An endless stream of barges hit Green Beach. How changed things were! On one wave not a single shot from shore molested them. Eight hundred Yanks on Kuralei without a casualty. How different that was! We got Admiral Kester's message: "Forty-eight minutes of daylight. A supreme effort."

At 1749 the Japs launched their big counter-attack. They swept from their blockhouse in wild assault. Our rockets sped among them, but did not stop them. It was the men in trench three that stopped them.

How they did so, I don't know. Japs swarmed upon them, screaming madly. With grenades and bayonets the banzai boys did devilish work. Eighty of our men died in that grim assault. Twelve had their heads completely severed.

But in the midst of the melee, two of our three tanks broke away from the burning Jap tanks and rumbled down between trench three and trench four. Up and down that tight area-way they growled. A Jap suicide squad stopped one by setting it afire. Their torches were their own gasoline-soaked bodies. Our tankmen, caught in an inferno, tried to escape. From trench three, fifty men leaped voluntarily to help them. Our men surrounded the flaming tank. The crewmen leaped to safety. In confusion, they ran not to our lines but into trench four. Our men, seeing them cut down, went mad. They raged into trench four and killed every Jap. In a wild spontaneous sweep they swamped trench five as well!

Aboard the LCS-108 we could not believe what we had seen. For in their rear were at least a hundred and twenty Japs still fighting. At this moment reinforcements from the amphibs arrived. The Japs were caught between heavy fire. Not a man escaped. The banzai charge from the blockhouse had ended in a complete rout.

At 1803 Admiral Kester sent his message: "You can do it. Twenty-seven minutes to Line Albany!" We were then four rows from the blockhouse. But we were sure that beyond trench seven no trenches had been dug. But we also knew that trenches six and seven were tougher than anything we had yet tackled. So for the last time Admiral Kester sent his beloved planes in to soften up the trenches. In the glowering dusk they roared up and down between the charred trees, hiccuping vitriol. The grim, terrible planes withdrew. There was a moment of waiting. We waited for our next assault. We waited for new tanks to stumble out of the promontory. We waited in itching dismay for that tropic night. We were so far from the blockhouse! The sun was almost sunk into the sea.

What we waited for did not come. Something else did. From our left flank, toward the cliffs, a large concentration of Jap reinforcements broke from heavy cover and attacked the space between trenches one and two. It was seen in a flash that we had inadequate troops at that point. LCS-108 and several other ships made an instantaneous decision. We threw all our fire power at the point of invasion. Rockets, five-inchers, eight-inchers and intermediate fire hit the Japs. The were stopped cold. Our lines held.

But I can still see one flight of rockets we launched that day at dusk. When the men in trench two saw the surprise attack coming on their flank, they turned sideways to face the new threat. Three Americans nearest the Japs never hesitated. Without waiting for a command to duty they leaped out of their trench to meet the enemy head on. Our rockets crashed into the advancing Japs. The three voluntary fighters were killed. By their own friends.

There was no possible escape from this tragedy. To be saved, all those men needed was less courage. It was nobody's fault but their own. Like war, rockets once launched cannot be stopped.

It was 1807. The sun was gone. The giant clouds hanging over Kuralei turned gold and crimson. Night birds started coming into the cacao grove. New Japs reported to the blockhouse for a last stand. Our own reinforcements shuddered as they stepped on dead Japs. Night hurried on.

At 1809, with guns spluttering, eight of our tanks from Sonova Beach burst out of the jungle. Four of them headed for the blockhouse. Four tore right down the alleyway between trenches five and six. These took a Jap reinforcement party head on. The fight was foul and unequal. Three Japs set fire to themselves and tried to immolate the tank crews. They were actually shot to pieces. The tanks rumbled on.

At the blockhouse it was a different story. Tank traps had been well built in that area. Our heavies could not get close to the walls. They stood off and hammered the resilient structure with shells.

"Move in the flame-throwers. Everything you have. Get the block-house." The orders were crisp. They reached the Marines in trench five just as the evening star became visible. Eight husky young men with nearly a hundred pounds of gear apiece climbed out of the trench. Making an exceptional target, they blazed their way across six and seven with hundreds of protectors. They drew a slanting hailstorm of enemy fire. But if one man was killed, somebody else grabbed the cumbersome machinery. In the gathering darkness they made a weird procession.

A sergeant threw up his hands and jumped. "No trenches after row seven!" A tank whirled on its right tread and rumbled over. Now, with tanks on their right and riflemen on their left, the flame-throwers advanced. From every position shells hit the blockhouse. It stood. But its defenders were driven momentarily away from the portholes. This was the moment!

With hoarse cries our flame-throwers rushed forward. Some died and fell into their own conflagration. But three flame-throwers reached the portholes. There they held their spuming fire. They burned away the oxygen of the blockhouse. They seared eyes, lips, and more than lungs. When they stepped back from the portholes, the blockhouse was ours.

Now it was night! From all sides Japs tried to infiltrate our lines. When they were successful, our men died. We would find them in the morning with their throats cut. When you found them so, all thought of sorrow for the Japs burned alive in the blockhouse was erased. They were the enemy, the cruel, remorseless, bitter enemy. And they would remain so, every man of them, until their own red sun sank like the tired sun of Kuralei.

Field headquarters were set up that night on Green Beach. I went ashore in the dark. It was strange to think that so many men had died there. In the wan moonlight the earth was white like the hair of an old woman who has seen much life. But in spots it was red, too. Even in the moonlight.

Unit leaders reported. "Colonel, that schedule for building the airstrip is busted wide open. Transport carrying LARU-8 hit. Heavy casualties." I grabbed the man's arm.

"Was that the transport that took a direct hit?" I asked.

"Yes," he said, still dazed. "Right in the belly."

"What happened?" I rattled off the names of my friends in that unit. Benoway, in the leg. The cook, dead. The old skipper, dead. "What happened to Harbison?" I asked.

The man looked up at me in the yellow light. "Are you kidding, sir?"

"No! I know the guy."

"*You* know him? Hmmm. I guess you don't! You haven't heard?" His eyes were excited.

"No."

"Harbison pulled out four days before we came north. All the time we were on Efate he couldn't talk about anything but war. 'Hold me back, fellows. I want to get at them!' But when our orders came through he got white in the face. Arranged it by airmail through his wife's father. Right now he's back in New Mexico. Rest and rehabilitation leave."

"That little Jewish photographic officer you had?" I asked, sick at the stomach.

"He's dead," the man shouted. He jumped up. "The old man's dead. The cook's dead. But Harbison is back in New Mexico." He shouted and started to cry.

"Knock it off!" a Marine colonel cried.

"The man's a shock case," I said. The colonel came over.

"Yeah. He's the guy from the transport. Fished him out of the drink. Give him some morphine. But for Christ's sake shut him up. Now where the hell is that extra .50 caliber ammo?"

The reports dragged in. We were exactly where Alligator said we should be. Everything according to plan. That is, all but one detail. Casualties were far above estimate. It was that bastard Hyaichi. We hadn't figured on him. We hadn't expected a Cal Tech honors graduate to be waiting for us on the very beach we wanted.

"We'll have to appoint a new beachmaster," a young officer reported to the colonel.

"Ours get it?" the colonel asked.

"Yessir. He went inland with the troops."

"Goddam it!" the colonel shouted. "I told Fry a hundred times…"

"It wasn't his fault, sir. Came when the Japs made that surprise attack on the flank."

There was sound of furious firing to the west. The colonel looked up.

"Well," he said. "We lost a damned good beachmaster. You take over tomorrow. And get that ammo in and up."

I grabbed the new beachmaster by the arm. "What did you say?" I whispered.

"Fry got his."

"Tony Fry?"

"Yes. You know him?"

"Yes," I said weakly. "How?"

"If you know him, you can guess." The young officer wiped his face. "His job on the beach was done. No more craft coming in. We were attacking the blockhouse. Fry followed us in. Our captain said, 'Better stay back there, lieutenant. This is Marines' work.' Fry laughed and turned back. That was when the Japs hit from the cliffs. Our own rockets wiped out some of our men. Fry grabbed a carbine. But the japs got him right away. Two slugs in the belly. He kept plugging along. Finally fell over. Didn't even fire the carbine once."

I felt sick. "Thanks," I said.

The colonel came over to look at the man from LARU-8. He grabbed my arm. "What's the matter, son? You better take a shot of that sleeping stuff yourself," he said.

"I'm all right," I said. "I was thinking about a couple of guys."

"We all are," the colonel said. He had the sad, tired look that old men wear when they have sent young men to die.

Looking at him, I suddenly realized that I didn't give a damn about Bill Harbison. I was mad for Tony Fry. That free, kind, independent man. In my bitterness I dimly perceived what battle means. In civilian life I was ashamed until I went into uniform. In the States I was uncomfortable while others were overseas. At Noumea I thought, "The guys on Guadal! They're the heroes!" But when I reached Guadal I found that all the heroes were somewhere farther up the line. And while I sat in safety aboard the LCS-108 I knew where the heroes were. They were on Kuralei. Yet, on the beach itself only a few men ever really fought the Japs. I suddenly realized that from the farms, and towns, and cities all over America an unbroken line ran straight to the few who stormed the blockhouses. No matter where along that line you stood, if you were not the man at the end of it, the ultimate man with his sweating hands upon the blockhouse, you didn't know what war was. You had only an intimation, as of a bugle blown far in the distance. You might have flashing insights, but you did not know. By the grace of God you would never know.

Alone, a stranger from these men who had hit the beaches, I went out to dig a place to sleep. Two men in a foxhole were talking. Eager for some kind of companionship, I listened in the darkness.

"Don't give me that stuff," one was saying. "Europe is twice as tough as this!"

"You talk like nuts," a younger voice retaliated. "These yellows is the toughest fighters in the world."

"I tell you not to give me that crap!" the older man repeated. "My brother was in Africa. He hit Sicily. He says the Krauts is the best all round men in uniform!"

"Lend me your lighter." There was a pause as the younger man used the flameless lighter.

"Keep your damned head down," his friend warned.

"If the Japs is such poor stuff, why worry?"

"Like I said," the other reasoned. "Where did you see any artillery barrage today? Now if this was the Germans, that bay would have been filled with shells."

"I think I saw a lot of barges get hell," the young man argued.

"You ain't seen nothing! You mark my words. Wait till we try to hit France! I doubt we get a ship ashore. Them Krauts is plenty tough. They got mechanized, that's what they got!"

"You read too many papers!" the second Marine argued. "You think when they write up this war they won't say the Japs was the toughest soldier we ever met?"

"Look! I tell you a thousand times. We ain't met the Jap yet. Mark my words. When we finally tangle with him in some place like the Philippines…"

"What were we doin' today? Who was them little yellow fellows? Snow White and the Seven Dwarfs? Well, where the hell was Snow White?"

"Now wait! Now wait just a minute! Answer me one question. Just one question! Will you answer me one question?"

"Shoot!"

"No *ifs* and *ands* and *buts*?"

"Shoot!"

"All right! Now answer me one question. Was it as tough as you thought it would be?"

There was a long moment of silence. These were the men who had landed in the first wave. The young man carefully considered the facts. "No," he said.

"See what I mean?" his heckler reasoned.

"But it wasn't no pushover, neither," the young man defended himself.

"No, I didn't say it was. But it's a fact that the Nips wasn't as tough as they said. We got ashore. We got to the blockhouse. Little while ago I hear we made just about where we was expected to make."

"But on the other hand," the young Marine said, "it wasn't no picnic. Maybe it was as tough as I thought last night!"

"Don't give me that stuff! Last night we told each other what we thought. And it wasn't half that bad. Was it? Just a good tough tussle. I don't think these Japs is such hot stuff. Honest to God I don't!"

"You think the way the Germans surrendered in Africa makes them tougher?"

"Listen, listen. I tell you a hundred times. They was pushed to the wall. But wait till we hit France. I doubt we get a boat ashore. That's one party I sure want to miss."

There was a moment of silence. Then the young man spoke again. "Burke?" he asked. "About last night. Do you really think he'll run for a fourth term?"

"Listen! I tell you a hundred times! The American public won't stand for it. Mark my words. They won't stand for it. I thought we settled that last night."

"But I heard Colonel Hendricks saying …"

"Please, Eddie! You ain't quotin' that fathead as an authority, are you?"

"He didn't do so bad gettin' us on this beach, did he?"

"Yeah, but look how he done it. A slaughter!"

"You just said it was easier than you expected."

"I was thinkin' of over there," Burke said. "Them other guys at Red Beach. Poor bastards. We did all right. But this knuckle-brain Hendricks. You know, Eddie, honest to God, if I had a full bladder I wouldn't let that guy lead me to a bathroom!"

"Yeah, maybe you're right. He's so dumb he's a colonel. That's all. A full colonel."

"Please, Eddie! We been through all that before. I got a brother wet the bed till he was eleven. He's a captain in the Army. So what? He's so dumb I wouldn't let him make change in my store. Now he's a captain! So I'm supposed to be impressed with a guy that's a colonel! He's a butcher, that's what he is. Like I tell you a hundred times, the guy don't understand tactics."

This time there was a long silence. Then Eddie spoke, enthusiastically. "Oh, boy! When I get back to Bakersfield!" Burke made no comment. Then Eddie asked, "Tell me one thing, Burke."

"Shoot."

"Do you think they softened this beach up enough before we landed?"

Burke considered a long time. Then he gave his opinion: "It's like I tell you back in Noumea. They got to learn."

"But you don't think they softened it up enough, do you, Burke?"

"Well, we could of used a few more big ones in there where the Japs had their guns. We could of used a few more in there."

Silence again. Then: "Burke, I was scared when we hit the beach."

"Just a rough tussle!" the older man assured him. "You thank your lucky stars you ain't goin' up against the Krauts. That's big league stuff!"

Silence and then another question: "But if the Japs is such pushovers, why you want me to stand guard tonight while you sleep?"

Burke's patience and tolerance could stand no more. "God-dammit," he muttered. "It's war! If we was fighting the Eyetalians, we'd still stand guard! Plain common sense! Call me at midnight. I'll let you get some sleep."

Shall I Live for a Ghost?
(from *The Last Enemy*)

Richard Hillary

I was falling. Falling slowly through a dark pit. I was dead. My body, headless, circled in front of me. I saw it with my mind, my mind that was the redness in front of the eye, the dull scream in the ear, the grinning of the mouth, the skin crawling on the skull. It was death and resurrection. Terror, moving with me, touched my cheek with hers and I felt the flesh wince. Faster, faster…I was hot now, hot, again one with my body, on fire and screaming soundlessly. Dear God, no! No! Not that, not again. The sickly smell of death was in my nostrils and a confused roar of sound. Then was all quiet. I was back.

Someone was holding my arms.

"Quiet now. There's a good boy. You're going to be all right. You've been very ill and you mustn't talk."

I tried to reach up my hand but could not.

"Is that you, nurse? What have they done to me?"

"Well, they've put something on your face and hands to stop them hurting and you won't be able to see for a little while. But you mustn't talk: you're not strong enough yet."

Gradually I realized what had happened. My face and hands had been scrubbed and then sprayed with tannic acid. The acid had formed into a hard black cement. My eyes alone had received different treatment; they were coated with a thick layer of gential violet. My arms were propped up in front of me, the fingers extended like witches' claws, and my body was hung loosely on straps just clear of the bed.

I can recollect no moments of acute agony in the four days which I spent in that hospital; only a great sea of pain in which I floated almost with comfort. Every three hours I was injected with morphia, so while imagining myself quite coherent, I was for the most part in a semi-stupor. The memory of it has remained a confused blur.

Two days without eating, and then periodic doses of liquid food taken through a tube. An appalling thirst, and hundreds of bottles of ginger beer. Being blind, and not really feeling strong enough to care. Imagining myself back in my plane, unable to get out, and waking to find myself shouting and bathed in sweat. My parents coming down to see me and their wonderful self-control.

They arrived in the late afternoon of my second day in bed, having with admirable restraint done nothing the first day. On the morning of the crash my mother had been on her way to the Red Cross, when she felt a premonition that she must go home. She told the taxi-driver to turn about and arrived at the flat to hear the telephone ringing. It was our Squadron Adjutant, trying to reach my father. Embarrassed by finding himself talking to my mother, he started in on a glamorized history of my exploits in the air and was bewildered by my mother cutting him short to ask where I was. He managed somehow after about five minutes of incoherent stuttering to get over his news.

They arrived in the afternoon and were met by Matron. Outside my ward a twittery nurse explained that they must not expect to find me looking quite normal, and they were ushered in. The room was in darkness; I just a dim shape in one corner. Then the blinds were shot up, all the lights switched on, and there I was. As my mother remarked later, the performance lacked only the rolling of drums and a spotlight. For the sake of decorum my face had been covered with white gauze, with a slit in the middle through which protruded my lips.

We spoke little, my only coherent remark being that I had no wish to go on living if I were to look like Alice. Alice was a large country girl who had once been our maid. As a child she had been burned and disfigured by a Primus stove. I was not aware that she had made any impression on me, but now I was unable to get her out of my mind. It was not so much her looks as her smell I had continually in my nostrils and which I couldn't dissociate from the disfigurement.

They sat quietly and listened to me rambling for an hour. Then it was time for my dressings and they took their leave.

The smell of ether. Matron once doing my dressing with three orderlies holding my arms; a nurse weeping quietly at the head of the bed, and no remembered sign of a doctor. A visit from the lifeboat crew that had picked me up, and a terrible longing to make sense when talking to them. Their inarticulate sympathy and assurance of quick recovery. Their discovery that an ancestor of mine had founded the lifeboats, and my pompous and unsolicited promise of a subscription. The expectation of an American ambulance to drive me up to the Masonic Hospital (for Margate was used only as a clearing station). Believing that I was already in it and on my way, and waking to the disappointment that I had not been moved. A dream that I was fighting to open my eyes and could not: waking in a sweat to realize it was a dream and then finding it to be true. A sensation of time slowing down, of words and actions, all in slow motion. Sweat, pain, smells, cheering messages from the Squadron, and an overriding apathy.

Finally I was moved. The ambulance appeared with a cargo of two somewhat nervous ATS women who were to drive me to London, and, with my nurse in attendance, and wrapped in an old grandmother's shawl, I was carried aboard and we were off. For the first few miles I felt quite well, dictated letters to my nurse, drank bottle after bottle of ginger beer, and gossiped with the drivers. They described the countryside for me, told me they were new to the job, expressed satisfaction at having me for a consignment, asked me if I felt fine. Yes, I said, I felt fine; asked my nurse if the drivers were pretty, heard her answer yes, heard them simpering, and we were all very matey. But after about half an hour my arms began to throb from the rhythmical jolting of the road. I stopped dictating, drank no more ginger beer, and didn't care whether they were pretty or not. Then they lost their way. Wasn't it awful and shouldn't they stop and ask? No, they certainly shouldn't: they could call out the names of the streets and I would tell them where to go. By the time we arrived at Ravenscourt Park I was pretty much all-in. I was carried into the hospital and once again felt the warm September sun burning my face. I was put in a private ward and had the impression of a hundred excited ants buzzing around me. My nurse said good-bye and started to sob. For no earthly reason I found myself in tears. It had been a lousy hospital, I had never seen the nurse anyway, and I was now in very good hands; but I suppose I was in a fairly exhausted state. So there we all were, snivelling about the place and getting nowhere. Then the charge nurse came up and took my arm and asked me what my name was.

"Dick," I said.

"Ah," she said brightly. "We must call you Richard the Lion Heart." I made an attempt at a polite laugh but all that came out was a dismal groan and I fainted away. The house surgeon took the opportunity to give me an anaesthetic and removed all the tannic acid from my left hand.

At this time tannic acid was the recognized treatment for burns. The theory was that in forming a hard cement it protected the skin from the air, and encouraged it to heal up underneath. As the tannic started to crack, it was to be chipped off gradually with a scalpel, but after a few months of experience, it was discovered that nearly all pilots with third-degree burns so treated developed secondary infection and septicaemia. This caused its use to be discontinued and gave us the dubious satisfaction of knowing that we were suffering in the cause of science. Both my hands were suppurating, and the fingers were already contracting under the tannic and curling down into the palms. The risk of shock was considered too great for them to do both hands. I must have been under the anaesthetic for about fifteen minutes and in that time I saw Peter Pease killed.

He was after another machine, a tall figure leaning slightly forward with a smile at the corner of his mouth. Suddenly from nowhere a Messerschmitt was on his tail about 150 yards away. For two seconds nothing happened. I had a terrible feeling of futility. Then at the top of my voice I shouted, "Peter, for God's sake look out behind!"

I saw the Messerschmitt open up and a burst of fire hit Peter's machine. His expression did not change, and for a moment his machine hung motionless. Then it turned slowly on its back and dived to the ground. I came to, screaming his name, with two nurses and the doctor holding me down on the bed.

"All right now. Take it easy, you're not dead yet. That must have been a very bad dream."

I said nothing. There wasn't anything to say. Two days later I had a letter from Colin. My nurse read it to me. It was very short, hoping that I was getting better and telling me that Peter was dead.

Slowly I came back to life. My morphia injections were less frequent and my mind began to clear. Though I began to feel and think again coherently I still could not see. Two VADs fainted while helping with my dressings, the first during the day and the other at night. The second time I could not sleep and was calling out for someone to stop the beetles running down my face, when I heard my nurse say fiercely, "Get outside quick: don't make a fool of yourself here!" and the sound of footsteps moving towards the door. I remember cursing the unfortunate girl and telling her to put her head between her knees. I was told later that for my first three weeks I did little but curse and blaspheme, but I remember nothing of it. The nurses were wonderfully patient and never complained. Then one day I found that I could see. My nurse was bending over me doing my dressings, and she seemed to me very beautiful. She was. I watched her for a long time, grateful that my first glimpse of the world should be of anything so perfect. Finally I said:

"Sue, you never told me that your eyes were so blue."

For a moment she stared at me. Then, "Oh, Dick, how wonderful," she said. "I told you it wouldn't be long"; and she dashed out to bring in all the nurses on the block.

I felt absurdly elated and studied their faces eagerly, gradually connecting them with the voices that I knew.

"This is Anne," said Sue. "She is your special VAD and helps me with all your dressings. She was the only one of us you'd allow near you for about a week. You said you liked her voice." Before me stood an attractive fair-haired girl of about twenty-three. She smiled and her teeth were as enchanting as her voice. I began to feel that hospital had its compensations. The nurses called me Dick and I knew them all by their Christian names. Quite how irregular this was I did not discover until I moved to another hospital where I was considerably less ill and not so outrageously spoiled. At first my dressings had to be changed every two hours in the daytime. As this took over an hour to do, it meant that Sue and Anne had practically no time off. But they seemed not to care. It was largely due to them that both my hands were not amputated.

Sue, who had been nursing since seventeen, had been allocated as my special nurse because of her previous experience of burns, and because, as Matron said, "She's our best girl and very human." Anne had been married to a naval officer killed in the *Courageous*, and had taken up nursing after his death.

At this time there was a very definite prejudice among the regular nurses against VADs. They were regarded as painted society girls, attracted to nursing by the prospect of sitting on the officers' beds and holding their hands. The VADs were rapidly disabused of this idea, and, if they were lucky, were finally graduated from washing bed-pans to polishing bed-tables. I never heard that any of them grumbled, and they gradually won a reluctant recognition. This prejudice was considerably less noticeable in the Masonic than in most hospitals: Sue, certainly, looked on Anne as a companionable and very useful lieutenant to whom she could safely entrust my dressings and general upkeep in her absence. I think I was a little in love with both of them.

The Masonic is perhaps the best hospital in England, though at the time I was unaware how lucky I was. When war broke out the Masons handed over a part of it to the services; but owing to its vulnerable position very few action casualties were kept there long. Pilots were pretty quickly moved out to the main Air Force Hospital, which I was not in the least eager to visit. Thanks to the kind-hearted duplicity of my house surgeon, I never had to; for every time they ran up and asked for me he would say that I was too ill to be moved. The Masonic's great charm lay in that it in no way resembled a hospital; if anything it was like the inside of a ship. The nursing staff were very carefully chosen, and during the regular blitzing of the district, which took place every night, they were magnificent.

The Germans were presumably attempting to hit Hammersmith Bridge, but their efforts were somewhat erratic and we were treated night after night to an orchestra of the scream and crump of falling bombs. They always seemed to choose a moment when my eyes were being irrigated, when my poor nurse was poised above me with a glass undine in her hand. At night we were moved into the corridor, away from the outside wall, but such was the snoring of my fellow sufferers that I persuaded Bertha to allow me back in my own room after Matron had made her rounds.

Bertha was my night nurse. I never discovered her real name, but to me she was Bertha from the instant that I saw her. She was large and gaunt with an Eton crop and a heart of gold. She was engaged to a merchant seaman who was on his way to Australia. She made it quite clear that she had no intention of letting me get round her as I did the day staff, and ended by spoiling me even more. At night when I couldn't sleep we would hold long and heated arguments on the subject of sex. She expressed horror at my ideas of love and on her preference for a cup of tea. I gave her a present of four pounds of it when I was discharged. One night the Germans were particularly persistent, and I had the unpleasant sensation of hearing a stick of bombs gradually approaching the hospital, the first some way off, the next closer, and the third shaking the building. Bertha threw herself across my bed; but the fourth bomb never fell. She got up quickly, looking embarrassed, and arranged her cap.

"Nice fool I'd look if you got hit in your own room when you're supposed to be out in the corridor," she said, and stumped out of the room.

An RASC officer who had been admitted to the hospital with the painful but unromantic complaint of piles protested at the amount of favouritism shown to me merely because I was in the RAF. A patriotic captain who was in the same ward turned on him and said: "At least he was shot down defending his country and didn't come in here with a pimple on his bottom. The Government will buy him a new Spitfire, but I'm damned if it will buy you a new arse."

One day my doctor came in and said that I could get up. Soon after I was able to totter about the passages and could be given a proper bath. I was still unable to use my hands and everything had to be done for me. One evening during a blitz, my nurse, having led me along to the lavatory, placed a prodigiously long cigarette-holder in my mouth and lighted the cigarette in the end of it. Then she went off to get some coffee. I was puffing away contentedly when the lighted cigarette fell into my pyjama trousers and started smouldering. There was little danger that I would go up in flames, but I thought it advisable to draw attention to the fact that all was not well. I therefore shouted "Oi!" Nobody heard me. "Help!" I shouted somewhat louder. Still nothing happened, so I delivered myself of my imitation of Tarzan's elephant call of which I was quite proud. It happened that in the ward opposite there was an old gentleman who had been operated on for a hernia. The combination of the scream of the falling bombs and my animal cries could mean only one thing. Someone had been seriously injured, and he made haste to dive over the side of the bed. In doing so he caused himself considerable discomfort: convinced of the ruin of his operation and the imminence of his death, he added his cries to mine. His fears finally calmed, he could see nothing humorous in the matter and insisted on being moved to another ward. From then on I was literally never left alone for a minute.

For the first few weeks, only my parents were allowed to visit me and they came every day. My mother would sit and read to me by the hour. Quite how much she suffered I could only guess, for she gave no sign. One remark of hers I shall never forget. She said: "You should be glad this has to happen to you. Too many people told you how attractive you were and you believed them. You were well on the way to becoming something of a cad. Now you'll find out who your real friends are." I did.

When I was allowed to see people, one of my first visitors was Michael Cary (who had been at Trinity with me and had a First in Greats). He was then private secretary to the Chief of Air Staff. He was allowed to stay only a short time before being shoo'd away by my nurses, but I think it may have been time enough to shake him. A short while afterwards he joined the Navy as an AB. I hope it was not as a result of seeing me, for he had too good a brain to waste polishing brass. Colin came down whenever he had leave from Hornchurch and brought me news of the Squadron.

Ken MacDonald, Don's brother who had been with "A" Flight at Dyce, had been killed. He had been seen about to bale out of his blazing machine at 1,000 feet; but as he was over a thickly populated area he had climbed in again and crashed the machine in the Thames.

Pip Cardell had been killed. Returning from a chase over the Channel with Dexter, one of the new members of the Squadron, he appeared to be in trouble just before reaching the English coast. He jumped; but his parachute failed to open and he came down in the sea. Dexter flew low and saw him move. He was still alive, so Dexter flew right along the shore and out to sea, waggling his wings to draw attention and calling up the base on the RT. No boat put out from the shore, and Dexter made a crash landing on the beach, drawing up ten yards from a nest of buried mines. But when they got up to Pip he was dead.

Howes had been killed, even as he had said. His Squadron had been moved from Hornchurch to a quieter area, a few days after I was shot down. But he had been transferred to our Squadron, still deeply worried because as yet he had failed to bring anything down. The inevitable happened; and from his second flight with us he failed to return.

Rusty was missing, but a clairvoyant had written to Uncle George swearing that he was neither dead nor captured. Rusty, he said (whom he had never seen), had crashed in France, badly burned, and was being looked after by a French peasant.

As a counter to this depressing news Colin told me that Brian, Raspberry, and Sheep all had the DFC, and Brian was shortly to get a bar to his. The Squadron's confirmed score was nearing the hundred mark. We had also had the pleasure of dealing with the Italians. They had come over before breakfast, and together with 41 Squadron we were looking for them. Suddenly Uncle George called out:

"Wops ahead."

"Where are they?" asked 41 Squadron.

"Shan't tell you," came back the answer. "We're only outnumbered three to one."

Colin told me that it was the most unsporting thing he had ever had to do, rather like shooting sitting birds, as he so typically put it. We got down eight of them without loss to ourselves and much to the annoyance of 41 Squadron.

Then one day I had an unexpected visitor. Matron opened the door and said "Someone to see you," and Denise walked in. I knew at once who she was. It was unnecessary for her to speak. Her slight figure was in mourning and she wore no make-up. She was the most beautiful person I have ever seen.

Much has been written on Beauty. Poets have excelled themselves in similes for a woman's eye, mouth, hair; novelists have devoted pages to a geometrically accurate description of their heroines' features. I can write no such description of Denise. I did not see her like that. For me she had an inner beauty, a serenity which no listing of features can convey. She had a perfection of carriage and a grace of movement that were strikingly reminiscent of Peter Pease, and when she spoke it might have been Peter speaking.

"I hope you'll excuse me coming to see you like this," she said; "but I was going to be married to Peter. He often spoke of you and wanted so much to see you. So I hope you won't mind me coming instead."

There was so much I wanted to say, so many things for us to talk over, but the room seemed of a sudden unbearably full of hurrying jolly nurses who would not go away. The bustle and excitement did little to put her at her ease, and her shyness was painful to me. Time came for her to leave, and I had said nothing I wanted to say. As soon as she was gone I dictated a note, begging her to come again and to give me a little warning. She did. From then until I was able to get out, her visits did more to help my recovery than all the expert nursing and medical attention. For she was the very spirit of courage. It was useless for me to say to her any of the usual words of comfort for the loss of a fiancé, and I did not try. She and Peter were two halves of the same person. They even wrote alike. I could only pray that time would cure that awful numbness and bring her back to the fullness of life. Not that she was broken. She seemed somehow to have gathered his strength, to feel him always near her, and was determined to go on to the end in the cause for which he had given his life, hoping that she too might be allowed to die, but feeling guilty at the selfishness of the thought.

She believed passionately in freedom, in freedom from fear and oppression and tyranny, not only for herself but for the whole world.

"For the whole world." Did I believe that? I still wasn't sure. There was a time—only the other day—when it hadn't mattered to me if it was true or not that a man could want freedom for others more than himself. She made me feel that this might be no mere catch-phrase of politicians, since it was something to which the two finest people I had ever known had willingly dedicated themselves. I was impressed. I saw there a spirit far purer than mine. But was it for me? I didn't know. I just didn't know.

I lay in that hospital and watched summer turn to winter. Through my window I watched the leaves of my solitary tree gradually turn brown, and then, shaken by an ever-freshening wind, fall one by one. I watched the sun change from a great ball of fire to a watery glimmer, watched the rain beating on the glass and the small broken clouds drifting a few hundred feet above, and in that time I had ample opportunity for thinking.

I thought of the men I had known, of the men who were living and the men who were dead; and I came to this conclusion. It was to the Carburys and the Berrys of this war that Britain must look, to the tough practical men who had come up the hard way, who were not fighting this war for any philosophical principles or economic ideals; who, unlike the average Oxford undergraduate, were not flying for aesthetic reasons, but because of an instinctive knowledge that this was the job for which they were most suited. These were the men who had blasted and would continue to blast the Luftwaffe out of the sky while their more intellectual comrades would alas, in the main be killed. They might answer, if asked why they fought, "To smash Hitler!" But instinctively, inarticulately, they too were fighting for the things that Peter had died to preserve.

Was there perhaps a new race of Englishmen arising out of this war, a race of men bred by the war, a harmonious synthesis of the governing class and the great rest of England; that synthesis of disparate backgrounds and upbringings to be seen at its most obvious best in RAF squadrons? While they were now possessed of no other thought than to win the war, yet having won it, would they this time refuse to step aside and remain indifferent to the peace-time fate of the country, once again leave government to the old governing class? I thought it possible. Indeed, the process might be said to have already begun. They now had as their representative Churchill, a man of initiative, determination, and no Party. But they would not always have him; and what then? Would they see to it that there arose from their fusion representatives, not of the old gang, deciding at Lady Cufuffie's that Henry should have the Foreign Office and George the Ministry of Food, nor figureheads for an angry but ineffectual Labour Party, but true representatives of the new England that should emerge from this struggle? And if they did, what then? Could they unite on a policy of humanity and sense to arrive at the settlement of problems which six thousand years of civilization had failed to solve? And even though they should fail, was there an obligation for the more thinking of them to try to contribute, at whatever personal cost "their little drop," however small, to the betterment of mankind? Was there that obligation, was that the goal towards which all those should strive who were left, strengthened and confirmed by those who had died? Or was it still possible for men to lead the egocentric life, to work out their own salvation without concern for the rest; could they simply look to themselves—or, more important, could I? I still thought so.

The day came when I was allowed out of the hospital for a few hours. Sue got me dressed, and with a pair of dark glasses, cotton-wool under my eyes, and my right arm in a sling, I looked fairly presentable. I walked out through the swing-doors and took a deep breath.

London in the morning was still the best place in the world. The smell of wet streets, of sawdust in the butchers' shops, of tar melted on the blocks, was exhilarating. Peter had been right: I loved the capital. The wind on the heath might call for a time, but the facile glitter of the city was the stronger. Self-esteem, I suppose, is one cause; for in the city, work of man, one is somebody, feet on the pavement, suit on the body, anybody's equal and nobody's fool; but in the country, work of God, one is nothing, less than the earth, the birds, and the trees; one is discordant—a blot.

I walked slowly through Ravenscourt Park and looked into many faces. Life was good, but if I hoped to find some reflection of my feeling, I was disappointed. One or two looked at me with pity, and for a moment I was angry; but when I gazed again at their faces, closed in as on some dread secret, their owners hurrying along, unseeing, unfeeling, eager to get to their jobs, unaware of the life within them, I was sorry for them. I felt a desire to stop and shake them and say: "You fools, it's you who should be pitied and not I; for this day I am alive while you are dead."

And yet there were some who pleased me, some in whom all youth had not died. I passed one girl, and gazing into her face became aware of her as a woman: her lips were soft, her breasts firm, her legs long and graceful. It was many a month since any woman had stirred me, and I was pleased. I smiled at her and she smiled at me. I did not speak to her for fear of breaking the spell, but walked back to lunch on air. After this I was allowed out every day, and usually managed to stay out until nine o'clock, when I drove back through the blitz and the black-out.

"London can take it" was already becoming a truism; but I had been put out of action before the real fury of the night attacks had been let loose, and I had seen nothing of the damage. In the hospital, from the newspapers, and from people who came to see me, I gained a somewhat hazy idea of what was going on. On the one hand I saw London as a city hysterically gay, a city doomed, with nerves so strained that a life of synthetic gaiety alone prevented them from snapping. My other picture was of a London bloody but unbowed, of a people grimly determined to see this thing through, with manpower mobilized; a city unable, through a combined lack of inclination, facility, and time, to fritter away the war in the night-haunts of the capital. I set out to see for myself.

London night-life did exist. Though the sirens might scream and the bombs fall, restaurants and cocktail bars remained open and full every night of the week. I say restaurants and cocktail bars, for the bottle parties and strip-tease cabarets which had a mushroom growth at the beginning of the war had long been closed. Nor was prostitution abroad. Ladies of leisure whose business hours were from eleven till three were perhaps the only citizens to find themselves completely baffled by the black-out. London was not promiscuous: the diners-out in a West End restaurant were no longer the clientele of cafe society, for cafe society no longer existed in London. The majority of the so-called smart set felt at last with the outbreak of war a real vocation, felt finally a chance to realize themselves and to orientate themselves to a life of reality. They might be seen in a smart restaurant; but they were there in another guise—as soldiers, sailors, and airmen on forty-eight hours' leave; as members of one of the women's services seeking a few hours' relaxation before again applying themselves wholeheartedly to their jobs; or as civil servants and Government workers who, after a hard day's work, preferred to relax and enjoy the bombing in congenial company rather than return to a solitary dinner in their own flats.

While the bombs were dropping on London (and they were dropping every night in my time in the hospital), and while half of London was enjoying itself, the other half was not asleep. It was striving to make London as normal a city by night as it had become by day. Anti-aircraft crews, studded around fields, parks, and streets, were momentarily silhouetted against the sky by the sudden flash of their guns. The Auxiliary Fire Service, spread out in a network of squads through the capital, was standing by, ready at a moment's notice to deal with the inevitable fires; air-raid wardens, tireless in their care of shelters and work of rescue, patrolled their areas watchfully. One heavy night I poked my nose out of the Dorchester, which was rocking gently, to find a cab calmly coasting down Park Lane. I hailed it and was driven back to the hospital. The driver turned to me: "Thank God, sir," he said, "Jerry's wasting 'is time trying to break our morale, when 'e might be doing real damage on some small town."

With the break of day London shook herself and went back to work. Women with husbands in Government jobs were no longer to be seen at noon draped along the bars of the West End as their first appointment of the day. They were up and at work with determined efficiency in administrative posts of the Red Cross, the women's voluntary services, and the prisoners of war organizations. The Home Guards and air-raid wardens of the previous night would return home, take a bath, and go off to their respective offices. The soldier was back with his regiment, the airman with his squadron; the charming frivolous creatures with whom they had dined were themselves in uniform, effective in their jobs of driving, typing, or nursing.

That, I discovered, was a little of what London was doing. But what was London feeling? Perhaps a not irrelevant example was an experience of Sheep Gilroy's when flying with the Squadron. He was sitting in his bath when a "flap" was announced. Pulling on a few clothes and not bothering to put on his tunic, he dashed out to his plane and took off. A few minutes later he was hit by an incendiary bullet and the machine caught fire. He baled out, quite badly burned, and landed by a parachute in one of the poorer districts of London. With no identifying tunic, he was at once set upon by two hundred silent and coldy angry women, armed with knives and rolling-pins. For him no doubt it was a harrowing experience, until he finally established his nationality by producing all the most lurid words in his vocabulary; but as an omen for the day when the cream of Hitler's Aryan youth should attempt to land in Britain it was most interesting.

All this went on at a time when night after night the East End was taking a terrible beating, and it was rumoured that the people were ominously quiet. Could their morale be cracking? The answer was provided in a story that was going the rounds. A young man went down to see a chaplain whom he knew in the East End. He noticed not only that the damage was considerable but that the people were saying practically nothing at all. "How are they taking it?" He asked nervously. The chaplain shook his head. "I'm afraid," he said, "that my people have fallen from grace: they are beginning to feel a little bitter towards the Germans."

The understatement in that remark was impressive because it was typical. The war was practically never discussed except as a joke. The casual observer might easily have drawn one of two conclusions: either that London was spent of all feeling, or that it was a city waiting like a blind man, unseeing, uncaring, for the end. Either conclusions would have been wide of the mark. Londoners are slow to anger. They had shown for long enough that they could take it; now they were waiting on the time when it would be their turn to dish it out, when their cold rage would need more than a Panzer division to stamp it out.

Now and then I lunched at home with my mother, who was working all day in the Prisoners of War Organization, or my father would leave his desk long enough to give me lunch at his club. On one of these occasions we ran into Bill Aitken, and I had coffee with him afterwards. He was still in Army Co-operation and reminded me of our conversation at Old Sarum. "Do you remember," he asked, "telling me that I should have to eat my words about Nigel Bicknell and Frank Waldron? Well, you were certainly right about Nigel."

"I haven't heard anything," I said, "but you sound as though he had renounced his career as Air Force psychologist."

Bill laughed. "He's done more than that. He was flying his Blenheim to make some attack on France when one engine cut. He carried on, bombed his objective, and was on his way back when the other engine cut out, too, and his machine came down in the sea. For six hours, until dawn when a boat saw him, he held his observer up. He's got the DFC."

"I must write to him," I said. "But I was right about Frank too. Do you remember your quotation that war was "a period of great boredom, interspersed with moments of great excitement"; and how you said that the real test came in the periods of boredom, since anyone can rise to a crisis?"

"Yes, I remember."

"Well, I think I'm right in saying that Frank has come through on that score. He's in the Scots Guards with very little to do; but he's considerably more subdued than you'll remember him. When he first got out of the Air Force he thought he could waltz straight into the Guards, but they wouldn't take him until he had been through an OCTU. That was his first surprise. The second was when there was no vacancy in the OCTU for three months. Our Frank, undismayed, hied himself off to France and kicked up his heels in Megève with the *Chasseurs Alpins*, and then in Cannes with the local lovelies. But he came back and went through his course. He was a year behind all his friends—or rather all those that were left, and it sobered him up. I think you'd be surprised if you saw him now."

Bill got up to leave. "I should like to see him again," he said with a smile, "but of the ex-bad boys, I think you are the best example of a change for the better."

"Perhaps it's as well that you can't stay," I said. "I'm afraid it wouldn't take you long to see that you're mistaken. If anything, I believe even more strongly in the ideas which I held before. Sometime we'll discuss it."

I spent most evenings with Denise at the house in Eaton Place. It was the usual London house, tall, narrow, and comfortable. Denise was living there alone with a housekeeper, for her father was about to marry again and had moved to the country. At tea-time I would come and find her curled up on the sofa behind the tray, gazing into the fire; and from then until eight o'clock, when I had to drive back to the Masonic, we would sit and talk—mostly of Peter, for it eased her to speak of him, but also of the war, of life, and death, and many lesser things.

Two years before the war she had joined the ATS. Sensibility and shyness might well have made her unsuited for this service, but when her family said as much, they merely fortified her in her determination. After she was commissioned, she fainted on her first parade, but she was not deterred, and she succeeded. She had left the ATS to marry Peter. I was not surprised to learn that she had published a novel, nor that she refused to tell me under what pseudonym, in spite of all my accusations of inverted snobbery. She wished to see nobody but Colin and me, Peter's friends; and though often she would have preferred to be alone, she welcomed me every day, nevertheless. So warm and sincere was her nature, that I might almost have thought myself her only interest. Try as I would, I could not make her think of herself; it was as if she considered that as a person she was dead. Minutes would go by while she sat lost in reverie, her chin cupped in her hand. There seemed nothing I could do to rouse her to consciousness of herself, thaw out that terrible numbness, breathe life into that beautiful ghost. Concern with self was gone out of her. I tried pity, I tried understanding, and finally I tried brutality.

It was one evening before dinner, and Denise was leaning against the mantelpiece, one black heel resting on the fender.

"When are you coming out of mourning?" I asked.

She had been standing with her chin lowered; and now, without lifting it, she raised her eyes and looked at me a moment.

"I don't know," she said slowly. "Maybe I never shall."

I think she sensed that the seemingly innocent question had been put deliberately, though she couldn't yet see why. It had surprised her; it had hurt her, as I had meant it to. Up to now I had been at pains to tread delicately. Now the time had come, I felt, for a direct attack upon her sensibility under the guise of outward stupidity.

"Oh, come, Denise," I said. "That's not like you. You know life better than that. You know there's no creeping away to hide in a dream world. When something really tragic happens—the cutting-off of a man at a moment when he has most reason to live, when he has planned great things for himself—the result for those who love him isn't a whimpering pathos; it's growth, not decline. It makes you a richer person, not a poorer one; better fitted to tackle life, not less fitted for it. I loved Peter, too. But I'm not going to pretend I feel sorry for you; and you ought to be grateful to the gods for having enriched you. Instead, you mope."

I knew well enough that she wouldn't go under, that this present numb resignation was transitory. But I had been worried too long by her numbness, her rejection of life, and I wanted to end it. She said nothing, and I dared not look at her. I could see her fingers move as I went doggedly on.

"You can't run away from life," I said. "You're a living vital person. Your heart tells you that Peter will be with you always, but your senses know that absence blots people out. Your senses are the boundaries of your feeling world, and their power stops with death. To go back and back to places where you were happy with Peter, to touch his clothes, dress in black for him, say his name, is pure self-deception. You drug your senses in a world of dreams, but reality cannot be shut out for long."

Still she said nothing, and I had a quick look at her. This was far worse than badgering Peter in the train. Her face was tense, slightly flushed, and her eyes were wide open and staring with what I hoped was anger, not pain. I wished to rouse her, and prayed only that I would not reduce her to tears.

"Death is love's crucifixion," I said brutally. "Now you go out with Colin and me because we were his friends, we are a link. But we are not only his friends, we are men. When I leave you and say good night, it's not Peter's hand that takes yours, it's mine. It's Colin's touch you feel when he helps you on with your coat. Colin will go away. I shall go back to hospital. What are you going to do then? Live alone? You'll try, but you won't be able. You will go out again—and with people who didn't know Peter, people your senses will force you to accept as flesh and blood, and not fellow players in a tragedy."

She went over to a sofa opposite me and sat looking out of the window. I could see her breast rise and fall with her breathing. Her face was still tense. The set of her head on her shoulders was so graceful, the lines of her figure were so delicate as she sat outlined against the light, that I became aware with a shock of never before having thought of her as a woman, a creature of flesh and blood. I who had made the senses the crux of my argument had never thought of her except as a disembodied spirit. Minutes passed; she said no word; and her silence began almost to frighten me. If she should go on saying nothing, and I had to do all the talking, I didn't know quite what I should end by saying. I was about to attack her again when she spoke, but in a voice so gentle that at first I had trouble hearing her.

"You're wrong, Richard," she said. "You are so afraid of anything mystical, anything you can't analyse, that you always begin rationalizing instinctively, in self-defence, fearing your own blind spots. You like to think of yourself as a man who sees things too clearly, too realistically, to be able to have any respect for the emotions. Perhaps you don't feel sorry for me; but I do feel sorry for you.

"I *know* that everything is not over for Peter and me. I know it with all the faith that you are so contemptuous of. We *shall* be together again. We are together now. I feel him constantly close to me; and that is my answer to your cheap talk about the senses. Peter lives within me. He neither comes nor goes, he is ever-present. Even while he was alive there was never quite the tenderness and closeness between us that now is there."

She looked straight at me and there was a kind of triumph in her face. Her voice was now so strong that I felt there was no defeating her any more, no drawing her out of that morass of mysticism from which I so instinctively recoiled.

"I suppose you're trying to hurt me to give me strength, Richard," she said; "but you're only hurting yourself. I have the strength. And let me explain where it comes from, so that we need never revert to the subject again. I believe that in this life we live as in a room with the blinds down and the lights on. Once or twice, perhaps, it is granted us to switch off the lights and raise the blinds. Then for a moment the darkness outside becomes brightness, and we have a glimpse of what lies beyond this life. I believe not only in life after death, but in life before death. This life is to me an intermission lived in spiritual darkness. In this life we are in a state not of being, but of becoming."

"Peter and I are eternally bound up together; our destinies are the same. And you, with your unawakened heart, are in some curious way bound up with us. Oh, yes, you are! In spite of all your intellectual subterfuges and attempts to hide behind the cry of self-realization! You lay in hospital and saw Peter die as clearly as if you had been with him. You told me so yourself. Ever since Peter's death you have been different. It has worked on you; and it's only because it has that I tell you these things. Colin says he would never have believed that anyone could change as you have."

"That," said I, "was pure hallucination. I don't pretend to account for it exactly, but it was that hundredth example of instinct, or intuition, that people are always boasting of while they never mention the ninety-nine other premonitions that were pure fantasy."

"Please, Richard," she said, "let's not talk about Peter and me any more. Your self-realization theory is too glib to stand a real test. To pass coldly through the death and destruction of war, to stand aloof and watch your sensibility absorb experience like a photographic plate, so that you may store it away to use for your own self-development—that's what you had hoped to do, I believe?"

"Of course it is," I admitted. She was really roused now, and I was pleased.

"Well, you can't! You know you can't, despite that Machiavellian pose of yours. You tell me women are not as I am. I tell you, men are not as you are. Or rather, were. You remember those photographs taken of you before the crash that I saw the other day? Well, I believe that then, before the crash, you could and possibly did feel as you say you still do. I could never have liked you when you looked like that, looked like the man of the theory you still vaunt. Have you read Donne's *Devotions*?"

"Looked through them," I said.

"In one of them he says this: 'Any man's death diminishes me, because I am involved in Mankind.' You, too, are involved, Richard; and so deeply that you won't always be able to cover up and protect yourself from the feelings prompted in you by that involvement. You talk about my self-deception: do you really believe you can go through life to the end, always taking and never giving? And do you really imagine that you haven't given to me, haven't helped me? Well, you have. And what have you got out of it? Nothing! You have given to me in a way that would have been impossible for you before Peter's death. You are still giving. You are conferring value on life by feeling Peter's death as deeply as you do. And you are bound to feel the death, be re-created by the death, of the others in the Squadron—if not in the same degree, certainly in the same way. Certainly you are going to 'realize' yourself; but it won't be by leading the egocentric life. The effect that you will have on everybody you meet will come not only from your own personality, but from what has been added to you by all the others who are now dead—what you have so ungratefully absorbed from them."

She spoke with great feeling and much of what she said struck home. It was true that Peter was much in my thoughts, that I felt him somewhere near me, that he was in fact the touchstone of my sensibility at the moment. It was true that the mystical experience of his death was something which was outside my understanding, which had still to be assimilated, and yet, and yet...I could not help but feel that with the passage of time this sense of closeness, of affinity, must fade, that its very intensity was in part false, occasioned by being ill, and by meeting Denise so shortly afterwards; a Denise who was no mere shadow of Peter, but Peter's reincarnation; thus serving to keep the memory and the experience always before my eyes. While here were two people of an intense lyrical sensibility, two people so close in thought, feeling, and ideals, that although one was dead and the other living they were to me as one, yet I could not feel that their experience was mine, that it could do more than touch me in passing, for that I had been of any help to Denise was in a large part due to the fact that we were so dissimilar. While her thoughts came trailing clouds of glory, mine were of the earth earthy, and at such a time could help to strike a balance between the mystical flights of her mind and the material fact of high-explosive bombs landing in the next street. But though we might travel the same road for a time, lone voyagers eager for company, yet the time must come when our ways should part. Right or wrong, her way was not mine and I should be mistaken in attempting to make it so. We must live how we can.

Billy Pilgrim
(from *Slaughterhouse-Five*)

Kurt Vonnegut

Listen:

Billy Pilgrim has come unstuck in time.

Billy has gone to sleep a senile widower and awakened on his wedding day. He has walked through a door in 1955 and come out another one in 1941. He has gone back through that door to find himself in 1963. He has seen his birth and death many times, he says, and pays random visits to all the events in between.

He says.

Billy is spastic in time, has no control over where he is going next, and the trips aren't necessarily fun. He is in a constant state of stage fright, he says, because he never knows what part of his life he is going to have to act in next.

Billy was born in 1922 in Ilium, New York, the only child of a barber there. He was a funny-looking child who became a funny-looking youth—tall and weak, and shaped like a bottle of Coca-Cola. He graduated from Ilium High School in the upper third of his class, and attended night sessions at the Ilium School of Optometry for one semester before being drafted for military service in the Second World War. His father died in a hunting accident during the war. So it goes.

Billy saw service with the infantry in Europe, and was taken prisoner by the Germans. After his honourable discharge from the Army in 1945, Billy again enrolled in the Ilium School of Optometry. During his senior year there, he became engaged to the daughter of the founder and owner of the school, and then suffered a mild nervous collapse.

He was treated in a veteran's hospital near Lake Placid, and was given shock treatments and released. He married his fiancée, finished his education, and was set up in business in Ilium by his father-in-law. Ilium is a particularly good city for optometrists because the General Forge and Foundry Company is there. Every employee is required to own a pair of safety glasses, and to wear them in areas where manufacturing is going on. GF&F has sixty-eight thousand employees in Ilium. That calls for a lot of lenses and a lot of frames.

Frames are where the money is.

Billy became rich. He had two children, Barbara and Robert. In time, his daughter Barbara married another optometrist, and Billy set him up in business. Billy's son Robert had a lot of trouble in high school, but then he joined the famous Green

Berets. He straightened out, became a fine young man, and he fought in Vietnam.

Early in 1968, a group of optometrists, with Billy among them, chartered an airplane to fly them from Ilium to an international convention of optometrists in Montreal. The plane crashed on top of Sugarbush Mountain, in Vermont. Everybody was killed but Billy. So it goes.

While Billy was recuperating in a hospital in Vermont, his wife died accidentally of carbon-monoxide poisoning. So it goes.

When Billy finally got home to Ilium after the airplane crash, he was quiet for a while. He had a terrible scar across the top of his skull. He didn't resume practice. He had a housekeeper. His daughter came over almost every day.

And then, without any warning, Billy went to New York City, and got on an all-night radio program devoted to talk. He told about having come unstuck in time. He said, too, that he had been kidnapped by a flying saucer in 1967. The saucer was from the planet Tralfamadore, he said. He was taken to Tralfamadore, where he was displayed naked in a zoo, he said. He was mated there with a former Earthling movie star named Monatana Wildhack.

Some night owls in Ilium heard Billy on the radio, and one of them called Billy's daughter Barbara. Barbara was upset. She and her husband went down to New York and brought Billy home. Billy insisted mildly that everything he had said on the radio was true. He said he had been kidnapped by the Tralfamadorians on the night of his daughter's wedding. He hadn't been missed, he said, because the Tralfamadorians had taken him through a time warp, so that he could be on Tralfamadore for years, and still be away from Earth for only a microsecond.

Another month went by without incident, and then Billy wrote a letter to the Ilium *News Leader*, which the paper published. It described the creatures from Tralfamadore.

The letter said that they were two feet high, and green, and shaped like plumber's friends. Their suction cups were on the ground, and their shafts, which were extremely flexible, usually pointed to the sky. At the top of each shaft was a little hand with a green eye in its palm. The creatures were friendly, and they could see in four dimensions. They pitied Earthlings for being able to see only three. They had many wonderful things to teach Earthlings, especially about time. Billy promised to tell what some of those wonderful things were in his next letter.

Billy was working on his second letter when the first letter was published. The second letter started out like this:

"The most important thing I learned on Tralfamadore was that when a person dies he only *appears* to die. He is still very much alive in the past, so it is very silly for people to cry at his funeral. All moments, past, present, and future, always have existed, always will exist. The Tralfamadorians can look at all the different moments just the way we can look at a stretch of the Rocky Mountains, for instance. They can see how permanent all the moments are, and they can look at any moment that interests them. It is just an illusion we have here on Earth that one moment follows another one, like beads on a string, and that once a moment is gone it is gone forever.

"When a Tralfamadorian sees a corpse, all he thinks is that the dead person is in bad condition in that particular moment, but that the same person is just fine in plenty of other moments. Now, when I myself hear that somebody is dead, I simply shrug and say what the Tralfamadorians say about dead people, which is 'So it goes.'"

And so on.

Billy was working on this letter in the basement rumpus room of his empty house. It was his housekeeper's day off. There was an old typewriter in the rumpus room. It was a beast. It weighed as much as a storage battery. Billy couldn't carry it very far very easily, which was why he was writing in the rumpus room instead of somewhere else.

The oil burner had quit. A mouse had eaten through the insulation of a wire leading to the thermostat. The temperature in the house was down to fifty degrees, but Billy hadn't noticed. He wasn't warmly dressed, either. He was barefoot, and still in his pajamas and a bathrobe, though it was late afternoon. His bare feet were blue and ivory.

The cockles of Billy's heart, at any rate, were glowing coals. What made them so hot was Billy's belief that he was going to comfort so many people with the truth about time. His door chimes upstairs had been ringing and ringing. It was his daughter Barbara up there, wanting in. Now she let herself in with a key, crossed the floor over his head, calling, "Father? Daddy, where are you?" And so on.

Billy didn't answer her, so she was nearly hysterical, expecting to find his corpse. And then she looked into the very last place there was to look—which was the rumpus room.

"Why didn't you answer me when I called?" Barbara wanted to know, standing there in the door of the rumpus room. She had the afternoon paper with her, the one in which Billy described his friends from Tralfamadore.

"I didn't hear you," said Billy.

The orchestration of the moment was this: Barbara was only twenty-one years old, but she thought her father was senile, even though he was only forty-six—senile because of damage to his brain in the airplane crash. She also thought that she was head of the family, since she had had to manage her mother's funeral, since she had to get a housekeeper for Billy, and all that. Also, Barbara and her husband were having to look after Billy's business interests, which were considerable, since Billy didn't seem to give a damn for business any more. All this responsibility at such an early age made her a bitchy flibbertigibbet. And Billy meanwhile, was trying to hang onto his dignity, to persuade Barbara and everybody else that he was far from senile, that, on the contrary, he was devoting himself to a calling much higher than mere business.

He was doing nothing less now, he thought, than prescribing corrective lenses for Earthling souls. So many of those souls were lost and wretched, Billy believed, because they could not see as well as his little green friends on Tralfamadore.

"Don't lie to me, Father," said Barbara. "I know perfectly well you heard me when I called." This was a fairly pretty girl, except that she had legs like an Edwardian grand piano. Now she raised hell with him about the letter in the paper. She said he was making a laughing stock of himself and everybody associated with him.

"Father, Father, Father—" said Barbara, "what are we going to *do* with you? Are you going to force us to put you where your mother is?" Billy's mother was still alive. She was in bed in an old people's home called Pine Knoll on the edge of Ilium.

"What is it about my letter that makes you so mad?" Billy wanted to know.

"It's all just crazy. None of it's true!"

"It's all true." Billy's anger was not going to rise with hers. He never got mad at anything. He was wonderful that way.

"There is no such planet as Tralfamadore."

"It can't be detected from Earth, if that's what you mean," said Billy. "Earth can't be detected from Tralfamadore, as far as that goes. They're both very small. They're very far apart."

"Where did you get a crazy name like 'Tralfamadore?'"

"That's what the creatures who live there call it."

"Oh God," said Barbara, and she turned her back on him. She celebrated frustration by clapping her hands. "May I ask you a simple question?"

"Of course."

"Why is it you never mentioned any of this before the airplane crash?"

"I didn't think the time was *ripe*."

And so on. Billy says that he first came unstuck in time in 1944, long before his trip to Tralfamadore. The Tralfamadorians didn't have anything to do with his coming unstuck. They were simply able to give him insights into what was really going on.

Billy first came unstuck while World War Two was in progress. Billy was a chaplain's assistant in the war. A chaplain's assistant is customarily a figure of fun in the American Army. Billy was no exception. He was powerless to harm the enemy or to help his friends. In fact, he had no friends. He was a valet to a preacher, expected no promotions or medals, bore no arms, and had a meek faith in a loving Jesus which most soldiers found putrid.

While on maneuvers in South Carolina, Billy played hymns he knew from childhood, played them on a little black organ which was waterproof. It had thirty-nine keys and two stops—*vox humana* and *vox celeste*. Billy also had charge of a portable altar, an olive-drab attaché case with telescoping legs. It was lined with crimson plush, and nestled in that passionate plush were an anodized aluminium cross and a Bible.

The altar and the organ were made by a vacuum-cleaner company in Camden,

New Jersey—and said so.

One time on maneuvers Billy was playing "A Mighty Fortress Is Our God," with music by Johann Sebastian Bach and words by Martin Luther. It was Sunday morning. Billy and his chaplain had gathered a congregation of about fifty soldiers on a Carolina hillside. An umpire appeared. There were umpires everywhere, men who said who was winning or losing the theoretical battle, who was alive and who was dead.

The umpire had comical news. The congregation had been theoretically spotted from the air by a theoretical enemy. They were all theoretically dead now. The theoretical corpses laughed and ate a hearty noontime meal.

Remembering this incident years later, Billy was struck by what a Tralfamadorian adventure with death that had been, to be dead and to eat at the same time.

Toward the end of maneuvers, Billy was given an emergency furlough home because his father, a barber in Ilium, New York, was shot dead by a friend while they were out hunting deer. So it goes.

When Billy got back from his furlough, there were orders for him to go overseas. He was needed in the headquarters company of an infantry regiment fighting in Luxembourg. The regimental chaplain's assistant had been killed in action. So it goes.

When Billy joined the regiment, it was in the process of being destroyed by the Germans in the famous Battle of the Bulge. Billy never even got to meet the chaplain he was supposed to assist, was never even issued a steel helmet and combat boots. This was in December of 1944, during the last mighty German attack of the war.

Billy survived, but he was a dazed wanderer far behind the new German lines. Three other wanderers, not quite so dazed, allowed Billy to tag along. Two of them were scouts, and one was an antitank gunner. They were without food or maps. Avoiding Germans, they were delivering themselves into rural silences ever more profound. They ate snow.

They went Indian file. First came the scouts, clever, graceful, quiet. They had rifles. Next came the antitank gunner, clumsy and dense, warning Germans away with a Colt .45 automatic in one hand and a trench knife in the other.

Last came Billy Pilgrim, empty-handed, bleakly ready for death. Billy was preposterous—six feet and three inches tall, with a chest and shoulders like a box of kitchen matches. He had no helmet, no overcoat, no weapon, and no boots. On his feet were cheap, low-cut civilian shoes which he had bought for his father's funeral. Billy had lost a heel, which made him bob up-and-down, up-and-down. The involuntary dancing, up and down, up and down, made his hip joints sore.

Billy was wearing a thin field jacket, a shirt and trousers of scratchy wool, and long underwear that was soaked with sweat. He was the only one of the four who had a beard. It was a random, bristly beard, and some of the bristles were white, even though Billy was only twenty-one years old. He was also going bald. Wind and cold and violent exercise had turned his face crimson.

He didn't look like a soldier at all. He looked like a filthy flamingo.

And on the third day of wandering, somebody shot at the four from far away—shot four times as they crossed a narrow brick road. One shot was for the scouts. The next one was for the antitank gunner, whose name was Roland Weary.

The third bullet was for the filthy flamingo, who stopped dead center in the road when the lethal bee buzzed past his ear. Billy stood there politely, giving the marksman another chance. It was his addled understanding of the rules of warfare that the marksman *should* be given a second chance. The next shot missed Billy's kneecaps by inches, going end-on-end, from the sound of it.

Roland Weary and the scouts were safe in a ditch, and Weary growled at Billy, "Get out of the road, you dumb motherfucker." The last word was still a novelty in the speech of white people in 1944. It was fresh and astonishing to Billy, who had never fucked anybody—and it did its job. It woke him up and got him off the road.

"Saved your life again, you dumb bastard," Weary said to Billy in the ditch. He had been saving Billy's life for days cursing him, kicking him, slapping him, making him move. It was absolutely necessary that cruelty be used, because Billy wouldn't do anything to save himself. Billy wanted to quit. He was cold, hungry, embarrassed, incompetent. He could scarcely distinguish between sleep and wakefulness now, on the third day, found no important differences, either, between walking and standing still. He wished everybody would leave him alone. "You guys go on without me," he said again and again.

Weary was as new to war as Billy. He was a replacement, too. As a part of a gun crew, he had helped to fire one shot in anger—from a 57-millimeter antitank gun. The gun made a ripping sound like the opening of the zipper on the fly of God Almighty. The gun lapped up snow and vegetation with a blowtorch thirty feet long. The flame left a black arrow on the ground, showing the Germans exactly where the gun was hidden. The shot was a miss.

What had been missed was a Tiger tank. It swiveled its 88-millimeter snout around sniffingly, saw the arrow on the ground. It fired. It killed everybody on the gun crew but Weary. So it goes.

Roland Weary was only eighteen, was at the end of an unhappy childhood spent mostly in Pittsburgh, Pennsylvania. He had been unpopular in Pittsburgh. He had been unpopular because he was stupid and fat and mean, and smelled like bacon no matter how much be washed. He was always being ditched in Pittsburgh by people who did not want him with them.

It made Weary sick to be ditched. When Weary was ditched, he would find somebody who was even more unpopular than himself, and he would horse around with that person for a while, pretending to be friendly. And then he would find some pretext for beating the shit out of him.

It was a pattern. It was a crazy, sexy, murderous relationship Weary entered into with people he eventually beat up. He told them about his father's collection of guns and swords and torture instruments and leg irons and so on. Weary's father, who was a plumber, actually did collect such things, and his collection was insured for four thousand dollars. He wasn't alone. He belonged to a big club composed of people who collected things like that.

Weary's father once gave Weary's mother a Spanish thumbscrew in working condition—for a kitchen paperweight. Another time he gave her a table lamp whose base was a model one foot high of the famous "Iron Maiden of Nuremburg." The real Iron Maiden was a medieval torture instrument, a sort of boiler which was shaped like a woman on the outside—and lined with spikes. The front of the woman was composed of two hinged doors. The idea was to put a criminal inside and then close the doors slowly. There were two special spikes where his eyes would be. There was a drain in the bottom to let out all the blood. So it goes.

Weary had told Billy Pilgrim about the Iron Maiden, about the drain in her bottom—and what that was for. He had talked to Billy about dumdums. He told him about his father's Derringer pistol, which could be carried in a vest pocket, which was yet capable of making a hole in a man "which a bull bat could fly through without touching either wing."

Weary scornfully bet Billy one time that he didn't even know what a blood gutter was. Billy guessed that it was the drain in the bottom of the Iron Maiden, but that was wrong. A blood gutter, Billy learned, was the shallow groove in the side of the blade of a sword or bayonet.

Weary told Billy about neat tortures he'd read about or seen in the movies or heard on the radio—about other neat tortures he himself had invented. One of the inventions was sticking a dentist's drill into a guy's ear. He asked Billy what he thought the worst form of execution was. Billy had no opinion. The correct answer turned out to be this: "You stake a guy out on an anthill in the desert— see? He's facing upward, and you put honey all over his balls and pecker, and you cut off his eyelids so he has to stare at the sun till he dies." So it goes.

* * *

Now, lying in the ditch with Billy and the scouts after having been shot at, Weary made Billy take a very close look at his trench knife. It wasn't government issue. It was a present from his father. It had a ten-inch blade that was triangular in cross section. Its grip consisted of brass knuckles, was a chain of rings through which Weary slipped his stubby fingers. The rings weren't simple. They bristled with spikes.

Weary laid the spikes along Billy's cheek, roweled the cheek with savagely affectionate restraint. "How'd you like to be hit with this—hm? Hmmmmmmmmmm?" he wanted to know.

"I wouldn't," said Billy.

"Know why the blade's triangular?"

"No."

"Makes a wound that won't close up."

"Oh."

"Makes a three-sided hole in a guy. You stick an ordinary knife in a guy—makes a slit. Right? A slit closes right up. Right?"

"Right."

"Shit. What do you know? What the hell they teach in college?"

"I wasn't there very long," said Billy, which was true. He had had only six months of college, and the college hadn't been a regular college, either. It had been the night school of the Ilium School of Optometry.

"Joe College," said Weary scathingly.

Billy shrugged.

"There's more to life than what you read in books," said Weary. "You'll find that out."

Billy made no reply to this, either, there in the ditch, since he didn't want the conversation to go on any longer than necessary. He was dimly tempted to say, though, that he knew a thing or two about gore. Billy, after all, had contemplated torture and hideous wounds at the beginning and the end of nearly every day of his childhood. Billy had an extremely gruesome crucifix hanging on the wall of his little bedroom in Ilium. A military surgeon would have admired the clinical fidelity of the artist's rendition of all Christ's wounds—the spear wound, the thorn wounds, the holes that were made by the iron spikes. Billy's Christ died horribly. He was pitiful.

So it goes.

*   *   *

Billy wasn't a Catholic, even though he grew up with a ghastly crucifix on the wall. His father had no religion. His mother was a substitute organist for several churches around town. She took Billy with her whenever she played, taught him to play a little, too. She said she was going to join a church as soon as she decided which one was right.

She never *did* decide. She did develop a terrific hankering for a crucifix, though. And she bought one from a Santa Fe gift shop during a trip the little family made out West during the Great Depression. Like so many Americans, she was trying to construct a life that made sense from things she found in gift shops.

And the crucifix went up on the wall of Billy Pilgrim.

The two scouts, loving the walnut stocks of their rifles in the ditch, whispered that it was time to move out again. Ten minutes had gone by without anybody's coming to see if they were hit or not, to finish them off. Whoever had shot was evidently far away and all alone.

And the four crawled out of the ditch without drawing any more fire. They crawled into a forest like the big, unlucky mammals they were. Then they stood up and began to walk quickly. The forest was dark and old. The pines were planted in ranks and files. There was no undergrowth. Four inches of unmarked snow blanketed the ground. The Americans had no choice but to leave trails in the snow as unambiguous as diagrams in a book on ballroom dancing—*step, slide, rest—step, slide, rest.*

"Close it up and keep it closed!" Roland Weary warned Billy Pilgrim as they moved out. Weary looked like Tweedledum or Tweedledee, all bundled up for battle. He was short and thick.

He had every piece of equipment he had ever been issued, every present he'd received from home: helmet, helmet liner, wool cap, scarf, gloves, cotton undershirt, woolen undershirt, wool shirt, sweater, blouse, jacket, overcoat, cotton underpants, woolen under-pants, woolen trousers, cotton socks, woolen socks, combat boots, gas mask, canteen, mess kit, first-aid kit, trench knife, blanket, shelter-half, raincoat, bullet-proof Bible, a pamphlet entitled "Know Your Enemy," another pamphlet entitled "Why We Fight," and another pamphlet of German phrases rendered in English phonetics, which would enable Weary to ask Germans questions such as "Where is your headquarters?" and "How many howitzers have you?" or to tell them, "Surrender. Your situation is hopeless," and so on.

Weary had a block of balsa wood which was supposed to be a foxhole pillow. He had a prophylactic kit containing two tough condoms "For the Prevention of Disease Only!" He had a whistle he wasn't going to show anybody until he got promoted to corporal. He had a dirty picture of a woman attempting sexual intercourse with a Shetland pony. He had made Billy Pilgrim admire that picture several times.

The woman and the pony were posed before velvet draperies which were fringed with deedlee-balls. They were flanked by Doric columns. In front of one column was a potted palm. The picture that Weary had was a print of the first dirty photograph in history. The word *photography* was first used in 1839, and it was in that year, too, that Louis J. M. Daguerre revealed to the French Academy that an image formed on a silvered metal plate covered with a thin film of silver iodide could be developed in the presence of mercury vapor.

In 1841, only two years later, an assistant to Daguerre, André Le Fèvre, was arrested in the Tuileries Gardens for attempting to sell a gentleman a picture of the woman and the pony. That was where Weary bought his picture, too—in the Tuileries. Le Fèvre argued that the picture was fine art, and that his intention was to make Greek mythology come alive. He said the columns and the potted palm proved that.

When asked which myth he meant to represent, Le Fèvre replied that there were thousands of myths like that, with the woman a mortal and the pony a god.

He was sentenced to six months in prison. He died there of pneumonia. So it goes.

Billy and the scouts were skinny people. Roland Weary had fat to burn. He was a roaring furnace under all his layers of wool and straps and canvas. He had so much energy that he bustled back and forth between Billy and the scouts, delivering dumb messages which nobody had sent and which nobody was pleased to receive. He also began to suspect, since he was so much busier than anybody else, that he was the leader.

He was so hot and bundled up, in fact, that he had no sense of danger. His vision of the outside world was limited to what he could see through a narrow slit between the rim of his helmet and his scarf from home, which concealed his baby face from the bridge of his nose on down. He was so snug in there that he was able to pretend that he was safe at home, having survived the war, and that he was telling his parents and his sister a true war story—whereas the true war story was still going on.

Weary's version of the true war story went like this: There was a big German attack, and Weary and his antitank buddies fought like hell until everybody was killed but Weary. So it goes. And then Weary tied in with two scouts, and they became close friends immediately, and they decided to fight their way back to their own lines. They were going to travel fast. They were damned if they'd surrender. They shook hands all around. They called themselves "The Three Musketeers."

But then this damn college kid, who was so weak he shouldn't even have been in the army, asked if he could come along. He didn't even have a gun or a knife. He didn't even have a helmet or a cap. He couldn't even walk right—kept bobbing up-and-down, up-and-down, driving everybody crazy, giving their position away. He was pitiful. The Three Musketeers pushed and carried and dragged the college kid all the way back to their own lines, Weary's story went. They saved his God-damned hide for him.

In real life, Weary was retracing his steps, trying to find out what had happened to Billy. He had told the scouts to wait while he went back for the college bastard. He passed under a low branch now. It hit the top of his helmet with a *clonk*. Weary didn't hear it. Somewhere a big dog was barking. Weary didn't hear that, either. His war story was at a very exciting point. An officer was congratulating the Three Musketeers, telling them that he was going to put them in for Bronze Stars.

"Anything else I can do for you boys?" said the officer.

"Yes, sir," said one of the scouts. "We'd like to stick together for the rest of the war, sir. Is there some way you can fix it so nobody will ever break up the Three Musketeers?"

Billy Pilgrim had stopped in the forest. He was leaning against a tree with his eyes closed. His head was tilted back and his nostrils were flaring. He was like a poet in the Parthenon.

This was when Billy first came unstuck in time. His attention began to swing grandly through the full arc of his life, passing into death, which was violet light. There wasn't anybody else there, or any thing. There was just violet light—and a hum.

And then Billy swung into life again, going backwards until he was in pre-birth, which was red light and bubbling sounds. And then he swung into life again and stopped. He was a little boy taking a shower with his hairy father at the Ilium Y.M.C.A. He smelled chlorine from the swimming pool next door, heard the springboard boom.

Little Billy was terrified, because his father had said Billy was going to learn to swim by the method of sink-or-swim. His father was going to throw Billy into the deep end, and Billy was going to damn well swim.

It was like an execution. Billy was numb as his father carried him from the shower room to the pool. His eyes were closed. When he opened his eyes, he was on the bottom of the pool and there was beautiful music everywhere. He lost consciousness, but the music went on. He dimly sensed that somebody was rescuing him. Billy resented that.

From there he traveled in time to 1965. He was forty-one years old, and he was visiting his decrepit mother at Pine Knoll, an old people's home he had put her in only a month before. She had caught pneumonia, and wasn't expected to live. She did live, though, for years after that.

Her voice was nearly gone, so, in order to hear her, Billy had to put his ear right next to her papery lips. She evidently had something very important to say. "How...?" she began, and she stopped. She was too tired. She hoped that she wouldn't have to say the rest of the sentence, that Billy would finish it for her.

But Billy had no idea what was on her mind. "How *what*, Mother?" he prompted.

She swallowed hard, shed some tears. Then she gathered energy from all over her ruined body, even from her toes and fingertips. At last she had accumulated enough to whisper this complete sentence:

"How did I get so *old*?"

           *   *   *

Billy's antique mother passed out, and Billy was led from the room by a pretty nurse. The body of an old man covered by a sheet was wheeled by just as Billy entered the corridor. The man had been a famous marathon runner in his day. So it goes. This was before Billy had his head broken in an airplane crash, by the way—before he became so vocal about flying saucers and traveling in time.

Billy sat down in a waiting room. He wasn't a widower yet. He sensed something hard under the cushion of his overstuffed chair. He dug it out, discovered that it was a book, *The Execution of Private Slovik*, by William Bradford Huie. It was a true account of the death before an American firing squad of Private Eddie D. Slovik, 36896415, the only American soldier to be shot for cowardice since the Civil War. So it goes.

Billy read the opinion of a staff judge advocate who reviewed Slovik's case, which ended like this: *He has directly challenged the authority of the government, and future discipline depends upon a resolute reply to this challenge. If the death penalty is ever to be imposed for desertion, it should be imposed in this case, not as a punitive measure nor as retribution, but to maintain that discipline upon which alone an army can succeed against the enemy. There was no recommendation for clemency in the case and none is here recommended.* So it goes.

Billy blinked in 1965, traveled in time to 1958. He was at a banquet in honor of a Little League team of which his son Robert was a member. The coach, who had never been married, was speaking. He was all choked up. "Honest to God," he was saying, "I'd consider it an honor just to be *water* boy for these kids."

Billy blinked in 1958, traveled in time to 1961. It was New Year's Eve, and Billy was disgracefully drunk at a party where everybody was in optometry or married to an optometrist.

Billy usually didn't drink much, because the war had ruined his stomach, but he certainly had a snootful now, and he was being unfaithful to his wife Valencia for the first and only time. He had somehow persuaded a woman to come into the laundry room of the house, and then sit up on the gas dryer, which was running.

The woman was very drunk herself, and she helped Billy get her girdle off. "What was it you wanted to talk about?" she said.

"It's all right," said Billy. He honestly thought it was all right. He couldn't remember the name of the woman.

"How come they call you Billy instead of William?"

"Business reasons," said Billy. That was true. His father-in-law, who owned the Ilium School of Optometry, who had set Billy up in practice, was a genius in his field. He told Billy to encourage people to call him Billy—because it would stick in their memories. It would also make him seem slightly magical, since there weren't any other grown Billys around. It also compelled people to think of him as a friend right away.

Somewhere in there was an awful scene, with people expressing disgust for Billy and the woman, and Billy found himself out in his automobile, trying to find the steering wheel.

The main thing now was to find the steering wheel. At first, Billy windmilled his arms, hoping to find it by luck. When that didn't work, he became methodical, working in such a way that the wheel could not possibly escape him. He placed himself hard against the left-hand door, searched every square inch of the area before him. When he failed to find the wheel, he moved over six inches, and searched again. Amazingly, he was eventually hard against the right-hand door, without having found the wheel. He concluded that somebody had stolen it. This angered him as he passed out.

He was in the back seat of his car, which was why he couldn't find the steering wheel.

Now somebody was shaking Billy awake. Billy still felt drunk, was still angered by the stolen steering wheel. He was back in World War Two again, behind the German lines. The person who was shaking him was Roland Weary. Weary had gathered the front of Billy's field jacket into his hands. He banged Billy against a tree, then pulled him away from it, flung him in the direction he was supposed to take under his own power.

Billy stopped, shook his head. "You go on," he said.

"What?"

"You guys go on without me. I'm all right."

"You're what?"

"I'm O.K."

"Jesus—I'd hate to see somebody *sick*," said Weary, through five layers of humid scarf from home. Billy had never seen Weary's face. He had tried to imagine it one time, had imagined a toad in a fishbowl.

Weary kicked and shoved Billy for a quarter of a mile. The scouts were waiting between the banks of a frozen creek. They had heard the dog. They had heard men calling back and forth, too—calling like hunters who had a pretty good idea of where their quarry was.

The banks of the creek were high enough to allow the scouts to stand without being seen. Billy staggered down the bank ridiculously. After him came Weary, clanking and clinking and tinkling and hot.

"Here he is, boys," said Weary. "He don't want to live, but he's gonna live anyway. When he gets out of this, by God, he's gonna owe his life to the Three Musketeers." This was the first the scouts had heard that Weary thought of himself and them as the Three Musketeers.

Billy Pilgrim, there in the creekbed, thought he, Billy Pilgrim, was turning to steam painlessly. If everybody would leave him alone for just a little while, he thought, he wouldn't cause anybody any more trouble. He would turn to steam and float up among the treetops.

Somewhere the big dog barked again. With the help of fear and echoes and winter silences, that dog had a voice like a big bronze gong.

Roland Weary, eighteen years old, insinuated himself between the scouts, draped a heavy arm around the shoulder of each. "So what do the Three Musketeers do now?" he said.

Billy Pilgrim was having a delightful hallucination. He was wearing dry, warm, white sweatsocks, and he was skating on a ballroom floor. Thousands cheered. This wasn't time-travel. It had never happened, never would happen. It was the craziness of a dying young man with his shoes full of snow.

One scout hung his head, let spit fall from his lips. The other did the same. They studied the infinitesimal effects of spit on snow and history. They were small, graceful people. They had been behind German lines before many times—living like woods creatures, living from moment to moment in useful terror, thinking brainlessly with their spinal cords.

Now they twisted out from under Weary's loving arms. They told Weary that he and Billy had better find somebody to surrender to. The scouts weren't going to wait for them any more.

And they ditched Weary and Billy in the creekbed.

Billy Pilgrim went on skating, doing tricks in sweatsocks, tricks that most people would consider impossible—making turns, stopping on a dime and so on. The cheering went on, but its tone was altered as the hallucination gave way to time-travel.

Billy stopped skating, found himself at a lectern in a Chinese restaurant in

Ilium, New York, on an early afternoon in the autumn of 1957. He was receiving a standing ovation from the Lions Club. He had just been elected President, and it was necessary that he speak. He was scared stiff, thought a ghastly mistake had been made. All those prosperous, solid men out there would discover now that they had elected a ludicrous waif. They would hear his reedy voice, the one he'd had in the war. He swallowed, knew that all he had for a voice box was a little whistle cut from a willow switch. Worse—he had nothing to say. The crowd quieted down. Everybody was pink and beaming.

Billy opened his mouth, and out came a deep, resonant tone. His voice was a gorgeous instrument. It told jokes which brought down the house. It grew serious, told jokes again, and ended on a note of humility. The explanation of the miracle was this: Billy had taken a course in public speaking.

And then he was back in the bed of the frozen creek again. Roland Weary was about to beat the living shit out of him.

Weary was filled with a tragic wrath. He had been ditched again. He stuffed his pistol into its holster. He slipped his knife into its scabbard. Its triangular blade and blood gutters on all three faces. And then he shook Billy hard, rattled his skeleton, slammed him against a bank.

Weary barked and whimpered through his layers of scarf from home. He spoke unintelligibly of the sacrifices he had made on Billy's behalf. He dilated upon the piety and heroism of "The Three Musketeers," portrayed, in the most glowing and impassioned hues, their virtue and magnanimity, the imperishable honor they acquired for themselves, and the great services they rendered to Christianity.

It was entirely Billy's fault that this fighting organization no longer existed, Weary felt, and Billy was going to pay. Weary socked Billy a good one on the side of his jaw, knocked Billy away from the bank and onto the snow-covered ice of the creek. Billy was down on all fours on the ice, and Weary kicked him in the ribs, rolled him over on his side. Billy tried to form himself into a ball.

"You shouldn't even *be* in the Army," said Weary.

Billy was involuntarily making convulsive sounds that were a lot like laughter. "You think it's funny, huh?" Weary inquired. He walked around to Billy's back. Billy's jacket and shirt and undershirt had been hauled up around his shoulders by the violence, so his back was naked. There, inches from the tips of Weary's combat boots, were the pitiful buttons of Billy's spine.

Weary drew back his right boot, aimed a kick at the spine, at the tube which had so many of Billy's important wires in it. Weary was going to break that tube.

But then Weary saw that he had an audience. Five German soldiers and a police dog on a leash were looking down into the bed of the creek. The soldiers' blue eyes were filled with a bleary civilian curiosity as to why one American would try to murder another one so far from home, and why the victim should laugh.

Battalion in Defence

(from *Officers and Gentlemen*)

Evelyn Waugh

Guy was weary, hungry and thirsty, but he had fared better than Fido in the last four days and, compared with him, was in good heart, almost buoyant, as he tramped alone, eased at last of the lead weight of human company. He had paddled in this lustral freedom on the preceding morning when he caught X Commando among the slit trenches and olive trees. Now he wallowed.

Soon the road ran out and round, the face of a rocky spur—the place where Fido had found no cover—and here he met a straggling platoon of infantry coming fast towards him, a wan young officer well ahead.

"Have you seen anything of Hookforce?"

"Never heard of them."

The breathless officer paused as his men caught up with him and formed column. They still had their weapons and equipment.

"Or the Halberdiers?"

"Cut off. Surrounded. Surrendered."

"Are you sure?"

"Sure? For Christ's sake, there are parachutists everywhere. We've just been fired on coming round that corner. You can't get up the road. A machine-gun, the other side of the valley."

"Where exactly?"

"Any casualties?"

"I didn't wait to see. Can't wait now. I wouldn't try that road if you know what's healthy."

The platoon scuffled on. Guy looked down the empty exposed road and then studied his map. There was a track over the hill which rejoined the road at a village two miles on. Guy did not greatly believe in the machine-gun but he chose the short cut and painfully climbed until he found himself on the top of the spur. He could see the whole empty, silent valley. Nothing moved anywhere except the bees. He might have been standing in the hills behind Santa Dulcina any holiday morning of his lonely boyhood.

Then he descended to the village. Some of the cottage doors and windows were barred and shuttered, some rudely broken down. At first he met no one. A well stood before the church, built about with marble steps and a rutted plinth. He approached thirstily but found the rope hanging loose and short from its bronze staple. The bucket was gone and leaning over he saw far below a little shaving-glass of light and his own mocking head, dark and diminished.

He entered an open house and found an earthenware jar of classic shape. As he removed the straw stopper he heard and felt a hum and, tilting it to the light, found it full of bees and a residue of honey. Then looking about in the gloom he saw an old woman gazing at him. He smiled, showed his empty water-bottle, made signs of drinking. Still she gazed, quite blind. He searched his mind for vestiges of Greek and tried: "*Hudor. Hydro. Dipsa.*" Still she gazed, quite deaf, quite alone. Guy turned back into the sunlight. There a young girl, ruddy, barefooted and in tears, approached him frankly and took him by the sleeve. He showed her his empty bottle, but she shook her head, made little inarticulate noises and drew him resolutely towards a small yard on the edge of the village, which had once held live-stock but was now deserted except by a second, similar girl, a sister perhaps, and a young English soldier who lay on a stretcher motionless. The girls pointed helplessly towards this figure. Guy could not help. The young man was dead, undamaged it seemed. He lay as though at rest. The few corpses which Guy had seen in Crete had sprawled awkwardly. This soldier lay like an effigy on a tomb—like Sir Roger in his shadowy shrine at Santa Dulcina. Only the bluebottles that clustered round his lips and eyes proclaimed that he was flesh. Why was he lying here? Who were these girls? Had a weary stretcher-party left him in their care and had they watched him die? Had they closed his eyes and composed his limbs? Guy would never know. It remained one of the countless unexplained incidents of war. Meanwhile, lacking words the three of them stood by the body, stiff and mute as figures in a sculptured Deposition.

To bury the dead is one of the corporal works of charity. There were no tools here to break the stony ground. Later, perhaps, the enemy would scavenge the island and tip this body with others into a common pit and the boy's family would get no news of him and wait and hope month after month, year after year. A precept came to Guy's mind from his military education: "The officer in command of a burial party is responsible for collecting the red identity discs and forwarding them to Records. The green disc remains on the body. If in doubt, gentlemen, remember that green is the of putrefaction."

Guy knelt and took the disc from the cold breast. He read a number, a name, a designation, *RC*. "May his soul and the souls of all the faithful departed, in the mercy of God, rest in peace."

Guy stood. The bluebottles returned to the peaceful young face. Guy saluted and passed on.

The country opened and soon Guy came to another village. Toiling beside Fido in the darkness, he had barely noticed it. Now he found a place of some size, other roads and tracks converged on a market square; the houses had large barns behind them; a domed church stood open. Of the original inhabitants there was no sign; instead, English soldiers were posted in doorways—Halberdiers—and at the cross-roads sat Sarum-Smith, smoking a pipe.

"Hullo, uncle. The CO said you were about."

"I'm glad to find you. I met a windy officer on the road who said you were all in the bag."

"It doesn't look like it, does it? There was something of a schemozzle last night but we weren't in that."

Since Guy last saw him in West Africa, Sarum-Smith had matured. He was not a particularly attractive man, but man he was. "The CO's out with the Adj, going round the companies. You'll find the second-in-command at battalion headquarters, over there."

Guy went where he was directed, to a farm-house beside the church. Everything was in order. One notice pointed to the regimental aid post, another to the battalion-office. Guy passed the R S M and the clerks and in the further room of the house found Major Erskine. An army blanket had been spread on the kitchen table. It was, in replica, the orderly room at Penkirk.

Guy saluted.

"Hullo, uncle, you could do with a shave."

"I could do with some breakfast, sir."

"Lunch will be coming up as soon as the CO gets back. Brought us some more orders?"

"No, sir."

"Information?"

"None, sir."

"What's headquarters up to then?"

"Not functioning much at the moment. I came to get information from you."

"We don't know much."

He put Guy in the picture. The Commandos had lost two troops somehow during the night. An enemy patrol had wandered in from the flank during the morning and hurriedly retired. The Commandos were due to come through them soon and take up positions at Imbros. They had motor transport and should not have much difficulty in disengaging. The Second Halberdiers were to hold their present line till midnight and then fall back behind Hookforce to the beach perimeter. "After that we're in the hands of the navy. Those are the orders as I understand them. I don't know how they'll work out."

A Halberdier brought Guy a cup of tea.

"Crock," said Guy, "I hope you remember me?"

"Sir."

"Rather different from our last meeting."

"Sir," said Crock.

"The enemy aren't attacking in any strength yet," Major Erskine continued. "They're just pushing out patrols. As soon as they bump into anything, they stop and try working round. All quite elementary. We could hold them for ever if those blasted Q fellows would do their job. What are we running away for? It's not soldiering as I was taught it."

A vehicle stopped outside and Guy recognized Colonel Tickeridge's large commanding voice. He went out and found the Colonel and the Adjutant. They were directing the unloading from a lorry of three wounded men, two of them groggily walking, the third lying on a stretcher. As this man was carried past him he turned his white face and Guy recognized one of his former company. The man lay under a blanket. His wound was fresh and he was not yet in much pain. He smiled up quite cheerfully.

"Shanks," said Guy. "What have you been doing to yourself?"

"Must have been a mortar bomb, sir. Took us all by surprise, bursting right in the trench. I am lucky, considering. Chap next to me caught a packet."

This was Halberdier Shanks who, Guy remembered, used to win prizes for the Slow Valse. In the days of Dunkirk he had asked for compassionate leave in order to compete at Blackpool.

"I'll come and talk when the MO's had a look at you."

"Thank you, sir. Nice to have you back with us."

The other two men had limped off to the RAP. They must be from D Company too, Guy supposed. He did not remember them; only Halberdier Shanks, because of his Slow Valse.

"Well, uncle, come along in and tell me what I can do for you."

"I was wondering if there was anything *I* could do for *you*, Colonel."

"Yes, certainly. You will lay on hot dinners for the battalion, a bath for me, artillery support and a few squadrons of fighter aircraft. That's about all we want this morning, I think." Colonel Tickeridge was in high good humour. As he entered his headquarters he called: "Hi, there. Bring on the dancing-girls. Where's Halberdier Gold?"

"Just coming up, sir."

Halberdier Gold was an old friend, since the evening at Matchet when he had carried Guy's bag from the station, before the question even arose of Guy's joining the corps. He smiled broadly.

"Good morning, Gold; remember me?"

"Good morning, sir. Welcome back to the battalion."

"Vino," called Colonel Tickeridge. "Wine for our guest from the higher formation."

It was said with the utmost geniality but it struck a slight chill after the men's warmer greeting.

Gold laid a jug of wine on the table with the biscuits and bully beef. While they ate and drank, Colonel Tickeridge told Major Erskine:

"Quite a bit of excitement on the left flank. We were up with D Company and I was just warning Brent to expect fireworks in half an hour or so when the Commandos pull out, when I'm blessed if the blighters didn't start popping off at us with a heavy mortar from the other side of the rocks. De Souza's platoon caught it pretty hot. Lucky we had the truck there to bring back the pieces. We just stopped to watch Brent Winkle the mortar out. Then we came straight home. I've made some nice friends out there—a company of New Zealanders who rolled up and said please might they join in our battle—first-class fellows."

This seemed the moment for Guy to say what had been in his mind since meeting Shanks.

"That's exactly what I want to do, Colonel," he said. "Isn't there a platoon you could let me take over?"

Colonel Tickeridge regarded him benevolently. "No, uncle, of course there isn't."

"But later in the day, when you get casualties?"

"My good uncle, you aren't under my command. You can't start putting in for a cross-posting in the middle of a battle. That's not how the army works, you know that. You're a Hookforce body."

"But, Colonel, those New Zealanders—"

"Sorry, uncle. No can do."

And that, Guy knew from of old, was final.

Colonel Tickeridge began to explain the details of the rear-guard to Major Erskine. Sarum-Smith came to announce that the Commandos were coming through and Guy followed him out into the village and saw a line of dust and the back of the last Hookforce lorry disappearing to the south. There was a little firing, rifles and light machine-guns, and an occasional mortar bomb three-quarters of a mile to the north where the Halberdiers held their line. Guy stood between his friends, isolated.

A few hours earlier he had exulted in his loneliness. Now the case was altered. He was a "guest from the higher formation," a "Hookforce body," without place or function, a spectator. And all the deep sense of desolation which he had sought to cure, which from time to time momentarily seemed to be cured, overwhelmed him as of old. His heart sank. It seemed to him as though literally an organ of his body were displaced, subsiding, falling heavily like a feather in a vacuum jar; Philoctetes set apart from his fellows by an old festering wound; Philoctetes without his bow. Sir Roger without his sword.

Presently Colonel Tickeridge cheerfully intruded on his despondency.

"Well, uncle, nice to have seen you. I expect you want to get back to your own people. You'll have to walk, I'm afraid. The Adj and I are going round the companies again."

"Can I come too?"

Colonel Tickeridge hesitated, then said: "The more the merrier."

As they went forward he asked news of Matchet. "You staff wallahs get all the luck. We've had no mail since we went into Greece."

The Second Halberdiers and the New Zealanders lay across the main road, their flanks resting on the steep scree that enclosed the valley. D Company were on the far right flank, strung out along a water-course. To reach them there was open ground to be crossed. As Colonel Tickeridge and his party emerged from cover a burst of fire met them.

"Hullo," he said, "the Jerries are a lot nearer than they were this morning."

They ran for some rocks and approached cautiously and circuitously. When they finally dropped into the ditch they found Brent and Sergeant-Major Rawkes. Both were preoccupied and rather grim. They acknowledged Guy's greeting and then turned at once to their CO.

"They've brought up another mortar."

"Can you pin-point it?"

"They keep moving. They're going easy with their ammunition at present but they've got the range."

Colonel Tickeridge stood and searched the land ahead through his field-glasses. A bomb burst ten yards behind; all crouched low while a shower of stone and metal rang overhead.

"We haven't anything to spare for a counter-attack," said Colonel Tickeridge. "You'll have to give a bit of ground."

In training Guy had often wondered whether the exercises at Penkirk bore any semblance to real warfare. Here they did. This was no Armageddon, no torrent of uniformed migration, no clash of mechanical monsters; it was the conventional "battalion in defence," opposed by lightly armed, equally weary small forces. Ritchie-Hook had done little to inculcate the arts of withdrawal, but the present action conformed to pattern. While Colonel Tickeridge gave his orders, Guy moved down the bank. He found de Souza and his depleted platoon. He had a picturesque bandage round his head. Under it has sallow face was grave.

"Lost a bit of my ear," he said. "It doesn't hurt. But I'll be glad when today is over."

"You're retiring at midnight, I gather."

"'Retiring' is good. It sounds like a maiden aunt going to bed."

"I dare say you'll be in Alexandria before me," said Guy. "Hookforce is last out, covering the embarkation. I don't get the impression that the Germans are anxious to attack."

"D'you know what I think, uncle? I think they want to escort us quietly into the ships. Then they can sink us at their leisure from the air. A much tidier way of doing things."

A bomb exploded short of them.

"I wish I could spot that damned mortar," said de Souza.

Then an orderly summoned him to company headquarters. Guy went with him and rejoined Colonel Tickeridge.

It took little time to mount the withdrawal on the flank. Guy watched the battalion adjust itself to its new line. Everything was done correctly. Colonel Tickeridge gave his orders for the hours of darkness and for the final retreat. Guy made notes of times and lines of march in which the Halberdiers and New Zealanders would pass through Hookforce. Then he took his leave.

"If you run across any blue jobs," said Colonel Tickeridge, "tell them to wait for us."

For the third time Guy followed the road south. Night fell. The road filled with many men. Guy found the remnants of his headquarters where he had left them. He did not inquire for Major Hound. Sergeant Smiley offered no information. They fell in and set out into the darkness. They marched all night, one silent component of the procession of lagging, staggering men.

Another day; another night.

Anopopei
(from *The Naked and the Dead*)

Norman Mailer

At 0400, a few minutes after the false dawn had lapsed, the naval bombardment of Anopopei began. All the guns of the invasion fleet went off within two seconds of each other and the night rocked and shuddered like a great log foundering in the surf. The ships snapped and rolled from the discharge, lashing the water furiously. For one instant the night was jagged and immense, demoniac in its convulsion.

Then, after the first salvos the firing became irregular, and the storm almost subsided into darkness again. The great clanging noises of the guns became isolated once more, sounded like immense freight trains jerking and tugging up a grade. And afterward it was possible to hear the sighing wistful murmur of shells passing overhead. On Anopopei the few scattered campfires were snubbed out.

The first shells landed in the sea, throwing up remote playful spurts of water, but then a string of them snapped along the beach, and Anopopei came to life and glowed like an ember. Here and there little fires started where the jungle met the beach, and occasionally a shell which carried too far would light up a few hundred feet of brush. The line of beach became defined and twinkled like a seaport seen from a great distance at night.

An ammunition dump began to burn, spreading a rose-colored flush over a portion of the beach. When several shells landed in its midst, the flames sprouted fantastically high, and soared away in angry brown clouds of smoke. The shells continued to raze the beach and then began to shift inland. The firing had eased already into a steady, almost casual, pattern. A few ships at a time would discharge their volleys and then turn out to sea again while a new file attacked. The ammo dump still blazed, but most of the fires on the beach had smoldered down, and in the light which came with the first lifting of the dawn there was not nearly enough scud to hide the shore. About a mile inland, something had caught fire on the summit of a hill, and back of it, far away, Mount Anaka rose out of a base of maroon-colored smoke. Implacably, despite the new purple robes at its feet, the mountain sat on the island, and gazed out to sea. The bombardment was insignificant before it.

In the troop holds the sounds were duller and more persistent; they grated and rumbled like a subway train. The holds' electric lights, a wan yellow, had been turned on after breakfast, and they flickered dully, throwing many shadows over the hatches and through the tiers of bunks, lighting up the faces of the men assembled in the aisles and clustered around the ladder leading up to the top deck.

Martinez listened to the noises anxiously. He would not have been surprised if the hatch on which he was sitting had slid away from under him. He blinked his bloodshot eyes against the weary glare of the bulbs, tried to numb himself to everything. But his legs would twitch unconsciously every time a louder rumble beat against the steel bulkheads. For no apparent reason he kept repeating to himself the last line from an old joke, "I don't care if I do die, do die, do dy." Sitting there, his skin looked brown under the jaundiced light. He was a small, slim and handsome Mexican with neat wavy hair, small sharp features. His body, even now, had the poise and grace of a deer. No matter how quickly he might move the motion was always continuous and effortless. And like a deer his head was never quite still, his brown liquid eyes never completely at rest.

Above the steady droning of the guns, Martinez could hear voices separating for an instant and then being lost again. Separate babels of sound came from each platoon; the voice of a platoon leader would buzz against his ear like a passing insect, undefined and rather annoying. "Now, I don't want any of you to get lost when we hit the beach. Stick together, that's very important." He drew his knees up tighter, rolled back farther on his haunches until his hipbones grated against the tight flesh of his buttocks.

The men in recon looked small and lost in comparison to the other platoons. Croft was talking now about the landing craft embarkation, and Martinez listened dully, his attention wavering. "All right," Croft said softly, "it's gonna be the same as the last time we practised it. They ain't a reason why anything should go wrong, and it ain't goin' to."

Red guffawed scornfully. "Yeah, we'll all be up there," he said. "But sure as hell, some dumb sonofabitch is going to run up, and tell us to get back in the hold again."

"You think I'll piss if we have to stay here for the rest of the war?" Sergeant Brown said.

"Let's cut it out," Croft told them. "If you know what's going on better than I do, you can stand up here and talk." He frowned and then continued. "We're on boat-deck station twenty-eight. You all know where it is, but we're goin' up together just the same. If they's a man here suddenly discovers he's left anythin' behind, that'll be just t.s. We ain't gonna come back."

"Yeah, boys, don't forget to take your rubbers," Red suggested, and that drew a laugh. Croft looked angry for a second, but then he drawled, "I know Wilson ain't gonna forget his," and they laughed again. "You're fuggin ay," Gallagher snorted.

Wilson giggled infectiously. "Ah tell ya," he said, "Ah'd sooner leave my M-one behind, 'cause if they was to be a piece of pussy settin' up on that beach, and Ah didn't have a rubber, Ah'd just shoot myself anyway."

Martinez grinned, but their laughter, irritated him. "What's the matter, Japbait?" Croft asked quietly. Their eyes met with the intimate look of old friends. "Aaah, goddam stomach, she's no good," Martinez said. He spoke clearly, but in a low and hesitant voice as if he were translating from Spanish as he went along. Croft looked again at him, and then continued talking.

Martinez gazed about the hold. The aisles between the bunks were wide and unfamiliar now that the hammocks were lashed up, and it made him vaguely uneasy. He thought they looked like the stalls in a bit library in San Antonio and he remembered there was something unpleasant about it, some girl had spoken to him harshly. "I don't care if I do die, do die," went through his head. He shook himself. There was something terrible going to happen to him today. God always let you know things out of His goodness, and you had to…to watch out, to look out for yourself. He said the last part to himself in English.

The girl was a librarian and she had thought he was trying to steal a book. He was very little then, and he had got scared and answered in Spanish, and she had scolded him. Martinez's leg twitched. She had made him cry, he could remember that. Goddam girl. Today, he could screw with her. The idea fed him with a pleasurable malice. Little-tit librarian, he would spit on her now. But the library stalls were still a troop hold, and his fear returned.

A whistle blew, startling him. "Men for boat-deck fifteen," a voice shouted down, and one of the platoons started going up the ladder. Martinez could feel the tension in everyone around him, the way their voices had become quiet. Why could they not go first? he asked himself, hating the added tension which would come from waiting. Something was going to happen to him. He knew that now.

After an hour their signal came, and they jogged up the ladder, and stood milling outside the hatchway for almost a minute before they were told to move to their boat. The decks were very slippery in the dawn and they stumbled and cursed as they plodded along the deck. When they reached the davits which held their landing boat, they drew up in a rough file and began waiting again. Red shivered in the cold morning air. It was not yet six a.m., and the day had already the depressing quality which early mornings always had in the Army. It meant they were moving, it meant something new, something unpleasant.

All over the ship the debarkation activities were in different stages. A few landing craft were down in the water already, filled with troops and circling around the ship like puppies on a leash. The men in them waved at the ship the flesh color of their faces unreal against the gray paint of the landing craft, the dawn blue of the sea. The calm water looked like oil. Nearer the platoon, some men were boarding a landing craft, and another one, just loaded, was beginning its descent into the water, the davit pulleys creaking from time to time. But over most of the ship men were still waiting like themselves.

Red's shoulders were beginning to numb under the weight of his full pack, and his rifle muzzle kept clanging against his helmet. He was feeling irritable. "No matter how many times you wear a goddam pack, you never get used to it," he said.

"Have you got it adjusted right?" Hennessey asked. His voice was stiff and quivered a little.

"Fug the adjustments," Red said. "It just makes me ache somewhere else. I ain't built for a pack, I got too many bones." He kept on talking, glancing at Hennessey every now and then to see whether he was less nervous. The air was chill, and the sun at his left was still low and quiet without any heat. He stamped his feet, breathing the curious odor of a ship's deck, oil and tar and the fish smell of the water.

"When do we get into the boats?" Hennessey asked.

The shelling was still going on over the beach, and the island looked pale green in the dawn. A thin wispy line of smoke trailed along the shore.

Red laughed. "What! Do ya think this is gonna be any different today? I figure we'll be on deck all morning." But as he spoke, he noticed a group of landing craft circling about a mile from them in the water. "The first wave's still farting round," he reassured Hennessey. For an instant he thought again of the Motome invasion, and felt a trace of that panic catching him again. His fingertips still remembered the texture of the sides of the rubber boat as he had clung to it in the water. At the back of his throat he tasted salt water again, felt the dumb whimpering terror of ducking underwater when he was exhausted and the Jap guns would not stop. He looked out again, his shaggy face quite bleak for a moment.

In the distance the jungle near the beach had assumed the naked broken look which a shelling always gave it. The palm trees would be standing like pillars now, stripped of their leaves, and blackened if there had been a fire. Off the horizon Mount Anaka was almost invisible in the haze, a pale gray-blue color almost a compromise between the hues of the water and the sky. As he watched, a big shell landed on the shore and threw up a larger puff of smoke than the two to three that had preceded it. This was going to be an easy landing, Red told himself, but he was still thinking about the rubber boats. "I wish to hell they'd save some of that country for us," he said to Hennessey. "We're gonna have to live there." The morning had a raw expectant quality about it, and he drew a breath, and squatted on his heels.

Gallagher began to curse. "How fugging long we got to wait up here?"

"Hold your water," Croft told him. "Half the commo platoon is coming with us, and they ain't even up yet."

"Well, why ain't they?" Gallagher asked. He pushed his helmet farther back on his head. "It's just like the bastards to have us wait up on deck where we can have our fuggin heads blown off."

"You hear any artillery?" Croft asked.

"That don't mean they ain't got any," Gallagher said. He lit a cigarette and smoked moodily, his hand cupped over the butt as though he expected it to be snatched away from him any moment.

A shell sighed overhead, and unconsciously Martinez drew back against a gunhousing. He felt naked.

The davit machinery was complicated, and a portion of it hung over the water. When a man was harnessed into a pack and web belt and carried a rifle and two bandoliers and several grenades, a bayonet and a helmet, he felt as if he had a tourniquet over both shoulders and across his chest. It was hard to breathe and his limbs kept falling asleep. Climbing along the beam which led out to the landing craft became an adventure not unlike walking a tightrope while wearing a suit of armor.

When recon was given the signal to get into its landing boat, Sergeant Brown wet his mouth nervously. "They could've designed these better," he grumbled to Stanley as they inched out along the beam. The trick was not to look at the water. "You know, Gallagher ain't a bad guy, but he's a sorehead," Stanley was confiding.

"Yeah," Brown said abstractedly. He was thinking it would be a hell of a note if he, a noncom, were to fall in the water. My God, you'd sink, he realized. "I always hate this part," he said aloud.

He reached the lip of the landing craft, and jumped into it, the weight of his pack almost spilling him, jarring his ankle. Everyone was suddenly very merry in the little boat which was swaying gently under the davits. "Here comes old Red," Wilson yelled, and everybody laughed as Red worked gingerly along the beam, his face puckered like a prune. When he reached the side he looked over scornfully at them and said, "Goddam, got the wrong boat. They ain't no one stupid-looking enough here to be recon."

"C'mon in, y'old billygoat," Wilson chuckled, his laughter easy and phlegmy, "the water's nice and cold."

Red grinned. "I know one place on you that ain't cold. Right now it's red-hot."

Brown found himself laughing and laughing. What a bunch of good old boys they were in the platoon, he told himself. It seemed as if the worst part were over already.

"How's the General get into these boats?" Hennessey asked. "He ain't young like us."

Brown giggled. "They got two privates to carry him over." He basked in the laughter which greeted this.

Gallagher dropped into the boat. "The fuggin Army," he said, "I bet they get more fuggin casualties out of guys getting into boats."

Brown roared. Gallagher probably looked mad even when he was screwing his wife. For an instant he was tempted to say so, and it made him laugh even more. In the middle of his snickering he had a sudden image of his own wife in bed with another man at this exact moment, and there was a long empty second in his laughter when he felt nothing at all. "Hey, Gallagher," he said furiously, "I bet you even look pissed-off when you're with your wife."

Gallagher looked sullen and then unexpectedly began to laugh too. "Aaah, fug you," he said, and that made everyone roar even more.

The little assault craft with their blunt bows looked like hippopotami as they bulled and snorted through the water. They were perhaps forty feet long, ten feet wide, shaped like open shoe boxes with a motor at the rear. In the troop well, the waves made a loud jarring sound beating against the bow ramp, and already an inch or two of water had squeezed through the crevices and was sloshing around the bottom. Red gave up the effort to keep his feet dry. Their boat had been circling for over an hour and he was getting dizzy. Occasionally a cold fan of spray would drop on them, shocking and abrupt and a trifle painful.

The first wave of soldiers had landed about fifteen minutes ago, and the battle taking place on the beach crackled faintly in the distance like a bonfire. It seemed remote and insignificant. To relieve the monotony Red would peer over the side wall and scan the shore. It still looked untenanted from three miles out, but the ornament of battle was there—a thin foggy smoke drifted along the water. Occasionally a flight of three dive bombers would buzz overhead and lance towards shore, the sound of their motors filtering back in a subdued gentle rumble. When they dove on the beach it was difficult to follow them, for they were almost invisible, appearing as flecks of pure brilliant sunlight. The puff their bombs threw up looked small and harmless and the planes would be almost out of sight when the noise of the explosions came back over the water.

Red tried to ease the weight of his pack by compressing it against the bulkhead of the boat. The constant circling was annoying. As he looked at the thirty men squeezed in with him, and saw how unnaturally green their uniforms looked against the blue-gray of the troop well, he had to breathe deeply a few times and sit motionless. Sweat was breaking out along his back.

"How long is this gonna take?" Gallagher wanted to know. "The goddam Army, hurry up and wait, hurry up and wait."

Red had started to light a cigarette, his fifth since their boat had been lowered in the water, and it tasted flat and unpleasant. "What do you think?" Red asked. "I bet we don't go in till ten." Gallagher swore. It was not yet eight o'clock.

"Listen," Red went on, "if they really knew how to work these kind of things, we woulda been eating breakfast now, and we woulda got into these crates about two hours from now." He rubbed off the tiny ash which had formed on his cigarette. "But, naw, some sonofabitchin' looey, who's sleeping right now, wanted us to get off the goddam ship so he could stop worrying about us." Purposely, he spoke loud enough for the Lieutenant from the communications platoon to hear him and grinned as the officer turned his back.

Corporal Toglio, who was squatting next to Gallagher, looked at Red. "We're a lot safer out in the water," Toglio explained eagerly. "This is a pretty small target compared to a ship, and when we're moving like this it's a lot harder to hit us than you think."

Red grunted. "Balls."

"Listen," Brown said, "they ain't a time when I wouldn't rather be on that ship. I think it's a hell of a lot safer."

"I looked into this," Toglio protested. "The statistics prove you're a lot safer here than any other place during an invasion."

Red hated statistics. "Don't give me any of those figures," he told Corporal Toglio. "If you listen to them you give up taking a bath cause it's too dangerous."

"No, I'm serious," Toglio said. He was a heavy-set Italian of about middle height with a pear-shaped head which was broader in the jaw than in the temple. Although he had shaved the night before, his beard darkened all of his face under his eyes except for his mouth, which was wide and friendly. "I'm serious," he insisted, "I saw the statistics."

"You know what you can do with them," Red said.

Toglio smiled, but he was a little annoyed. Red was a pretty good guy, he was thinking, but too independent. Where would you be if everybody was like him? You'd get nowhere. It took co-operation in everything. Something like this invasion was planned, it was efficient, down to a timetable. You couldn't run trains if the engineer took off when he felt like it.

The idea impressed him, and he pointed one of his thick powerful fingers to tell Red when suddenly a Jap shell, the first in half an hour, threw up a column of water a few hundred yards from them. The sound was unexpectedly loud, and they all winced for a moment. In the complete silence that followed, Red yelled loud enough for the whole boat to hear, "Hey, Toglio, if I had to depend on you for my safety, I'd a been in hell a year ago." The laughter was loud enough to embarrass Toglio, who forced himself to grin. Wilson capped it by saying in his high soft voice, "Toglio, you can figger out more ways to make a man do something, and then it turns out all screwed up anyway. Ah never saw a man who was so particular over nothin'."

That wasn't true, Toglio said to himself. He liked to get things done right, and these fellows just didn't seem to appreciate it. Somebody like Red was always ruining your work by making everybody laugh.

The assault boat's motor grew louder suddenly, began to roar, and after completing a circle, the boat headed in toward shore. Immediately the waves began to pound against the forward ramp, and a long cascade of spray poured over the troops. There was a surprised groan and then a silence settled over the men. Croft unslung his rifle and held one finger over the muzzle to prevent any water from getting into the barrel. For an instant he felt as though he were riding a horse at a gallop. "Goddam, we're going in," someone said.

"I hope it's cleaned up at least," Brown murmured.

Croft felt superior and dejected. He had been disappointed when he had learned weeks before that recon was to be assigned to the beach detail for the first week. And he had felt a silent contempt when the men in the platoon had shown their pleasure at the news. "Chickenshit," he muttered to himself now. A man who was afraid to put his neck out on the line was no damn good. Leading the men was a responsibility he craved; he felt powerful and certain at such moments. He longed to be in the battle that was taking place inland from the beach, and he resented the decision which left the platoon on an unloading detail. He passed his hand along his gaunt hard cheek and looked silently about him.

Hennessey was standing near the stern. As Croft watched his white silent face, he decided that Hennessey was frightened and it amused him. The boy found it hard to be still; he kept bobbing about in his place, and once or twice he flinched noticeably at a sudden noise; his leg began to itch and he scratched it violently. Then, as Croft watched, Hennessey pulled his left trouser out of his legging, rolled it up to expose his knee, and with a great deal of care rubbed a little spittle over the irritated red spot on his knee. Croft gazed at the white flesh with its blond hairs, noticed the pains with which Hennessey replaced his trouser in the legging, and felt an odd excitement as if the motions were important. That boy is too careful, Croft told himself.

And then with a passionate certainty he thought, "Hennessey's going to get killed today." He felt like laughing to release the ferment in him. This time he was sure.

But, abruptly, Croft remembered the poker game the preceding night when he had failed to draw his full house, and he was confused and then disgusted. You figure you're getting a little too smart for yourself, he thought. His disgust came because he felt he could not trust such emotions, rather than from any conviction that they had no meaning at all. He shook his head and sat back on his haunches, feeling the assault boat race in toward land, his mind empty, waiting for what events would bring.

Martinez had his worst minute just before they landed. All the agonies of the previous night, all the fears he had experienced early that morning had reached their climax in him. He dreaded the moment when the ramp would go down and he would have to get out of the boat. He felt as if a shell would swallow all of them, or a machine-gun would be set up before the bow, would begin firing the moment they were exposed. None of the men was talking, and when Martinez closed his eyes, the sound of the water lashing past their craft seemed overwhelming as though he were sinking beneath it. He opened his eyes, pressed his nails desperately into his palms. "Buenos Dios," he muttered. The sweat was dripping from his brow into his eyes, and he wiped it out roughly. Why no sounds? he asked himself. And indeed there were none. The men were silent, and a hush had come over the beach; the lone machine-gun rapping in the distance sounded hollow and unreal.

A plane suddenly wailed past them, then roared over the jungle firing its guns. Martinez almost screamed at the noise. He felt his legs twitching again. Why didn't they land? By now he was almost ready to welcome the disaster that would meet him when the ramp went down.

In a high piping voice, Hennessey asked, "Do you think we'll be getting mail soon?" and his question was lost in a sudden roar of laughter. Martinez laughed and laughed, subsided into weak giggles, and then began laughing again.

"That fuggin Hennessey," he heard Gallagher say.

Suddenly Martinez realized that the boat had ground to a stop. The sound of its motors had altered, had become louder and a little uncertain, as if the propeller were no longer biting the water. After a moment he understood that they had landed.

For several long seconds, they remained motionless. Then the ramp clanked down, and Martinez trudged dumbly into the surf, almost stumbling when a knee-high wave broke behind him. He walked with his head down, looking at the water, and it was only when he was on shore that he realized nothing had happened to him. He looked about. Five other craft had landed at the same time, and then men were stringing over the beach. He saw an officer coming toward him, heard him ask Croft, "What platoon is this?"

"Intelligence and reconnaissance, sir, we're on beach detail," and then the instructions to wait over by a grove of coconut trees near the beach. Martinez fell into line, and stumbled along behind Red, as the platoon walked heavily through the soft sand. He was feeling nothing at all except a conviction that his judgment had been delayed.

The platoon marched about two hundred yards and then halted at the coconut grove. It was hot already, and most of the men threw off their packs and sprawled in the sand. There had been men here before them. Units of the first wave had assembled nearby, for the flat caked sand was trodden by many feet, and there was the inevitable minor refuse of empty cigarette packs and a discarded ration or two. But now these men were inland, moving somewhere through the jungle, and there was hardly anyone in sight. They could see for a distance of about two hundred yards in either direction before the beach curved out of view, and it was all quiet, relatively empty. Around either bend there might be a great deal of activity, but they could not tell this. It was still too early for the supplies to be brought in, and all the troops that had landed with them had been quickly dispersed. Over a hundred yards away to their right, the Navy had set up a command post which consisted merely of an officer at a small folding desk, and a jeep parked in the defilade where the jungle met the beach. To their left, just around the bend an eighth of a mile away, the Task Force Headquarters was beginning to function. A few orderlies were digging fox-holes for the General's staff, and two men were staggering down the beach in the opposite direction, unwinding an eighty-pound reel of telephone wire. A jeep motored by in the firm wet sand near the water's edge and disappeared beyond the Navy's CP. The landing boats which had beached near the colored pennants on the other side of Task Force Headquarters had backed off by now and were cruising out toward the invasion fleet. The water looked very blue and the ships seemed to quiver a little in the mid-morning haze. Occasionally one of the destroyers would fire a volley or two, and half a minute later the men would hear the soft whisper of the shell as it arched overhead into the jungle. Once in a while a machine-gun would start racketing in the jungle, and might be answered soon after with the shrill riveting sound of a Japanese light automatic.

Sergeant Brown looked at the coconut trees which were shorn at the top from the shelling. Farther down, another grove had remained untouched, and he shook his head. Plenty of men could have lived through that bombardment, he told himself. "This ain't such a bad shelling, compared to what they did to Motome," he said.

Red looked bitter. "Yeah, Motome." He turned over on his stomach in the sand, and lit a cigarette. "The beach stinks already," he announced.

"How can it stink?" Stanley asked. "It's too early."

"It just stinks," Red answered. He didn't like Stanley, and although he had exaggerated the faint brackish odor that came from the jungle, he was ready to defend his statement. He felt an old familiar depression seeping through him; he was bored and irritable, it was too early to eat, and he had smoked too many cigarettes. "There ain't any invasion going on," he said, "this is practice, amphibious maneuvers." He spat bitterly.

Croft hooked his cartridge belt about his waist, and slung his rifle. "I'm going to hunt for S-four," he told Brown. "You keep the men here till I get back."

"They forgot us," Red said. "We might as well go to sleep."

"That's why I'm going to get them," Croft said.

Red groaned. "Aaah, why don't you let us sit on our butts for the day?"

"Listen, Valsen," Croft said, "you can cut all the pissin' from here on."

Red looked at him warily. "What's the matter?" he asked. "You want to win the war all by yourself?" They stared tensely at each other for a few seconds, and then Croft strode off.

"You're picking the wrong boy to mess with," Sergeant Brown told him.

Red spat again. "I won't take no crap from nobody." He could feel his heart beating quickly. There were a few bodies lying in the surf about a hundred yards from them, and as Red looked a soldier from Task Force Headquarters began dragging them out of the water. A plane patrolled overhead.

"It's pretty fuggin quiet," Gallagher said.

Toglio nodded. "I'm going to dig a hole." He unstrapped his entrenching tool, and Wilson snickered. "You just better save your energy, boy," he told him.

Toglio ignored him and started digging. "I'm going to make one too," Hennessey piped, and began to work about twenty yards from Toglio. For a few seconds the scraping of their shovels against the sand was the only sound.

Oscar Ridges sighed. "Shoot," he said, "Ah might as well make one too." He guffawed with embarrassment after he spoke, and bent over his pack. His laughter had been loud and braying.

Stanley imitated him. "Waa-a-aaah!"

Ridges looked up and said mildly, "Well, shoot, Ah just cain't help the way Ah laugh. It's good enough, Ah reckon." He guffawed again to show his good will, but the laughter was much more chastened this time. When there was no answer, he began to dig. He had a short powerful body which was shaped like a squat pillar, for it tapered at neither end. His face was round and dumpy with a long slack jaw that made his mouth gape. His eyes goggled placidly to increase the impression he gave of dull-wittedness and good temper. As he dug, his motions were aggravatingly slow; he dumped each shovelful in exactly the same place, and paused every time to look about before he bent down again. There was a certain wariness about him, as though he were accustomed to practical jokes, expected them to be played on him.

Stanley watched him impatiently. "Hey, Ridges," he said, looking at Sergeant Brown for approbation, "if you were sitting on a fire, I guess you'd be too lazy to piss and put it out."

Ridges smiled vaguely. "Reckon so," he said quietly, watching Stanley walk toward him, and stand over the hole to examine his progress. Stanley was a tall youth of average build with a long face which looked vain usually and scornful and a little uncertain. He would have been handsome if it had not been for his long nose and sparse black mustache. He was only nineteen.

"Christ, you'll be digging all day," Stanley said with disgust. His voice was artificially rough like that of an actor who fumbles for a conception of how soldiers talk.

Ridges made no answer. Patiently he continued digging. Stanley watched him for another minute, trying to think of something clever to say. He was beginning to feel ridiculous just standing there, and on an impulse kicked some sand into Ridges's foxhole. Silently, Ridges shoveled it out, not breaking his rhythm. Stanley could feel the men in the platoon watching him. He was a little sorry he had started for he wasn't certain whether the men sided with him. But he had gone too far to renege. He kicked in quite a bit of sand.

Ridges laid down his shovel and looked at him. His face was patient but there was some concern in it. "What you trying to do, Stanley?" he asked.

"You don't like it?" Stanley sneered.

"No, sir, Ah don't."

Stanley grinned slowly. "You know what you can do."

Red had been watching with anger. He liked Ridges. "Listen, Stanley," Red shouted, "wipe your nose and start acting like a man."

Stanley swung round and glared at Red. The whole thing had gone wrong. He was afraid of Red, but he couldn't retreat.

"Red, you can blow it out," he said.

"Speaking of blowing it out," Red drawled, "will you tell me why you bother cultivating that weed under your nose when it grows wild in your ass-hole?" He spoke with a heavy sarcastic brogue which had the men laughing before he even finished. "Good ol' Red," Wilson chuckled.

Stanley flushed, took a step towards Red. "You ain't going to talk to me that way."

Red was angry, eager for a fight. He knew he could whip Stanley. There was something which he was not ready to face, and he let his anger ride over it. "Boy, I could break you in half," he warned Stanley.

Brown got to his feet. "Listen, Red," he interrupted, "you weren't spoiling that damn hard to have a fight with Croft."

Red paused, and was disgusted with himself. That was it. He stood there indecisively. "No, I wasn't," he said, "but there ain't any man I won't fight." He wondered if he had been afraid of Croft. "Aaah, fug it," he said, turning away.

But Stanley realized that Red would not fight, and he walked after him. "This ain't settled for me," he said.

Red looked at him. "Go blow, will ya."

To his amazement, Stanley heard himself saying, "What's the matter, you going chickenshit?" He was positive he had said too much.

"Stanley," Red told him, "I could knock your head off, but I ain't gonna fight today." His anger was returning, and he tried to force it back. "Let's cut out this crap."

Stanley watched him, and then spat in the sand. He was tempted to say something more, but he knew the victory was with him. He sat down by Brown.

Wilson turned to Gallagher and shook his head. "Ah never thought old Red would back down," he murmured.

Ridges, seeing he was unmolested, went back to his digging. He was brooding a little over the incident, but the satisfying heft of the shovel in his hand soothed him. Just a little-bitty tool, he told himself. Pa would git a laugh out of seein' something like that. He became lost in his work, feeling a comfortable familiarity in the labor. They ain't nothin' like work for bringin' a man round, he told himself. The hole was almost finished, and he began to tamp the bottom with his feet, setting them down heavily and evenly.

The men heard a vicious slapping sound like a fly-swatter being struck against a table. They looked around uneasily. "That's a Jap mortar," Brown muttered.

"He's very near," Martinez muttered. It was the first thing he had said since they had landed.

The men at Task Force Headquarters had dropped to the ground. Brown listened, heard an accelerating whine, and buried his face in the sand. The mortar exploded about a hundred and fifty yards away, and he lay motionless, listening to the clear terrifying sound of shrapnel cutting through the air, whipping the foliage in the jungle. Brown stifled a moan. The shell had landed a decent distance away, but…He was suffering an unreasonable panic. Whenever some combat started there was always a minute when he was completely unable to function, and did the first thing that occurred to him. Now, as the echo of the explosion damped itself in the air, he sprung excitedly to his feet. "Come on, let's get the hell out of here," he shouted.

"What about Croft?" Toglio asked.

Brown tried to think. He felt a desperate urgency to get away from this stretch of beach. An idea came to him, and he grasped it without deliberation. "Look, you got a hole, you stay here. We're gonna head down about half a mile, and when Croft comes back, you meet us there." He started gathering his equipment, dropped it suddenly, muttered, "Fug it, get it later," and began to jog down the beach. The other men looked at him in surprise, shrugged, and then Gallagher, Wilson, Red, Stanley and Martinez followed him, spread out in a long file. Hennessey watched them go, and looked over at Toglio and Ridges. He had dug his hole only a few yards away from the periphery of the coconut grove and he tried to peer into the grove now, but it was too thick to be able to see for more than fifty feet. Toglio's foxhole on his left was about twenty yards away but it seemed much farther. Ridges, who was on the other side of Toglio, seemed a very great distance away. "What shall I do?" he whispered to Toglio. He wished he had gone with the others, but he had been afraid to ask for fear they would laugh at him. Toglio took a look around, and then, crouching, ran over to Hennessey's hole. His broad dark face was sweating now. "I think it's a very serious situation," he said dramatically, and then looked into the jungle.

"What's up?" Hennessey asked. He felt a swelling in his throat which was impossible to define as pleasant or unpleasant.

"I think some Japs sneaked a mortar in near the beach, and maybe they're going to attack us." Toglio mopped his face. "I wish the fellows had dug holes here," he said.

"It was a dirty trick to run off," Hennessey said. He was surprised to hear his voice sound natural.

"I don't know," Toglio said. "Brown's got more experience than I have. You got to trust your noncoms." He sifted some sand through his fingers. "I'm getting back in my hole. You just sit tight and wait. If any Japs come, we've got to stop them." Toglio's voice was portentous, and Hennessey nodded eagerly. This was like a movie, he thought. Vague images overlapped in his mind. He saw himself standing up and repelling a charge. "Okay, kid," Toglio said, and clapped him on the back. Crouching again, Toglio ran past his own hole to talk to Ridges. Hennessey remembered Red's telling him that Toglio had come to the platoon after the worst of the Motome campaign. He wondered if he could trust him.

Hennessey squatted in his hole and watched the jungle. His mouth was dry and he kept wetting his lips; every time there seemed to be a movement in the bushes, his heart constricted. The beach was very quiet. A minute went by, and he began to get bored. He could hear a truck grinding its gears down the beach, and when he took a chance and turned around, he could see another wave of landing craft coming in about a mile from shore. Reinforcements for us, he told himself, and realized it was absurd.

The harsh slapping sound came out of the jungle and was followed by another discharge and another and another. That's the mortars, he thought, and decided he was catching on fast. And then he heard a screaming piercing sound almost overhead like the tearing squeals of a car braking to avert a crash. Instinctively he curled flat in his hole. The next instants were lost to him. He heard an awful exploding sound which seemed to fill every corner of his mind, and the earth shook and quivered underneath him in the hole. Numbly he felt dirt flying over him, and his body being pounded by some blast. The explosion came again, and the dirt and the shock, and then another and another blast. He found himself sobbing in the hole, terrified and resentful. When another mortar landed, he screamed out like a child, "That's enough, That's enough!" He lay there trembling for almost a minute after the shells had stopped. His thighs felt hot and wet, and at first he thought, I'm wounded. It was pleasant and peaceful, and he had a misty picture of a hospital bed. He moved his hand back, and realized with both revulsion and mirth that he had emptied his bowels.

Hennessey froze his body. If I don't move, I won't get any dirtier, he thought. He remembered Red and Wilson talking about "keeping a tight ass-hole," and now he understood what they meant. He began to get the giggles. The sides of his foxhole were crumbling, and he had a momentary pang of anxiety at the thought that they would collapse in the next shelling. He was beginning to smell himself and he felt a little sick. Should be change his pants? He wondered. There was only one other pair in his pack, and he might have to wear them for a month. If he threw these away, they might make him pay for them.

But no, that wasn't true, he told himself; you didn't have to pay for lost equipment overseas. He was beginning to get the giggles again. What a story this would make to tell Pop. He saw his father's face for a moment. A part of him was trying to needle his courage to look over the edge of his hole. He raised himself cautiously, as much from the fear of further soiling his pants as from an enemy he might see.

Toglio and Ridges were still beneath the surface of their slit-trenches. Hennessey began to suspect he had been left alone. "Toglio, Corporal Toglio," he called, but it came out in a hoarse croaking whisper. There was no answer; he didn't ask himself whether they had heard him. He was alone, all alone, he told himself, and he felt an awful dread at being so isolated. He wondered where the others were. He had never seen combat before, and it was unfair to leave him alone; Hennessey began to feel bitter at being deserted. The jungle looked dark and ominous like a sky blacking over with thunderclouds. Suddenly, he knew he couldn't stay here any longer. He got out of his hole, clutched his rifle, and started to crawl away from the hole.

"Hennessey, where are you going?" Toglio shouted. His head had suddenly appeared from the hole.

Hennessey started, and then began to babble, "I'm going to get the others. It's important, I got my pants dirty." He began to laugh.

"Come back," Toglio shouted.

The boy looked at his foxhole and knew it was impossible to return to it. The beach seemed so pure and open. "No, I got to go," he said, and began to run. He heard Toglio shout once more, and then he was conscious only of the sound of his breathing. Abruptly, he realized that something was sliding about in the pocket his pants made as they bellied over his leggings. In a little frenzy, he pulled his trouser loose, let the stool fall out, and then began to run again.

Hennessey passed by the place where the flags were put up for the boats to come in, and saw the Navy officer lying prone in a little hollow near the jungle. Abruptly, he heard the mortars again, and then right after it a machine-gun firing nearby. A couple of grenades exploded with a loud empty sound that paper bags make when they burst. He thought for an instant, There's some soldiers after them Japs with the mortar. Then, he heard the terrible siren of the mortar shell coming down on him. He pirouetted in a little circle, and threw himself to the ground. Perhaps he felt the explosion before a piece of shrapnel tore his brain in half.

Red found him when the platoon was coming back to meet Toglio. They had waited out the shelling in a long Zigzag trench which had been dug by a company of reserve troops farther along the beach. After word had come that the Jap mortar crew had been wiped out, Brown decided to go back. Red didn't feel like talking to anybody, and unconsciously he assumed the lead. He came around a bend in the beach and saw Hennessey lying facedown in the sand with a deep rent in his helmet and a small circle of blood about his head. One of his hands was turned palm upward, and his fingers clenched as though he were trying to hold something. Red felt sick. He had liked Hennessey, but it had been the kind of fondness he had for many of the men in the platoon—it included the possibility that it might be ended like this. What bothered Red was the memory of the night they had sat on deck during the air raid when Hennessey had inflated his life belt. It gave Red a moment of awe and panic as if someone, *something*, had been watching over their shoulders that night and laughing. There was a pattern where there shouldn't be one.

Brown came up behind him, and gazed at the body with a troubled look. "Should I have left him behind?" he asked. He tried not to consider whether he were responsible.

"Who takes care of the bodies?"

"Graves Registration."

"Well, I'm going to find them so they can carry him away," Red said. Brown scowled. "We're supposed to stick together." He stopped, and then went on angrily, "Goddam, Red, you're acting awful chicken today, picking fights and then backing out of them, throwing a fit over..." He looked at Hennessey and didn't finish.

Red was walking on already. For the rest of this day, that was one part of the beach he was going to keep away from. He spat, trying to exorcise the image of Hennessey's helmet, and the blood that had still been flowing through the rent in the metal.

The platoon followed him, and when they reached the place where they had left Toglio, the men began digging holes in the sand. Toglio walked around nervously, repeating continually that he had yelled for Hennessey to come back. Martinez tried to reassure him. "Okay, nothing you can do," Martinez said several times. He was digging quickly and easily in the soft sand, feeling calm for the first time that day. His terror had withered with Hennessey's death. Nothing would happen now.

When Croft came back he made no comment on the news Brown gave him. Brown was relieved and decided he did not have to blame himself. He stopped thinking about it.

But Croft brooded over the event all day. Later, as they worked on the beach unloading supplies, he caught himself thinking of it many times. His reaction was similar to the one he had felt at the moment he discovered his wife was unfaithful. At that instant, before his rage and pain had begun to operate, he had felt only a numb throbbing excitement and the knowledge that his life was changed to some degree and certain things would never be the same. He knew that again now. Hennessey's death had opened to Croft vistas of such omnipotence that he was afraid to consider it directly. All day the fact hovered about his head, tantalizing him with odd dreams and portents of power.

Some Were Unlucky
(from *Enemy Coast Ahead*)

Guy Gibson, VC

We had been flying for about an hour and ten minutes in complete silence, each one busy with his thoughts, while the waves were slopping by a few feet below with monotonous regularity. And the moon dancing in those waves had become almost a hypnotising crystal. As Terry spoke he jerked us into action. He said, "Five minutes to go to the Dutch coast, skip."

I said, "Good," and looked ahead. Pulford turned on the spotlights and told me to go down much lower; we were about 100 feet off the water. Jim Deering, in the front turret, began to swing it from either way, ready to deal with any flak ships, which might be watching for mine-layers off the coast. Hutch sat in his wireless cabin ready to send a flak warning to the rest of the boys who might run into trouble behind us. Trevor took off his Mae West and squeezed himself back into the rear turret. On either side the boys tucked their blunt-nosed Lancs in even closer than they were before, while the crews inside them were probably doing the same sort of thing as my own. Someone began whistling nervously over the intercom. Someone else said, "Shut up."

Then Spam said, "There's the coast."

I said, "No, it's not; that's just low cloud and shadows on the sea from the moon."

But he was right and I was wrong, and soon we could see the Dutch Islands approaching. They looked low and flat and evil in the full moon, squirting flak in many directions because their radar would now know we were coming. But we knew all about their defences, and as we drew near this squat and unfriendly expanse we began to look for the necessary landmarks which would indicate how to get through that barrage. We began to behave like a ship threading its way through a minefield, in danger of destruction on either side, but safe if we were lucky and on the right track. Terry came up beside me to check up on Spam. He opened the side windows and looked out to scan the coast with his night glasses. "Can't see much," he said. "We're too low, but I reckon we must be on track because there's so little wind."

"Hope so."

"Stand by, front gunner; we're going over."

"OK. All lights off. No talking. Here we go."

With a roar we hurtled over the Western Wall, skirting the defences and turning this way and that to keep to our thin line of safety; for a moment we held our breath. Then I gave a sigh of relief; no one had fired a shot. We had taken them by surprise.

"Good effort, Terry. Next course."

"105 degrees magnetic."

We had not been on the new course for more than two minutes before we came to more sea again; we had obviously just passed over a small island, and this was wrong. Our proper track should have taken us between the two islands, as both were fairly heavily defended, but by the grace of God, the gunners on the one we had just passed over were apparently asleep. We pulled up high to about 300 feet to have a look and find out where we were, then scrammed down on the desk again as Terry said, "OK—there's the windmill and those wireless masts. We must have drifted to starboard. Steer new course—095 degrees magnetic, and be careful of a little town that is coming up straight ahead."

"OK, Terry, I'll go around it."

We were turning to the left now, and as we turned I noticed with satisfaction that Hoppy and Mickey were still flying there in perfect formation.

We were flying low. We were flying so low that more than once Spam yelled at me to pull up quickly to avoid high-tension wires and tall trees. Away on the right we could see the small town, its chimneys outlined against the night sky; we thought we saw someone flash us a "V," but it may have been an innkeeper poking his head out of his bedroom window. The noise must have been terrific.

Our new course should have followed a very straight canal, which led to a T-shaped junction, and beyond that was the Dutch frontier and Germany. All eyes began looking out to see if we were right, because we could not afford to be wrong. Sure enough, the canal came up slowly from underneath the starboard wing and we began to follow it carefully, straight above it, for now we were mighty close to Eindhoven, which had the reputation of being very well defended. Then, after a few minutes, that too had passed behind and we saw a glint of silvery light straight ahead. This was the canal junction, the second turning point.

It did not take Spam long to see where we were; now we were right on track, and Terry again gave the new course for the River Rhine. A few minutes later we crossed the German frontier, and Terry said, in his matter-of-fact way: "We'll be at the target in an hour and a half. The next thing to see is the Rhine."

But we did not all get through. One aircraft, P/O Rice, had already hit the sea, bounced up, lost both its outboard engines and its weapon, and had flown back on the inboard two. Les Munro had been hit by flak a little later on, and his aircraft was so badly damaged that he was forced to return to base. I imagined the feelings of the crews of these aircraft who, after many weeks of intense practice and expectation, at the last moment could only hobble home and land with nothing accomplished. I felt very sorry for them. This left sixteen aircraft going on; 112 men.

The journey into the Ruhr Valley was not without excitement. They did not like our coming. And they knew we were coming. We were the only aircraft operating that night; it was too bright for the main forces. And so, deep down in their underground plotting-rooms, the Hun controllers stayed awake to watch us as we moved steadily on. We had a rough idea how they worked, these controllers, moving fighter squadrons to orbit points in front of us, sounding air-raid sirens here and there, tipping off the gun positions along our route and generally trying to make it pretty uncomfortable for the men who were bound for "Happy Valley." As yet they would not know where we were going, because our route was planned to make feint attacks and fox their control. Only the warning sirens would have sounded in all the cities from Bremen southwards. As yet, the fighters would be unable to get good plots on us because we were flying so low, but once we were there the job would have to take quite a time, and they would have their chance.

We flew on. Germany seemed dead. Not a sign of movement, of light of a moving creature stirred the ground. There was no flak, there was nothing. Just us.

And so we came to the Rhine. This is virtually the entrance to the Ruhr Valley; the barrier our armies must cross before they march into the big towns of Essen and Dortmund. It looked white and calm and sinister in the moonlight. But it presented no difficulties to us. As it came up, Spam said, "We are six miles south. Better turn right, skip. Duisburg is not far away."

As soon as he mentioned Duisburg my hands acted before my brain, for they were more used to this sort of thing, and the Lanc banked steeply to follow the Rhine up to our crossing point. For Duisburg is not a healthy place to fly over at 100 feet. There are hundreds of guns there, both light and heavy, apart from all those searchlights, and the defences have had plenty of experience…

As we flew up—"How did that happen?"

"Don't know, skip. Compass u/s?"

"Couldn't be."

"Hold on, I will just check my figures."

Later—"I'm afraid I misread my writing, skip. The course I gave you should have been another ten degrees to port."

"OK, Terry. That might have been an expensive mistake."

During our steep turn the boys had lost contact, but now they were just beginning to form up again; it was my fault the turn had been too steep, but the name Duisburg or Essen, or any of the rest of them, always does that to me. As we flew along the Rhine there were barges on the river equipped with quick-firing guns and they shot at us as we flew over, but our gunners gave back as good as they got; then we found what we wanted, a sort of small inland harbour, and we turned slowly towards the east. Terry said monotonously, "Thirty minutes to go and we are there."

As we passed on into the Ruhr Valley we came to more and more trouble, for now we were in the outer light-flak defences, and these were very active, but by weaving and jinking we were able to escape most of them. Time and again searchlights would pick us up, but we were flying very low and, although it may sound foolish and untrue when I say so, we avoided a great number of them by dodging behind the trees. Once we went over a brand-new aerodrome which was very heavily defended and which had not been marked on our combat charts. Immediately all three of us in front were picked up by the searchlights and held. Suddenly Trevor, in the rear turret, began firing away trying to scare them enough to turn out their lights, then he shouted that they had gone behind some tall trees. At the same time Spam was yelling that he would soon be shaving himself by the tops of some corn in a field. Hutch immediately sent out a flak warning to all the boys behind so that they could avoid this unattractive area. On either side of me, Mickey and Hoppy, who were a little higher, were flying along brightly illuminated; I could see their letters quite clearly, "TAJ" and "MAJ", standing out like Broadway signs. Then a long string of tracer came out from Hoppy's rear turret and I lost him in the momentary darkness as the searchlights popped out. One of the pilots, a grand Englishman from Derbyshire, was not so lucky. He was flying well out to the left. He got blinded in the searchlights and, for a second, lost control. His aircraft reared up like a stricken horse, plunged on to the deck and burst into flames; five seconds later his mine blew up with a tremendous explosion. Bill Astell had gone.

The minutes passed slowly as we all sweated on this summer's night, sweated at working the controls and sweated with fear as we flew on. Every railway train, every hamlet and every bridge we passed was a potential danger, for our Lancasters were sitting targets at that height and speed. We fought our way past Dortmund, past Hamm—the well-known Hamm which has been bombed so many times; we could see it quite clearly now, its tall chimneys, factories and balloons capped by its umbrella of flak like a Christmas tree about five miles to our right; then we began turning to the right in between Hamm and the little town of Soest, where I nearly got shot down in 1940. Soest was sleepy now and did not open up, and out of the haze ahead appeared the Ruhr hills.

"We're there," said Spam.

"Thank God," said I, feelingly.

As we came over the hill, we saw the Möhne Lake. Then we saw the dam itself. In that light it looked squat and heavy and unconquerable; it looked grey and solid in the moonlight, as though it were part of the countryside itself and just as immovable. A structure like a battleship was showering out flak all along its length, but some came from the power-house below it and nearby. There were no search-lights. It was light flak, mostly green, yellow and red, and the colours of the tracer reflected upon the face of the water in the lake. The reflections on the dead calm of the black water made it seem there was twice as much as there really was.

"Did you say these gunners were out of practice?" asked Spam, sarcastically.

"They certainly seem awake now," said Terry.

They were awake all right. No matter what people say, the Germans certainly have a good warning system. I scowled to myself as I remembered telling the boys an hour or so ago that they would probably only be the German equivalent of the Home Guard and in bed by the time we arrived.

It was hard to say exactly how many guns there were, but tracers seemed to be coming from about five positions, probably making twelve guns in all. It was hard at first to tell the calibre of the shells, but after one of the boys had been hit, we were informed over the RT that they were either 20-mm type or 37-mm, which, as everyone knows, are nasty little things.

We circled around stealthily, picking up the various landmarks upon which we had planned our method of attack, making use of some and avoiding others;

every time we came within range of those bloody-minded flak-gunners they let us have it. "Bit aggressive, aren't they?" said Trevor.

"Too right they are."

I said to Terry, "God, this light flak gives me the creeps."

"Me, too," someone answered.

For a time there was a general bind on the subject of light flak, and the only man who didn't say anything was Hutch, because he could not see it and because he never said anything about flak, anyway. But this was not the time for talking. I called up each member of our formation and found, to my relief, that they had all arrived, except, of course, Bill Astell. Away to the south, Joe McCarthy had just begun his diversionary attack on the Sorpe. But not all of them had been able to get there; both Byers and Barlow had been shot down by light flak after crossing the coast; these had been replaced by other aircraft of the rear formation. Bad luck, this being shot down after crossing the coast, because it could have happened to anybody; they must have been a mile or so off track and had got the hammer. This is the way things are in flying; you are either lucky or you aren't. We, too, had crossed the coast at the wrong place and had got away with it. We were lucky.

Down below, the Möhne Lake was silent and black and deep, and I spoke to my crew.

"Well, boys, I suppose we had better start the ball rolling." This with no enthusiasm whatsoever. "Hello, all Cooler aircraft. I am going to attack. Stand by to come in to attack in your order when I tell you."

Then to Hoppy: "Hello, 'M Mother'. Stand by to take over if anything happens."

Hoppy's clear and casual voice came back. "OK, Leader. Good luck."

Then the boys dispersed to the pre-arranged hiding-spots in the hills, so that they should not be seen either from the ground or from the air, and we began to get into position for our approach. We circled wide and came around down moon, over the high hills at the eastern end of the lake. On straightening up we began to dive towards the flat, ominous water two miles away. Over the front turret was the dam silhouetted against the haze of the Ruhr Valley. We could see the towers. We could see the sluices. We could see everything. Spam, the bomb-aimer, said "Good show. This is wizard." He had been a bit worried, as all bomb-aimers are, in case they cannot see their aiming points, but as we came in over the tall fir trees his voice came up again rather quickly. "You're going to hit them. You're going to hit those trees."

"That's all right, Spam. I'm just getting my height."

To Terry: "Check height, Terry."

To Pulford: "Speed control, Flight-Engineer."

To Trevor: "All guns ready, gunners."

To Spam: "Coming up, Spam."

Terry turned on the spotlights and began giving directions—"Down—down—down. Steady—steady." We were then exactly sixty feet.

Pulford began working the speed; first he put on a little flap to slow us down, then he opened the throttles to get the air-speed indicator exactly against the red mark. Spam began lining up his sights against the towers. He had turned the fusing switch to the "ON" position. I began flying.

The gunners had seen us coming. They could see us coming with our spotlights on for over two miles away. Now they opened up and the tracers began swirling towards us; some were even bouncing off the smooth surface of the lake. This was a horrible moment: we were being dragged along at four miles in a minute, almost against our will, towards the things we were going to destroy. I think at that moment the boys did not want to go. I know I did not want to go. I thought to myself, "In another minute we shall all be dead—so what?" I thought again, "This is terrible—this feeling of fear—if it is fear." By now we were a few hundred yards away, and I said quickly to Pulford, under my breath, "Better leave the throttles open now and stand by to pull me out of the seat if I get hit." As I glanced at him I thought he looked a little glum on hearing this.

The Lancaster was really moving and I began looking through the special sight on my windscreen. Spam had his eyes glued to the bombsight in front, his hand on his button; a special mechanism on board had already begun to work so that the mine would drop (we hoped) in the right spot. Terry was still checking the height. Joe and Trev began to raise their guns. The flak could see us quite clearly now. It was not exactly inferno. I have been through far worse flak fire than that; but we were very low. There was something sinister and slightly unnerving about the whole operation. My aircraft was so small and the dam was so large; it was thick and solid, and now it was angry. My aircraft was very small. We skimmed along the surface of the lake, and as we went my gunner was firing into the defences, and the defences were firing back with vigour, their shells whistling past us. For some reason, we were not being hit.

Spam said, "Left—little more left—steady—steady—coming up."

Of the next few seconds I remember only a series of kaleidoscopic incidents. The chatter from Joe's front guns pushing out tracers which bounced off the left-hand flak tower.

Pulford crouching beside me.

The smell of burnt cordite.

The cold sweat underneath my oxygen mask.

The tracers flashing past the windows—they all seemed the same colour now—and the inaccuracy of the gun positions near the power-station; they were firing in the wrong direction.

The closeness of the dam wall.

Spam's exultant, "Mine gone."

Hutch's red Very lights to blind the flak-gunners.

The speed of the whole thing.

Someone saying over the RT, "Good show, leader. Nice work."

Then it was all over, and at last we were out of range, and there came over us all, I think, an immense feeling of relief and confidence.

Trevor said, "I will get those bastards," and he began to spray the dam with bullets until at last he, too, was out of range. As we circled round we could see a great, 1,000-feet column of whiteness still hanging in the air where our mine had exploded. We could see with satisfaction that Spam had been good, and it had gone off in the right position. Then, as we came closer, we could see that the explosion of the mine had caused a great disturbance upon the surface of the lake and the water had become broken and furious, as though it were being lashed by a gale. At first we thought that the dam itself had broken, because great sheets of water were slopping over the top of the wall like a gigantic basin. This caused some delay, because our mines could only be dropped in calm water, and we would have to wait until all became still again.

We waited.

We waited about ten minutes, but it seemed hours to us. It must have seemed even longer to Hoppy, who was the next to attack. Meanwhile, all the fighters had now collected over our target. They knew our game by now, but we were flying too low for them; they could not see us and there were no attacks.

"At last—"Hello, 'M Mother'. You may attack now. Good luck."

"OK. Attacking."

Hoppy, the Englishman, casual, but very efficient, keen now on only one thing, which was war. He began his attack.

He began going down over the trees where I had come from a few moments before. We could see his spotlights quite clearly, slowly closing together as he ran across the water. We saw him approach.

The flak, by now, had got an idea from which direction the attack was coming, and they let him have it. When he was about 100 yards away someone said, hoarsely, over the RT: "Hell! He has been hit."

"M Mother" was on fire; an unlucky shot had got him in one of the inboard petrol tanks and a long jet of flame was beginning to stream out. I saw him drop his mine, but his bomb-aimer must have been wounded, because it fell straight on to the power-house on the other side of the dam. But Hoppy staggered on, trying to gain altitude so that his crew could bale out. When he had got up to 500 feet there was a vivid flash in the sky and one wing fell off; his aircraft disintegrated and fell to the ground in cascading, flaming fragments. There it began to burn quite gently and rather sinisterly in a field some three miles beyond the dam.

Someone said, "Poor old Hoppy!"

Another said, "We'll get those bastards for this."

A furious rage surged up inside my own crew, and Trevor said, "Let's go in and murder those gunners." As he spoke, Hoppy's mine went up. It went up behind the power-house with a tremendous yellow explosion and left in the air a great ball of black smoke; again there was a long wait while we watched for this to clear. There was so little wind that it took a long time.

Many minutes later I told Mickey to attack; he seemed quite confident, and we ran in beside him and a little in front; as we turned, Trevor did his best to get those gunners as he promised.

Bob Hay, Mickey's bomb-aimer, did a good job, and his mine dropped in exactly the right place. There was again a gigantic explosion as the whole surface of the lake shook, then spewed forth its cascade of white water. Mickey was all right; he got through. But he had been hit several times and one wing-tank lost all its petrol. I could see the vicious tracer from his rear-gunner giving one gun position a hail of bullets as he swept over. Then he called up, "OK. Attack completed." It was then that I thought that the dam wall had moved. Of course we could not see anything, but if Jeff's theory had been correct, it should have cracked by now. If only we could go on pushing it by dropping more successful mines, it would surely move back on its axis and collapse.

Once again we watched for the water to calm down. Then in came Melvyn Young in "D Dog." I yelled to him, "Be careful of the flak. It's pretty hot."

He said, "OK."

I yelled again, "Trevor's going to beat them up on the other side. He'll take most of it off you."

Melvyn's voice again. "OK. Thanks." And so as "D Dog" ran in we stayed at a fairly safe distance on the other side, firing with all guns at the defences, and the defences, like the stooges they were, firing back at us. We were both out of range of each other, but the ruse seemed to work, and we flicked on our identification lights to let them see us even more clearly. Melvyn's mine went in, again in exactly the right spot, and this time a colossal wall of water swept right over the dam and kept on going. Melvyn said, "I think I've done it. I've broken it." But we were in a better position to see than he, and it had not rolled down yet. We were all getting pretty excited by now, and I screamed like a schoolboy over the RT: "Wizard show, Melvyn. I think it'll go on the next one."

Now we had been over the Möhne for quite a long time, and all the while I had been in contact with Scampton Base. We were in close contact with the Air Officer Commanding and the Commander-in-Chief of Bomber Command, and with the scientist, observing his own greatest scientific experiment in Damology. He was sitting in the operations room, his head in his hands, listening to the reports as one after another the aircraft attacked. On the other side of the room the Commander-in-Chief paced up and down. In a way their job of waiting was worse than mine. The only difference was that they did not know that the structure was shifting as I knew, even though I could not see anything clearly.

When at last the water had all subsided I called up No. 5—David Maltby—and told him to attack. He came in fast, and I saw his mine fall within feet of the right spot; once again the flak, the explosion and wall of water. But this time we were on the wrong side of the wall and could see what had happened. We watched for about five minutes, and it was rather hard to see anything, for by now the air was full of spray from these explosions, which had settled like mist on our windscreens. Time was getting short, so I called up Dave Shannon and told him to come in.

As I turned I got close to the dam wall and then saw what had happened. It had rolled over, but I could not believe my eyes. I heard someone shout, "I think she has gone! I think she has gone!" Other voices took up the cry and quickly I said, "Stand by until I make a recco." I remembered that Dave was going in to attack and told him to turn away and not to approach the target. We had a closer look. Now there was no doubt about it; there was a great breach 100 yards across, and the water, looking like stirred porridge in the moonlight, was gushing out and rolling into the Ruhr Valley towards the industrial centres of Germany's

Third Reich.

Nearly all the flak had now stopped, and the other boys came down from the hills to have a closer look to see what had been done. There was no doubt about it at all—the Möhne Dam had been breached and the gunners on top of the dam, except for one man, had all run for their lives towards the safety of solid ground; this remaining gunner was a brave man, but one of the boys quickly extinguished his flak with a burst of well-aimed tracer. Now it was all quiet, except for the roar of the water which steamed and hissed its way from its 150-foot head. Then we began to shout and scream and act like madmen over the RT, for this was a tremendous sight, a sight which probably no man will ever see again.

Quickly I told Hutch to tap out the message, "Nigger," to my station, and when this was handed to the Air Officer Commanding there was (I heard afterwards) great excitement in the operations room. The scientist jumped up and danced round the room.

Then I looked again at the dam and at the water, while all around me the boys were doing the same. It was the most amazing sight. The whole valley was beginning to fill with fog from the steam of the gushing water, and down in the foggy valley we saw cars speeding along the roads in front of this great wave of water, which was chasing them and going faster than they could ever hope to go. I saw their headlights burning and I saw water overtake them, wave by wave, and then the colour of the headlights under the water changing from light blue to green, from green to dark purple, until there was no longer anything except the water bouncing down in great waves. The floods raced on, carrying with them as they went—viaducts, railways, bridges and everything that stood in their path. Three miles beyond the dam the remains of Hoppy's aircraft was still burning gently, a dull red glow on the ground. Hoppy had been avenged.

Then I felt a little remote and unreal sitting up there in the warm cockpit of my Lancaster, watching this mighty power which we had unleashed; then glad, because I knew that this was the heart of Germany, and the heart of her industries, the place which itself had unleashed so much misery upon the whole world.

We knew, as we watched, that this flood-water would not win the war; it would not do anything like that, but it was a catastrophe for Germany.

I circled round for about three minutes, then called up all aircraft and told Mickey and David Maltby to go home and the rest to follow me to Eder, where we would try to repeat the performance.

We set our course from the southern tip of the Mohne Lake, which was already fast emptying itself—we could see that even now—and flew on in the clear light of the early morning towards the south-east. We flew on over little towns tucked away in the valleys underneath the Ruhr Mountains. Little places, these, the Exeters and Baths of Germany; they seemed quiet and undisturbed and picturesque as they lay sleeping there on the morning of May 17. The thought crossed my mind of the amazing mentality of German airmen, who went out of their way to bomb such defenceless districts. At the same time a bomb or two on board would not have been out of place to wake them up as a reprisal.

At the Sorpe Dam, Joe McCarthy and Joe Brown had already finished their work. They had both made twelve dummy runs and had dropped their mines along the lip of the concrete wall in the right spot. But they had not been able to see anything spectacular, for these earthen dams are difficult nuts to crack and would require a lot of explosive to shirt them. It looked as if we would not have enough aircraft to finish that job successfully because of our losses on the way in. However, the Sorpe was not a priority target, and only contributed a small amount of water to the Ruhr Valley Catchment Area.

After flying low across the treetops, up and down the valleys, we at last reached the Eder Lake and, by flying down it for some five minutes, we arrived over the Eder Dam. It took some finding because fog was already beginning to form in the valleys, and it was pretty hard to tell one part of the reservoir filled with water, from another valley filled with fog. We circled up for a few minutes waiting for Henry, Dave and Les to catch up; we had lost them on the way. Then I called up on the RT.

"Hello, Cooler aircraft—can you see the target?"

Dave answered faintly, "I think I'm in the vicinity. I can't see anything. I cannot find the dam."

"Stand by—I will fire a red Very light—right over the dam." No sooner had Hutch fired his Very pistol than Dave called up again. "OK—I was a bit south. I'm coming up."

The other boys had seen the signal too, and after a few minutes we rendezvous'd in a left-hand orbit over the target. But time was getting short now; the glow in the north had begun to get brighter, heralding the coming dawn. Soon it would be daylight, and we did not want this in our ill-armed and unarmoured Lancasters.

I said, "OK, Dave. You begin your attack."

It was very hilly all round. The dam was situated, beautifully, I thought, in a deep valley with high hills all around densely covered with fir trees. At the far end, overlooking it, was rather a fine Gothic castle with magnificent grounds. In order to make a successful approach our aircraft would have to dive steeply over this castle, dropping down on to the water from 1,000 feet to 60 feet—level out let go the mine—then do a steep climbing turn to starboard to avoid a rocky mountain about a mile on the other side of the dam. It was much more inaccessible than the Möhne Valley and called for a much higher degree of skill in flying. There did not seem to be any defences, though, probably because it was an out-of-the-way spot and the gunners would not have got the warning. Maybe they had just been warned and were now getting out of their beds in the nearby village before cycling up the steep hill to get to their gun emplacements. Dave circled wide and then turned to go in. He dived down rather too steeply and sparks came from his engine, as he had to pull out at full boost to avoid hitting the mountain on the north side. As he was doing so…

"Sorry, leader. I made a mess of that. I'll try again." He tried again.

He tried five times, but each time he was not satisfied and would not allow his bomb-aimer to drop his mine. He spoke again on the RT "I think I had better circle round a bit and try and get used to this place."

"OK, Dave. You hang around for a bit, and I'll get another aircraft to have a crack—Hello, 'Z Zebra'" (this was Henry). "You can go in now."

Henry made two attempts. He said he found it very difficult, and gave the other boys some advice on the best way to go about it. Then he called up and told us that he was going in to make his final run. We could see him running in. Suddenly he pulled away; something seemed to be wrong, but he turned quickly, climbed up over the mountain and put his nose right down, literally flinging his machine into the valley. This time he was running straight and true for the middle of the wall. We saw his spotlights together, so he must have been at 60 feet. We saw the red ball of his Very light shooting out behind his tail, and we knew he had dropped his weapon. A split second later we saw something else; Henry Maudsley had dropped his mine too late. It had hit the top of the parapet and had exploded immediately on impact with a slow, yellow, vivid flame which lit up the whole valley like daylight for just a few seconds. We could see him quite clearly banking steeply a few feet above it. Perhaps the blast was doing that. It all seemed so sudden and vicious and the flame seemed so very cruel. Someone said, "He has blown himself up."

Trevor said, "Bomb-aimer must have been wounded."

It looked as though Henry had been unlucky enough to do the thing we all might have done. I spoke to him quickly, "Henry—Henry. 'Z Zebra'—'Z Zebra'. Are you OK?" No answer. I called again. Then we all thought we heard a very faint, tired voice say, "I think so—stand by." It seemed as though he was dazed, and his voice did not sound natural. But Henry had disappeared. There was no burning wreckage on the ground; there was no aircraft on fire in the air. There was nothing. Henry had disappeared. He never came back.

Once more the smoke from his explosion filled the valley, and we all had to wait for a few minutes. The glow in the north was much brighter, and we would have to hurry up if we wanted to get back.

We waited patiently for it to clear away.

At last to Dave—"OK. Attack now, David. Good luck."

Dave went in and, after a good dummy run, managed to put his mine up against the wall, more or less in the middle. He turned on his landing light as he pulled away and we saw the spot of light climbing steeply over the mountain as he jerked his great Lancaster almost vertically over the top. Behind me there was that explosion which, by now, we had got used to, but the wall of the Eder Dam did not move.

Meanwhile, Les Knight had been circling very patiently, not saying a word. I told him to get ready, and when the water had calmed down he began his attack. Les, the Australian, had some difficulty too, and after a while Dave began to give him some advice on how to do it. We all joined in on the RT, and there was a continuous back-chat going on.

"Come on, Les. Come in down the moon; dive towards the point and then turn left."

"OK, Digger. It's pretty difficult."

"Not that way, Dig. This way."

"Too right it's difficult. I'm climbing up to have another crack."

After a while I called up rather impatiently and told them that a joke was a joke and that we would have to be getting back. Then Les dived in to make his final attack. His was the last weapon left in the squadron. If he did not succeed in breaching the Eder now, then it would never be breached; at least, not tonight.

I saw him run in. I crossed my fingers. But Les was a good pilot and he made as perfect a run as any seen that night. We were flying above him, and about 400 yards to the right, and saw his mine hit the water. We saw where it sank. We saw the tremendous earthquake which shook the base of the dam, and then, as if a gigantic hand had punched a hole through cardboard, the whole thing collapsed. A great mass of water began running down the valley into Kassel. Les was very excited. He kept his radio transmitter on by mistake for quite some time. His crew's remarks were something to be heard, but they couldn't be put into print here. Dave was very excited and said, "Good show, Dig!" I called them up and told them to go home immediately. I would meet them in the Mess afterwards for the biggest party of all time.

The valley below the Eder was steeper than the Ruhr, and we followed the water down for some way. We watched it swirling and slopping in a 30-foot wall as it tore round the steep bends of the countryside. We saw it crash down in six great waves, swiping off power-stations and roads as it went. We saw it extinguish all the lights in the neighbourhood as though a great black shadow had been drawn across the earth. It all reminded us of a vast moving train. But we knew that a few miles farther on lay some of the Lutfwaffe's largest training bases. We knew that it was a modern field with every convenience, including underground hangars and underground sleeping quarters…We turned for home.

Dave and Les, still jabbering at each other on RT, had by now turned for home as well. Their voices died away in the distance as we set our course for the Möhne Lake to see how far it was empty. Hutch sent out a signal to Base using the code word, "Dinghy," telling them the good news—and they asked us if we had anymore aircraft available to prang the third target. "No, none," I said. "None," tapped Hutch.

Now we were out of RT range of our base and were relying on WT for communication. Gradually, by code words, we were told of the movements of the other aircraft. Peter Townsend and Anderson of the rear formation had been sent out to make one attack against the Sorpe. We heard Peter say that he had been successful, but heard nothing from Anderson.

"Let's tell Base we're coming home, and tell them to lay on a party," suggested Spam.

We told them we were coming home.

We had reached the Möhne by now and circled twice. We looked at the level of the lake. Already bridges were beginning to stick up out of the lowering water. Already mudbanks with pleasure-boats sitting on their sides could be seen. Below the dam the torpedo nets had been washed to one side of the valley. The power-station had disappeared. The map had completely changed as a new silver lake had formed, a lake of no strict dimensions; a lake slowly moving down towards the west.

Base would probably be panicking a bit, so Hutch sent out another message telling them that there was no doubt about it. Then we took one final look at what we had done and afterwards turned north to the Zuider Zee.

Trevor asked a question—Trevor, who had fired nearly 12,000 rounds of ammunition in the past two hours. "I am almost out of ammo," he called, "but I have got one or two incendiaries back here. Would you mind if Spam tells me when a village is coming up, so that I can drop one out? It might pay for Hoppy, Henry and Bill."

I answered, "Go ahead."

We flew north in the silence of the morning, hugging the ground and wanting to get home. It was quite light now, and we could see things that we could not see on the way in—cattle in the fields, chickens getting airborne as we rushed over them. On the left someone flew over Hamm at 500 feet. He got the chop. No one knew who it was. Spam said he thought it was a German night-fighter which had been chasing us.

I suppose they were all after us. Now that we were being plotted on our retreat to the coast, the enemy fighter controllers would be working overtime. I could imagine the Führer himself giving orders to "stop those air pirates at all costs." After all, we had done something which no one else had ever done. Water when released can be one of the most powerful things in the world—similar to an earthquake—and the Ruhr Valley had never had an earthquake.

Someone on board pointed out that Duisburg had been pranged the night before and that our water might put the fires out there. Someone else said—rather callously, I thought—If you can't burn em, drown 'em." But we had not tried to do this; we had merely destroyed a legitimate industrial objective so as to hinder the Ruhr Valley output of war munitions. The fact that people were in the way was incidental. The fact that they might drown had not occurred to us. But we hoped that the dam wardens would warn those living below in time, even if they were Germans. No one likes mass slaughter, and we did not like being the authors of it. Besides, it brought us in line with Himmler and his boys.

Terry looked up from his chart-board. "About an hour to the coast," he said.

I turned to Pulford. "Put her into maximum cruising. Don't worry about petrol consumption." Then to Terry—"I think we had better go the shortest way home, crossing the coast at Edmond—you know the gap there. We're the last one, and they'll probably try to get us if we lag behind."

Terry smiled and watched the air-speed needle creep round. We were now doing a smooth 240 indicated, and the exhaust stubs glowed red hot with the power she was throwing out. Trevor's warning light came on the panel, then his voice—"Unidentified enemy aircraft behind."

"OK. I'll sink to the west—it's dark there."

As we turned—"OK. You've lost it."

"Right. On course. Terry, we'd better fly really low."

These fighters meant business, but they were hampered by the conditions of light during the early morning. We could see them before they saw us.

Down went the Lanc until we were a few feet off the ground, for this was the only way to survive. And we wanted to survive. Two hours before we had wanted to burst dams. Now we wanted to get home—quickly. Then we could have a party.

Some minutes later Terry spoke. "Thirty minutes to the coast."

"OK. More revs."

The needle crept round. It got very noisy inside.

We were flying home—we knew that. We did not know whether we were safe. We did not know how the other boys had got on. Bill, Hoppy, Henry, Barlow, Byers and Ottley had all gone. They had all got the hammer. The light flak had given it to most of them, as it always will to low-flying aircraft—that is, the unlucky ones. They had all gone quickly, except perhaps for Henry. Henry, the born leader. A great loss, but he gave his life for a cause for which men should be proud. Boys like Henry are the cream of our youth. They die bravely and they die young.

And Burpee, the Canadian? His English wife about to have a baby. His father who kept a large store in Ottawa. He was not coming back because they had got him, too. They had got him somewhere between Hamm and the target. Burpee, slow of speech and slow of movement, but a good pilot. He was Terry's countryman and so were his crew. I like their ways and manners, their free-and-easy outlook, their openness. I was going to miss them a lot—even when they chewed gum.

I called up Melvyn on the RT. He had been with me all the way round as deputy-leader when Mickey had gone home with his leaking petrol tank. He was quite all right at the Eder. Now there was no reply. We wondered what had happened.

Terry said, "Fifteen minutes to go."

Fifteen minutes. Quite a way yet. A long way, and we might not make it. We were in the black territory. They had closed the gates of their fortress and were locked inside; but we knew the gap—the gap by those wireless masts at Edmond. If we could find that, we should get through safely.

Back at the base they would be waiting for us. We did not know that when they received the code word "Dinghy" there was a scene in the operations room such as the WAAF Ops Clerks had never seen before. The Air Officer Commanding had jumped up and had shaken Jeff by the hand, almost embracing him. The Commander-in-Chief had picked up the phone and asked for Washington. At Washington another US-Great Britain conference was in progress. Sir Charles Portal, the CAS, was giving a dinner-party. He was called away to the telephone. Back at Scampton the C.-in-C. yelled, "Downwood successful—yes". At Washington, CAS was having difficulty in hearing. At last members of the dinner-party heard him say quietly, "Good show." From then on the dinner-party was a roaring success.

We did not know anything about the fuss, the Press, the publicity which would go round the world after this effort. Or of the honours to be given to the squadron or of trips to America and Canada, or of visits by important people. We did not care about anything like that. We only wanted to get home.

We did not know that we had started something new in the history of aviation, that our squadron was to become a byword throughout the RAF as a precision-bombing unit—a unit which could pick off anything from Viaducts to gun emplacements, from low level or high level, by day or by night. A squadron consisting of crack crews using all the latest new equipment and the largest bombs, even earthquake bombs. A squadron flying new aeroplanes, and flying them as well as any in the world.

Terry was saying, "Rotterdam's 20 miles on the port bow. We will be getting to the gap in five minutes." Now they could see where we were going, the fighters would be streaking across Holland to close that gap. Then they could hack us down.

I called up Melvyn, but he never answered. I was not to know that Melvyn had crashed into the sea a few miles in front of me. He had come all the way from California to fight this war and had survived sixty trips at home and in the Middle East, including a double ditching. Now he had ditched for the last time. Melvyn had been responsible for a good deal of the training that made their raid possible. He had endeared himself to the boys, and now he had gone.

Of the sixteen aircraft which had crossed the coast to carry out this mission, eight had been shot down, including both Flight Commanders. Only two men escaped to become prisoners of war. Only two out of fifty-six, for there is not much chance at 50 feet.

They had gone. Had it been worth it? Or were their lives just thrown away on a spectacular mission? Militarily, it was cheap at the price. The damage done to the German war effort was substantial. But there is another side to the question. We would soon begin our fifth year of war—a war in which the casualties had been lighter than the last; nevertheless, in Bomber Command there have been some heavy losses. These fifty-five boys who had lost their lives were some of many. The scythe of war, and a very bloody one at that, had reaped a good harvest in Bomber Command. As we flew on over the low fields of Holland, past dykes and ditches, we could not help thinking, "Why must we make war every twenty-five years? Why must men fight? How can we stop it? Can we make countries live normal lives in a peaceful way?" But no one knows the answer to that one.

The answer may lie in being strong. A powerful, strategic bomber force based so that it would control the vital waterways of the world, could prevent and strangle the aggressor from the word "Go." But it rests with the people themselves; for it is the people who forget. After many years they will probably slip and ask for disarmament so that they can do away with taxes and raise their standards of living. If the people forget, they bring wars on themselves, and they can blame no one but themselves.

Yes, the decent people of this world would have to remember war. Movies and radio records should remind this and the future generations of what happened between 1936 and 1942. It should be possible to keep this danger in everyone's mind so that we can never be caught on the wrong foot again. So that our children will have a chance to live. After all, that is why we are born. We aren't born to die.

But we ourselves must learn. We must learn to know and respect our great Allies who have made the chance of victory possible. We must learn to understand them, their ways and their customs. We British are apt to consider ourselves the yardstick upon which everything else should be based. We must not delude ourselves. We have plenty to learn.

We must learn about politics. We must vote for the right things, and not necessarily the traditional things. We want to see our country remain as great as it is today—for ever. It all depends on the people, their common-sense and their memory.

Can we hope for this? Can all this be done? Can we be certain that we can find the answer to a peaceful world for generations to come?

"North Sea ahead, boys," said Spam.

There it was. Beyond the gap, in the distance, lay the calm and silvery sea, and freedom. It looked beautiful to us then—perhaps the most wonderful thing in the world.

We climbed up a little to about 300 feet.

Then—"Full revs and boost, Pulford."

As he opened her right up, I shoved the nose down to get up extra speed and we sat down on the deck at about 260 indicated.

"Keep to the left of this little lake," said Terry, map in hand.

This was flying.

"Now over this railway bridge."

More speed.

"Along this canal…" We flew along that canal as low as we had flown that day. Our belly nearly scraped the water, our wings would have knocked horses off the towpath.

"See those radio masts?"

"Yeah."

"About 200 yards to the right."

"OK."

The sea came closer. It came closer quickly as we tore towards it. There was a sudden tenseness on board.

"Keep going; you're OK now."

"Right. Stand by, from gunner."

"Guns ready."

Then we came to the Western Wall. We whistled over the anti-tank ditches and beach obstacles. We saw the yellow sand-dunes slide below us silently, yellow in the pale morning.

Then we were over the sea with the rollers breaking on the beaches and the moon casting its long reflections straight in front of us—and there was England.

We were free. We had got through the gap. It was a wonderful feeling of relief and safety. Now for the party.

"Nice work," said Trevor from the back.

"Course home?" I asked.

Behind us lay the Dutch coast, squat, desolate and bleak, still squirting flak in many directions.

We would be coming back.

Major Major Major Major
(from *Catch-22*)

Joseph Heller

Major Major Major Major had had a difficult time from the start.

Like Minniver Cheevy, he had been born too late—exactly thirty-six hours too late for the physical well-being of his mother, a gentle, ailing woman who, after a full day and a half's agony in the rigors of childbirth, was depleted of all resolve to pursue further the argument over the new child's name. In the hospital corridor, her husband moved ahead with the unsmiling determination of someone who knew what he was about. Major Major's father was a towering, gaunt man in heavy shoes and a black woolen suit. He filled out the birth certificate without faltering, betraying no emotion at all as he handed the completed form to the floor nurse. The nurse took it from him without comment and padded out of sight. He watched her go, wondering what she had on underneath.

Back in the ward, he found his wife lying vanquished beneath the blankets like a desiccated old vegetable, wrinkled, dry and white, her enfeebled tissues absolutely still. Her bed was at the very end of the ward, near a cracked window thickened with grime. Rain splashed from a moiling sky and the day was dreary and cold. In other parts of the hospital chalky people with aged, blue lips were dying on time. The man stood erect beside the bed and gazed down at the woman a long time.

"I have named the boy Caleb," he announced to her finally in a soft voice. "In accordance with your wishes." The woman made no answer, and slowly the man smiled. He had planned it all perfectly, for his wife was asleep and would never know that he had lied to her as she lay on her sickbed in the poor ward of the country hospital.

From this meager beginning had sprung the ineffectual squadron commander who was now spending the better part of each working day in Pianosa forging Washington Irving's name to official documents. Major Major forged diligently with his left hand to elude identification, insulated against intrusion by his own undesired authority and camouflaged in his false mustache and dark glasses as an additional safeguard against detection by anyone chancing to peer in through the dowdy celluloid window from which some thief had carved out a slice. In between these two low points of his birth and his success lay thirty-one dismal years of loneliness and frustration.

Major Major had been born too late and too mediocre. Some men are born mediocre, some men achieve mediocrity, and some men have mediocrity thrust upon them. With Major Major it had been all three. Even among men lacking all distinction he inevitably stood out as a man lacking more distinction than all

130

the rest, and people who met him were always impressed by how unimpressive he was.

Major Major had three strikes on him from the beginning—his mother, his father and Henry Fonda, to whom he bore a sickly resemblance almost from the moment of his birth. Long before he even suspected who Henry Fonda was, he found himself the subject of unflattering comparisons everywhere he went. Total strangers saw fit to deprecate him, with the result that he was stricken early with a guilty fear of people and an obsequious impulse to apologize to society for the fact that he was *not* Henry Fonda. It was not an easy task for him to go through life looking something like Henry Fonda, but he never once thought of quitting, having inherited his perseverance from his father, a lanky man with a good sense of humour.

Major Major's father was a sober God-fearing man whose idea of a good joke was to lie about his age. He was a long-limbed farmer, a God-fearing, freedom-loving, law-abiding rugged individualist who held that federal aid to anyone but farmers was creeping socialism. He advocated thrift and hard work and disapproved of loose women who turned him down. His speciality was alfalfa, and he made a good thing out of not growing any. The government paid him well for every bushel of alfalfa he did not grow. The more alfalfa he did not grow, the more money the government gave him, and he spent every penny he didn't earn on new land to increase the amount of alfalfa he did not produce. Major Major's father worked without rest at not growing alfalfa. On long winter evenings he remained indoors and did not mend harnesses, and he sprang out of bed at the crack of noon every day just to make certain that the chores would not be done. He invested in land wisely and soon was not growing more alfalfa than any other man in the country. Neighbors sought him out for advice on all subjects, for he had made much money and was therefore wise. "As ye sow, so shall ye reap," he counseled one and all, and everyone said, "Amen."

Major Major's father was an outspoken champion of economy in government, provided it did not interfere with the sacred duty of government to pay farmers as much as they could get for all the alfalfa they produced that no one else wanted or for not producing any alfalfa at all. He was a proud and independent man who was opposed to unemployment insurance and never hesitated to whine, whimper, wheedle, and extort for as much as he could get from whomever he could. He was a devout man whose pulpit was everywhere.

"The Lord gave us good farmers two strong hands so that we could take as much as we could grab with both of them," he preached with ardor on the courthouse steps or in front of the A & P as he waited for the bad-tempered gum-chewing young cashier he was after to step outside and give him a nasty look. "If the Lord didn't want us to take as much as we could get," he preached, "He wouldn't have given us too good hands to take it with." And the others murmured, "Amen."

Major Major's father had a Calvinist's faith in predestination and could perceive distinctly how everyone's misfortunes but his own were expressions of God's will. He smoked cigarettes and drank whiskey, and he thrived on good wit and stimulating intellectual conversation, particularly his own when he was lying about his age or telling that good one about God and his wife's difficulties in delivering Major Major. The good one about God and his wife's difficulties had to do with the fact that it had taken God only six days to produce the whole world, whereas his wife had spent a full day and a half in labor just to produce Major Major. A lesser man might have wavered that day in the hospital corridor, a weaker man might have compromised on such excellent substitutes as Drum Major, Minor Major, Sergeant Major, or C. Sharp Major, but Major Major's father had waited fourteen years for just such an opportunity, and he was not a person to waste it. Major Major's father had a good joke about opportunity. "Opportunity only knocks once in this world," he would say. Major Major's father repeated his good joke at every opportunity.

Being born with a sickly resemblance to Henry Fonda was the first of a long series of practical jokes of which destiny was to make Major Major the unhappy victim throughout his joyless life. Being born Major Major Major was the second. The fact that he had been born Major Major Major was a secret known only to his father. Not until Major Major was enrolling in kindergarten was the discovery of his real name made, and then the effects were disastrous. The news killed his mother, who just lost her will to live and wasted away and died, which was just fine with his father, who had decided to marry the bad-tempered girl at the A & P if he had to and who had not been optimistic about his chances of getting his wife off the land without paying her some money or flogging her.

On Major Major himself the consequences were only slightly less severe. It was a harsh and stunning realization that was forced upon him at so tender an age, the realization that he was not, as he had always been led to believe, Caleb Major, but instead was some total stranger named Major Major Major about whom he knew absolutely nothing and about whom nobody else had ever heard before. What playmates he had withdrew from him and never returned, disposed, as they were, to distrust all strangers, especially one who had already deceived them by pretending to be someone they had known for years. Nobody would have anything to do with him. He began to drop things and to trip. He had a shy and hopeful manner in each new contact, and he was always disappointed. Because he needed a friend so desperately, he never found one. He grew awkwardly into a tall, strange, dreamy boy with fragile eyes and a very delicate mouth whose tentative, groping smile collapsed instantly into hurt disorder at every fresh rebuff.

He was polite to his elders, who disliked him. Whatever his elders told him to do, he did. They told him to look before he leaped, and he always looked before he leaped. They told him never to put off until the next day what he could do the day before, and he never did. He was told to honor his father and his mother, and he honored his father and his mother. He was told that he should not kill, and he did not kill, until he got into the Army. Then he was told to kill, and he killed. He turned the other cheek on every occasion and always did unto others exactly as he would have had others do unto him. When he gave to charity, his left hand never knew what his right hand was doing. He never once took the name of the Lord his God in vain, committed adultery or coveted his neighbor's ass. In fact, he loved his neighbor and never even bore false witness against him. Major Major's elders disliked him because he was such a flagrant nonconformist.

Since he had nothing better to do well in, he did well in school. At the state university he took his studies so seriously that he was suspected by the homosexuals of being a Communist and suspected by the Communists of being a homosexual. He majored in English history, which was a mistake.

"*English* history!" roared the silver-maned senior Senator from his state indignantly. "What's the matter with American history? American history is as good as any history in the world!"

Major Major switched immediately to American literature, but not before the FBI had opened a file on him. There were six people and a Scotch terrier inhabiting the remote farmhouse Major Major called home, and five of them and the Scotch terrier turned out to be agents for the FBI. Soon they had enough derogatory information on Major Major to do whatever they wanted to with him. The only thing they could find to do with him, however, was take him into the Army as a private and make him a major four days later so that Congressmen with nothing else on their minds could go trotting back and forth through the streets of Washington, DC, chanting, "Who promoted Major Major? Who promoted Major Major?"

Actually, Major Major had been promoted by an IBM machine with a sense of humor almost as keen as his father's. When war broke out, he was still docile and compliant. They told him to enlist, and he enlisted. They told him to apply for aviation cadet training, and he applied for aviation cadet training, and the very next night found himself standing barefoot in icy mud at three o'clock in the morning before a tough and belligerent sergeant from the Southwest who told them he could beat hell out of any man in his outfit and was ready to prove it. The recruits in his squadron had all been shaken roughly awake only minutes before by the sergeant's corporals and told to assemble in front of the administration tent. It was still raining on Major Major. They fell into ranks in the civilian clothes they had brought into the Army with them three days before. Those who had lingered to put shoes and socks on were sent back to their cold, wet, dark tents to remove them, and they were all barefoot in the mud as the sergeant ran his stony eyes over their faces and told them he could beat hell out of any man in his outfit. No one was inclined to dispute him.

Major Major's unexpected promotion to major the next day plunged the belligerent sergeant into a bottomless gloom, for he was no longer able to boast that he could beat hell out of any man in his outfit. He brooded for hours in his tent like Saul, receiving no visitors, while his elite guard of corporals stood discouraged watch outside. At three o'clock in the morning he found his solution, and Major Major and the other recruits were again shaken roughly awake and ordered to assemble barefoot in the drizzly glare at the administration tent, where the sergeant was already waiting, his fists clenched on his hips cockily, so eager to speak that he could hardly wait for them to arrive.

"Me and Major Major," he boasted, in the same tough, clipped tones of the night before, "can beat hell out of any man in my outfit."

The officers on the base took action on the Major Major problem later that same day. How could they cope with a major like Major Major? To demean him personally would be to demean all other officers of equal or lesser rank. To treat him with courtesy, on the other hand, was unthinkable. Fortunately, Major Major had applied for aviation cadet training. Orders transferring him away were sent to the mimeograph room late in the afternoon, and at three o'clock in the morning Major Major was again shaken roughly awake, bidden Godspeed by the sergeant and placed aboard a plane heading west.

Lieutenant Scheisskopf turned white as a sheet when Major Major reported to him in California with bare feet and mud-caked toes. Major Major had taken it for granted that he was being shaken roughly awake again to stand barefoot in the mud and had left his shoes and socks in the tent. The civilian clothing in which he reported for duty to Lieutenant Scheisskopf was rumpled and dirty. Lieutenant Scheisskopf, who had not yet made his reputation as a parader, shuddered violently at the picture Major Major would make marching barefoot in his squadron that coming Sunday.

"Go to the hospital quickly," he mumbled, when he had recovered sufficiently to speak, "and tell them you're sick. Stay there until your allowance for uniforms catches up with you and you have some money to buy some clothes. And some shoes. Buy some shoes."

"Yes, sir." "I don't think you have to call me 'sir', sir," Lieutenant Scheisskopf pointed out. "You outrank me."

"Yes, sir. I may outrank you, sir, but you're still my commanding officer."

"Yes, sir, that's right," Lieutenant Scheisskopf agreed. "You may outrank me, sir, but I'm still your commanding officer. So you better do what I tell you, sir, or you'll get into trouble. Go to the hospital and tell them you're sick, sir. Stay there until your uniform allowance catches up with you and you have some money to buy some uniforms."

"Yes, sir."

"And some shoes, sir. Buy some shoes the first chance you get, sir."

"Yes, sir. I will, sir."

"Thank you, sir."

Life in cadet school for Major Major was no different than life had been for him all along. Whoever he was with always wanted him to be with someone else. His instructors gave him preferred treatment at every stage in order to push him along quickly and be rid of him. In almost no time he had his pilot's wings and found himself overseas, where things began suddenly to improve. All his life, Major Major had longed for but one thing, to be absorbed, and in Pianosa, for a while, he finally was. Rank meant little to the men on combat duty, and relations between officers and enlisted men were relaxed and informal. Men whose names he didn't even know said "Hi" and invited him to go swimming or play basketball. His ripest hours were spent in the day-long basketball games no one gave a damn about winning. Score was never kept, and the number of players might vary from one to thirty-five. Major Major had never played basketball or any other game before, but his great, bobbing height and rapturous enthusiasm helped make up for his innate clumsiness and lack of experience. Major Major found true happiness there on the lopsided basketball court with the officers and enlisted men who were almost his friends. If there were no winners, there were no losers, and Major Major enjoyed every gamboling moment right up till the day Colonel Cathcart roared up in his jeep after Major Duluth was killed and made it impossible for him ever to enjoy playing basketball there again.

"You're the new squadron commander," Colonel Cathcart had shouted rudely across the railroad ditch to him. "But don't think it means anything, because it doesn't. All it means is that you're the new squadron commander."

Colonel Cathcart had nursed an implacable grudge against Major Major for a long time. A superfluous major on his rolls meant an untidy table of organization and gave ammunition to the men at Twenty-seventh Air Force Headquarters who Colonel Cathcart was positive were his enemies and rivals. Colonel Cathcart had been praying for just some stroke of good luck like Major Duluth's death. He had been plagued by one extra major; he now had an opening for one major. He appointed Major Major squadron commander and roared away in his jeep as abruptly as he had come.

For Major Major, it meant the end of the game. His face flushed with discomfort, and he was rooted to the spot in disbelief as the rain clouds gathered above him again. When he turned to his teammates, he encountered a reef of curious, reflective faces all gazing at him woodenly with morose and inscrutable animosity. He shivered with shame. When the game resumed, it was not good any longer. When he dribbled, no one tried to stop him; when he called for a pass, whoever had the ball passed it; and when he missed a basket, no one raced him for the rebound. The only voice was his own. The next day was the same, and the day after that he did not come back.

Almost on cue, everyone in the squadron stopped talking to him and started staring at him. He walked through life self-consciously with downcast eyes and burning cheeks, the object of contempt, envy, suspicion, resentment and malicious innuendo everywhere he went. People who had hardly noticed his resemblance to Henry Fonda before now never ceased discussing it, and there were even those who hinted sinisterly that Major Major had been elevated to squadron commander *because* he resembled Henry Fonda. Captain Black, who had aspired to the position himself, maintained that Major Major really *was* Henry Fonda but *was* too chickenshit to admit it.

Major Major floundered bewilderedly from one embarrassing catastrophe to another. Without consulting him, Sergeant Towser had his belongings moved into the roomy trailer Major Duluth had occupied alone, and when Major Major came rushing breathlessly into the orderly room to report the theft of his things, the young corporal there scared him half out of his wits by leaping to his feet and shouting "*Attention!*" the moment he appeared. Major Major snapped to attention with all the rest in the orderly room, wondering what important personage had entered behind him. Minutes passed in rigid silence, and the whole lot of them might have stood there at attention till doomsday if Major Danby had not dropped by from Group to congratulate Major Major twenty minutes later and put them all at ease.

Major Major fared even more lamentably at the mess hall, where Milo, his face fluttery with smiles, was waiting to usher him proudly to a small table he had set up in front and decorated with an embroidered tablecloth and a nosegay of posies in a pink cut-glass vase. Major Major hung back with horror, but he was not bold enough to resist with all the others watching. Even Havermeyer had lifted his head from his plate to gape at him with his heavy, pendulous jaw. Major Major submitted meekly to Milo's tugging and cowered in disgrace at his private table throughout the whole meal. The food was ashes in his mouth, but he swallowed every mouthful rather than risk offending any of the men connected with its preparation. Alone with Milo later, Major Major felt protest stir for the first time and said he would prefer to continue eating with the other officers. Milo told him it wouldn't work.

"I don't see what there is to work," Major Major argued. "Nothing ever happened before."

"You were never the squadron commander before."

"Major Duluth was the squadron commander and he always ate at the same table with the rest of the men."

"It was different with Major Duluth, sir."

"In what way was it different with Major Duluth?"

"I wish you wouldn't ask me that, sir," said Milo.

"Is it because I look like Henry Fonda?" Major Major mustered the courage to demand.

"Some people say you are Henry Fonda," Milo answered.

"Well, I'm not Henry Fonda," Major Major exclaimed, in a voice quavering with exasperation. "And I don't look the least bit like him. And even if I do look like Henry Fonda, what difference does that make?"

"It doesn't make any difference. That's what I'm trying to tell you, sir. It's just not the same with you as it was with Major Duluth."

And it just wasn't the same, for when Major Major, at the next meal, stepped from the food counter to sit with the others at the regular tables, he was frozen in his tracks by the impenetrable wall of antagonism thrown up by their faces and stood petrified with his tray quivering in his hands until Milo glided forward wordlessly to rescue him, by leading him tamely to his private table. Major Major gave up after that and always ate at his table alone with his back to the others. He was certain they resented him because he seemed too good to eat with them now that he was squadron commander. There was never any conversation in the mess tent when Major Major was present. He was conscious that other officers tried to avoid eating at the same time, and everyone was greatly relieved when he stopped coming there altogether and began taking his meals in his trailer.

Major Major began forging Washington Irving's name to official documents the day after the first CID man showed up to interrogate him about somebody at the hospital who had been doing it and gave him the idea. He had been bored and dissatisfied in his new position. He had been made squadron commander but had no idea what he was supposed to *do* as squadron commander, unless all he was supposed to do was forge Washington Irving's name to official documents and listen to the isolated clinks and thumps of Major—de Coverley's horseshoes falling to the ground outside the window of his small office in the rear of the orderly-room tent. He was hounded incessantly by an impression of vital duties left unfulfilled and waited in vain for his responsibilities to overtake him. He seldom went out unless it was absolutely necessary, for he could not get used to being stared at. Occasionally, the monotony was broken by some officer or enlisted man Sergeant Towser referred to him on some matter that Major Major was unable to cope with and referred right back to Sergeant Towser for sensible disposition. Whatever he was supposed to get done as squadron commander apparently was getting done without any assistance from him. He grew moody and depressed. At times he thought seriously of going with all his sorrows to see the chaplain, but the chaplain seemed so overburdened with miseries of his own that Major Major shrank from adding to his troubles. Besides, he was not quite sure if chaplains were for squadron commanders.

He had never been quite sure about Major—de Coverley, either, who, when he was not away renting apartments or kidnapping foreign laborers, had nothing more pressing to do than pitch horseshoes. Major Major often paid strict attention to the horseshoes falling softly against the earth or riding down around the small steel pegs in the ground. He peeked out at Major—de Coverley for hours and marveled that someone so august had nothing more important to do. He was often tempted to join Major—de Coverley, but pitching horseshoes all day long seemed almost as dull as signing "Major Major Major" to official documents, and Major—de Coverley's countenance was so forbidding that Major Major was in awe of approaching him.

Major Major wondered about his relationship to Major—de Coverley and about Major—de Coverley's relationship to him. He knew that Major—de Coverley was his executive officer, but he did not know what that meant, and he could not decide whether in Major—de Coverley he was blessed with a lenient superior or cursed with a delinquent subordinate. He did not want to ask Sergeant Towser, of whom he was secretly afraid, and there was no one else he could ask, least of all Major—de Coverley. Few people ever dared approach Major—de Coverley about anything and the only officer foolish enough to pitch one of his horseshoes was stricken the very next day with the worst case of Pianosan crud that Gus or Wes or even Doc Daneeka had ever seen or even heard about. Everyone was positive the disease had been inflicted upon the poor officer in retribution by Major—de Coverley, although no one was sure how.

Most of the official documents that came to Major Major's desk did not concern him at all. The vast majority consisted of allusions to prior communications which Major Major had never seen or heard of. There was never any need to look them up, for the instructions were invariably to disregard. In the space of a single productive minute, therefore, he might endorse twenty separate documents each advising him to pay absolutely no attention to any of the others. From General Peckem's office on the mainland came prolix bulletins each day headed by such cheery homilies as "Procrastination is the Thief of Time" and "Cleanliness is Next to Godliness."

General Peckem's communications about cleanliness and procrastination made Major Major feel like a filthy procrastinator, and he always got those out of the way as quickly as he could. The only official documents that interested him were those occasional ones pertaining to the unfortunate second lieutenant who had been killed on the mission over Orvieto less than two hours after he arrived on Pianosa and whose partly unpacked belongings were still in Yossarian's tent. Since the unfortunate lieutenant had reported to the operations tent instead of to the orderly room, Sergeant Towser had decided that it would be safest to report him as never having reported to the squadron at all, and the occasional documents relating to him dealt with the fact that he seemed to have vanished into thin air, which, in one way, was exactly what did happen to him. In the long run, Major Major was grateful for the official documents that came to his desk, for sitting in his office signing them all day long was a lot better than sitting in his office all day long not signing them. They gave him something to do.

Inevitably, every document he signed came back with a fresh page added for a new signature by him after intervals of from two to ten days. They were always much thicker than formerly, for in between the sheet bearing his last endorsement and the sheet added for his new endorsement were the sheets bearing the most recent endorsements of all the other officers in scattered locations who were also occupied in signing their names to that same official document. Major Major grew despondent as he watched simple communications swell prodigiously into huge manuscripts. No matter how many times he signed one, it always came back for still another signature, and he began to despair of ever being free of any of them. One day—it was the day after the CID man's first visit—Major Major signed Washington Irving's name to one of the documents instead of his own, just to see how it would feel. He liked it. He liked it so much that for the rest of the afternoon he did the same with all the official documents. It was an act of impulsive frivolity and rebellion for which he knew afterward he would be punished severely. The next morning he entered his office in trepidation and waited to see what would happen. Nothing happened.

He had sinned, and it was good, for none of the documents to which he had signed Washington Irving's name ever came back! Here, at last, was progress, and Major Major threw himself into his new career with uninhibited gusto. Signing Washington Irving's name to official documents was not much of a career, perhaps, but it was less monotonous than signing "Major Major Major." When Washington Irving did grow monotonous, he could reverse the order and sign Irving Washington until that grew monotonous. And he was getting something done, for none of the documents signed with either of these names ever came back to the squadron.

What did come back, eventually, was a *second* CID man, masquerading as a pilot. The men knew he was a CID man because he confided to them he was and urged each of them not to reveal his true identity to any of the other men to whom he had already confided that he was a CID man.

"You're the only one in the squadron who knows I'm a CID man," he confided to Major Major, "and it's absolutely essential that it remain a secret so that my efficiency won't be impaired. Do you understand?"

"Sergeant Towser knows."

"Yes, I know. I had to tell him in order to get in to see you. But I know he won't tell a soul under any circumstances."

"He told me," said Major Major. "He told me there was a CID man outside to see me."

"That bastard. I'll have to throw a security check on him. I wouldn't leave any top-secret documents lying around here if I were you. At least not until I make my report."

"I don't get any top-secret documents," said Major Major. "That's the kind I mean. Lock them in your cabinets where Sergeant Towser can't get his hands on them."

"Sergeant Towser has the only key to the cabinet."

"I'm afraid we're wasting time," said the second CID man rather stiffly. He was a brisk, pudgy, high-strung person whose movements were swift and certain. He took a number of photostats out of a large red expansion envelope he had been hiding conspicuously beneath a leather flying jacket painted garishly with pictures of airplanes flying through orange bursts of flak and with orderly rows of little bombs signifying fifty-five combat missions flown. "Have you ever seen any of these?"

Major Major looked with a blank expression at copies of personal correspondence from the hospital on which the censoring officer had written "Washington Irving" or "Irving Washington."

"No."

"How about these?"

Major Major gazed next at copies of official documents addressed to him to which he had been signing the same signatures.

"No."

"Is the man who signed these names in your squadron?"

"Which one? There are two names here."

"Either one. We figure that Washington Irving and Irving Washington are one man and that he's using two names just to throw us off the track. That's done very often you know."

"I don't think there's a man with either of those names in my squadron."

A look of disappointment crossed the second CID man's face. "He's a lot cleverer than we thought," he observed. "He's using a third name and posing as someone else. And I think...yes, I think I know what that third name is." With excitement and inspiration, he held another photostat out for Major Major to study. "How about this?"

Major Major bent forward slightly and saw a copy of the piece of V mail from which Yossarian had blacked out everything but the name Mary and on which he had written, "I yearn for you tragically. R. O. Shipman, Chaplain, US Army." Major Major shook his head.

"I've never seen it before."

"Do you know who R. O. Shipman is?"

"He's the group chaplain."

"That locks it up," said the second CID man. "Washington Irving is the group chaplain."

Major Major felt a twinge of alarm. "R. O. Shipman is the group chaplain," he corrected.

"Are you sure?"

"Yes."

"Why should the group chaplain write this on a letter?"

"Perhaps somebody else wrote it and forged his name."

"Why should somebody want to forge the group chaplain's name?"

"To escape detection."

"You may be right," the second CID man decided after an instant's hesitation, and smacked his lips crisply. "Maybe we're confronted with a gang, with two men working together who just happen to have opposite names. Yes, I'm sure that's it. One of them here in the squadron, one of them up at the hospital and one of them with the chaplain. That makes three men, doesn't it? Are you absolutely sure you never saw any of these official documents before?"

"I would have signed them if I had."

"With whose name?" asked the second CID man cunningly. "Yours or Washington Irving's?"

"With my own name," Major Major told him. "I don't even know Washington Irving's name."

The second CID man broke into a smile.

"Major, I'm glad you're in the clear. It means we'll be able to work together, and I'm going to need every man I can get. Somewhere in the European theater of operations is a man who's getting his hands on communications addressed to you. Have you any idea who it can be?"

"No."

"Well, I have a pretty good idea," said the second CID man, and leaned forward to whisper confidentially. "That bastard Towser. Why else would he go around shooting his mouth off about me? Now, you keep your eyes open and let me know the minute you hear anyone even talking about Washington Irving. I'll throw a security check on the chaplain and everyone else around here."

The moment he was gone, the first CID man jumped into Major Major's office through the window and wanted to know who the second CID man was. Major Major barely recognized him.

"He was a CID man," Major Major told him.

"Like hell he was," said the first CID man. "I'm the CID man around here."

Major Major barely recognized him because he was wearing a faded maroon corduroy bathrobe with open seams under both arms, linty flannel pajamas, and worn house slippers with one flapping sole. This was regulation hospital dress, Major Major recalled. The man had added about twenty pounds and seemed bursting with good health.

"I'm really a very sick man," he whined. "I caught cold in the hospital from a fighter pilot and came down with a very serious case of pneumonia."

"I'm very sorry," Major Major said.

"A lot of good that does me," the CID man sniveled. "I don't want your sympathy. I just want you to know what I'm going through. I came down to warn you that Washington Irving seems to have shifted his base of operations from the hospital to your squadron. You haven't heard anyone around here talking about Washington Irving, have you?"

"As a matter of fact, I have," Major Major answered. "That man who was just in here. He was talking about Washington Irving."

"Was he really?" the first CID man cried with delight. "This might be just what we needed to crack the case wide open! You keep him under surveillance twenty-four hours while I rush back to the hospital and write my superiors for further instructions." The CID man jumped out of Major Major's office through the window and was gone.

A minute later, the flap separating Major Major's office from the orderly room flew open and the second CID man was back, puffing frantically in haste. Gasping for breath, he shouted. "I just saw a man in red pajamas jumping out of your window and go running up the road! Didn't you see him?"

"He was here talking to me," Major Major answered. "I thought that looked mighty suspicious, a man jumping out the window in red pajamas." The man paced about the small office in vigorous circles. "At first I thought it was you, hightailing it for Mexico. But now I see it wasn't you. He didn't say anything about Washington Irving, did he?"

"As a matter of fact," said Major Major, "he did."

"He did?" cried the second CID man. "That's fine! This might be just the break we needed to crack the case wide open. Do you know where we can find him?"

"At the hospital. He's really a very sick man."

"That's great!" exclaimed the second CID man. "I'll go right up there after him. It would be best if I went incognito. I'll go explain the situation at the medical tent and have them send me there as a patient."

"They won't send me to the hospital as a patient unless I'm sick," he reported back to Major Major. "Actually, I am pretty sick. I've been meaning to turn myself in for a checkup, and this will be a good opportunity. I'll go back to the medical tent and tell them I'm sick, and I'll get sent to the hospital that way."

"Look what they did to me," he reported back to Major Major with purple gums. His distress was inconsolable. He carried his shoes and socks in his hands, and his toes had been painted with gentian-violet solution, too. "Who ever heard of a CID man with purple gums?" he moaned.

He walked away from the orderly room with his head down and tumbled into a slit trench and broke his nose. His temperature was still normal, but Gus and Wes made an exception of him and sent him to the hospital in an ambulance.

Major Major had lied, and it was good. He was not really surprised that it was good, for he had observed that people who did lie were, on the whole, more resourceful and ambitious and successful than people who did not lie. Had he told the truth to the second CID man, he would have found himself in trouble.

Instead he had lied and he was free to continue his work.

He became more circumspect in his work as a result of the visit from the second CID man. He did all his signing with his left hand and only while wearing the dark glasses and false mustache he had used unsuccessfully to help him begin playing basketball again. As an additional precaution, he made a happy switch from Washington Irving to John Milton. John Milton was supple and concise. Like Washington Irving, he could be reversed with good effect whenever he grew monotonous. Furthermore, he enabled Major Major to double his output, for John Milton was so much shorter than either his own name or Washington Irving's and took so much less time to write. John Milton proved fruitful in still one more respect. He was versatile, and Major Major soon found himself incorporating the signature in fragments of imaginary dialogues. Thus, typical endorsements on the official documents might read, "John, Milton is a sadist" or "Have you seen Milton, John?" One signature of which he was especially proud read, "Is anybody in the John, Milton?" John Milton threw open whole new vistas filled with charming, inexhaustible possibilities that promised to ward off monotony forever. Major Major went back to Washington Irving when John Milton grew monotonous.

Major Major had bought the dark glasses and false mustache in Rome in a final, futile attempt to save himself from the swampy degradation into which he was steadily sinking. First there had been the awful humiliation of the Great Loyalty Oath Crusade, when not one of the thirty or forty people circulating competitive loyalty oaths would even allow him to sign. Then, just when that was blowing over, there was the matter of Clevinger's plane disappearing so mysteriously in thin air with every member of the crew, and blame for the strange mishap centering balefully on him because he had never signed any of the loyalty oaths.

The dark glasses had large magenta rims. The false black mustache was a flamboyant organ grinder's, and he wore them both to the basketball game one day when he felt he could endure his loneliness no longer. He affected an air of jaunty familiarity as he sauntered to the court and prayed silently that he would not be recognized. The others pretended not to recognize him, and he began to have fun. Just as he finished congratulating himself on his innocent ruse he was bumped hard by one of his opponents and knocked to his knees. Soon he was bumped hard again, and it dawned on him that they did recognize him and that they were using his disguise as a license to elbow, trip and maul him. They did not want him at all. And just as he did realize this, the players on his team fused instinctively with the players on the other team into a single, howling, bloodthirsty mob that descended upon him from all sides with foul curses and swinging fists. They knocked him to the ground, kicked him while he was on the ground, attacked him again after he had struggled blindly to his feet. He covered his face with his hands and could not see. They swarmed all over each other in their frenzied compulsion to bludgeon him, kick him, gouge him, trample him. He was pummeled spinning to the edge of the ditch and sent slithering down on his head and shoulders. At the bottom he found his footing, clambered up the other wall and staggered away beneath the hail of hoots and stones with which they pelted him until he lurched into shelter around a corner of the orderly room tent. His paramount concern throughout the entire assault was to keep his dark glasses and false mustache in place so that he might continue pretending he was somebody else and be spared the dreaded necessity of having to confront them with his authority.

Back in his office, he wept; and when he finished weeping he washed the blood from his mouth and nose, scrubbed the dirt from the abrasions on his cheek and forehead, and summoned Sergeant Towser.

"From now on," he said, "I don't want anyone to come in to see me while I'm here. Is that clear?"

"Yes, sir," said Sergeant Towser. "Does that include me?"

"Yes."

"I see. Will that be all?"

"Yes."

"What shall I say to the people who do come to see you while you're here?"

"Tell them I'm in and ask them to wait."

"Yes, sir. For how long?"

"Until I've left."

"And then what shall I do with them?"

"I don't care."

"May I send them in to see you after you've left?"

"Yes."

"But you won't be here then, will you?"

"No."

"Yes, sir. Will that be all?"

"Yes."

"Yes, sir."

"From now on," Major Major said to the middle-aged enlisted man who took care of his trailer, "I don't want you to come here while I'm here to ask me if there's anything you can do for me. Is that clear?"

"Yes, sir," said the orderly. "When should I come here to find out if there's anything you want me to do for you?"

"When I'm not here."

"Yes, sir. And what should I do?"

"Whatever I tell you to."

"But you won't be here to tell me. Will you?"

"No."

"Then what should I do?"

"Whatever has to be done."

"Yes, sir."

"That will be all," said Major Major.

"Yes, sir," said the orderly. "Will that be all?"

"No," said Major Major. "Don't come in to clean, either. Don't come in for anything unless you're sure I'm not here."

"Yes, sir. But how can I always be sure?"

"If you're not sure, just assume that I am here and go away until you are sure. Is that clear?"

"Yes, sir."

"I'm sorry to have to talk to you in this way, but I have to. Goodbye."

"Goodbye, sir."

"And thank you. For everything."

"Yes, sir."

"From now on," Major Major said to Milo Minderbinder, "I'm not going to come to the mess hall any more. I'll have all my meals brought to me in my trailer."

"I think that's a good idea, sir," Milo answered. "Now I'll be able to serve you special dishes that the others will never know about. I'm sure you'll enjoy them. Colonel Cathcart always does."

"I don't want any special dishes. I want exactly what you serve all the other officers. Just have whoever brings it knock once on my door and leave the tray on the step. Is that clear?"

"Yes, sir," said Milo. "That's very clear. I've got some live Maine lobsters hidden away that I can serve you tonight with an excellent Roquefort salad and two frozen éclairs that were smuggled out of Paris only yesterday together with an important member of the French underground. Will that do for a start?"

"No."

"Yes, sir. I understand."

For dinner that night Milo served him broiled Maine lobster with excellent Roquefort salad and two frozen éclairs. Major Major was annoyed. If he sent it back, though, it would only go to waste or to somebody else, and Major Major had a weakness for broiled lobster. He ate with a guilty conscience. The next day for lunch there was terrapin Maryland with a whole quart of Dom Pérignon 1937, and Major Major gulped it down without a thought.

After Milo, there remained only the men in the orderly room, and Major Major avoided them by entering and leaving every time through the dingy celluloid window of his office. The window unbuttoned and was low and large and easy to jump through from either side. He managed the distance between the orderly room and his trailer by darting around the corner of the tent when the coast was clear, leaping down into the railroad ditch and dashing along with his head bowed until he attained the sanctuary of the forest. Abreast of his trailer, he left the ditch and wove his way speedily toward home through the dense underbrush, in which the only person he ever encountered was Captain Flume, who, drawn and ghostly, frightened him half to death one twilight by materializing without warning out of a patch of dewberry bushes to complain that Chief White Halfoat had threatened to slit his throat open from ear to ear.

"If you ever frighten me like that again," Major Major told him. "I'll slit your throat open from ear to ear."

Captain Flume gasped and dissolved right back into the patch of dewberry bushes, and Major Major never set eyes on him again.

When Major Major looked back on what he had accomplished, he was pleased. In the midst of a few foreign acres teeming with more than two hundred people, he had succeeded in becoming a recluse. With a little ingenuity and vision, he had made it all but impossible for anyone in the squadron to talk to him, which was just fine with everyone, he noticed, since no one wanted to talk to him anyway. No one, it turned out, but that madman Yossarian, who brought him down with a flying tackle one day as he was scooting along the bottom of the ditch to his trailer for lunch.

The last person in the squadron Major Major wanted to be brought down with a flying tackle by was Yossarian. There was something inherently disreputable about Yossarian, always carrying on so disgracefully about that dead man in his tent who wasn't even there and then taking off all his clothes after the Avignon mission and going around without them right up to the day General Dreedle stepped up to pin a medal on him for his heroism over Ferrera and found him standing in formation stark naked. No one in the world had the power to remove the dead man's disorganized effects from Yossarian's tent. Major Major had forfeited the authority when he permitted Sergeant Towser to report the lieutenant who had been killed over Orvieto less than two hours after he arrived in the squadron as never having arrived in the squadron at all. The only one with any right to remove his belongings from Yossarian's tent, it seemed to Major Major, was Yossarian himself, and Yossarian, it seemed to Major Major, had no right.

Major Major groaned after Yossarian brought him down with a flying tackle, and tried to wiggle to his feet. Yossarian wouldn't let him.

"Captain Yossarian," Yossarian said, "requests permission to speak to the major at once about a matter of life or death."

"Let me up, please," Major Major bid him in cranky discomfort. "I can't return your salute while I'm lying on my arm."

Yossarian released him. They stood up slowly. Yossarian saluted again and repeated his request.

"Let's go to my office," Major Major said. "I don't think this is the best place to talk."

"Yes, sir," answered Yossarian.

They smacked the gravel from their clothing and walked in constrained silence to the entrance of the orderly room.

"Give me a minute or two to put some mercurochrome on these cuts. Then have Sergeant Towser send you in."

"Yes, sir."

Major Major strode with dignity to the rear of the orderly room without glancing at any of the clerks and typists working at the desks and filing cabinets. He let the flap leading to his office fall closed behind him. As soon as he was alone in his office, he raced across the room to the window and jumped outside to dash away. He found Yossarian blocking his path. Yossarian was waiting at attention and saluted again.

"Captain Yossarian requests permission to speak to the major at once about a matter of life or death," he repeated determinedly.

"Permission denied," Major Major snapped.

"That won't do it."

Major Major gave in. "All right," he conceded wearily. "I'll talk to you. Please jump inside my office."

"After you."

They jumped inside the office. Major Major sat down, and Yossarian moved around in front of his desk and told him that he did not want to fly any more combat missions. What could he do? Major Major asked himself. All he could do was what he had been instructed to do by Colonel Korn and hope for the best.

"Why not?" he asked.

"I'm afraid."

"That's nothing to be ashamed of," Major Major counseled him kindly. "We're all afraid."

"I'm not ashamed," Yossarian said. "I'm just afraid."

"You wouldn't be normal if you were never afraid. Even the bravest men experience fear. One of the biggest jobs we all face in combat is to overcome our fear."

"Oh, come on, Major. Can't we do without that horseshit?"

Major Major lowered his gaze sheepishly and fiddled with his fingers. "What do you want me to tell you?"

"That I've flown enough missions and can go home."

"How many have you flown?"

"Fifty-one."

"You've only got four more to fly."

"He'll raise them. Every time I get close he raises them."

"Perhaps he won't this time."

"He never sends anyone home, anyway. He just keeps them around waiting for rotation orders until he doesn't have enough men left for the crews, and then raises the number of missions and throws them all back on combat status. He's been doing that ever since he got here."

"You mustn't blame Colonel Cathcart for any delay with the orders," Major Major advised. "It's Twenty-seventh Air Force's responsibility to process the orders promptly once they get them from us."

"He could still ask for replacements and send us home when the orders did come back. Anyway, I've been told that Twenty-seventh Air Force wants only forty missions and that it's only his own idea to get us to fly fifty-five."

"I wouldn't know anything about that," Major Major answered. "Colonel Cathcart is our commanding officer and we must obey him. Why don't you fly the four more missions and see what happens?"

"I don't want to."

What could you do? Major Major asked himself again. What could you do with a man who looked you squarely in the eye and said he would rather die than be killed in combat, a man who was at least as mature and intelligent as you were and who you had to pretend was not? What could you say to him?

"Suppose we let you pick your missions and fly milk runs," Major Major said. "That way you can fly the four missions and not run any risks."

"I don't want to fly milk runs. I don't want to be in the war any more."

"Would you like to see our country lose?" Major Major asked.

"We won't lose. We've got more men, more money and more material. There are ten million men in uniform who could replace me. Some people are getting killed and a lot more are making money and having fun. Let somebody else get killed."

"But suppose everybody on our side felt that way."

"Then I'd certainly be a damned fool to feel any other way. Wouldn't I?"

What could you possibly say to him? Major Major wondered forlornly. One thing he could not say was that there was nothing he could do. To say there was nothing he could do would suggest he *would* do something if he could and imply the existence of an error or injustice in Colonel Korn's policy. Colonel Korn had been most explicit about that. He must never say there was nothing he could do.

"I'm sorry," he said. "But there's nothing I can do."

The Invasion of Papau
(from *Retreat from Kokoda*)

Raymond Paull

Lieutenant Kienzle set out from Uberi on 6th July, intending to inspect the track through to Kokoda, and by preceding Captain Templeton and his troops, organize their stages on the march. However, Templeton joined him at Uberi on the following day, and they went on together with 120 carriers on the morning of the 8th. The Australians enjoyed the rare luxury of travelling light across the Kokoda Trail. The natives carried their packs and rations, while the lugger *Gili Gili* carried their bulk supplies and equipment. Templeton was instructed to meet and discharge the lugger on arrival at Buna.

An alert and capable leader, Templeton had seen active service as Leading Seaman (Gunner) in the Royal Naval Reserve during the First World War. He was a man of great physical and mental stamina, but his age excluded him from the Second A.I.F. His men knew him as "Uncle Sam"—a somewhat gruff, kindly Company Commander who shirked nothing, and they were unreservedly devoted to him. At Iorabaiwa, having struggled to the top of the ridge after the first day's march, Templeton walked back for two hours along the track, and returned with six rifles and two packs taken from footsore men.

From Iorabaiwa next morning, the Australians and natives reached Nauro after four and a half hours. Although not greatly encumbered, the troops were sorely taxed by the steep descents and equally stiff climbing, so Templeton, out of consideration for their aching muscles, rested them on the 10th, and they pushed on through Menari to Efogi on the 11th. Lieutenant Peter Brewer awaited them at Kagi with 186 carriers from Kokoda, so Kienzle sent back the carriers brought from Ilolo, with instructions to build up the depots established at the intermediate stages. He believed that he would obtain the best results if he confined the carriers' work to one stage. Accustomed mainly to the milder coastal climate, the chill air and the rigours of their tasks in the mountains easily distressed them.

The Australians left Kagi after breakfast on 13 July with the Kokoda carriers. It was a miserable journey. They marched in a heavy, continuous downpour, the track swirling with water. The men fell through the thin, mossy carpet, or floundered on roots concealed by the mud. The perpetual drip of the moss forest subdued them. This was *keru gabuna*, the Cold Place. They were happier on the descent into the upper reaches of Iora Creek, arriving at the first crossing at noon, and after three hours more, at Iora Creek village.

Continuing next morning, Kienzle and Templeton left the troops and carriers at Deniki and went down into Kokoda. Kienzle also took this opportunity of visiting his own plantation at Yodda, and returned to Deniki in the afternoon with fresh foodstuffs and five homestead natives.

While the carriers rested on the 16th, he sorted stores for the southward journey, and at Kokoda next day, bade farewell to Templeton and B Company before going back along the roadway through the plantation on the long march to Port Moresby. Arriving at Kagi on the afternoon of the 19th, Kienzle checked over the supplies delivered in the wake of the advance party. They consisted of 42 tins of biscuits, 42 loads of rations and 2,700 lb. of rice.

An "old hand," experienced in the use of native labour, Kienzle realized that to maintain a supply line over such a long, difficult route was not a simple matter of porterage. Not only did the limited number of carriers available aggravate the problem; on such a route too many natives were laden with supplies to sustain themselves and their fellow carriers. The longer the journey, the greater the aggregate weight of the carrier line's own rations, and the smaller the weight of supplies—Australian rations, ammunition, equipment, medical stores and the many other items needed by the troops—delivered at their destination. In proportion to the number of carriers employed, the quantity of supplies of all kinds delivered at Kokoda would be negligible.

The supply problem would be simplified if, on the other hand, the carriers' loads were flown from Port Moresby to a convenient dropping place sufficiently far forward. Kienzle considered that Kagi fulfilled this qualification. It did not provide an extensive dropping area, and it might often be obscured by cloud, but deliveries to Kagi by aircraft would reduce the number of carrying stages forward to Kokoda, and have the effect of increasing the supply of native labour. He decided to discuss this proposal fully on his return to New Guinea Force Headquarters.

The *Gili Gili*, a Thursday Island lugger, sailed from Port Moresby on 4th July with 20 tons of Templeton's stores, equipment and ammunition. Staff-Sergeant A. L. Collyer and three other men of the 39th Battalion travelled in the ship, and directed the discharge of her cargo at Buna. When it had been cleared from the beach, they followed the laden carriers along the Kokoda road. At Awala three days later, Collyer reported to Templeton, proceeding with Pte. John McBride from Kokoda to Buna. They returned to Awala on 21st July. As they rested there from the heat, they heard but disregarded a distant rumbling noise which seemed to emanate from the massive banks of cloud, the seat of tropical thunder, in the direction of the coast. The same rumbling noise went unheeded by the troops Templeton had left at Kokoda.

In the Buna Government Station, Lieutenant Alan Champion and Sergeant Harper were studying a newly arrived cypher at 3.30 p.m. on 21st July when a police-boy burst in. He said warningly, "Air-plane, taubada." As they accompanied him on to the beach, they saw a Kawanisi float-plane approaching over Holnicote Bay. It passed the station building and flew along the coast, turned back, and strafed the station as it crossed the clearing.

Half an hour after the plane's appearance, the police-boy called again from beneath the coconut palms above the beach, "Ssip i kom taubada." The ship he indicated lay six miles off to the north-west, and there were more silhouetted beyond her. Champion and Harper identified the foremost as a cruiser, which opened fire as they watched. They saw the flashes of her gunfire clearly from the Buna beach, but when no shells fell around them, the two men assumed her target to be Gona or Sanananda Point.

Harper ran quickly to the radio hut. He tuned his transmitter to the emergency frequency, and in plain language reported what he had seen: "A Japanese warship is shelling off Buna, apparently to cover a landing at Gona or Sanananda. Acknowledge, Moresby. Over…" He listened for Port Morseby's response. The receiver was silent.

Harper repeated his message again and again, while the boom of the cruiser's gunfire echoed across the bay.

The legendary figure of the Kokoda Trail was Doctor Geoffrey Hamden Vernon. A tall, elderly Australian, Vernon cheerfully took upon himself the care of the native carriers toiling over the trail beneath loads of supplies and equipment and returning with stretcher casualties. The Australian people, who generously extolled the praises of the "Fuzzy Wuzzy Angels" in the months ahead, failed to realize that the carriers' patience, tenderness and fortitude with wounded Australians rewarded, in part, Vernon's unsparing services on their behalf.

A son of a Sydney city architect, Vernon graduated in medicine and surgery from the University of Sydney to a practice in the distant Queensland town of Winton. He relinquished this to serve in the First A.I.F. As Regimental Medical Officer in the 11th Light Horse Regiment, and returned to Australia with the Military Cross and a deafness caused by a bursting shell on Gallipoli in 1915. During his Kokoda days, unable to hear normal speech, Vernon remarked wryly that his deafness was an advantage, because he heard none of the wild rumours that circulated with the stamp of gospel truth among the troops around him.

The outbreak of the Second World War found him at Misima. Knowing that his age and disability excluded him from active service, he volunteered to substitute anywhere in the Territory for a younger man. A walker on a marathon scale, he combined duty with enjoyment in the next two years on patrols for the Medical Service. When the Australian Government evacuated the women, children and older men from Papua in December, 1941, Vernon flatly refused to go. The authorities threatened him with arrest and compulsory expulsion. He ignored them, determined to find his own useful niche.

Towards the end of June, 1942, after serving as medical officer at the native hospital at Sapphire Creek, below Rouna Pass, Vernon transferred to Ilolo and there became responsible for the carrier lines on the Kokoda Trail. One of his first decisions gave two days' rest to a carrier line which, having just arrived from Kagi, had been ordered to make another outward journey next morning. Vernon went himself, to inspect conditions and medical posts along the track.

On the heights above Nauro, the morning was clear and pleasant, the air fresh and invigorating. A breeze stirred the trees, and the grass had a dewiness and fragrance. The little outpost at Iorabaiwa, separated from the ridge by the deep valley of the Ofi River, seemed far below. Vernon stopped on the ridge for a pannikin of hot soup. As he sat there, relishing the peace and remoteness of this upland place, Kienzle halted on his journey back from Kokoda. The two men exchanged views while they shared the soup.

During the late afternoon, Vernon scrambled over the boulders on the river crossing and climbed up to Efogi. Weary from the day's march, he saw much still to be done, especially in the native hospital, where a single, busy orderly treated injured feet, abraded shoulders, respiratory infections and other ailments. Nearly every patient showed positive evidence of hard work and exposure.

Vernon stayed at Efogi on the following day to supervise the treatment of these natives. He noted also a shortage of blankets. Although a biting mountain cold prevailed at these altitudes, Efogi did not possess enough blankets to issue one to each man.

Resuming his journey on 25th July with Sergeant Jarrett, of Angau, a police-boy carrying a note overtook them at the foot of the hill below the village. Jarrett read and passed the note without comment to Vernon. It related that Japanese troops had landed at Gona, and were advancing inland towards Kokoda.

"I'll go on," said Vernon. "There's no M.O. with those 39th youngsters." He continued on his way, while Jarrett returned to improve the staging conditions at Efogi.

The blue-print for the first stage of the Japanese campaign to capture Port Moresby gave a major part to the 15th Independent Engineer Regiment. Its role combined the construction of roads and bridges during the advance inland with that of strengthening the fighting potential of the striking force. The regiment embarked at Talamo on 29th June in the transports *Ryoyo Mara* and *Ayatozan Mam* to join the Nankia Shitai at Rabaul.

The Commander of this regiment, Colonel Yokoyama, issued a remarkable document on 14 July towards the end of the voyage: "From today, we are entering an area subject to air attack. Hereafter, there will be no more exercises; any attack will be the real thing. Get out on deck before the enemy's arrival. Those who are slow will be regarded as cowards. When sinking, remain calm until the water touches the feet, and when in the water, take the necessary precautions. Those who hurriedly jump into the sea will drown. When in the water, sections or platoons should gather together and sing military songs. All must be calm, even when awaiting rescue for perhaps two days and night." Yokoyama was unduly pessimistic. Both ships entered Rabaul harbour unmolested early next morning.

From the units available there, and en route, the Japanese Command chose a highly mobile advance force, known as the Yokoyama Advance Butai, its commander being the author of the homily on air attacks at sea.

Documents captured at a later stage of the Owen Stanley campaign showed the composition of the Yokoyama Advance Butai as:

Unit	Commander
15th Indep. Engr. Regt	Colonel Yokoyama
1st. Bn. 144th Inf. Regt	Lieut.-Colonel Tsukamoto
No. 5 Coy. 2nd Bn. 144th Inf. Regt	1st. Lieut. Kamimura
No. 7 Coy. 2nd Bn. 4lst Inf. Regt	1st Lieut. Kamida
No. 2 Bty. 47th Fd. A/A Bn	1st Lieut. Nakashima
No. 1 Bty. 55th Mtn. Arty. Bn	1st Lieut. Hamada
Two Coys. Sasebo No. 5 Special Naval Landing	Commander Tsukioka
Party (Marines)	
Part of 15th Naval Pnr. Unit.	
2 Pl. No. 2 Coy. and Eqpt. Pl. No. 3	
Coy. Indep. Engrs.	
2 Sec. 144th Regt. Sig. Unit.	

A separate document calculated, for provisioning purposes, the strength of the Yokoyama Advance Butai at 7,000 troops, with 1,200 natives and 2,630 horses. These figures included 1,700 infantry and attached personnel, and 1,000 personnel of the 15th Independent Engineer Regiment. The provisioning plan envisaged ration supplies for thirty days, together with emergency rations for twelve days, and additional rations for ten days to be sent to the battlefield.

Beneath these calculations, however, were more figures purporting to show the combined strength of the advance force, including its supply column:

	Strength	Horses
Main Force	3,800	330
Waggon Transport, 1 Coy	400	300
Packhorse Transport, 4 Coys	2,800	2,000
Total	7,000	2,630

Against the figures, 3,800, shown for "main force," was a pencilled amendment, 2,700. From this document, therefore, it would appear that the combined strength of the Yokoyama Advance Butai was not less than 2,700 combat troops, 3,200 supply and base troops—a total of 5,900 Japanese—and 1,200 natives for porterage and other menial tasks.

The Yokoyama Advance Butai embarked in the transports *Ryoyo Mam* and *Ayatozan Mam* at Rabaul on 19th July, and sailed on the 20th with an escort of two cruisers and two destroyers for Basabua, about 1,000 yards east of the Gona Mission. The convoy passed through St George's Channel and down the east coast of New Britain without incident, and made its landfall on the Papuan coast in clear, warm weather, on the afternoon of 21st July.

The naval bombardment seen from Buna by Champion and Harper lifted at 4 o'clock, and the Japanese landed from barges on the empty beach. The landing went on uninterrupted all night long; not until the coming dawn was the first offensive action taken against it. Dispatched from Port Moresby in the early morning of the 22nd to reconnoitre the enemy's strength, Flight Lieutenant L. W. Manning, of 32 (Hudson) Squadron, RAAF, flew for some miles beyond the north coast, doubled back, and approached Gona from the direction of Rabaul. His bomb-racks held four 250 lb. bombs.

Manning first sighted a destroyer. He passed over the ship at 1,000 feet, and examined another ship which proved to be a cruiser. Circling, Manning found another destroyer and cruiser and the two transports. The *Ryoyo Maru* and *Ayatozan Maru* lay 500 yards from the beach, and the cruisers about two miles out. The destroyers steamed slowly a little farther off. Hearing the Hudson's approach from the north, the Japanese apparently believed it to be one of their own aircraft. The two transports and one of the cruisers were motionless; the second cruiser scarcely moved in the water. None challenged the solitary aircraft flying overhead in the darkness.

Seeing only the six ships, Manning headed out to sea to make his radio report to Port Moresby. Then, in the half dark that precedes the day, he turned for his attack run, choosing one of the transports as his target. He dived from 1,500 feet. This was the moment Manning and his crew had dreamed about, yet when the opportunity presented itself, tension and eagerness conspired to spoil their judgement. The four bombs fell into the sea, the nearest drenching the ship from a distance of 40 yards. Manning pulled the Hudson's nose up and climbed away over the coast, eluding the enemy's angry fire, and leaving the bombers from Port Moresby to find their prey.

The crew of the *Ryoyo Maru*, probably the ship Manning attacked, soon had her under way. The horses had not yet been put ashore, and cargo lay in her open holds. She escaped unscathed. The *Ayatozan Maru*, not so fortunate, received a direct bombing hit and began to burn, although the survivors of the attack turned her head towards the beach and ran her aground. The *Ayatozan Maru* afterwards assumed the familiarity of a landmark, known to troops and air crew as the "Gona wreck."

A communiqué issued on 23rd July from General Douglas MacArthur's headquarters* conceded the fresh Japanese gains: "The enemy effected a landing at Gona Mission, on the north coast of Papua, a point not occupied by the Allied Forces. The enemy convoy was discovered by reconnaissance, and our Air Forces executed a series of bombing attacks throughout the day on enemy shipping, landing barges and personnel on shore. One large transport and one barge were sunk, and heavy casualties were inflicted on debarking troops. An enemy float-plane was shot down in combat. Two of our fighters are missing."

In spite of air attacks, the Japanese established and consolidated their beachhead. The vanguard—marines, infantry and engineers—had already set out, some on foot, some on bicycles, to reconnoitre the road to Kokoda. The main strength of the Yokoyama Butai followed.

*MacArthur, escaping from the Philippines to Australia, had been appointed Supreme Allied Commander, South-West Pacific Area.

The strip of country between the north coast and the foothills of the Owen Stanley Range is flat and perpetually swampy. It is subject to widespread inundation with each daily deluge. From its spongy ground rises a dense jungle, dank and foetid, broken occasionally by patches of kunai, and intersected by the native pads connecting the villages and crossing the Buna-Kokoda road. In July, 1942, the Kokoda road was no more than a narrow muddy vehicle track extending to the Kumusi River, which was spanned by a stout suspension footbridge, the crossing-place being known as Wairopi, or Wire Rope.

The Kumusi at this point is a stream about eighty yards wide, its depth varying from hour to hour according to the rains falling over its vast headwaters to the east of the Kokoda Trail. Normally, the flow of its current is between eight and ten knots, but it can change in a few minutes to a roaring torrent. Beyond the river, the track follows the course of Oivi Creek, crossing its tributaries, passing Ilimo and Gorari villages, and climbing 800 feet to the summit of the steep Oivi spur, which protrudes from the base of the Owen Stanleys to separate the Kumusi and Mambare waters. The spur is clothed with a dense rain forest of tangled undergrowth, trees and vines. The Oivi rest huts stood then in a clearing on the crest of the slope, providing shelter for the passing traveller. The track passes through the clearing, falls gradually with an even grade to the crossing on Iora Creek, and ascends the escarpment above the Mambare into Kokoda.

In the advance to Kokoda, the Japanese vanguard wore green uniforms, and steel helmets garnished with leaves. Some wore scarlet helmets. They carried abundant supplies of ammunition, mess tins of cooked rice, and equipment which included a light shovel slung across the back, and a machete for cutting a pathway through the jungle.

Their tactics appeared to follow a definite pattern. A mobile spearhead advanced rapidly until opposing forces barred further progress. While the spearhead deployed and engaged the opposition, support troops would site a machine-gun, and might also bring up one or more mortars. Feint or deliberate attacks disclosed the width and strength of the defensive position by drawing the enemy's fire. For this purpose, advance scouts often risked and forfeited their lives. The stronger support elements, coming forward, cut their way round their opponents' flanks, either to force a withdrawal or to annihilate the defenders in a surprise attack from the rear.

Out-flanking tactics were sometimes varied to confuse, bluff or frighten the opposition. If the Japanese thought that a threatened encirclement would compel their adversaries to retire without fighting, they indulged in shouting, noisy scrub-cutting and wasteful fire. They employed some badly chosen English phrases and scraps of pidgin to entrap an unwary enemy. A bird-like whistle or a single rifle-shot sometimes signalled the attack. In a frontal attack, the Japanese were dogged and persistent, probing ceaselessly for weak spots in the enemy's defences.

Communiqués issued from GHQ on 24th and 25th July contained brief references to attacks made by bombers, dive-bombers and strafing aircraft against the Japanese beachhead. On the 27th the communiqué reported that "our patrols engaged the enemy in light skirmishes at Awala." It chronicled, on the 28th, the bare fact of contact between "Australian patrols" and the enemy in the vicinity of Oivi.

In Sydney on the same day, the veteran Australian politician, William Morris Hughes, inquired how and why the enemy had succeeded so easily in gaining their foothold in Papua. "We must wake up to the fact," said Mr Hughes, "that we are fighting an enemy who is not afraid to die; an enemy who is on the offensive everywhere. To reach Buna, the Japanese had to come in a convoy, with barges and troopships. We have an Air Force on duty there, day and night. The Japanese ought not to have got there. Every day, they are creeping nearer and nearer. Soon, they may have established sufficient bases to make a major attack on Australia itself…"

Kokoda was lost while the newspapers reporting Mr Hughes' words tumbled from the presses in Australia early next morning.

RETREAT TO OIVI

Port Moresby never picked up the message sent by Sergeant Harper from Buna on 21st July, but heard a simultaneous warning from Sergeant Hanna at Ambasi, forty miles to the north-west. In the absence of any response to his call on the emergency frequency, Harper dispatched a police-boy to Awala with a written message, instructing him not to stop until he had delivered it. Lieutenant Champion and Harper then considered their own means of escape before the enemy isolated and captured them. They left the Government Station just before 6 o'clock. They were barely out of the clearing when enemy bombers attacked the building.

Champion and Harper dined that evening at Higaturu with Captain Austin, but in spite of their persuasions, he declined to accompany them, saying the journey would too greatly tax his strength, whereas he would be safe enough in his well-stocked refuge in the hills. They left him collecting the few personal belongings and treasures he was loath to leave for the Japanese. At Awala on the following morning, having travelled throughout the night, Champion and Harper reported to Captain Grahamslaw.

The unexpected appearance of the Japanese, and their rapid advance inland, trapped many of the Europeans at the hospitals, missions and plantations on the Buna coast. Few succeeded in eluding the enemy and crossing the mountains to the south coast. Lieutenant Louis Austin and an Anglican mission party— Miss Margaret Branchley, Miss Lilian Lashman, the Reverend Henry Holland, the Reverend Vivian Hedlich, Mr John Duffill, two half-caste mission workers, Louise Artango and Anthony Gore, and Gore's six-year-old son—travelling from Ioma to Tufi, were betrayed to the Japanese by the natives of Perembata village. At Buna on 12th August, outside the headquarters of the Sasebo No. 5 Special Naval Landing Party, the entire party were beheaded one by one with the sword—the boy last of all.

The self-appointed executioner responsible for this inhuman massacre of

Christian mission workers was Sub-Lieutenant Komai,* a Company Commander of this Marine Butai.

A traitorous guide betrayed Miss Hayman and Miss Parkinson from the Gona Mission. After a night under guard in the coffee-house at Popondetta, the Japanese took the two women to a spot where graves had been dug, and repeatedly bayoneted their prisoners until death mercifully ended their agonies. Their bodies, recovered some months later by Sergeant-Major Arek, a Wanigela native, received Christian burial at Sangara Mission. Father Benson alone survived captivity.

Near Popondetta also, the Japanese captured and killed Hanna and a small band of American Airacobra pilots forced down on various missions over the north coast.

The advancing Japanese encountered their first resistance near the Isivita-Sangara track junction, 1,000 yards east of Awala, on 22nd July. Against them, the Australians mustered the 39th Battalion's 11 Platoon, under Lieutnat H. E. Mortimore, and Major Watson's handful of Papuan Infantry. They possessed no better weapons than rifles, a few revolvers and Thompson sub-marine guns, and a single Lewis gun with one drum of ammunition.

An urgent message from Templeton on the previous day had instructed Mortimore to proceed from Kokoda with his men. Meanwhile, Watson had disposed the PIB in defensive positions covering Awala. Mortimore and his platoon, arriving at 11 o'clock after marching all night, had barely shed their packs when the Japanese scouts appeared. With the exchange of the first shots, the enemy threw out flanking patrols and brought up machine-guns, a mortar and an infantry support gun, like a well rehearsed exercise. The Australians attempted to provide covering fire for the withdrawal, to find that the speed of the enemy's attack had dispersed the PIB. Watson, with the remnants of his patrol and the Australians extricated themselves and fell back across the Kumusi, where Sergeant Collyer and Private McBride attacked the bridge. Unable to cut the cables, they broke up the footplates and loosened the lock-nuts with which the cables were secured. The bridge collapsed into the river's broad channel.

Templeton left a section of 11 Platoon at Wairopi to delay the enemy's crossing while the remainder of the force withdrew to Gorari Creek, a stream with a channel twenty yards wide flowing through a deep defile into Oivi Creek. A wire suspension bridge also spanned Gorari Creek, but the Australians left it untouched for ambush purposes, and sited two Lewis guns at the side of the track covering the bridge. Templeton placed a section of the platoon on either side, and kept a third in reserve. He also brought 12 Platoon forward from Kokoda.

---

*Komai was identified also as the executioner of Flight-Lieutenant William Ellis Newton, v.c., at Salamaua on 29th March, 1943. The Marine Commander, Torashige Tsukioka, and his Adjutant, Lieutenant Kagahito Okabayashi, were both killed during a bombing attack on Salamaua three months after the callous "Bushido" murder of Newton. An Australian War Crimes Investigation team traced Komai to the point where his death was established beyond doubt. The natives responsible for the betrayal of the mission party were hanged.

Lieutenant-Colonel Owen joined Templeton at Gorari, having flown across to Kokoda in the late afternoon of the 24th (the pilot had turned back on the first attempt on the previous day), and gone forward immediately. New Guinea Force on the 18th had instructed Owen to send his rifle companies across the range, and on the 22nd, extended his command to that of Maroubra Force, the name given to the combined Australian and Papuan force on the northern side of the Owen Stanleys. Captain A. C. Dean and C Company, the first of the troops to follow Templeton, left Ilolo on the same day.

The oncoming Japanese soon crossed the Kumusi's wide channel under a barrage of mortar and machine-gun fire, and on the 25th ran into the Gorari trap. The Australians succeeded at first in holding them on the far side of the creek, and thwarted their customary encircling tactics on the steep, open crossing. Japanese snipers finally broke the deadlock by climbing high up into the foliage of the jungle trees and pouring an accurate fire on to the Australians.

Returning to Kokoda late that night, Owen dispatched a signal to Port Moresby saying: "Clashed at Gorari and inflicted approximately 15 casualties at noon. At 5 p.m., our position was heavily engaged, and two tired platoons are now at Oivi. Third platoon now at Kokoda is moving to Oivi at 6 a.m. Must have more troops, otherwise there is nobody between Oivi and Dean, who is three days out from Ilolo. Will have drome open for landing. Must have two fresh companies to avoid being outflanked at Oivi. Advise me before 3 a.m. if air-borne troops not available."

Owen received thirty-two reinforcements next day—Lieutenant D. I. H. McClean and 16 Platoon of D Company. The other platoons of this company made the journey over the mountain and back with pilots reluctant to risk landing at Kokoda. These troops, returning to the 7-Mile, set out on the long overland journey in the wake of C Company.

McClean and fourteen of his men made the first crossing in a civilian Douglas airliner devoid of camouflage, preceding Sergeant E. J. Morrison with sixteen men and the platoon's two Bren guns still immersed in the original protective layer of grease in their boxes.

As the plane approached the Mambare, McClean and his men saw the Kokoda airfield bestrewn with obstacles. The Douglas circled, pitching in the valley's turbulence, while the troops vomited despondently into their tin hats, and 10 Platoon and a few natives removed the obstacles.

McClean's troops were still shaky from their air-sickness when the plane landed and taxied to the end of the runway where Owen awaited them. As they emerged from the cabin, Owen said, "Sorry I can't give you a spell Mac. B Company is in trouble at Oivi, and I'll have to send you off right away. It's half a day's march." The new arrivals picked up their packs and rifles, stumbled across the Kokoda plateau, and in the early afternoon toiled up the spur into Oivi. B Company, resting there, were hollow-eyed and exhausted, having had little sleep or food in four days.

Nobody could suggest that Oivi provided a good defensive position. The troops manned a perimeter along the edge of the high jungle wall, and positions overlooking the track from Gorari. A standing patrol of one section, under Corporal R. Stent, lay in the jungle across the track below the clearing, until the Japanese set up a heavy machine-gun, the Juki, nearby, and two scouts flushed the Australians. They retaliated by shooting the two Japanese, and returned unharmed into the perimeter, with the enemy vanguard of Marines close behind.

By three o'clock, Templeton could not conceal his anxiety about the prospects of holding the Japanese. He had learned from McClean that the balance of 16 Platoon expected to join him at Oivi, as well as the main strength of D Company. Templeton reasoned that if the Japanese overwhelmed his small force there, Garland's platoon at Kokoda could not hope to survive, and the enemy then might march unchecked to the top of the main range before they encountered Dean. Before the full weight of the attack developed, Templeton decided to go back along the track towards Kokoda with the object of bringing up the reinforcements. Ten minutes after his departure, Collyer heard the single, sharp crack of a rifle. Templeton did not return, nor did a small patrol sent out to find him. A burst of machine-gun fire, falling suddenly around Collyer and Stent on the Kokoda side of the clearing, warned the Australians that the enemy had penetrated along the flank. The Japanese launched their attack in the late afternoon, but when it failed to dislodge the Australians, it subsided at dusk.

Every man at Oivi felt Templeton's loss keenly, for he was a courageous and efficient officer. They cursed their easy acquiescence in allowing him to go unescorted. The sole evidence of his fate discovered much later in the campaign suggests that the Japanese ambushed and captured Templeton, badly wounded him, and killed him to rid themselves of an unwanted encumbrance.

At Oivi, the remaining officers agreed at nightfall that to continue the battle there invited annihilation. The noise of scrub-cutting on all sides, and the discovery of a Juki, newly sited on the north-western flank for a dawn attack, lent strength to this decision. Lance-Corporal Sinopa, a tall, reliable police-boy, suggested the means of escape, by volunteering to guide the Australians by a circuitous route back to Kokoda. Sinopa's success earned him promotion and the Military Medal.

The Australians struck out into the jungle on the north-eastern side of the clearing at 10 o'clock. They descended a steep bank into Oivi Creek, and travelled along the course of the stream, sometimes waist deep in its icy waters, until Sinopa led them up the right-hand bank into dense jungle. The men groped their way blindly in the intense darkness, clutching the bayonet scabbard or webbing straps of the man immediately ahead, yet even this journey provided its sample of the Australian soldier's irrepressible humour, in the advice addressed to the column by a man who had seized a handful of phosphorescent fungus: "Grab yourself some headlights, fellas."

The weary column emerged just before dawn on to the foothills track between Gebara and Sangai. Sitting there on the narrow pathway, the men had broken open their emergency rations when from the direction of Oivi, a distant din proclaimed the Japanese attack on the empty clearing.

By an unfortunate accident of omission, five Australians still manned a section of the perimeter when the withdrawal occurred. Finding themselves alone in the clearing at some undetermined hour of the night, they departed with considerable haste, skirted the enemy's positions safely, and returned to the main track to meet Morrison's party. Unable to break through the Japanese lines into Oivi, Morrison had disposed his men defensively across the track forward of Kokoda, awaiting fresh instructions or an opportunity of assisting B Company by attacking the Japanese from the rear. Morrison also had gathered up several men of the patrol sent out from Oivi in search of Templeton.

Another lad of this patrol whom Morrison failed to intercept stumbled into Kokoda with grave news—Oivi surrounded and Templeton missing. Owen proceeded at once to mobilize his meagre resources for the defence of the Kokoda Trail. This he regarded as the task of paramount importance. Having barely fifty men on hand, he knew that he could not hope to hold the Kokoda plateau, airfield and track against the enemy, and he saw no likelihood of relief for some days. After consulting Garland, Owen sent a police-boy with a message for Morrison. It is a gem among military orders: "Withdraw patrol through me at Kokoda at 10 a.m. Be careful that enemy do not catch up to you unexpectedly on bicycles." The police-boy also carried a bunch of bananas which served as lunch for Morrison and his men.

Meanwhile, the Australians at Kokoda buried in the rubber plantation the grenades and ammunition they were unable to carry, and set out up the Deniki hill after midnight to positions above a waterfall, which offered the nearest perimeter defences.

Travelling westward along the foothills track, the column from Oivi reached the outskirts of Kokoda to find the plateau silent and deserted. Watson and Captain Stevenson, who had been Templeton's Second-in-Command, and now commanded B Company, could understand Owen's withdrawal, but the absence of the Japanese puzzled them. Suspecting a trap, they retired warily, followed Iora Creek upstream, and climbed the Deniki hill, where Owen welcomed them heartily.

Vernon, going forward on his voluntary mission, reported to Owen on the same day, saying he would remain to assist until Captain J. A. McK. Shera, the 39th Battalion's Medical Officer, arrived from Port Moresby.

The night was cheerless and cold. Vernon did not have the comfort of a single blanket for his shake-down in the improvised Aid Post. The wind blew a chill draught through the gaping fissures in the floor, and a miniature shower-bath fell through the roof. At 10 o'clock next morning, when a reconnaissance of Kokoda showed it still to be unoccupied, the Australians descended the hill and again took up the defence of the plateau. Vernon also began packing his few belongings until Owen, misled by the doctor's grey hairs and gaunt figure, interrupted him.

"I think you should remain here at Deniki, doctor," he said.

Vernon shook his head. "Sorry, I'm rather deaf. I didn't hear you."

"I suggest that you should remain here at Deniki," Owen shouted.

"Nonsense," said Vernon scornfully. "Where do you think the wounded will be—here, or down at Kokoda?" He followed the troops early in the afternoon.

At 11.30 a.m., Owen signalled Port Moresby, saying, "Reoccupied Kokoda. Fly in reinforcements, including 2 Platoon and four detachments of mortars. Drome opened."

The opportunity afforded by his advice to reinforce Kokoda was lost that day. At dusk, the Japanese attacked in strength.

KOKODA—THE FIRST BATTLE

Lieutenant-Colonel Owen anticipated correctly that the Japanese would attack along the Mambare River and the Oivi track, so he prepared his main defensive positions on the plateau at the northern end, where the plateau narrows to an abrupt point, with steep slopes falling to the river. He protected his rear with a trench dug along the line of the rubber trees.

Approaching cautiously in the failing light, the enemy attacked with an estimated strength of 400 troops, but withdrew under the steady rifle-fire from the men along the top of the escarpment. Returning again after nightfall, the Japanese tried to climb the escarpment on to the point of the plateau, without gaining ground. Their mortars, emplanted across the Mambare, bombarded the plateau, and they renewed the attack under the covering fire of their Jukis.

The grenades and savage fire pouring down from the plateau halted the Japanese momentarily, before they pressed forward again, clinging precariously to the slope, winning a piecemeal yard of cover, and falling back. The Japanese commander committed more troops and added an infantry support gun to the bombardment.

A chance enemy bullet at this stage of the battle hastened the end. It mortally wounded Owen as he threw a grenade from a trench at the point of the plateau where the fighting was heaviest. Owen fell back into the trench. He died while the Japanese swarmed over the plateau and the Australians withdrew up the hill-side. Owen's command of the 39th Battalion lasted no more than twenty-two days, yet he left with his men an indelible impression of courage and determination that inspired them in their ordeal by battle until Papua was won again for Australia.

The most graphic description of this first Battle of Kokoda lies in the pages of Doctor Vernon's personal diary. Acute deafness and advancing years never impaired his sharp impressions and keen memory.

"The night of the 28th and the early morning of the 29th of July will not easily fade from my memory," he wrote. "Kokoda is approached from a range through a grove of rubber trees about three-quarters of a mile in depth. The rubber trees, as deeply shaded as a natural forest, suddenly give way to the grass and gardens of the station…

"On arrival, I reported to the 39th Battalion and then inspected and arranged the police house, which had been converted into the RAP. In front of this was a large scorched area, where a quantity of Army and Canteen stores had been burnt before the withdrawal on the 26th. Our Angau OC took me at dusk into the HQ kitchen and gave me a very solid meal. I was tired after the forced march from Efogi, and want of sleep the night before at Deniki, and I said I would have a rest in Graham's house near the RAP, arranging to be called for the first casualty. I selected a lounge and lay down, in company with a fine ginger cat whose acquaintance I had already made when visiting the Grahams eight months previously. I fed the cat with pieces of scone. He seemed hungry and grateful for the snack, and nestling up against me, we both fell asleep. I hung my last few remaining treasures on a hook, where I could grab them in an emergency, but eventually I had to leave them there. When the time came to retrieve them, it was too late to enter the house, as it was being riddled with bullets from a Jap machine-gun, posted just below it on the upper slope of the escarpment.

"Dusk fell early, a grey, misty, cheerless evening though the moon was at the full. Jap scouts had already been reported, and about 7.30, cat-calls and a stray mortar shot or so came ringing across the Mambare. Thereafter, there was increasing noise and salvoes of firing, mostly I think, from the Japs, who had a big mortar with them, at shorter and shorter intervals. By midnight, the firing on both sides had become almost continuous. It was warm and comfortable in the lounge, and I slept secure in the knowledge that I would be called when wanted.

"About one o'clock on the 29th a hand touched my shoulder. It was Brewer, with news that Colonel Owen had been wounded. The moon was now in full strength, and shone brightly through the white mountain mist as I hurried with Brewer past the old magistrate's house, now the HQ, where we picked up a stretcher and several bearers.

"We crept down a shallow communication trench leading forward to a firing pit at the very edge of the escarpment. The CO was propped up in the narrow space, struggling violently yet more than semi-conscious, quite unable to realize where he was, or to help us get him out. Removal was difficult, but we got him on to the stretcher at last and carried him to the RAP where Wilkinson* was waiting with a lantern, and the instruments laid out for operating. Lieutenant-Colonel Owen had received a single GSW** at the outer edge of the right frontal bone just above the eyebrows. There appeared to be no wound of exit, and a little bleeding was controlled by gauze packing. Skull and brain had, of course, been penetrated. He was now quite unconscious, with occasional convulsive seizures which lessened as he grew weaker. At the time of our withdrawal he had become quite still, and was on the point of death. He probably did not survive another fifteen minutes.

"Major Watson came in to see him, and then we had four or five casualties in rapid succession who, when dressed, were told to get back to Deniki as soon as they could. Wilkinson held the lantern for me, and every time he raised it, a salvo of machine-gun bullets was fired at the building. This particular enemy machine-gun was as yet a little below the edge of the escarpment, probably just behind Graham's back premises, so its range was bound to be too high, and while

---

*WO John Wilkinson.

**T Gun-shot wound.

the roof was riddled, those working below could feel reasonably safe. I was very glad to have Jack Wilkinson with me. He had been an old friend on Misima, and thanks to his experience in Greece and Crete, I felt every confidence in him. There are many Angau men who treated me with the utmost kindness and consideration during the whole campaign, always ready to shield me from any personal danger or discomfort, and I am glad to be able to acknowledge their care.

"We had now evacuated our walking wounded, and there was a lull in our work. Presently, Wilkinson came bursting into the RAP and said that an order for all to retreat at once had been given. I spoke of returning to Graham's house for my bag, but already it was a death-trap, and I was advised to let the Japs have my things. Before leaving, I spent some five or ten minutes in the RAP during which we fixed up Colonel Owen, who was now dying as comfortably as possible moistening his mouth and cleaning him up. Then I stuffed our operating instruments and a few dressings into my pocket, seized the lantern, and went out towards the rubber. The rest of the medical equipment had to be abandoned, but it was not very extensive, and I think we saved all the instruments.

"Outside, the mist had grown very dense, but the moonlight allowed me to see where I was going. Thick white streams of vapour stole between the rubber trees, and changed the whole scene into a weird combination of light and shadow. The mist was greatly to our advantage; our own line of retreat remained perfectly plain, but it must have slowed down the enemy's advance considerably, another chance factor that helped to save the Kokoda force. After a hasty look round the almost deserted plateau, I walked into the rubber. The firing was still heavy, coming, I suppose, from the Japs, as many of our men had left. I stayed awhile on the edge of the rubber, hoping to strike someone in authority, but as all the men were hurrying out to Deniki, I slowly followed them.

"I had not gone far before I felt uneasy at leaving the combat area while any troops who might have been wounded remained there. In the 1914–18 Sinai campaign, it was dinned into me that the place of the MO was at the tail of a retreating column, in company with the Second-in-Command. I had many a scramble over the sandhills with two or three AMC men, and no one else between us and the Turks, and usually found such hurried escapes somewhat exhilarating. Hence, at Kokoda, where my orders had been second-hand, I thought on reflection that I should remain for a while, at least till I had met some responsible officer, and I called to several withdrawing parties to ask if there were any officers amongst them. The men seemed neither to know, or greatly to care; their orders to leave had been definite enough, and they were carrying them out. By now, I had gone nearly half a mile through the rubber, and I turned back and hid behind the trunk of a tree just at the edge of the Kokoda clearing, in sight of the RAP and the station garden. The firing had almost died down, and the parties making for the hills were smaller and came less frequently. Finally, after a long period, during which no one passed and I was beginning to think I had better leave too, Major Watson, in company with Lieutenant Brewer and a couple of officers of the 39th passed along the track. I felt considerably relieved, and leaving my hiding place, called to Watson, who said, 'Come on, we are the last out.' Actually, two men followed us a little later. I heard afterwards that the station was then full of Japs, but in the mist, I recognized none, nor was I molested in any way.

"The Major sent Brewer on ahead, and walked very leisurely through the plantation. At the time, his dawdling walk rather mystified me, but I put it down to his being very tired. This was not the case. Later, he explained that he had dallied purposely to see that all the men got out, and his subsequent good spirits as we got well away from the battle area showed me he had not turned a hair over the night's events. A mile and a half along the track, we passed Skinner's signal post. This had been hurriedly evacuated, and several boxes of soldiers' treasures lay open and abandoned. I was told to help myself, and thus only an hour or two later, I more or less made up my involuntary gift to some Jap or other in Kokoda.

"Dawn on the 29th found us approaching the foothills and when it was full daylight, we passed a detachment acting as rearguard. This party, I believe, was unmolested for two or three days, and then fell back on Deniki. At 9 a.m., we reached our assembly point at Deniki. On arrival, I checked off our wounded from Kokoda, finding several who had not gone through the RAP. One man had a bullet lying superficially over the knee, so we laid him down on the track and removed it under a local anaesthetic. Then we had a meal and a rest, and thus ended the retreat from Kokoda. Apparently everyone was accounted for, as regards the Army, but I still had one worry on my mind—what had become of my pal, the ginger cat?

"Looking back on the Japanese assault on Kokoda, I can now see that by withdrawing, we took the wisest course. That we were considerably out-manned by the enemy was only too certain; we had but about ninety combatants, not counting a detachment of the PIB, whereas the Japanese force was variably estimated at from three hundred to five hundred men. Besides this advantage in numbers, they had others, particularly in that our line of retreat was practically undefended, and open to them had they worked around to our rear. In that case, the entire force would have been surrounded, and capture or death the fate of every individual. By withdrawing in good time, we saved men who later held up the Japs till reinforcements arrived, a very good example of the military axiom that the only conclusive victory consists in the complete annihilation of enemy forces.

"Our casualties amounted to one killed; one, I believe, missing—a man named Maloney posted on the right flank—and about seven or eight wounded. This trifling loss may indicate a somewhat brief resistance, but there was no reason to wait till more were killed. The result must have been the same in any case—retreat, and when that was cut off, annihilation.

"I was told that the Japs fell freely as they stormed the escarpment, but that there were too many of them to account for all. Their casualties must have been far heavier than ours—this was the case throughout the Owen Stanley campaign—and I was given different accounts of thirty to seventy killed during the assault.

"Taking it all round, though our early retreat prevented full resistance, the results could hardly have been bettered.

"Setting aside small clashes around Sangara, and the more extensive delaying actions at Wire Rope and Oivi, the assault on Kokoda can be called the first pitched battle on Papuan soil. It was an experience I would not have cared to miss, and among the impressions of that exciting night, none stands out more clearly than the weirdness of the natural conditions—the thick white mist dimming the moonlight, the mysterious veiling of trees, houses and men, the drip of moisture from the foliage, and at the last, the almost complete silence, as if the rubber groves of Kokoda were sleeping as usual in the depths of the night, and men had not brought disturbance."

The two men mentioned by Vernon who overtook the officers in the plantation were Pte. "Snowy" Parr, a Brenn-gunner in 16 Platoon, and Pte. "Rusty" Hollow, a lad acting as Parr's, "offsider." Parr bestowed his respect in the battalion on a limited field—Owen, Sergeant Morrison, and his Bren-gun.

From his position alongside Owen, Parr swept the escarpment with bursts of fire during the worst of the fighting, and a cold rage moved him when Owen fell back, mortally wounded, into the trench. Until the withdrawal began, the fighting was too close and too general for Parr to particularize in his vengeance. Then, retiring slowly with Hollow as the enemy came over the far side of the escarpment, he crossed the plateau unnoticed, to find a group of perhaps fifteen Japanese celebrating their victory on what once had been Brewer's lawn. From a range of less than sixty yards, he expended a full Bren magazine on the group, keeping his trigger finger hard against the metal, directing the muzzle accurately on to the Japanese so that none would survive, nor any round be wasted.

When the muzzle spat out the last round, Parr turned and spoke, "Come on, Rusty." Without haste, almost satisfied, he walked into the shelter of the rubber plantation, with Hollow silent at his side.

Vernon's estimate of Australian casualties is short of the true figure. Apart from Owen, the official record shows six men missing and presumed dead; one who died of wounds, and five wounded. Fourteen others originally reported missing were eventually recovered. This one inaccuracy in Vernon's moving narrative of the Battle of Kokoda may perhaps be attributed to his deafness.

Until Dean arrived with C Company, the 39th Battalion had five officers and 67 other ranks to hold Deniki. At 7 am. on 29th July, Captain Stevenson reported by signal to Port Moresby: "Kokoda lost from this morning. Blow the drome and road east of Oivi. Owen mortally wounded and captured. Templeton missing." Two hours after Stevenson sent this message, the GHQ communique issued in Brisbane announced: "Gona—Allied ground patrols attacked and drove back the enemy from his advance outpost positions." Twenty-four hours later, such were the intricacies of military censorship, the only reference to North-Eastern Papua in the communiqué stated: "Kokoda—Allied and enemy forward elements engaged in skirmishes in this area," and correspondents, still unaware of the loss of Kokoda, were permitted to speculate on its strategic importance.

Two Japanese documents, captured some months later, provide other glimpses of the battle. A "Report from the Front Line" declared that "No. 1 Company Commander—1st Lieutenant Yukio Ogawa was killed in action. The Australians left forty dead." A methodical officer of the 3rd (Kuwada) Battalion, 144th Regiment, 2nd Lieutenant Hidetaka Noda, after noting the weather, "Overcast, occasionally fine," quotes a report received at Rabaul: "In the Kokoda area, our Advance Force has been engaged in battle with 1,200 Australians, and has suffered unexpectedly heavy casualties…

Stalingrad—The Story of the Battle
(from *Stalingrad: Point of Return*)

Ronald Seth

When Hitler had marched into Poland, Vyacheslav Mikhailovich Molotov had made a speech which was broadcast throughout the length and breadth of the Union of Soviet Socialist Republics. In Stalingrad the people had gathered in the Square of 9th January to listen to it. Russia, they had heard him say, had no intention of going to war with anyone. If any assurance were needed the Non-Aggression Pact just signed with National-Socialist Germany, Russia's greatest ideological enemy, gave ample proof of the Soviet Union's peaceful intentions. The people of Stalingrad, like the people of the rest of Russia, had believed him, and had settled down to their own peaceful lives, from time to time indulging a new pastime—that of standing on the side-lines watching the German fascists and the western bourgeoisies trying to cut each other's throats. Even when it looked as if the detested Hitler was winning easily, no one was greatly perturbed, for not even Hitler would be mad enough to attack mighty Mother Russia.

So when, without warning, on 22nd June, 1941, Hitler did prove that he was certifiably insane, all the Russian people were taken by surprise, and none more so than the inhabitants of Stalingrad. But surprise was quickly translated into apprehension as the German armies penetrated one hundred, two hundred, three hundred miles towards the heart of Russia in an unbelievably few short weeks, rolling back the Red Army before them as though it were a roll of carpet, repeating the pattern of German invincibility first fashioned in the west.

However, not merely the Red Army was involved. Every Russian—man, woman and child old enough to walk—was involved. It was not a way of life that was at stake, nor fear of a foreign master, nor the Constitution, nor what the Kremlin stood for, that inspired the resistance of two hundred million Russians. The source of their inspiration was the fact that the very soil of Holy Russia, the actual physical soil, had been desecrated by alien feet, who trod it not in peace but in enmity.

It is difficult for the western mind to apprehend exactly the motives which impelled the Russians to defend their country as they did. We in the west gave everything we could to help our country ward off the same invader, not because we loved just this side of the lakes of Cumberland, the Downs of Sussex, the Highlands of Scotland, the rich black earth of the Fens, the Yorkshire Moors, the plot of land behind our house we call our garden, the geraniums in our window-boxes. We joined the Services, we worked at unaccustomed factory benches, we parted from homes and families, we offered and gave our lives, because we valued freedom of conscience, freedom of religion, freedom of thought, liberty of action within certain well-defined limits, in fact, all the nebulous indefinable things which make up our way of life and to which we have given the name democracy. We fought to preserve institutions rather than some physical concrete object which we could touch and see. It is not to be denied that something of the same motives activated the Russians, but these primary sources of inspiration with us were secondary considerations with them. Not even the houses that stood on the land, nor the crops that grew out of the land, nor the ore that was dug out of the land, nor the machinery made out of the ore were so precious that they could not be destroyed, if need be, without a qualm; but the soil of Mother Russia must remain inviolate.

That, of course, meant fighting, ruthless fighting with no quarter given and none expected; and it meant that every soldier must be supported by every man, woman and child who did not bear arms. The soldiers must be given food, they must be clothed, they must be given arms.

To the people of Stalingrad it meant tanks to protect the soldiers and to destroy the enemy, and lorries to carry them to the front and to take them food and clothing and ammunition. The Tractor Factory began modifications on 25th June, 1941, to transform the tractor-producing assembly lines into tank-producing lines. Work was carried out at such speed that by mid-July a steady stream of tanks was leaving the factory for the fronts. The motor-car factory had made a similarly rapid change-over and soon heavy army lorries and other essential vehicles were being added to the contribution of tanks. But as yet, despite the rate of the German advances on all sectors of the front, the battle itself was hundreds of miles from Stalingrad. Proud and defiant by the broad waters of the Volga, on the very frontier between Europe and Asia, the city felt itself secure. The armchair strategists explained away the speed of the German advances in the only terms patriots might use without being accused of creating alarm and despondency.

"It's plain enough what the High Command are doing," they said. "They are falling back like this to entice the Germans on, until their lines of communication are stretched to breaking point. Stalin's scorched-earth policy is all part of the plan. By destroying everything in the path of the oncoming armies our men force them to rely on their own supplies which have to be brought up all the way from Germany. There aren't half enough railways to provide all the supplies and reinforcements such armies need, and when autumn comes the roads will be out of commission, too, on account of the mud. By the time the mud freezes with the winter frosts our people will have regrouped, and before the Germans can bring up what they need our men will attack and destroy them wherever they can find them."

It was comforting talk, even if one did wonder why the Germans did not see that they were being led into a trap. Even when Leningrad was surrounded and when the German armies advanced with frightening speed on Moscow, and Field-Marshal von Rundstedt's panzers took Rostov, there was still no need for alarm. And when Marshal Timoshenko's armies in the centre suddenly turned on von Bock in September and forced the Germans on to the defensive, the pundits could say: "We told you, so!" though, since they did not know the true position, they could not explain that the Marshal's strategy was not identical with theirs.

Even when German aircraft made their first bombing attack on the city in October 1941, the Stalingraders were not unduly perturbed. In fact, it gave them a kind of inner warmth—they were now actively involved in the fighting. Their factories were making a contribution to the Russian war effort which was hardly bettered by any other city with identical resources, so it was perfectly natural that the Germans should try to destroy the factories and kill the people. Besides, if what they achieved on this first raid was the best they could do, clearly they had been grossly overrated, for not a single factory was hit. Dwelling-houses and a kindergarten were destroyed, though no airman had ever wished for bigger and better targets than the Dzerzhinsky Tractor Factory, the Red October Factory and the oil refinery, conspicuous with its squat rotund storage-tanks reflected in the very waters of the Volga. "Prestige raid," the armchair pundits called it. "They want to make their people think they have got to the boundary of Asia."

It was the coldest winter Leningrad and Moscow had experienced for a long time. Even down in Stalingrad it was colder than usual. But the production lines in the factories did not falter; non-stop, manned by men and women for twenty-four hours a day, seven days a week—how many days a month? why bother to count?—they turned out the tanks and the lorries, the weapons and the ammunition and sent them off to the front.

But when the spring came the Germans started coming forward again. No one could tell exactly where they were eventually making for yet. It might be the south, where the oil was, though Hitler would gain much greater prestige if he succeeded in doing what Napoleon had failed to do—capture Moscow.

In May 1942 German aircraft began to visit Stalingrad again. The raids were not exceptionally heavy and though they did some damage it was not critically serious, but they were frequent now. At first the people hurried to the shelters as soon as the sirens of the Volga ferries gave the warning. But this slowed down production, which was what the Germans wanted as the next best thing to destroying a plant. Somehow a way had to be found which would protect the bulk of the people and at the same time not stop the machines. The men of the Tractor Factory found the answer. They set aside temporarily one of the smaller shops and soon were producing reinforced steel pill-boxes large enough to take one man. A heavy steel door swung to when the man had stepped inside, and through a narrow hooded slit in it he would watch the machines which were now left running instead of being turned off. One of these pill-boxes was placed at all strategic points throughout the factory, and men were detailed to stay with them when the bombs began to fall on the factory itself, for now the workers remained at the benches and by the machines until the danger warning was given. In this way much time was saved, and though some production was still lost, it was only a fraction of what the losses had formerly been; and this procedure was adopted in all factories producing war materials.

Then when the Germans started their offensive in June the people of Stalingrad still did not expect to see anything of them except their aircraft. The fighting was still 125 miles away to the east, and was not the Don, almost as mighty a river as the Volga and a defence barrier that would take some breaching, between the fighting and the city, and was not the general direction of the German advance north-eastwards towards Moscow?

Then quite suddenly even the armchair strategists changed their tune. Whichever way the Germans went now, Stalingrad must be threatened, for they could never leave such a strong-point on one or other of their flanks.

By mid-July the German intention had become a certainty. The German Fourth Panzer Army had crossed the Don and reached the heights of Kotelnikovo, and its spearhead, instead of pointing south, as though to protect the flank of First Panzer Army, was pointing north, and obviously coming up towards Stalingrad. Not only that, German activity in the great bend of the Don seemed to indicate the probability of a drive being made across the river, and that could only be interpreted to mean one thing—a full attack on Stalingrad.

Once it became obvious that the city might soon be in dire danger, the Soviet Government lost no time in preparing it and its people to withstand any assault which might be launched against it. What was called the Stalingrad Front was formed, with the Russian Sixty-second, Sixty-fourth and Fifty-seventh Armies under the command of General Yeryomenko.

At the same time a City Defence Council was set up under the leadership of Chuyanov, chairman of the Party Committee. This Council organised the civilians of Stalingrad, and liaised closely with the Military Council of the Commander-in-Chief. In the Red Army, in units above division level, authority had always been vested in a Military Council which was normally composed of three men: one, the Commanding General; two, his Chief of Staff; and three, a gentleman always referred to in Russian as "The Member of the Military Council." Before the War, the Member of the Military Council was always a highly trusted member of the Communist Party, and he stood in relation to the Commanding General as the Political Commissar stood to the C.O. in lower units. This form of dual control gradually tended to disappear during the War, and the Member of the Military Council more often than not filled the role of Deputy to the Commanding General dealing mainly with political and strategic questions rather than being involved with tactics.

With regard to the Member of the Military Council in Stalingrad, history repeated itself once more. In 1918, no one, even those in the inner conclaves of the Party, had an inkling that Stalin, who had filled this position in this place then, would rise to the supreme position in Russia after the death of Lenin; in 1942, no one could have guessed that the Member of the Military Council, Nikita Kruschev, would succeed Stalin on the same pinnacle of power.

Marshal Timoshenko, who had so successfully brought pressure to bear on Field-Marshal von Back's armies in the September and October of the previous year, was no longer able to hold the greatly reinforced Germans. Fighting fierce delaying actions with comparatively small forces, he withdrew the bulk of his men across the Don, across the steppes and across the Volga, there to reorganise and re-equip them. The longer he delayed the German advance, the more men would he save for another day, and the longer would Stalingrad be safe.

But it could not be long before the attack was launched, and everything that could be done for the defence of the city must be done with all speed. It was decided that an anti-tank trench must be dug, and at first workers in non-essential industries, those, that is, not engaged in war production, and office workers were organised into labour battalions under the direction of military commanders. Such soldiers of Yeryomenko's city defence as could be spared were also set to work digging; but they were slow at the work, protesting they would rather fight any day than dig. So the colleges and schools were closed and all students, boys and girls above the age of twelve, and all men and women who could be released from their normal work, whatever it was, were given spades and forks and picks and buckets and asked to dig.

The response of the civilian population was one of the many miraculous factors which contributed to the Russian defence of Stalingrad. The main anti-tank trench, fifteen feet deep and twelve feet wide, was to stretch from the Tractor Factory in the extreme northern suburb, along the western boundary of the city, to the ravine at Beketovskaya in the south. From the Tractor Factory to Beketovskaya is twenty-five miles; only the ten southernmost miles of the city's entire length were not protected by the great ditch.

In itself the digging of this trench was a wonder. The people of Stalingrad, from young boys and girls to old men and ancient crones, dug with pick and fork and shovel, dug deep and piled up the earth on the westward edge of the trench.

There were not enough tools to go round, but that did not matter. The organisation was such that as soon as a worker paused for a second to wipe the sweat from his brow or ease an aching back his tool was snatched from him and a fresh digger took his place. In two weeks the great ditch was completed.

While this main work was going on, other much shorter stretches of trenches were being dug at salient points, and barricades were being erected across the western mouths of streets. In the central and northern sectors of the city, that is, in the new city, which had sprung up over the old Tsaritsyn since 1927, the lay-out had been as regular as the planning of Manhattan's financial section. By that I mean that though many of the streets were set obliquely to the river—contrary to the layout of the post-war Stalingrad—they were straight and broad. At the western limit old carts and sandbags and above all the precious proud trees of the streets and the courtyards were piled across the entrances, and by the time all were closed in this way the city was sealed off against all normal intruders from the west. Other barricades were also erected in the depths of the city, so that if the first line were breached there could be no forward surge of the enemy which would press back the defenders by the sheer weight of its impetus.

Behind these defence works were posted the men of General Chuikov's understrength Sixty-second Army. (Shumilov with the Sixty-fourth and Tolbukhin with the Fifty-seventh were away to the south-western approaches.) Their backs were to the Volga, over which there has never been and still is not a bridge of any sort by which they might retreat. They had one order: to prevent the Germans from capturing the city. If they could not do that they must die where they stood or throw themselves into the river.

Behind Sixty-second Army stood all the men of Stalingrad and many of the women, too. In late June all the healthy males of the city from fifteen to fifty years of age had been registered, called up and organised into military units. Some were given uniforms, but the majority of them had only armbands. Even before the digging of the trenches began and the barricades were erected, the men who had been organised started work on other types of defences. These were mostly dug-in tanks, that is to say, tanks buried in holes in the ground with only their turrets and guns exposed. Sometimes they would be covered with a shell of concrete before the earth was replaced over them, though even just a covering of earth made them extremely effective strong-points if their siting had been expertly done.

During this period of making preparations, apart from the strange work they were called upon to do, the people of Stalingrad began to experience a totally new way of life. The men already allotted their units, and the units given their tasks to perform, assumed at once the separation from their families and homes which is normally caused by military service. They were fed by the authorities and they slept wherever they happened to find themselves when the time came for sleeping. In the northern and central sectors more often than not it was in the streets or in the courtyards of the flats. Fortunately it was summer time with even the night-temperatures well above a hundred degrees Fahrenheit, and the likelihood of rain extremely remote. In the south, where the wooden one-storey houses of the old Tsaritsyn still stood in apparent disorder among a maze of deep-rutted, dirt-surfaced lanes, the surrounding fields were thicker with men than with grass during the dark hours. Nor was it merely the husbands whom the wives and mothers did not see for days at a time. Their sons and daughters might be digging or building the crazy-looking defence walls in some alien part of the city and they, too, getting food wherever it was obtainable, slept at night wherever they happened to be when sleep overtook them. Many of the younger ones were taken into nearby flats and given mattresses and cushions or a space on the bare floors of sitting-room or kitchen, but the majority slept in the courts under the trees and in the squares under the stars.

The atmosphere in which all this was carried out was unreal, tense and very brittle. Those in authority urged all to their work with words of encouragement and patriotic slogans. Perhaps one of the reasons why revolutions have been so few among the English-speaking peoples is because English is so matter-of-fact, so uninflammatory that the words needed to suspend the reason of rabbles are entirely lacking. The Romance languages, on the other hand, have not this disability, and the Slavonic languages seem to have been invented for the purpose of expressing or arousing the most intimate emotions without embarrassing either oneself or ones hearers. The constant exhortations of the leaders added to the natural national and civic patriotism of the Stalingraders was more than enough to stimulate to tremendous physical efforts every man, woman and child in the city, and to raise their morale and imbue them with a determination to resist the enemy when he came at all costs, even of life itself.

Outwardly, then, there was confidence and defiance, though the excitement, which was inevitable among adults and young alike, tended to undermine the eventual degree of effectiveness. But underneath the outward courage there was also fear and a shaken morale which had affected the soldiers as well as the civilians. Indeed, it has been expressed to me recently in Stalingrad by people who went through the battle that the morale of the soldiers was much lower than that of the civilians at the beginning.

"It was natural that this should be so, I think," Andrei Galishev said to me. "You see, the soldiers knew what the advances of the Germans really meant; that the Germans had better and more numerous weapons than we had, and that their soldiers were much more highly trained. Our armies had *fallen back*, had been pushed back, a very long way; and the enemy armies had *advanced* just that same distance. When you go on retreating for hundreds and hundreds of miles you must sometime begin to get despondent. Lots of our soldiers in Stalingrad, though they were prepared to fight until they had given their last drop of blood, believed that they would never be able to hold the city. Well, if you think those things, whether you whisper them to your bosom friend or keep them strictly to yourself, some of your potential as a soldier is taken away. There was another thing, too, which disturbed many secretly, and it applied to civilians as well as soldiers. This was the terrible brutality with which the Germans treated prisoners of war and our civilians. Soldiers who had come from the west, where we had retreated first and then advanced a little and retreated again, brought terrible stories of men beaten up until they died, little twelve-year-old girls raped, young men sexually mutilated—this was a form of sport for the German soldiers—and multiple gallows by the roadsides bearing our men and our women hanging side by side, young and old alike. Now and again, too, a prisoner of war had escaped and the stories they had to tell of the treatment they received from the Germans were so horrible that they turned your stomach upside down. These stories were true, but even had they not been, the best they could have been in the minds of the people were exaggerations. Once stories like this begin to circulate, though they may be so wild as to seem patently untrue, something of them lingers in the mind. Courage is unsettled then, and it takes longer to get used to being brave."

But whatever happened, whether schools or offices or shops were closed, or ditches were dug or barricades raised, or you slept on the kitchen floor of somebody else's house or a strange courtyard under the stars, you worked to the limit of your powers to defend the city, and if you were making tanks or heavy lorries or guns or ammunition, you doubled your efforts, and at the same time prepared for the future.

In the Tractor Factory, for example, the workers were organised into armoured battalions, and raised a complete regiment. When they were not making tanks they were learning to drive the tanks they made and to fire the guns and to know the tactics of mobile warfare. What they did in the Tractor Factory they did elsewhere. In the Red October Factory the women workers formed themselves into a so-called brigade under the command of Sergeant Kovalova, who was to meet her death at the head of her "men" when she led them out to the defence of her factory.

By the end of July it was clear that the German offensive against the city could not be long in coming. The very old, it was decided, and the very young, where the mother could be spared by the rest of her family to go with them, should be evacuated from the city across the Volga. This was not easy to propose nor to accomplish, for the old people were strongly attached to their city, and the mothers of the very young were afraid that if they were separated from the rest of their families they might never find one another again; and the authorities were hard put to it to know what to do with them once they were across the great river. On the east bank of the Volga just here the naked steppe looks like the edge of the world. For miles upon miles there are no rivers, no towns, nothing; and to get them away from this void, nothing could be spared them but their own old and tired legs to carry them under the scorching summer sun to the nearest little town many miles away to the north-east out of the way of the bombs and from under the feet of the defenders.

This first evacuation was a limited movement. It had to be. So as the days of August slipped by, and the tension mounted, and the life of the city changed every hour, you began to wish something would happen; either that Tomoshenko and his men would hold the Germans on the other side of the Don, though you knew that could not happen without a miracle, or that the German would come to your city so that he could be sent staggering back.

But then news reached the city that a German tank army had come up to within eighteen miles in the south. The city authorities called the people together in the afternoon of 22nd August to tell them and to urge them to remain calm. The attack would come very soon now. Exactly when, it was difficult to say. It might be tomorrow; it might be the day after, or the day after that. But whenever it came, let them not panic whatever happened; both the Army and the city had everything in hand.

The exhortation came not a day too soon, for the day the Germans had chosen was tomorrow. Almost before it was light on 23rd August, high above the city, so high that the eastern rising sun made them look like a cloud of silver dust no bigger than a man's hand, Junkers of German VIII Air Corps came over the city and before you could turn your eyes away to shade them, the earth seemed to be leaping up to the sky, and the noise in your ears threatened to burst open your skull.

THE ASSAULT BEGINS

No one in Stalingrad could say with certainty how many German aeroplanes came over the city and dropped their bombs that day. They came with the first morning light, and with hardly a pause they droned over the city until nightfall, and after nightfall, still they came. Some of the Russian air-observer corps insist that on 23rd August, 1942, the Germans flew over two thousand sorties to the city in the hours of daylight alone.

As the sun came up over the eastern steppes of Asia on the other side of the river, the stifling night gave way to a burnished, breathless day, and through the shimmering heat, with a whistling rush of terrified air, the bombs rained down and shook the earth to the skies. Never before had so many German aircraft come to the city at one time, nor had so many bombs been dropped. In the same way that the artillery barrage in the Kaiser's War had heralded an imminent attack, so this attack from the air was the signal that the assault on the city had begun. At least, so the Russians believed; and they were to be proved right.

The air-attack on Stalingrad on this and the two following days is in some way comparable with the destruction of Rotterdam on 14th May, 1940, but with this difference—only the centre of the Dutch city was razed, whereas scarcely a single quarter of Stalingrad escaped. The German's chief aim was to create panic among the civilian population and by so doing impede all the attempts of the military to function effectively. Though from the ground it appeared at the time as if the Richthofen squadron—Colonel-General Baron von Richthofen, the most outstanding Luftwaffe leader of the War, was commanding Fourth Air Fleet, whose VIII Air Corps was supporting Sixth Army—were dropping their bombs haphazardly, when the damage was plotted on a map it could be seen that Stalingrad was being annihilated according to a plan. The main point of effort was directed initially at the residential and administrative sectors. There was little sense in attacking those industries you hoped to turn to your own good account when you had captured the city. Nevertheless, despite the intention, the human element varied the results. If at first bombs fell on factories and other industrial undertakings by mistake, in a week or two there would be no discrimination, for by then the city had to be taken even if it were only a heap of rubble and stinking, grotesquely maimed corpses.

On the shore of the river almost exactly opposite the centre stood a field of oil-storage tanks, and it was not long before German bombs had hit the tanks. The city was already burning, but now the dense black smoke of oil was adding its pall to the thick canopy of smoke and dust and quivering heat haze which hung over the city. This smoke and dust blotted the sun for the most part completely from sight, though here and there, if you glanced up, you could see a strange extinguished moon of a sun which seemed to be cowering in pale stature behind the veil of awfulness. But beneath the smoke and through it fierce flames shot up so high that it seemed as if they were trying to escape by taking to the air. And the oil was running away, too, with a fat man's agility which surprises by its speed. The ground about the tanks sloped down to the river so gently that you scarcely noticed it. But the oil found the slope and let itself slip irresistibly down and into the river. Yet the water could not quench its flames. As more and more oil forced its way into the river it pushed the first rim farther and farther out into the middle stream, in a great blazing mass of flame which was carried by the currents here almost across the kilometre-wide Volga until it seemed that the Volga itself was on fire.

A small river-barge, one of the many which plied between city and city, bringing grain from Yenotaevsk to the people of Saratov and Kuibyshev, and taking back manufactured goods, had been damaged by a near-missing bomb which fell into the river and exploded not far from it. The engine had died of the shock and nothing that Andrei Parfenov could do would restore it to life. The boat meant livelihood to Andrei and for many years now he and it had worked together and become attached to one another. They had come to Stalingrad as soon as they had heard that the city was threatened because Andrei thought that they could be useful in such jobs as helping the old and the children across the river, thus relieving the ferries.

As he bent over the engine he could see nothing wrong, and yet it would not go. Cursing softly at it and then with increasing vigour, he unscrewed this and that, looked at it closely, blew on it and put it back, and tried again. But without result.

"Andrei! Andrei!" a voice almost shrill with scarcely controlled fear shouted down to him.

"What is it?" he called back impatiently.

Since he had come down to look at the engine he had left behind the pandemonium of whistling and exploding bombs, the crash of buildings and the cries of anxious men. Only now and again did a near or excessively loud noise impinge on his pre-occupation with the engine.

"What is it?"

"It's the river, Andrei," the voice shouted back. "The river's on fire."

"Talk sense, Matsve!" Andrei called. "I've worries enough without your lunacy."

"But it's true, Andrei!" Matsve insisted. "The oil is on fire and it's spread on to the river and the flames are coming this way."

"What's that?" Andrei looked up at the white face peering down at him, white even against the black and white picture framed in the hatch.

"The flames are coming this way quickly, I tell you."

Andrei, spanner still in hand, came quickly up the companion-way on to the deck. He looked across to the city and could not see it, only the great blanket of smoke and the tossing sheets of flame. The boy was right! The river was on fire, and the fire was spreading rapidly across the river to where he had moored his barge, a little east of mid-stream, until he could repair the engine.

"Can't you mend the engine?" Matsve asked.

"No…not yet. Can you swim?"

The boy nodded.

"It's a long way," Andrei pointed out.

"I can do it. But what about you?"

"It will be some time before the fire reaches here. I shall stay…"

"Then so shall I!"

Andrei made a little gesture of annoyance.

"Listen to what I've got to say, will you?" he snapped. "Swim ashore as quickly as you can and ask anyone who has a dinghy to lend it to you to come and fetch me off. I can't swim. Understand?"

"Yes, Andrei." Already the boy was pulling his shirt over his head. "Will you listen?" Andrei repeated. "If no one will lend you one, take the first you find. Be as quick as you can."

The boy stripped off his trousers, paused for a brief moment on the edge of the barge, then drawing in his breath he plunged head-first into the river. Andrei watched his slick, sun-darkened body sliding through the water for a dozen yards or so. The boy could swim like an eel. They all could these days; yet here he was, he'd lived on the river fifty years and by the river five before that and hadn't learned to swim. He wasn't the only one who made a living off the river who couldn't swim, but they were all born before the Revolution, when nobody took much notice of teaching children anything except how to work. It was a good thing he'd taken the boy aboard, and just as well that Vassiliev and Mosha were in the city, because they couldn't swim either. But what was he thinking? If anyone survived what was going on in the city, it would be a miracle!

He turned back and looked towards the great wall of flame and pall of smoke. The oil on the water was spreading out slowly, with the relentless forward creeping of lava. You could not see it move, and yet you could divine the perpetual motion of the flames.

He hoped the boy would waste no time. He swung round and looked towards the sandy east bank. The smoke from the burning oil was being driven across the river to the east by the light breeze which had been blowing almost constantly these last three weeks. Fortunately it was billowing obliquely across the wide water, and just on the clear northern edge of it he saw the shining body of Matsve wading ashore. The boy stood at the water's edge for a moment, looking back towards the barge and waving. Andrei waved back; the boy answered and then went scrambling up the bank on all fours and out of sight.

The difficulty which was facing Andrei derived in great part from the currents, which here flowed right into the path of the burning oil and carried it downstream and across the river. Now that he was without any means of motivation, if he pulled up his anchor, before he would know where he was he would be running right among the flames, which, in their turn, while being carried down-river were also spreading outwards with ever-extending perimeter like a grease-spot on flannel; so even if he stayed where he was it would not be long before they crept up on him.

The barge was empty and riding high in the water, for since he had only come down the river from Nikolayevskij, intending to take a shipment of cured hides on board at Stalingrad, it had not been worth while taking on ballast. If he had had a pole long enough he would have tried poling the barge to the other side of the river, provided the lightness of it had not allowed the stream to carry it too quickly down into the flames. The thought had occurred to him when he had sent the boy to fetch the dinghy that they might be able to tow the barge to safety—but, again, only if the stream were not too strong and the barge too light.

He glanced round to the east bank, but there was no sight of the boy. The heat from the leaping flames was now added to the heat of the smoke-hidden sun; but it was a particular heat, for he could feel the scorch of it on his cheeks. Supposing the boy couldn't find a dinghy? Then it would be all up, not only with the barge but with him, too. He was fond of the barge and would hate to lose her, she had been more than a good friend; but he wasn't going to let a silly sort of sentimentality make him take foolish risks. He was keen to go on living, even though he was over sixty. He liked being alive, and besides he could do his bit against—what did they call them?—the fascist barbarians, and if they went on behaving like this, Mother Russia would be wanting the help of every man she could lay hands on, whether boys like Matsve or ancients like himself. It had been a wonderful and beautiful city, and now, in the three or four hours since daybreak and the first enemy bombs had fallen, the fine, tall buildings had come tumbling down, filling the streets with debris, and under the smoke heavens knew what was happening. Now the enemy bombers were coming back again. You could hear them above the crackle of burning and the distance-muted shouts of men and the thunder-crackle of anti-aircraft guns. What were the Germans hoping to do? Destroy the city utterly and its people?

On the top of the east bank Matsve heard the dull drone of the German bombers, too, and paused in his scrambling, the soles of his feet tingling with the branding heat of the soft sand into which they sank over the ankles, to look across the river at the city. Into his mind came the same question as the one Andrei had asked himself. Yet, what good would a ruined city be to them? Not that they were ever going to capture the city. The people and the soldiers would see to that, and when he had rescued Andrei from the barge he was going to cross the river and go into the city and help them.

He looked at the near-edge of the river to the north, searching for a dinghy, but could not see one. There were two or three long-boats, used chiefly for ferry work on short distances, capable of carrying half a dozen people and their sacks and baskets and parcels, but requiring a small motor to propel them, or two or three men with oars. These were packed now with old people, women and children and the few pitiful belongings they had been able to snatch up in their flight from the city. One was already on its way back to the west bank, to fetch another load, Matsve supposed. They were going to save several lives. He could not ask one of them to go and rescue Andrei from his barge.

At that moment he heard a shrill woman's voice on the other side of him, to the south, and on the edge of the smoke-cloud he saw two women with four or five children, one of whom was coughing and being sick and crying all at the same time, while the others were carrying bundles and baskets up the bank from a rowing-boat. With a private cry of joy he ran obliquely down the bank to where one of the women and an older girl were unloading the boat.

"Is that your boat?" he asked.

Without stopping, the woman said: "It is ours. Why?"

"Please could you lend it to me?" he pleaded. "You see that barge out there in the middle of the river, near the burning oil? The engine's broken down, my friend is on board, an old man, but in any case he can't swim, and every minute the flames are getting nearer."

The woman looked out across the river, then turned her head back.

"Yes," she said simply. "You may have the boat, but it is too heavy for you to row on your own against the river. Anya will take an oar with you. Help us with these things, otherwise you will be too late to save your friend."

Within two or three minutes the last of the bundles had been removed from the boat.

"I can manage on my own," Matsve said to the fifteen- or sixteen-year-old girl.

"We shall get there quicker if I help you," the girl answered, sitting down and taking an oar.

Matsve pushed the boat off the sand and as it floated jumped in.

Sitting in front of the girl, he took up the other oar.

"Now, together—pull!" he called over his shoulder, as they came out into the stream. "You'll have to keep us on course."

On the barge Andrei had lost sight of the boy after answering his wave. There was nothing he could do, only hope that the burning oil would stay away from the barge until Matsve could get back. They would make an attempt to tow the barge to the east bank, but if the current was too strong, well—it would just have to take whatever came to it.

While he was waiting, he prepared a rope. One end he fixed to a cleat in the stern, and coiled the rest and put it down beside the cleat ready to throw into the dinghy. Another shorter length he fixed to a second cleat, and threw the running end over the side of the barge into the river. Down this rope he would slide into the dinghy—if Matsve could find one and if he arrived in time.

Over the city droned the German bombers, though you could not hear this noise now; it was drowned by the barking of the A-A guns and the whistle of bombs falling and the tremendous blasts of exploding bombs. The heat from the blazing oil was beginning to burn one's eyeballs; that was how near it was now. Matsve had to come soon or not at all.

Andrei turned away from the city and looked towards the east and his heart turned over.

"Row, boy! Row, daughter! You're doing fine!" he yelled.

Less than fifty strokes away was the big dinghy. He was saved! But only just, for as he shouted a billowing, acrid darkness swirled over him, and when it had cleared he saw flames dancing over the point of the bows. He ran to the side and looked down. The oil had come up to the barge now and the flames were lapping at it. It would be useless to try to save it. He heard Matsve calling out to him.

"The barge is alight!" the boy shouted.

"I know," Andrei shouted back. "Come under the stern; under this rope!"

The boy and girl manoeuvred the boat under the stern, and in no time at all the old man had lowered himself over the side of the barge and into it. Almost before he had righted himself Matsve and the girl were pulling away, and not until they were thirty or forty yards from the barge did they pause and sit looking at it as it blazed from end to end.

"Well-seasoned timber and many coats of pitch," Andrei commented. "That's why she burns so well."

"I read once in a book at school," Anya said, "that in the old times in one of the northern countries where the people were great sailors and sailed across the seas and conquered many countries…"

"I've read about them, too," Matsve said. "You mean the…the…Oh, I can't remember! But when their great chiefs died they put them in one of their long-boats and set fire to the boat. Why do you remember that?"

"The barge looks like such a boat, I imagine," the girl said. "I'm sorry for you, Comrade."

"She's been a good friend," Andrei said. "I shall miss her."

"Perhaps, when the war is over and the Germans have gone, they will give you another barge," the girl suggested.

"Perhaps…Well, let's get to the bank," Andrei said.

One of the women was with the children on top of the bank, but the other came down to the water's edge and held the bow steady while Anya, Matsve and old Andrei got out. When they had pulled the dinghy up on to the sand, she held out a pair of trousers to Matsve.

"You'll need these," she said. "I suppose you've left all your things in the barge."

For the first time Matsve realised that ever since he had gone into the water he had been naked. Under the skin of his cheeks the blood which rushed there heightened his tan. Turning to Anya he said: "I'm sorry. I was so anxious…"

"It's of no consequence," the woman said. "She has brothers. They're in the city. They would not come with us."

"I must go to the city, too," Matsve said. "They will need all the help we can give them."

"I shall come with you," Andrei said.

"I will row you over," Anya offered.

"No. It's not safe. Up there they are bringing people over in the little ferries and then going back to the city. We shall go back with them," Matsve answered.

"What will you do?" Andrei asked the woman.

"Try to find somewhere to live not too far away," the woman with the sick child said. "But what shall we do to find our husbands and our sons? Do you think we shall ever see them again?"

"Of course you will see them again," Andrei answered. "My advice is, go and join those people down there. If there is a crowd of people they must do something for them. Let us all go to them together."

Anya took the sick child from its mother, and Matsve walked beside her carrying a heavy bundle of belongings.

"Thank you for helping me," he said. "I hope we shall meet again some day."

"Yes," she replied. "I hope so."

But as their homes over the river buckled and burned under the enemy bombs their hopes could be little more than politenesses. Yet they did meet again and fifteen years later were telling their story to an Englishman in the sitting-room of their brand-new flat in the brand-new city of Stalingrad.

When Matsve and Andrei at last got back to the city, they found a strange and terrible confusion. Though the Germans had not created the panic they had planned, the weight and length of the bombing attacks had knocked the authorities off balance. They had not expected that the main attacks would be directed on the women and children in the residential quarters of the city, but rather in the northern suburbs. It was there that the majority of the anti-aircraft artillery had been sited. Though even then the A-A defences were nothing like so strong as they ought to have been; but if equipment just is not available, you have to make the best of what you have.

The people had been taken unawares by the first bombs. Most had believed that the first raid was merely a repetition of the raids on the industrial sector which the Germans had been making since the previous February, and scarcely anyone had bothered to go to the shelters. But as the second wave came in something seemed to tell the people that they were the chosen targets, and there was a scurrying rush for the cellars. Nevertheless, hundreds of women and children were killed and maimed before the survivors went underground for safety.

One of the great difficulties facing the military and civil authorities in Stalingrad was the almost complete absence of any air-warning system. The Germans were operating from airfields one hundred and two hundred miles away, and they were routed across almost empty steppe. There had been no time to erect forward warning stations, and, in any case, the military situation out in the steppe was extremely fluid, the Russian forces either fighting delaying actions or retreating. In such conditions it was not possible to plot aircraft and send back information. Almost the first news of the Germans' approach, therefore, was the sound of their engines followed by the quick sight of them.

In the circumstances the most satisfactory procedure would have been to keep the city under constant alert, since, though you knew the aircraft had gone when you could not hear them any more, you could not know when the next wave would come over. But how can you keep a city under constant alert, down in cellars which were never intended to be in any degree comfortable, nor equipped with any kind of conveniences? The people had to feed themselves and relieve themselves. In any case, so many were trapped and killed and injured, so many houses were heaps of rubble above the cellars, so many had lost all their belongings, including their food, that to have kept them shut up would have denied assistance to the helpless and suffering and those who could help themselves.

By the afternoon of the first day it was clear to the civilian authorities that all women and children and old men who could not be of any help would have to be evacuated. Where they would go no one had any idea, but the main thing was to get them out of the city and across the Volga. Once there it would be time enough to decide on the next step. Fortunately the city organisation for peacetime purposes was so good that very soon a plan had been worked out, and arrangements made for the first contingents to be shipped across the river before dawn next day.

Happily, though a large section of the city telephone network had been destroyed in the bombing, there was a telephone link with all of the local administrative centres. The word was passed to these, and the rest was done orally by the local officials. As a piece of *ad hoc* organisation it possessed that quality of native genius which was to stamp so much that the Russians did in their struggle against the Germans, not only here in Stalingrad—though here it was extremely marked—but everywhere else where Russians met Germans, and which very largely enabled the Russians to turn disaster into ultimate victory. When the Russo-German campaign opened, stories trickled through to us of German hilarity caused by the matchboard characteristics of Russian armour-plating and the primitive nature of Russian tanks. It is true that, compared with the German, or British, or French, Russian armour-plating was of inferior quality and their tanks were merely mobile engines mounted with guns lacking the thousand and one refinements which adorned Western tanks, most of which on the battle-field proved useless, and often an impediment. But the Russians had no time for refinements. They wanted tanks able to carry out the simple functions of tanks in modern warfare without any of the frills, and they built tanks which performed these functions. Many Russian tanks were knocked out but they also knocked out many of the enemy; and if many were knocked out the Russians did not mind all that much, for their production was more than double the German production, simply because the finish was less polished and the gadgets less numerous, though neither lack of polish nor gadgets detracted from the functions of the tank as the Russian experts saw the role of these machines. We English, too, pride ourselves on our ability to extemporise in times of crisis. We are justifiably proud of this knack—we may look upon Dunkirk as one of the supreme examples of this ability—but we shall delude ourselves if we believe that we are unique in our achievements in this field. Again and again on every sector of the Eastern Front the Russians proved they were our equals and often our masters in extemporisation, and here in Stalingrad they were to save their city very largely by the ability to adapt themselves to a kind of fighting quite unknown to them and by making use of every conceivable advantage that presented itself on the spur of the moment.

The heaviest raid of this first day came between two and three in the afternoon. The smoke of the burning buildings and the smoke from the oil-storage tanks still drew its veil across the blue of the sky. The fire-fighters were hampered by streets blocked by fallen houses and by lack of water, particularly in those parts of the city farthest from the river. In most cases there was little that could be done except let the burning buildings burn themselves out. But even when water was available in satisfactory quantities, the appliances were often inadequate to deal with the fierce intensity of the fires.

This was what happened when the dockyards caught fire during this raid. The yards were built chiefly of wood, and though the Volga lapped at the jetties and stocks and at the walls of dry-docks, it could do nothing to quell the fire, for the wood was old and seasoned and dry, and when it was attacked by flames it went up like the driest tinder, despite the efforts of the men there to pump up the river to quench the swiftly destroying flames. The men were standing by the pumps and the hoses when the bombs fell. Many of them were killed by the same bombs which set fire to the docks, and before their surviving companions could shake the dust out of their eyes and grasp their heads to stop the vibrations of the brain-cells which the noise and the blast had set up, the flames had taken such hold that the men were helpless.

All day long the voluntary evacuations, mostly of mothers with young children, had been going on, and since midday the larger ferries had been brought into use for this. Several naval monitors had also joined the few which had been at Stalingrad when the raids began. By chance entirely, for the German aircraft stayed high up above the city, a number of the ferries and the monitors received damage from bomb splinters and the blast from near-misses; and two monitors and three civilian boats were sunk by freak direct hits.

While this raid was going on news reached the military command of the situation out in the steppe, and word was sent to the northern sector, where the factories had been working more or less at the wartime normal, of the threat that was coming up on their northern flank. The main weight of the Russian defence was concentrated to the south, where the Fifty-seventh and Sixty-fourth Armies had gone out to meet the German Fourth Panzer Army, leaving General Chuikov and his Sixty-second Army to guard the city and the northern flank. There could be no possible doubt now that this was the beginning of the assault on the city, and it looked as if the German plan was to come into Stalingrad from the north, where the General would have to rely for the most part upon the workers in the factories to defend the factories and the streets while he moved his soldiers out into the steppe to ward off the blow as long as they could.

So in the mid-afternoon the first phase of defence was put into effect. The specified formations of civilians were instructed to report to their depots, where they were issued with rifles, ammunition and armbands.

It is not possible to appreciate the state of mind in which the men of Stalingrad went to the barricades that night. Duty demanded that they should not go to their homes to allay apprehensions concerning their families, but should stay at their posts conscious of other men's wives and children, brothers and sisters, fathers and mothers lying dead all round them and not knowing whether they themselves might not now be alone in the world. True, the bombs had begun to fall while they were on their way to work; but who was to tell them that this was not a raid like all the others, despite the unusual timing? And once at their bench or by their machine they could not go rushing home as the raid developed, to make sure their families were safe or to die with them. But the fate of their families and the ruin of their homes instilled in them an even greater determination to frustrate the fascist plans. Already men were saying: "We can build the city again, but we cannot refurbish honour"—wisely they did not say, "We can make other families to replace the old"—and every man vowed in his heart that if ever the city were taken it would be over his lifeless body.

Gone now, dispersed by the brutal destruction of this one day, was the belief that the Germans were so superior as to be invincible. By attempting to destroy morale Hitler had restored it to full vigour.

As the afternoon light flickered into the indeterminate half-light of dusk the General's soldiers sent back the news that the Germans had reached the Volga to the north of the city. They were only mobile columns, however, and neither so numerous nor so strong that they could not be held out of the city should they attempt to attack before reinforcements of tanks or infantry arrived.

The news was both surprising and reassuring: surprising that these forces should have crossed the steppe so easily, and reassuring because any imminent attack by these forces could be decisively in their favour. But in getting where they had, the Germans had not had it entirely their own way. The General's men had stood in their way and his tanks had given battle. Many of those tanks would never fight again, nor would their crews; but many were crippled, yet still had fight in them. When the light had failed to such an extent that it was dangerous trying to distinguish friend from enemy, the crippled hobbled back to the city and to the factory from which they had emerged in shining eagerness only a day or two before. From this first day they formed a habit in which they were to persist so long as the Tractor Factor could offer them shelter; a habit which they transferred to the workers in the factory. By day they went out and fought, both tanks and workers; by night they returned to the factory to have their wounds patched and their damage repaired.

And if the senseless destruction of helpless life that day had not hardened the determinations of the men of Stalingrad, these stories which the tank-crews told them as they worked on through the night could not have failed to stir them by example. If youngsters still in their teens could conquer their misgivings, forget the dangers and fight with complete disregard for their lives so that the soil of the city might not be fouled by German possession, then men of experience in life and love of Russia could no longer have wavering doubts.

Such a story they were telling about Ivan Khvastantsev, a Sergeant in charge of an anti-tank gun squad. About eleven miles to the south and three to the east of Kotleban, Sergeant Khvastantsev established his squad in a small farm-house and the surrounding out-buildings. Khvastantsev's little group was one of the most advanced elements of the Sixty-second Army which had gone to the city.

"This farm where you are to go," said his battalion* commander, who was with his company commander when he went to receive his orders, "this farm where you are to go lies almost directly in the path of the German XIVth Panzer Corps which is advancing from Vartiachii. Your orders are simple. You will engage and destroy as many enemy tanks as you can. That is all. You do not retreat until you have no ammunition left. Do you understand, Comrade Sergeant?"

"Yes, Comrade Captain, I understand," Sergeant Khvastantsev answered, and without another word had returned to his men and told them just as economically what was expected of them.

With all the speed they could get out of their vehicles they had dashed across the steppe to the farm. The farmer was young, his wife younger and they had four small children, the oldest of whom was six.

"You must take your wife and children to safety," the Sergeant had said, when he had explained to the farmer why he and his men had come.

"But when will it be safe?" the young man had asked.

"Go towards the city, but to the south," the Sergeant suggested, almost unable

---

*In the Red Army four companies = one battalion, four battalions = one regiment, four regiments = one division.

to answer the man's question. "In that way, you will not be in the way of our soldiers who are coming out of the city. In the city you can be of some help, and they will send your wife and the children across the river to safety."

"Very well," the farmer replied, and while Sergeant Khvastantsev deposed his men, the strongest horse was harnessed to the cart, and clothes and cushions and other precious belongings were loaded into it, and finally the children, frightened by the soldiers and excited at the same time, were placed on the cushions with their mother beside them, the youngest at her breast.

"Go as quickly as you can," Khvastantsev urged the man. "It may be difficult in the city, but there will be many there to help you and to tell you what to do. Goodbye, and don't worry about your farm or your house. Whatever you lose will be made up to you again when we've beaten the Germans. But now the chief thing is to defeat the enemy."

He stood watching them until they had turned into the roadway, and then he went back to the house. There his men had almost completed their arrangements. Overhead an aircraft engine could be heard throbbing, but the machine must have been in the sun, for wherever you could look in the sky unblinded, you could see nothing. It could be either Russian or German, for it was obviously on a reconnaissance mission, since it was going on a circular route—round and round over the steppe, searching no doubt for signs of dust or columns of lorries or lumbering tanks which would tell the advance of one side or another.

He had detailed a look-out to sit on the gable of the barn with field-glasses to keep a constant watch to the west. The first he knew of the advance of the enemy, therefore, was from him.

"What are they?" Khvastantsev called up to the man.

"MGs they look like," the man shouted down, peering all the time through the glasses.

Khvastantsev climbed up on to an upturned cart and through his own glasses searched the steppe. But all he could distinguish was the bow of the leading tank and the dust which the column was sending up into the air.

"Can you see how many there are?" he asked the look-out.

"Not properly, but five or six, I think, all fairly close together. Then there's quite a gap, and way back more dust…Yes, the second lot are armoured lorries."

"No infantry?"

"No, Comrade Sergeant, no infantry."

"Right! Keep out of sight," Khvastantsev told the man. "And let me know what happens. How far are they away now?"

"Half a mile perhaps, but advancing quickly."

Khvastantsev's men knew what to do. Between them they were armed with two Soviet-type bazookas, three anti-tank rifles and several dozen hand grenades. They would not open fire until they got the word from him, and then they would fire at their own discretion until the enemy retreated or were destroyed, or they themselves were killed.

From his point of vantage, standing in the rickety cart, the Sergeant was soon able to pick out the leading tank. Not until it was level with the entrance to the farm would he give the order to fire. His look-out was well enough hidden by the low chimney behind which he sprawled on his belly on the farmhouse thatch. It was not essential that the German should be unaware of his squad's presence at the farm, but the element of surprise was always a valuable ally in any encounter. If he judged his time well, the first four or five tanks could be knocked out before they knew from which direction the attack was coming or their companies could come to their assistance. If they could be stopped in the roadway they could prove quite an obstacle to the following column, until they were cleared out of the way.

"The leader is only three hundred yards off," the look-out called down.

"Yes, I can see him," Khvastantsev called back. "Now, don't move, anybody— especially you up there on the roof. Take aim!"

Khvastantsev lowered his glasses. The leading German tanks were near enough now to be seen quite clearly without them. Under his breath, the Sergeant began to count softly to himself, and as the first tank appeared by the entrance he shouted: "Fire!"

The pandemonium, which cut short the single-syllabled cry, made a shiver of excitement course down his backbone. It always had done from the first time in front of Moscow; a hundred, two hundred times and more he must have given the order, but it was an order you could never become accustomed to, for every time it was a challenge both to your enemy and yourself.

The shell from a bazooka hit the leading enemy tank amid-ship. With a violent stagger it turned across the road obliquely and came to a stop, completely blocking the way. While the second tank was concentrating on taking avoiding action, the second bazooka found its mark, and almost at once the third came into range of the first bazooka, whose rocket carried away part of the tank's track; its momentum sent it hurtling forward into the rear of the tank in front.

By this time the two rear tanks had realised that they had run into an ambush, and had also determined the source of the attack. They turned off the road and came hurtling like awkward automatons across the field towards Khvastantsev and his man, their guns blazing.

The Germans always reacted in this way. Whenever they ran into this kind of trap, those tanks which were not immobilised at once made a head-on attack on the attackers. It had happened to Khvastantsev and his men again and again. But they had camouflaged their positions so well that the Germans could not draw accurate aim and were firing blind. Holding their fire, without any order from their leader, until the German tanks were within most effective range, the bazookas then let fly and within seconds the two tanks were smoking, motionless wrecks.

Khvastantsev called up to the look-out to ask what was happening farther away. The column had stopped, the man said, and more tanks were coming up.

"What sort of a force is it? Can you see?" the Sergeant shouted.

"Light tanks, MGs like these and lorries of infantry, they look like," came the answer.

"Then they'll have to clear the road before they can go on," the Sergeant muttered. "The lorries would get bogged down if they left the road. That means they'll have to push us out of here."

He knew at once what that meant. There had been no mention of reinforcements coming up. His orders had been simple: stop the enemy as long as you can. He said nothing to his men. They would fight until the enemy retreated or they themselves were killed. They would not run away whatever happened; but it was as well that they should be able to concentrate on the battle, for knowledge of certain death can deflect even the most courageous from singleness of purpose.

"Another five tanks are advancing, Comrade Sergeant," the lookout called down. "It looks as if they're going to try and surround us."

But the look-out was wrong. The tanks advanced in a semi-circle, and it needed only the slightest variation of his disposition to meet this threat. Half an hour later four more German tanks lay smoking and silent in the fields to the west of the house, and the fifth was retreating lamely to out-of-range safety.

It was an hour before the Germans made their next move. This time eight tanks came forward; but this time the aim of the Russians faltered, and when once again the enemy withdrew, leaving another four casualties on the field, they had taken their toll of the Sergeant's force. Out of fifteen men, six were dead and three so seriously wounded that they could take no further part in the battle. But still the three first tanks blocked the advance.

In the next attack one of the bazookas was put out of action and three of the six still unharmed men were killed. Taking over the remaining bazooka and somehow performing the almost miraculous feat of loading and firing himself, Khvastantsev was presently by himself and must have known that it would not be long now before he joined his companions.

A splinter from a shell struck his left arm and the arm fell to his side limp and useless. Now, with only one hand, he could not load and fire the bazooka.

Two tanks, realising from the now very intermittent fire that the opposition was broken, came rumbling forward to administer the coup de grace. With his still usable right hand Khvastantsev fumbled at his belt and somehow managed to free one of the grenades attached to it. Drawing the pin with his teeth, he waited until the nearer tank was almost upon him, then raising himself on one knee he lobbed the grenade at it, in the same moment getting to his feet. Almost before the grenade exploded he had seized another and drawn the pin, and with it still in his hand he ran at the tank and deliberately threw himself beneath it, and as he died claimed his last victim. Now, and only now, when all firing had stopped did the Germans come forward to clear the road, and when they went on, as a result of the courage and outstanding bravery of Sergeant Khvastantsev and his men they were weaker by no fewer than twenty tanks.

Only one of all Khvastantsev's little band survived—Philip Sharupov, radio-operator, who, through the entire engagement, had sent a running report of all that was happening. The last words that came from Sharupov's radio was his simple description of his leader's final act. Then the transmitter went dead, and Sharupov has never been seen or heard of since. But the story which he told, as the battle in the farmhouse raged, reached not only those who awarded Khvastantsev the honour of Hero of the Soviet Union, but the men, the ordinary men, of Stalingrad, and gave them heart as they themselves prepared to meet the enemy.

The speed with which the Germans advanced on the northern flank was bewildering. By mid-afternoon it became clear to the defenders that the enemy would reach the Volga by nightfall. Steps had been taken to contain them within a fairly narrow corridor by troops pressing down from the north and by elements of Sixty-second Army sent out from the city pressing up from the south, and, in fact, the German front along the Volga eventually extended for only three miles. Nevertheless, the Russians expected next day to receive the full weight of a determined attack on the northern sector of the city.

But the attack did not come. As usual the German van had outrun not only the main body, but supplies and reinforcements through the totally unexpected absence of fierce opposition. Instead, they continued the systematic bombing of the city, street by street, block by block, dropping an estimated two thousand bombs on every square kilometre. From the east bank of the Volga and from the western steppe, it appeared that the whole city was ablaze.

From first-light the official evacuation of the civilian population who were not bearing arms was speeded up. A constant stream of women and children were led down to the river and put upon ferries and any kind of boat that was at hand. Stukas were now accompanying the German bombers, and seeing the ceaseless to-and-fro trans-river traffic they swooped down and bombed and machine-gunned the helpless refugees, killing and maiming, and frightening the women and children into near panic. When news of what was happening on the river reached other parts of the city, an unofficial evacuation began. Soon old men, women and children were leaving the city, their pitiful belongings in sacks and hand-carts. They passed through the defences and made towards the west. There was no attempt to stop them. In the city they were a liability as well as a responsibility, and the steppe was vastly wide.

On this and the following days the exodus in both directions continued, and by the end of the month fewer than ten thousand civilians remained in the city. These included a few children whose mothers refused to leave the one place in the world they knew—home. If they were to die, they said, they would prefer to die there than on the road to the Don or across the river in the strange east. But mostly they were women prepared to act as nurses, or to look after the men, or even to bear arms as soldiers.

These events made even an attempt at orderly life and living no longer possible, and on 25th August the authorities declared martial law. Already the form that the battle was ultimately to take had begun to emerge, for the majority of all who remained in the city were forced into the cellars and basements which, they discovered now for the first time, offered shelter against the German terror and a strange security. In these underground fastnesses they were already beginning to acquire the determination to defy the enemy when, logically, they should have caved in and cried *Kamerad*.

In the north the hedgehog formed by the forward German troops came under relentless Russian pressure from the Don army, striking southwards against it.

For a time, until reinforcements and supplies of ammunition were brought up, the situation looked critical for the 16th Panzer Division. The pressure from the south by the Russian Sixty-second Army gradually weakened, however, as the advance of the main forces of Sixth Army on the central sector compelled it to retire within the city's defences. In the south, too, the Fourth Panzer Army was slowly but surely pushing back the Russian south-western armies.

Taken all in all, the future of Lieutenant-General Paulus and his men looked rosy indeed. The main danger seemed to come from the speed of their own advance; the forward elements were outstripping their supplies. However, the Army High Command were jubilant, and began to calculate the days until Stalingrad would be in German hands. Then, imperceptibly at first, and dangerously on that account but with increasing certainty, it began to dawn on them that Sixth Army's future was not so assured as that.

As the Germans approached nearer the city the Russian resistance began to stiffen. On the airfield of Gumrak, a long, fierce battle was waged, an augury, if only the Germans had been able to read it, of what was to come. Soon, however, it became apparent to their Commanders at all levels that the strength of the divisions was being whittled away with the same attritional inevitability as water wears out a stone. Losses could not entirely be avoided; in fact, they were to be expected. But equally to be expected was that the losses would be made good. But they were not. Reinforcements and replacements were coming up irregularly and when they did arrive they were, more often than not, totally inadequate.

The Russians, on the other hand, were strengthening their forces all the time on the northern sector, and they were bringing up men, too, opposite the city, on the east bank of the Volga. So far, however, the latter were only in such numbers as to provide encouragement for the men in the city, who were gradually being crushed between vastly superior enemy odds—despite the increasingly heavy German losses—and the river.

By the end of the first week of September the German Sixth Army had come up to the western limits of the city almost along the whole of its length, with the Fourth Panzer Army at the southern limits. Now the battle proper for the city began.

Ditches and barricades proved no lasting barriers to the weight of German pressure; only men could hold the enemy back. The air-attacks had stopped, for only a freak building here and there stood practically untouched among the vast devastation. The great blocks of flats, the fine public buildings were now crazy, hollow shells. Only the basements were peopled.

It was for this crazy shell of a city that the fiercest of all city-battles of the Second World War was joined. For the Russians its factories could no longer contribute to the Soviet war-effort; for the Germans it was useless as a shelter. Even its strategic value either to Germans or Russians was now extremely doubtful. For Hitler, as we shall see, it was to become the object of a Führer-prestige obsession; for Stalin, it was to become the symbol of the ultimate in Russian defiance. For the Germans it was to achieve synonymity with final defeat; for the Russians it was to mark the beginning of final victory.

So, under Hitler's direct and personal orders, with everything they possessed the Germans attacked, street by street, house by house. The Russians fell back and the Germans came on. As they fell back the Russians mined the streets and set booby traps in every nook and cranny, and these claimed almost as many victims as the rifles and grenades.

By the middle of September, Fourth Panzer Army had reached the Tsaritsa and occupied the southern suburbs of the city. But the area they were occupying needed a great deal of mopping up, and at Beketovka the Russians held a deep, bell-shaped bridgehead on the west bank of the Volga, which extended seven miles along the shore of the river, having a width of two miles, and including the important industrial districts of Krasno and Sarepta up to Beketovka. From this bridgehead Fourth Panzer Army could not dislodge them without reinforcements, and these were not forthcoming.

On 15th September, Fourth Panzer Army withdrew its northern boundary from the Tsaritsa to the south side of the railway line, and at the same time Lieutenant-General Paulus took over control of all German operations in the city north of the railway. That is to say, while Fourth Panzer Army held the unimportant southern districts right up to the Volga, as far as the railway, Sixth Army had to contend with the gradual, and terrifyingly bloody, wearing-down conflict in the central sector.

But by now, besides losses of men, the Russians were beginning to be faced with a particularly difficult problem of food supplies. Such supplies as had been in the city when the battle began were rapidly running down, and it had not yet been possible to organise a regular system of replacements from across the river. It would appear, however, by a strange incident which took place on 15th September on the boundary of Fourth Panzer Army and the Russian Sixty-second Army, that the Germans were, surprisingly, in equally straitened circumstances.

A vast elevator stuffed with several thousand tons of grain was set on fire during operations that day and neither side could do anything to put out the flames, which very soon spread from the actual building to its contents. Fighting for the time-being forgotten, Russians from the north and Germans from the south strove long and hard to save the precious grain, but the combined amounts rescued by both sides added up to only a fraction of the whole. At the time the loss of so much food constituted a real tragedy for the Russians, but before the battle was concluded the rations of the garrison would be overflowing plenty compared with the terrible privations which the Germans were to suffer.

When the Luftwaffe decided that it had done enough and withdrew, both sides began to rely more and more on artillery. The Russians were helped in this by monitors of the Soviet navy, small shallow-draught ships with extremely heavy gun-power which presented difficult problems for the Germans, for, unlike their own fixed heavy artillery they could be constantly moved, and their positions could not be pin-pointed to allow eliminating attacks to be made on them. The guns of both sides carried on the destruction of the city where the Luftwaffe had left off, the Germans using theirs to attack the derelict houses whose crazy roofs and shattered upper stories harboured nests of snipers; their deadly aim took heavy toll of advancing troops and their defences could not be reached except by well-directed artillery fire.

The Russian defence grew more and more tenacious as each day passed, and though the Germans advanced yard by yard, their losses were fantastically high. By the beginning of October it was clear to Lieutenant-General Paulus that the date of the capture of Stalingrad was no longer predictable. Each street, each house in each street, even each room in each house, would have to be fought for; and as the Russians were pushed ever nearer to the river, so did their resistance increase, and soon it took a day to take a house where formerly it had taken half a day to take a street.

With each day that passed Hitler became more and more insistent that not one free Russian should be left in the ruins of Stalingrad. But he did not know how fanatically the Russians were defending their ruins. Nor did he know, nor did the Commander-in-Chief of his Sixty Army know, how hard pressed these same fanatical Russians were.

"Stalingrad must be taken!" Hitler commanded, and in anticipation announced the fall of the city in his communiqués.

"If the city falls, you will die with it!" Stalin bluntly told the defenders of his city.

So a quarter of a million men pressed hard upon a force less than one quarter of their own strength, and by sheer disregard for losses they pushed the Russians back until all the city was in their hands except for a few pockets of resistance here and there in the factories and in the north and except for the main area, six square miles in extent, in the central sector, known by the Germans as *Der Tennisschläger*, the Tennis Racquet.

The railway system of Stalingrad is industrially strategic; that is to say, it has been planned to meet the requirements of the factories rather than the citizens, who are more inclined to use the river as their chief highway for moving from one part of the city to another. One line runs from Kuibyshev, some six hundred miles north of Stalingrad, right through the city and out at the southern end to Krasnodar, not far from the north-eastern Black Sea coast. Two other links enter the city from the north-west and south-west coming respectively from Moscow and Rostov. The former meets the Kuibyshev-Krasnodar line in the central sector of the city, and at the time of the battle this feature has been eliminated—the main marshalling yards were situated here. The Central Station was connected by a loop to the marshalling yards, which were much nearer to the river. The loop began to the north of the station, curved east and south-east and rejoined the main line south of the station, and the shape of the area enclosed by the loop was exactly that of a tennis-racquet's head.

This area, together with the larger portion of the Mamai heights to the north-west of it, and the streets and squares lying between it and the river, the Soviet Sixty-second Army resolutely refused to surrender. We shall see later that what is generally called the Battle of Stalingrad was, for the greater part of its later stages, really two battles which were waged simultaneously—the battle for German survival fought in the steppes to the west from the Volga to the Don, and the battle for the city itself, fought, with even greater intensity, in this area of the Tennis Racquet. Out in the steppes the Russians were triumphantly on the offensive, the Germans surrounded and in as grave a situation as can face any army completely encircled by vastly superior forces. In the city, in the basements and ruins of the Tennis Racquet, the Germans struggled to satisfy a personal whim of their Führer, and the Russians struggled to thwart that whim.

It was this concentration on the battle of the Tennis Racquet, where alone victory could allow Hitler to proclaim: "I have captured Stalin's own city," which was to prove the undoing of Lieutenant-General Paulus and his Sixth Army, and was to be the proving of Russian arms. Judged by any standard, it was a strange battle, as we shall see.

The White Mouse and the Maquis d'Auvergue

(from *The White Mouse*)

Nancy Wake

Hubert and I were parachuted into France near Montlucon, and were taken to the nearby village of Cosne-d'Allier, where I did my meet-the-people in the village square.

I did not meet the farmer on whose property we had landed. Had the Germans made any enquiries regarding the activity so close to his farmhouse on the night in question, he wanted to be able to say he had gone to bed early and had not heard any strange noises.

Although we would have been happier and felt safer away from Cosne-d'Allier, we were waiting for someone called Hector to contact us, as he was our only link to Gaspard, the leader of the Maquis d'Auvergne. This was the group we were to work with, but we had to be taken to them by an intermediary.

By now I had given Hubert a watered-down version of my social début in the village and he was even more anxious to find another place to live. We discussed the pros and cons fully and agreed we would wait another day, but miraculously Hector arrived the next morning. Trouble in his own area had been the cause of his delay.

There was no bathroom in this old house and I had been washing myself from neck to knee in a tiny *cabinet de toilette*. I was tired of standing up in the cramped roomette, so I got a big basin, filled it with water, took it back to the bedroom, sat down and started to wash my feet, at the same time discussing our immediate plans with Hubert. My revolver was by my side.

In walked Hector, who took one look at me, my feet and my revolver and laughed for at least two minutes. Actually neither of us thought it was very amusing but perhaps the long delay we had experienced had made us lose our sense of humour. Every time he recounts this tale my feet get bigger and the basin gets smaller, and the last time I heard the story I had a Bren gun by my side!

We were greatly relieved to see him in spite of the fact that he did not have the information or addresses we required, but as he promised to send them with his courier in two days' time we were both happy to think our troubles were over.

Our happiness was short-lived as the courier did not arrive. And we did not see Hector again until after the war. He was arrested, survived Buchenwald and now lives on the outskirts of Paris. Sadly we had to face the cold truth. For the time being we were up the proverbial creek without a paddle. Hubert and I both decided we would have to forget all about security and confide to a certain extent in our host Jean and his wife. This done, he thought he might be able to find Laurent's hideout. Laurent was one of the leaders of a local Maquis group, and he would be able to take us to Gaspard, who was in charge of all the separate groups of the Maquis in the area.

We started out early in the morning in Jean's *gazogène* (a charcoal-fuelled car). He seemed to know all the secondary roads extremely well and assured us there was not much danger of running into the Germans. We looked at each other in silence as we had been briefed in London only to travel by bicycle or train, or better still on foot. Hubert was white in the face; as for me, once again I decided I was going to play it by ear.

Jean drove from one contact to another until, when it was late evening, we found Laurent. I was always grateful to Jean and his wife for delivering us into the safe hands of Laurent, who was a tall, handsome man. When I knew him better we became great friends. I respected him, too, because he was a man who knew no fear. He conducted us to an old château near Saint-Flour in the Cantal and went to inform Gaspard of our arrival.

The purpose of our mission was to meet Gaspard, who was believed to have three to four thousand men hiding in the departments of the Allier, Puy-de-Dôme, Haute Loire and Gantal. We were to make our own assessment not only of the leader Gaspard, but also of the manner in which his considerable army had been formed and was now being operated and controlled. If we felt reasonably sure that he and his Maquis would be an asset to the Allies when and after they landed on D-day, then the French Section of SOE, commanded by Colonel Buckmaster in England would assist them with finance and arms.

Laurent had been gone for days before Gaspard arrived at the château and our meeting was not a happy one. He maintained he had no knowledge of Hector and had therefore not been expecting any assistance from SOE. He did not inform us that he was hoping for the support of an Inter-Allied team, a fact that London, for reasons of their own, had failed to mention in our briefings.

If Hubert and I had possessed all the cards in the pack we would not have wasted the time we did when we first landed. It was also unfortunate that, owing to the arrest of Hector, we had not received the detailed local information promised to us in London. The fact that our wireless operator chose to spend some time with a friend before joining us did not diminish our problems.

Hubert and I had the good fortune to overhear the group discussing us while they were sitting in the big kitchen where they congregated all the time. They seemed sure we had some money and they were plotting to relieve me of it and get rid of me at the same time. At a later period when Gaspard and I had more respect for each other he assured me the men had been joking. That could be true, but when I am stranded in an old, empty château, many kilometres from civilization, surrounded by a gang of unshaven, disreputable-looking men, I tend to be cautious and take things seriously.

Without any radio contact with London we were not in an enviable position, so when Gaspard suggested he would send us to Chaudes-Aigues in the Cantal, where a man called Henri Fournier was in charge of the local Maquis, we readily agreed.

In retrospect I can guess why Gaspard adopted the attitude he did. He was banking on the support of the Inter-Allied group but in the event it did not materialize he did not want to antagonize us irreparably. We were of no use to him without a radio and the money, which we said (quite untruthfully) we did not possess. He would kill two birds with one stone. He would dispatch us to a man he disliked who would have us on his hands if we failed to become functional. When many years had passed, after reading information that was gradually coming to light, I concluded that Gaspard had been under the misapprehension that an elaborate military scheme involving a French airborne force being dropped in the Massif Central area before D-day would become operational. It did not materialize, probably another case of the left hand not letting the right hand know what it was doing.

In normal times Henri Fournier was an executive in hotel management. He detested the Germans and he and his wife had come to live in Chaudes-Aigues for the duration of the Occupation. He was puzzled by our arrival but when we explained the situation I think the mystery was clarified because, when we became friends, he admitted to me in confidence that he heartily disliked Gaspard.

Fournier arranged accommodation for us in a funny little hotel high up in the hills, in a village called Lieutades. It was freezing cold, both inside the hotel and outside, and there was little to eat. We had absolutely nothing to do and we were both beginning to worry as our radio operator, Denis Rake, was long overdue.

Denis (or Denden, as he was called) had been one of our instructors at SOE school, the one arguing with the French-woman. Even in those days when homosexuality was illegal he had never concealed the fact that he was queer. Indeed it was always the first thing he mentioned, especially to women, who often found him too attractive for his liking. We were both fond of him but knew he could be completely unreliable.

Denden arrived by car just as we were beginning to give up hope. He found me sitting on the wall of the local cemetery and wanted to know if I was picking a suitable grave! He realized that his late arrival had caused us needless anxiety and in true Denden fashion he told us a cock-and-bull story which neither of us believed. However, a radio operator is an important person in the field, and we were not going to give him a reason to leave us and go straight back to his lover, which was exactly where he had been. On landing in France by Lysander he had met the man he had been having an affair with several weeks before in London, and they had decided to have a last fling.

Nevertheless, we were absolutely delighted to see him for now we could put our plans into action. While waiting for Denden we had decided that if he did arrive we would help Fournier first of all. We had been impressed by what we had seen of his group. We respected him and knew that he had spent a lot of his savings on the Resistance. We packed our bags and left for Chaudes-Aigues.

Fournier was overwhelmed with joy when told that we would shortly be in radio contact with London and that his group would be the first to receive our report. He and Hubert were busy making out the lists of weapons and explosives they hoped would be sent from England, and Denden and I were busy coding the messages to be transmitted.

When the day and hour of the transmission arrived the room was full of Maquisards anxious to witness this exciting event. They appeared to be making Denden nervous so I asked them to leave the room. Reluctantly they filed out, all except Fournier, who refused to budge. Denden looked more nervous than before. He told me why. He was transmitting on the wrong schedule. He was twenty-four hours too soon. The three of us managed to restrain our laughter and started the proceedings all over again the following day. There were no more hitches and soon we were preparing for our first operation.

The plateaux on top of the mountains which surround Chaudes-Aigues were ideal for air-drops. Fournier and his group had surveyed the whole area and were of the opinion that we could receive, unpack and distribute the contents of the containers on the field and return to our homes without any interference. As soon as London had received our messages and we were all organized we received air-drops on six consecutive nights. It continued to be a roaring success until later on when Gaspard arrived with his men and was followed almost immediately by the Germans.

We manned the fields from ten at night until four in the morning, unless the planes arrived beforehand. We would unpack the containers immediately. The weapons had to be cleaned and all the protective grease removed before we handed them over to the leaders of the individual groups. Every available man assisted. Nevertheless, sometimes it would be noon before we finished and after lunch before we could snatch a few hours' sleep. It was a strenuous time for everyone; we were kept on the go continuously, but it was also rewarding to witness the enthusiasm of Fornier and his Maquis.

Every now and then Hubert, Denis and I would receive parcels from London which would arrive in a special container. Words cannot describe the thrill it gave me to open mine, stamped all over with "Personal for Hélène." Here we were, in the middle of a war, high up in the mountains of Central France, yet because of the thoughtfulness of SOE Headquarters we felt close to London.

My parcel always contained personal items unobtainable in France during the Occupation, plus supplies of Lizzie Arden's products, Brooke Bond tea, chocolates or confectionery. Without fail there'd be a note and a small gift from Claire Wolf, the only girl I'd been friendly with at headquarters. We remained staunch friends, and when she died at her home on the Isle of Man in 1984 I was grief-stricken.

Once, to my delight, I received a letter from my old pal, Richard Broad. I remember jumping up and down shouting, "I've got a letter from R.B.!" Hubert and Denis weren't a bit interested—they'd never heard of him! But I kissed every page as I read the letter. I still have it—and it's still covered in lipstick.

I was thankful that Hubert and I had arranged the tasks we would perform to our mutual satisfaction. He would deal with all matters of a military nature and meet Gaspard whenever necessary and possible. I would be in charge of finance and its distribution to the group leaders. I would visit the groups, assess the merit of their demands and arrange for their air-drops, which we would both attend if possible. The tables had turned. After being regarded as a bloody nuisance by Gaspard when I first arrived, I now carried a lot of weight. *I* was the one who decided which groups were to get arms and money. Denden was in charge of coding and decoding the messages he transmitted and received. German detectors looking for illegal transmitters had to be evaded, and when we were expecting a message from London about a drop of arms, we listened to the five BBC news broadcasts a day. It was time-consuming, exacting work.

For my part, I had found a different attitude in France when I returned and joined the Maquis. By the spring of 1944 anyone with a brain could see that the Allies would beat the Germans and consequently some French people were already preparing to play politics. This exasperated me as the memory of the colossal harm caused by politics in the thirties still rankled. The majority of the men wanted to kick the Germans out of their country, return to their homes and pick up the threads of their lives. Liberation was on the horizon; now it was no longer a battle between "cops and robbers," it was becoming a battle of wits.

When Fournier told me Colonel Gaspard was promoted to general, I snorted and Fournier laughed. Hubert was inclined to be impressed and a little in awe of rank. I was not. Not that I did not respect genuine rank, but in the Resistance, especially in the Maquis, some of them upgraded themselves in such a fashion that the chap you met one week as a solider or civilian suddenly appeared as a colonel a few days later. If you enquired about such a rapid promotion you would be given the name of someone you had never heard of, or the initials of some secret organization equally unknown to you. Furthermore, the alleged promotion would be promulgated after the Liberation. Some of the newly promoted officers tried to pull rank with me.

Fournier laughed when I told him what I wanted to do. In View of the importance of my department—finance and air-drops—I promoted myself to the rank of field marshal, to be promulgated after the war! No one would pull rank on me and get away with it. I continued to arm and assist, to the best of my ability, the worthwhile and dedicated groups in the Maquis, irrespective of the rank of their leaders.

During May, as a direct outcome of the large concentration of men in the mountains, a continuity of pitched battles were being fought between the Germans and our Maquis d'Auvergne. The Maquisards defended themselves brilliantly. Although they were always outnumbered by the enemy, sometimes comprising crack SS troops, the losses inflicted on the Germans were staggering. A few days before the Allies landed in Normandy the Germans attacked Gaspard's group in Mont Mouchet. They were stopped by the Maquis and driven back in defeat.

It was soon clear that the Germans were becoming concerned about the steadily increasing strength and actions of the Maquis. It was either just before or after this battle that the traitor Roger the Légionnaire was in our region. He and another German agent had managed to infiltrate Gaspard's Maquis, stating they wished to join his group. Their story and their odd behaviour aroused suspicions almost immediately, and in the cross-firing which subsequently took place, one Maquisard was killed and both German agents were seriously wounded. Roger received three bullets in the chest from a Colt .45 but as he was wearing a bullet-proof vest he did not die immediately. Interrogated under extreme pressure, he confessed to having been responsible for initiating a series of unbelievably inhuman punishments inflicted on captured members of the Resistance. He also stated that he had been directly responsible for the arrest of O'Leary at Toulouse on 2 March 1943. His confessions were taken down and I was given a copy to forward to London. Shortly afterwards Roger and the other German agent were shot and buried on Mont Mouchet.

I shivered when I read the report. One of the Resistance members Roger was seeking was the person who obtained the arms from England. Little did he know that he had passed me as he drove along the narrow mountain track. It was unbelievable that I had missed him in Toulouse and been so close to him on this mountain.

I left the area as soon as possible. I could understand the hatred the Maquisards had for the Germans who behaved like crazed wild animals in their dealings with the Resistance. I hated and loathed them too, but personally I favoured an accurate bullet and a quick death. Nevertheless there is a lot to be said for the proverb "an eye for an eye," and when all is said and done Roger was only paying for some of the abominable treatment meted out to his victims. Torture is horrible. But before any outsiders form an opinion they should study both sides of the story closely.

On 4 June 1944 I received a special message from London stating that "Anselm" was being dropped that night in the Montluçon area, in the *départment* of the Allier, and I was ordered to collect him. That was easier said than done. Hector had been arrested before he had time to give us details of safe houses, contacts and passwords. I knew that a Madame Renard was one of the contacts and I thought I had heard that she had been the housekeeper of an ambassador in Paris and also that she made good cakes.

Fourner gave me his best car and driver plus a bicycle, which we put on the roof. The area between Chaudes-Aigues and Montluçon was swarming with Germans and Maquis each thirsting for revenge. In those days the only petrol-driven cars belonged to either the Germans or the Resistance. We were inclined to be more afraid of the Maquis than we were of the Germans because some Maquisards had been known to shoot first and ask questions afterwards. We didn't want them to mistake us for the enemy.

However, all went well. We enquired at each village along our route as to the whereabouts of Germans and Maquisards and, thanks to the help and information given us, we reached Montluçon safely. We hid the car in some bushes and my driver concealed himself a little distance away so he could observe anyone who discovered our vehicle.

I had promised one of the men in my group that I would call on his wife who was pregnant. She was happy to have news of her husband but had never heard of a Madame Renard. She did give me the name and address of a friend who, she said, might be able to help. I cycled to her home. Although the name Renard did not ring a bell, when I mentioned the fact that she had been in the employ of an ambassador she was able to help me trace her. The town was full of Germans and there were patrols and road-blocks everywhere.

Madame Renard opened the door when I rang. I tried to explain as best I could the predicament I was in and how I had found her. She just stood there staring at me intently. Suddenly I could smell rum baba and I told her I knew all about her cakes. She laughed and led me into the kitchen. She called to "Anselm," who came out of a cupboard pointing a Colt A5 clutched in his hand. We looked at each other in astonishment. It was René Dusacq, whom I had met during my training in England. He was also one of the men who had kissed me goodbye when I left on my mission. He was to become known as Bazooka.

Dusacq nearly passed out when I said we would be going by car to Chaudes-Aigues. He sat in the back with his Colt at the ready, while I was in the front with the driver, a couple of Sten guns and half a dozen grenades. It was a smooth trip back to our headquarters where, to my bitter disappointment, I learnt that during my absence the Allies had landed and I had missed all the fun of blowing up our targets.

On 10 June the Germans attacked Mont Mouchet, this time supported by another 11,000 troops, with artillery, tanks and armoured cars, as against Gaspard's 3,000 Maquisards with light arms. Incredibly, they captured an armoured car and two cannons. During the night the Germans withdrew which gave the Maquis the opportunity to remove some of their vehicles, food and clothing over to our region. The attack recommenced at dawn. The Maquis were ordered to pull out at nightfall but in the meantime they fought like tigers. They were magnificent. The German losses were always anything from 4 to 10 per cent more than the casualties of the Maquis. Is it any wonder that the next time they attacked the Maquis d'Auvergne, they doubled their strength? I was destined to find myself in the centre of their mighty battle array. The wonder is that I was not captured or killed.

From our headquarters we could hear the sound of the battle raging. Alas, we could offer no assistance to our colleagues in arms. The nature of the terrain between our position and the Maquis under attack made it impossible. All through the day our scouts kept us informed of the fighting going on. All we could do was get on with our work.

It was unfortunate that hundreds of new recruits were streaming into our area, ready to be armed. Hubert and Fournier and his lieutenants had no time to worry about the conflict going on over the mountain. They were trying desperately to interview, however briefly, and arm the new recruits. It was a fantastic sight. The men were coming into Chaudes-Aigues from all directions. Not even the sound of the fighting nearby dampened their enthusiasm.

Denden was forever coding and decoding; not only for the night operation but for the daylight parachutage from 150 planes we had been promised. I had been designated to the footwear department! Every man had to be fitted with one pair of British army boots and two pairs of socks. When the supplies in the village ran out I went up to the plateau and opened more containers. As soon as they had been fitted with boots they were passed on to Bazooka, who all day long and far into the night would be instructing them on how to use our weapons.

Gaspard and his men arrived soon after their battle with the Germans and installed themselves on top of one of the plateaux surrounding Chaudes-Aigues. Hubert tried diplomatically to get him to form his men into smaller groups but Gaspard waved aside the suggestion. He was rightly proud of the way he and his men had faced up to the German attack but he was a stubborn man and very self-opinionated.

We were receiving more and more air-drops. Night after night the planes would fly over our plateau and drop our precious containers. We were so occupied unpacking them, degreasing and assembling the weapons before distributing them we had little time for sleep, but the atmosphere of the Maquisards with whom we were in daily contact was so exhilarating and gratifying that we never worried. I don't think any of the reception committees ever got over the thrill of seeing the parachutes drop from the planes. Least of all Fournier, who never missed a drop and who made sure that his men were in position at the correct time. It was bitterly cold on the plateau and from ten at night the ground would be soaking wet with the heavy dew. We used to soak loaf sugar in *eau de vie* (plum brandy) and suck them to try to keep warm.

Now that Gaspard was a "General" he proceeded to turn the little village of Saint-Martial (I seem to remember it had been deserted by its inhabitants) into a pukka headquarters. He had a colonel from the regular Army with him on his staff, who had brought his wife with him. The colonel obviously had not forgotten the regular eating hours in the officers' mess and he introduced the same system in their headquarters. We had been used to eating when it was convenient and thought this was a bit of a joke. I kept out of the way and continued to eat in Chaudes-Aigues if possible.

Hubert attended the "mess meals" on several days and begged me to at least put in an appearance. For the sake of peace I agreed to accompany him the next day. The "general" sat at one end of the table, the colonel at the other end next to his wife, and the British and American members with the other French leaders were seated in between. I thought I heard someone address the colonel's wife as "Madame la Colonel" and decided I must be mistaken, but after a while I realized they really were addressing her in this manner. That was enough for me. The Maquis and the way we were forced to live did not merit such French Army formality. Denden, Bazooka and I always found excuses to be too occupied at noon to join the "High Command," as we called them, and soon Hubert followed suit whenever he could. He knew that with us at least he would have a laugh.

In spite of the danger and hard work we were enjoying working together with Fournier and his men. We all pulled together and there was never any friction between us. We could not say the same about Gaspard. We agreed unanimously that he was an extremely difficult man to get along with. I must admit that I personally never had any trouble with him after the first meeting. He may not have liked to admit it but he had met his match with me. And I intended to keep it that way.

I was glad to have René Dusacq with us. Although we had not yet received any bazookas, they were his favourite weapon after his Colt 45, which never left his side; hence his nickname. Also he helped me keep Denden under control. When I returned from visiting other groups an irate farmer came to see me, stating that his son had complained about an alleged advance from Denden. I managed to calm him down but it was embarrassing for our team. We had to be so careful the way we handled Denden because we knew he was just itching for an excuse to go and join his current lover further north. Bazooka, like us, was fond of him, but we could not close our eyes to the problems which would arise if we let him run wild amongst the good-looking young men in the Maquis. The trouble with Denden was that he actually believed most men were homosexual and if they were not, then they should be!

It always amuses me when I look back on those days with Denden. I often wonder why London decided to send him with us. Did they think our mission so hopeless it did not matter whom they sent? Did they think I was some kind of "Den Mother"? This much I do know. Not many heterosexual men from SOE headquarters would have cared to go into the midst of 7,000 full-blooded Maquisards with a self-proclaimed homosexual. They owe us a special debt of gratitude that, because of our understanding and handling of the affair, there were no court cases after the war, and that Denden was not torn to pieces or, alternatively, shot to death by an irate father.

Apart from that particular problem we were a happy team with Fournier, when he could get away from his nagging wife. We would laugh about the antics of the would-be politicians and others seeking power after the Liberation. For my part I always admired the men, so many of whom had been forced to leave their families unprovided for, either to escape the relève or the Germans. To me they will always represent the true spirit of the Resistance.

More and more recruits were joining Gaspard on the plateaux. The numbers of men assembling within the one area was getting completely out of control and our team felt it was courting trouble. Readily we agreed with Hubert's suggestion that we move further north. Unfortunately we had an air-drop that night and the next, plus our first daylight parachutage, in which we had been promised 150 planes. It had been so hard to organize and the arms would mean such a lot to the Maquis that we decided to postpone our departure for a few more days.

We came down from the plateau just before dawn, we were all exhausted and suffering from lack of sleep. Chaudes-Aigues has natural hot water springs so I went over to the public baths and soaked myself before popping into bed to snatch a few hours' sleep. It was not to be. The sound of gunfire made me leap out of bed. Hurriedly I dressed myself and raced down to the hall of the hotel where we lived.

The Germans were attacking us. Our look-outs came into the village to report. The whole area surrounding the mountains was literally swarming with Germans. When it was all over we learnt that they had been 22,000 strong, supported by over 1,000 vehicles, including tanks and armoured cars, trench mortars, artillery to back up the infantry, plus ten planes.

Several weeks previously I'd met Graham Buchanan, an Australian who'd been shot down near Nevers and rescued by a Maquis group. He was just as surprised as I was to meet another Australian in the French mountains.

From Nevers he and several other Allied airmen had been sent to Chaudes-Aigues where they were billeted in our hotel. I assured them there was nothing to worry about as I wished them goodnight. But a few hours later I had to tell them there was lots to worry about, that we were being attacked and would have to withdraw. Despite the panic and confusion which followed, all of this group eventually got back to England safely. (Graham Buchanan now lives near Murwillumbah in New South Wales, where he's a farmer.)

We packed as much as we could in our cars and raced up to Fridfont on the plateau to join the Maquis, which was 7,000 strong by now. Hubert left to confer with Gaspard who was on the other end of the plateau. He refused to consider withdrawal and stated he would fight to the death with his own group. I coded the message while Denden tried to contact London, not an easy thing to do when an operator's call is not expected. He persevered for hours and eventually received an instruction to transmit in one hour's time. Our message cancelled all our drops and requested Gaspard be ordered to withdraw.

Many of the containers had not been opened the night before as the planes had arrived late. I went along to the dropping zone and finished unpacking and putting the weapons in working order. Then I drove to all the positions where I could see our men, and once the arms and ammunition had been distributed I went back to Denden. We were the only two people not fighting. The men were holding back the onslaught and displaying outstanding bravery and enthusiasm as they defended the plateaux.

By now I was so exhausted I could hardly move. I was thirsty, hungry, sleepy and every bone in my body ached. As I could not help Denden until he received the final message from London I told him I was going to have a little kip and to wake me when I was needed.

I went to bed in a farmhouse where we had been authorized to take refuge. Just as I was dropping off to sleep Fournier came in and made me get up as he said it was too dangerous to stay inside. I was so sleepy I didn't care what happened. The only thing that would have wakened me completely was if I had come face to face with a German. I slept for a couple of hours under a tree which I thought was just as dangerous and less comfortable than in the bed.

Finally, the message came through. We were all ordered to withdraw and a personal message for Gaspard ordered him to follow suit. Knowing how stubborn he could be, I asked Denden to sign the message as if coming from Konig, de Gaulle's General who led the Free French Forces of the Interior. I think the signature of a genuine general did the trick as Gaspard was as meek as a lamb when he took delivery of the signal.

Several planes bombed Saint-Martial as I left the village, and as my car became visible on the road to Fridfont one pilot of a Henschel left his group and started to chase my car. I could see his helmet and goggles as he banked to continue the pursuit, and I could hear the bullets whizzing as his aim got closer and closer. Suddenly a young Maquisard who was hiding in some bushes signalled me, shouting at the same time to jump. We flung ourselves into a culvert by the roadside as the plane flew overhead. The young man explained that Fridfont was being evacuated and that Bazooka was waiting for me further down the mountain. We dashed from cover to cover as the German pilot kept up the chase.

By the time I regained Fridfont everyone had been evacuated. Denden had already left with a group, Hubert with another. A young man who had waited for me conducted me to where my group was hiding and where I was delighted to find Bazooka. He always looked after me when he was around.

The withdrawal from the plateaux was a credit to the leaders of the Maquis. When the Germans arrived there was not a soul left. They must have felt very frustrated when, after the fierce fighting and their huge losses of life, they reached the top of the mountain only to find the entire Maquis had evaporated.

We had been formed into groups of fifty to 100, each one being led by one or two men familiar with the terrain we would be covering. Our leader had been a non-commissioned officer in the French Army. He originated from Alsace but although he was not a local man, he was an experienced tracker so we had no qualms about getting lost in the tough mountains we would have to cross.

The Germans were patrolling all the bridges over the river Truyére which was deep, rapid and dangerous in most parts. They were also guarding closely any part of the river they thought we might attempt to cross. Thanks to Fournier and his men, we were able to cross the river in all the most dangerous places.

When Hubert and I first went to Ghaudes-Aigues we were a little dubious about Fournier's suggestion that we use the plateaux as dropping zones, mainly because we were afraid we could get trapped by the Germans, without an escape route. It was then he showed us the ingenious scheme they had devised for crossing the river well away from bridges and secluded by heavy foliage.

They had installed layer after layer of heavy slabs of local stone on the river-bed and covered them by secured dead tree-trunks. They were not visible from above as they were at least 45 cm below the level of the water. All we had to do was remove our footwear, release the logs, balance ourselves with a walking stick or the branch of a tree, and cross in absolute safety. It worked perfectly.

Our destination was Saint-Santin, north-west of our present position. We headed south, crossed more mountains and gradually proceeded north in a round-about fashion. All the groups were taking different routes and we aimed to keep well away from each other whenever possible.

It took us about four days to reach Saint-Santin. It was tough going all the way. We were miles from the German infantry but their planes circled the entire region for days. They criss-crossed the area where we had been, dropping bombs, then systematically bombed all the surrounding mountains and forests hoping, presumably, to flush out the Maquisards, who luckily were not there.

After two days we were all thirsty and starving. We were out of immediate danger so we approached a prosperous-looking farm asking for water and a little food. They offered milk and food to "L'anglaise," which I did not accept as they treated the bedraggled looking men as if they were lepers. The poorer farmers and their wives gave as much food as they could spare and let us sleep in their barns overnight. I could not help thinking of the old saying, "The rich get richer and the poor get poorer."

At last we reached our destination. We ran into Gaspard and his group. I will always remember this meeting with him. He looked at me and said, "Alors, Andrée," took my arm and walked the rest of the way with me and Bazooka. I do not know what he was thinking at that moment but for my part it was something special, as if from then on we would understand each other. He was a man of few words, and I knew from those two that he respected me as a comrade-in-arms.

From the information London had been able to give us at our briefings, we got the impression that the German garrisons in the Auvergne were manned by elderly men and puny boys. I don't know what happened to them, perhaps they were too tired or too weak to take part in the conflict. We only saw crack German troops plus some mighty tough Mongol warriors who cared for little else but slaughter and plundering. Some of them were found lying on the battlefields with their pockets full of watches and human fingers with gold wedding-rings still on them. Nevertheless, hundreds and hundreds of the enemy lay wounded and over 1,400 were dead. The Maquis lost over a hundred and about the same number were wounded. What a glorious victory for Gaspard and his Maquis d'Auvergne, but from then on the Germans would be all out for revenge.

About thirty of us installed ourselves in an unfinished house on the outskirts of Saint-Santin. It belonged to the parents of a good-looking young man in our group on whom Denden had designs. Therefore, Bazooka, who was never without his Colt .45, was detailed to watch over this young man's honour.

For several days groups of men kept arriving with exciting tales of their long cross-country hike. Denden turned up, footsore and weary, without his transmitter, which he had buried, or his codes, which he had destroyed. We were back to square one, out of contact with London and useless to everyone. From that day on until the end of the Occupation I don't think I ever stopped for more than two or three hours. If I wasn't walking or riding a bicycle, or fighting, or being chased by the Germans, or the Vichyites, it just wasn't a normal day.

Fortunately, through contacts I learnt of the whereabouts of a Free French radio operator living just over the adjacent mountain. It was hoped that he would co-operate if I mentioned the name of our mutual acquaintance. Someone lent me a man's bicycle which I half pushed and carried up the mountain but literally flew down the other side. The bike was getting up such speed that the brakes were useless, and I fell off several times. I pedalled about twenty kilometres only to find that because of all the German activity in the region, the Frenchman had left the day before. The mountain lying between me and Saint-Santin did little to lift the disappointment I felt.

Denden knew there was an SOE operator in Chateauroux because that is where he had spent his idyllic week while we were waiting for him in the Auvergne. He gave me as much information as he could remember and it was decided I would leave as soon as I could make myself presentable, even though it was 200 kilometres away.

We had been given the address of a friendly tailor in Aurillac but I had to wash and mend my slacks and blouse before I could appear anywhere without raising suspicion. Just then Laurent drove up in a car of all things; he had driven right around the Germans without any trouble. We were so happy to see him but livid when we thought of his comfortable trip, whereas we were all exhausted.

Laurent wouldn't give me a car to drive to Chateauroux as he said that since our battle the Germans had tightened up all regulations, and road-blocks had been installed all over the entire region. Furthermore any identity cards issued in the Cantal were suspect and by law had to be exchanged at the local police stations under the supervisIon of the Germans. As my identity card was from the Cantal I would have to travel without any papers. Added to which I doubted that I would get to Châteauroux on a bicycle, let alone return, and be strongly counselled Hubert to prevent me from continuing with my plan. Laurent thought that quite apart from the problems with identity cards, papers and tighter regulations, 200 kilometres was just too far to cycle. But, as I pointed out, we were useless without our radio, and this was our only immediate hope.

Once Laurent accepted the fact that I would make the trip irrespective of all the obstacles he put in my way, he lost no time in doing everything he could to make my journey less dangerous. Men were sent in all directions to collect local information about German movements and then when he had studied all the details be mapped out the route he advised me to take. I would have to cycle about 200 kilometres of the roundabout route, without an identity card or a licence for the beautiful new ladies' bicycle a Maquisard had been able to purchase for me "under the counter." If I reached Châtearou safely I would have to return by the best way I could.

While all these preparations were going on I was busy trying to get my wardrobe together. I needed an entire new outfit plus some walking shoes. I cycled into Aurillac where the tailor agreed to make me a costume in twenty-four hours, with one fitting in two hours' time. He also gave me the name and address of a cobbler who could supply me with shoes without a coupon. When I arrived at the cobbler's shop I was dismayed to hear the tailor had phoned to warn me not to return for the fitting as the Milice who were next door to his shop had already been enquiring about the woman in slacks.

The Germans had, meantime, placed road-blocks on all the main roads leading into town. I escaped by crossing several fields and heading north between two main roads until I could cross one of them and regain Saint-Santin, which lay to the west. All the way back I had been trying to think of a way to go back for my fitting. I had to find a disguise. But what? Then I had an idea.

The parents of the handsome young man in whose house we were hiding lived in the village. I went to see them and asked if they had any old clothes I could borrow. His grandmother had an old trunk with an amazing array. I borrowed a long white piqué dress which must have been fashionable before World War I. They introduced me to a farmer who was taking his horse and cart to the market in Aurillac early the next morning. I became secretive about my plans as I knew Hubert, and Denden in particular, would rag me if they saw me in my disguise. I crept out of the house early and waited for the farmer. Unfortunately, just as

I had installed myself in the front of the cart beside the farmer with a pair of his trousers on my lap, which was my reason for the visit to the tailor, Denden appeared and alerted everyone else. Of course they had a good hearty laugh at my expense. Who wouldn't? There I was sitting up in the cart surrounded by fruit and vegetables looking like a real country bumpkin, wet hair pulled back tight, no make-up, an old-fashioned dress, and wearing a pair of the farmer's old boots.

Our cart and the produce were inspected several times by the Germans as we entered Aurillac; they did not give me a second look, even their first glance was rather disdainful. I did not blame them. I did not look very fetching. The only thing that boosted my morale that day was when the tailor failed to recognize me as I entered his shop. My costume was delivered the following day, and I set off for Châteauroux the day after.

On the eve of my departure Laurent sent several men on ahead to warn as many villages as they could in the Cantal and the Puy-de-Dôme to look out for me and to warn me if trouble lay ahead. In the Allier he had not been able to make any contacts so I just had to trust to luck. I had company as far as Montluçon. A Maquisard was going to visit his wife, who was ill. When we had to take the National Route we pushed our bikes instead of riding them in case any Germans approached, in which event we would have time to dive into the culverts by the side of the road until they passed.

I by-passed Montluçon and was heading for Saint-Amand. It was getting dark and I wanted to make a few enquiries. I went into a bistro and had a simple meal and a glass of wine. Listening to the conversation of the other customers, I gathered that the Germans in the area were quiet for the time being. I found a barn not far away, removed my costume and slept until the sound of an air raid awakened me.

At Saint-Amand I stopped for a coffee and overheard that Bourges had been raided the day before. When I arrived there I thought the place was quiet—not a soul in the streets and all the shutters were closed. It was only afterwards I found out that the Germans had shot some hostages that morning. I passed two groups of Germans but they made no attempt to stop me.

At Issoudon I stopped for a black-market meal, cleaned myself up and entered into conversation with the owner of the restaurant, who shared some of my wine and brandy. The dangerous part was yet to come and I needed all the local information I could obtain. There is nothing like brandy to loosen the tongue! I cycled to the local markets and filled my string bag with all the fruit and vegetables I could buy without food coupons, hoping that I would pass for a housewife out shopping. I was still making good time although my legs were beginning to ache because of the mountainous terrain I had crossed. I had cycled 200 kilometres.

There were continuous streams of German vehicles leaving Issoudon for Châteauroux so I cycled west to Brion then south-west to Villedieu-sur-Indre, and entered the city without any trouble. One German patrol was checking on the opposite side of the road but they waved me on when they saw me hesitate. I pedalled round and round the town and was just about to give in, with much despair, when I came across the bistro I was looking for. It was exactly as Denden had described it. But when I called at the SOE house they refused to help me; they refused to send a message to London. Actually their performance was completely stupid because if I had been a German or one of their agents, they would have been arrested on the spot. I left the house in disgust and returned to the bistro.

They must have been saying prayers for me back in the Auvergne because as I was pedalling around Châteauroux I had run into a Maquisard I had met several weeks before in the Corrèze. He was looking for a Free French radio operator as their operator had been killed in action. We had both agreed to help each other if one of us found our contacts and I had left him at the bistro where he was waiting when I returned with the bad news.

Off we pedalled to find his contact, who was also a patron of a bistro which was situated opposite the home of the radio operator. He warned us that the Germans had not caught the radio operator but they were in the house waiting to trap any callers.

The town was literally swarming with Germans. They were completely surrounding areas and checking the houses systematically, so we decided to leave immediately. We separated and arranged to meet outside the town. Both of us were able to by-pass the road-blocks and, wasting no time, we headed for a Maquis group my companion knew in the Creuse. The leader belonged to the Free French and had come from Algiers, where his headquarters were. He was understanding when I told him the trouble I was in and said that if his radio operator did not object to sending my message, neither would he. The operator agreed to my request to send a message to Colonel Buckmaster in London via the Free French in Algiers. I wished my travelling companion good luck and was on my way.

By now I was so tired I resolved to take the quickest route home. Every kilometre I pedalled was sheer agony. I knew that if I ever got off the bike, I could never get on it again, so I kept pedalling. Halfway across the Allier the companion I had left in Montluçon was looking out for me. He had guessed the road I would take if all went well. His wife had presented him with a baby son and they were both well, so he was happy. I arrived back in Saint-Santin twenty-four hours before the time they had anticipated I would, even though they were well aware I might never return. I had pedalled 500 kilometres in seventy-two hours.

They greeted me with open arms and shouts of joy. All I could do was cry. When I got off that damned bike I felt as if I had a fire between my legs and the inside of my thighs were raw. I couldn't stand up, I couldn't sit down, I couldn't walk and I didn't sleep for days. But thanks to all the help I had been given by one and all, I had succeeded and all we had to do now was to wait and see if Algiers sent our signal on to Colonel Buckmaster. They did. As I said to Hubert, Denden and Bazooka, I never wanted to be told any more that the Free French agents in the field would not help the British ones, because I knew better. I never heard of that group in the Creuse after that so I have never been able to say "thank you" in peacetime.

It took me a few days to recover. The doctor from the village had dressed my thighs which were in a horrible state but there was little else anyone could do. My three close colleagues looked in frequently to see how I was faring, but I just wanted to be left alone. When I'm asked what I'm most proud of doing during the war, I say "the bike ride."

Finally the day came when I could move without experiencing too much pain, and I dressed and went out to lunch. To my surprise a strange Frenchman, to whom I was not introduced, was sitting at my table. He had arrived during my absence, stating that he was a full Colonel in the regular French Army and that he was going to take over our outfit and run it on correct military lines. Hubert had not been game to tell me that this man had been our uninvited guest for days.

Normally one could ask for identity papers but in those days it was pointless to do so as everybody's papers in the Resistance were false. Perhaps he was a Colonel. I neither knew or cared. All I could see was that now victory was so close too many people wanted to jump on the bandwagon and play that ugly game of politics. I had been a budding journalist in the thirties and witnessed the havoc caused by politicians and other power-hungry individuals, so I was not impressed by this "Colonel's" speech.

When he had finished his pep-talk, obviously for my ears as the others had heard it before, I asked him what he was going to do for money and arms, because I certainly was not going to give him any of ours. Hubert looked embarrassed but Bazooka, Denden and the rest of our group did not try to conceal their joy. The four of us discussed this new situation later and they agreed with my suggestion that we all move further north towards Tardivat, the gallant French man who greeted me when I dropped into France. Tardivat was not a politician. From then on until the end of the Occupation we never looked back.

When Hubert and I drove up north to the *département* of the Allier and towards Tardivat, Bazooka was left in charge, with Denden detailed to listen to all the BBC personal messages in the event we received a signal from London acknowledging our SOS and perhaps confirming the parachutage we requested.

Tardivat was delighted to see us. Immediately he found a suitable site for our group not far from Ygrande and near a field we had been using for air-drops. Hubert remained with him to prepare the camp, while I returned to Saint-Santin to fetch our belongings and the men, who were 200 strong.

Not only did I find London had received our signal, they had already sent me my own radio operator, who would share his codes with Denden. Roger was a good-looking American Marine, aged nineteen. He spoke very little French but they all liked him and he fitted into our life-style smoothly. Unhappily for us all, Bazooka had been ordered to the Clermont-Ferrand area to instruct another Maquis group.

Hubert had been working hard setting up our camp and we all settled in straight away. The men were still part of the Maquis d'Auvergne but they were more or less our own special group attached to our Allied team. We were lucky to have them with us; they were all good men, we knew them personally and, like the Americans and British, they had no political aspirations. They only wanted to get rid of the enemy and return to their families. That night we were joined by thirty young Frenchmen, all evaders from the *relève*—the German compulsory labour force. They were enthusiastic but as yet untrained.

I was heartily sick of sleeping on the damp ground and when one day Tarvidat asked me for an extra quantity of Bren guns which were in short supply, I bribed him by promising Brens for a bus. However, I stipulated a bus with two long seats in the rear, facing each other, so I could balance the big mattress (also procured by Tardivat) on top of them. He took a few men down to a main road and set up a road-block. As each bus reached the barriers he made all the passengers alight while he inspected the rear. This procedure continued until a suitable bus arrived. The poor passengers must have been petrified by the sight of the Maquisards, all armed to the teeth and looking fierce. The passengers in the unsuitable buses must have been mystified also when they were allowed to continue their journey. Naturally he received his Bren guns. He was going to get them anyway. So I used to sleep in the back of the bus, on a beautiful soft mattress with nylon parachutes for sheets, and entertain in the front.

Somehow or other I'd managed to have with me a couple of pretty nighties, leftovers from another life. No matter how tired I was, after a day in a male world, wearing trousers, I'd change into a frilly nightie to sleep in my bus.

Our immediate plan at Ygrande was to increase the level of security which had been impossible when we were attached to the oversized groups further south. We had a conference with our men and it was decided unanimously that we would never remain in one spot more than three or four days. If the site happened to be in a particularly favourable position we could stay one week, but no longer. As soon as we moved to one place we would agree on the next one and the leaders would be informed. In the case of a sudden attack my bus would be loaded immediately with wireless equipment, the operators themselves and my bicycle, and proceed to our rendezvous point. A driver and one man were detailed to enforce this rule.

We had not been in Ygrande two days when our lookouts warned us that a large body of Germans were approaching. Our withdrawal went like clockwork. Three thousand Huns wasted all their ammunition to capture one empty farmhouse. We were all delighted, as can well be imagined.

Two American weapons instructors were to be dropped at a field nearby that same night. Remembering the complete lack of security when I had been introduced to the entire village of Cosne-d'Allier, I determined that things would be different when these two arrived. And they were different, almost unique, in fact.

They arrived safely, although one of them had lost his suitcase and we took them straight back to our camp, where we entertained them in the bus. Naturally we greeted these two Americans, John Alsop and Reeve Schley, with French champagne. They did not speak much French but we didn't mind as long as they could instruct the Maquis groups in the use of our weapons. They gave us news from London and we carried on talking and drinking until about four in the morning.

They looked smart in their uniforms, especially Schley who had on beautiful leather cavalry boots. I knew that when our men saw how well dressed they were they would start moaning again about our uniforms. All we could give them were socks, boots, khaki trousers and shirts, and they were dying to have decent uniforms. We took them to their simple quarters which Denden and I had cleaned up; we had even put some wildflowers in a jam jar next to their beds. As we left, one of them asked quite casually if we ever got attacked, and quite casually I replied that we had just been attacked the day before but I didn't think the Germans would be back that day. That proved to be the understatement of the year. They were already at our back door.

I woke up when the Germans started firing and yelled out to the Americans who were close by to get up—we were being attacked. We couldn't find Hubert; he had disappeared. As we learned much later, he had got up early to find the missing suitcase before anyone else did. Schley must have been in such a hurry to get dressed that he put on his cavalry boots first and couldn't get his trousers on, so reckoning he didn't have time to start all over again, he cut his trousers with a knife and appeared in front of me in short scalloped trousers. I wasn't much better—I hadn't time to take my pink satin nightdress off and it was showing under my shirt.

Our 200 men had disappeared to fight and our "High Command," consisting only of Denden and me, were packing everything into my bus which had started to leave when I noticed the bicycle was left behind. Denden raced over and threw it on top of the bus, and immediately started screaming blue murder. He had got caught on some electric wires! Roger and the driver were laughing their heads off. I was doubled up, tears running down my face. All this time the Americans were standing there surveying the scene amidst the sound of machine-gun fire, grenades and what have you.

Thank goodness they didn't understand much French, as the scouts soon came back with the news that we were being attacked by 6,000 Germans. We were 200 plus two in the High Command, two newly arrived Americans and thirty new recruits. We were definitely outnumbered. For a while we hoped Hubert would arrive with some reinforcements, but he was trapped, kilometres away.

Then some of our defenders came back and said the Germans were well entrenched but why couldn't we try the bazookas that had been dropped the previous night and which they were obviously dying to try out. The problem was that the two instructors were the only ones who knew how to use them, and they couldn't speak French. But our men insisted they could knock out a few German posts if only someone would show them what to do. Those poor Americans! It was like a scene from a comic opera.

The wounded were being brought in so I put the other member of the High Command, Denden, in charge of them, irrespective of his plea that he didn't like the sight of blood. I gave him plenty of bandages and a gallon of pure alcohol. I didn't issue him with any arms as he didn't like them either.

We collected all the bazookas and prepared to face the enemy, the two non-French-speaking instructors, the interpreter (me), and two men for each bazooka. I think our new recruits must have thought it was going to be a piece of cake because twenty of them volunteered to carry some of our material. I warned them to stick to the woods but they unfortunately disobeyed my orders and took a short-cut. Seven of them were killed immediately by the German machine-guns. The other thirteen fled back to our camp.

The rest of us carried on regardless. Everything was put in place, the Americans instructed on bazookas, firing off. I ran from one crew to another translating. They knocked out several German posts and when we had exhausted our supply of ammunition (some had not been unpacked) we withdrew. This may have been a first for the Americans but it was also a first for me. I had never been on a battlefield translating from English into French on how to fire a bazooka.

We returned to our camp to find Denden with a loaded carbine slung over his shoulder, a row of grenades fastened on to his belt, and a Colt. The man who was afraid of guns! He was also very, very drunk. He had been drinking the pure alcohol as he tended the wounded, and it had given him Dutch courage. I removed the grenades as he could have not only killed himself, he could have killed us too, and I had enough trouble on my plate.

I kept my fingers crossed as I told Alsop and Schley that everything would be all right and asked one of our scouts to show me the way to the Spaniards' camp. We crawled across several fields and when I reached one of their outposts I asked the sentry on duty to ask his Colonel to send my SOS to Tardivat.

When I returned to our camp Schley said he didn't want the Germans to smoke the Havana cigars his father had given him back in New York, so the three of us sat down and puffed away as if we didn't have a care in the world. Suddenly we heard the sound of Bren guns and mortars to the rear of the Germans. I yelled out to everyone: "Tardivat, let's go!" He gave us time to retreat, then retreated himself, leaving the Germans to conquer a deserted campsite.

Tardivat and his men had been sitting down to lunch when he received my SOS. I was amazed that Frenchmen would leave their meal, and said so flippantly. All he said was, "Aren't you glad you gave me all those Bren guns?" However, he had saved our lives. We had smoked those cigars for nothing! All this happened during the first twelve hours after the Americans' arrival, and I had planned such a pleasant and relaxed day for them, a day they would remember. They would certainly remember it, but for entirely different reasons.

We found Hubert hiding in a barn. Having retrieved Schley's suitcase he had been cut off from us when the fighting had begun and had therefore been unable to assist in any way.

Several of our badly wounded men were smuggled into a private hospital run by a religious order. The seven reckless young men who had died so tragically were laid to rest in a nearby cemetery. They were buried with all the military honours possible considering the danger of conducting such a service.

We stayed near the Spanish camp for a couple of days and moved onto a good site in the Forêt de Tronçais. It was well concealed, protected by Tardivat's groups and, to our delight, near a large pond where we were able to enjoy the pleasure of bathing ourselves, instead of having to carry out our ablutions from a small bucket of water. If we were bathing during the daytime we either dived under the water or made a dash for the forest when German planes flew overhead.

We were receiving new recruits every day. Alsop and Schley were kept busy all day long instructing them on the use of weapons and explosives, fortunately within the peace of our forest and not on the battlefield!

The Americans had brought their cameras with them and they had, unknown to me, taken a snap of me getting out of my pink satin nightdress. Denden had told them of my famous satin nightdresses, one pink and one blue. However mannish I looked by day, I always slept in satin.

I determined to get even. I waited until Schley went into bathe one morning. He undressed and left his clothes and camera by a tree. I took the camera and sat by the water's edge, waiting for him to emerge. After being in the icy cold water for thirty minutes he was blue in the face but he would not admit defeat. The German planes appeared on the horizon and he was forced to reassess his predicament. We always found time to play jokes on one another and enjoy a good laugh. It became a battle of wits between the sexes.

There had been nothing violent about my nature before the war yet the years would see a great change. But in spite of my virulent attitude to the enemy I could not condone torture and brutality on our part, although I was not foolish enough to believe they would extend me the same courtesy. Consequently the day I was informed confidentially by a man in our Maquis that a group nearby were holding three females, one of whom was a German spy. I threatened to disarm them if they did not release the poor unfortunate women into my custody. All three had been ill-treated and used as if they were prostitutes.

The leader of the group concerned was a married man. I had accepted his hospitality before he had joined the Maquis. When I learnt his wife had been aware of the brutality meted out to the women I was horrified to think I had been friendly with them both.

The two French girls were no problem, but the German girl could not be set free. I interrogated her and she admitted she had been sent to spy on the Maquis and then to report back to the Gestapo. She hated the French and the British as much as I hated her people. Reluctantly I informed her she would have to be shot as there was no alternative under the circumstances.

At first the men refused to shoot a woman and agreed to form a firing squad only after I had announced I would undertake the task myself. She spat at me as she passed and shouted "Heil Hitler" before she died.

For my part I showed absolutely no emotion as she walked to her death. How had this been possible? How bad I become so aggressive? It was simple. I remembered Vienna, Berlin and the Jews. I remembered seeing a poor French woman, seven months pregnant, tied to a stake and bayonetted, criss-cross, in the stomach by a German soldier. Her screaming two-year-old held her hand and she was left to die with her unborn child. A German officer stood by and watched the soldier carry out his orders. I remembered my friend in the escape-route network who was beheaded with an axe after he had been captured by the Gestapo. The enemy had made me tough. I had no pity for them nor would I expect any in return.

I have returned to Germany many times since their defeat. They have worked hard to rebuild their Fatherland. It is a lovely country to visit and although I am quite happy to be friendly with some young Germans I keep well away from the older generation in case I become involved with some ex-Nazi. I will never be able to forget the misery and death they caused to so many millions of innocent people; the savage brutality, the sadism, the unnecessary bloodshed, the slaughter and inhuman acts they performed on other human beings. I am inclined to feel sorry for the young Germans of today, knowing how utterly miserable I would be if I was descended from a Nazi.

War is a calamity. It is destructive and brings great sorrow and loss of life. But at least it is, or should be, a clear-cut manoeuvre between two opposing nations fighting each other until one side admits defeat. Civil war is disastrous because it means two or more parts of a nation fighting for supremacy. Although I did not go to Spain during the Civil War I was always in close touch with people who did.

By July 1944 there were so many branches of the Resistance it was difficult to keep track of them. They were right-wingers, left-wingers, red-hot Communists, government officials, civil servants, ex-Vichyites, ex-Milicians, secret army, regular army and dozens more, besides masses of individuals trying to get on the bandwagon. We kept our distance from the would-be politicians, concentrating on arming the Maquisards as efficiently and rapidly as possible.

Hubert was fully occupied with the leaders of the adjacent groups, discussing and executing plans that would frustrate the Germans wherever and whenever the opportunity arose. They attacked the enemy convoys on the road, they intercepted and stole hundreds of wagon-loads of food being transported to Germany, they set up ambushes in the most unlikely places and generally made the existence of the Germans in the area a perilous one. Apart from these activities they manned the dropping zones at night and in their spare time they prepared the explosives needed to destroy the targets we had been assigned.

Laurent had provided me with a new car and a driver who knew the Allier and the Puy-de-Dôme like the back of his hand. I would contact dozens and dozens of groups of men hiding in forests. After meeting their leaders I would assess their groups, most of whom impressed me, and would promise to arm their men and also contribute a certain amount of money towards their subsistence.

Sometimes Roger accompanied me. He was not as good or experienced an operator as Denden but he was more relaxed and never complained about the conditions under which he worked. If he had to transmit or receive messages while we were travelling by car we would pull into the side of the road, he would throw the aerial over a tree, sit on the wheel or bumper bar, balance his set on his knee and tap away in Morse code. If we ran out of distilled water he never made a fuss like Denden did, he would simply substitute ordinary water.

I had to find new fields where we could organize our air-drops. This was becoming more and more difficult as the Germans were attacking Maquis groups every day in retaliation. Roger and I had to shoot our way out of a road-block on two occasions and we were extremely fortunate to escape capture.

One day I was obliged to go to Vichy. When my business there was concluded

I decided to treat myself to a good meal in an expensive black-market restaurant before returning to the forest. A member of an unruly group of men (whom, incidentally, I had refused to arm) had apparently been informed of my extravagance and decided I had been spending money to which his so-called "Resistance" group was entitled. He was quite wrong as Hubert, Denden and I always received our own personal allowances from London. This ignorant and uncouth individual was airing his views about our British team in a café in a little village where I was due at midday. My visit had obviously been discussed there. He became very, very inebriated and announced he was going to kill me. He then opened a case and displayed several grenades. The patron of the café became alarmed and was going to dispatch someone to warn me as soon as I arrived on the outskirts of the village.

This village was old, with narrow streets. The only way a motorist could drive through it was to take a blind alleyway where a reflecting mirror warned of the traffic ahead. The café was only a few metres away.

I was early, and blissfully unaware of the drama about to unfold. When the would-be assassin heard a car approaching he took a grenade out of the case, removed the pin and held it in his hand. When he saw a woman in the car he went to throw it but he was so drunk he had forgotten the pin was out and it blew up in his hand. I saw the explosion and bits of human flesh all over the place, but it was a few minutes before I heard the story. I could not feel sorry for him. He and his men were the types who pretended to be members of the Resistance and at times gave it a bad name.

This story reached the forest via "bush wireless" before I returned. It was decided there and then that I would have a bodyguard whenever I travelled by car. Tardivat suggested we approach the Spanish group and their colonel immediately delegated six of his best men to protect me.

We must have made an impressive sight as our three cars sped along the roads. They had installed a Bren machine-gun in the windscreen of each car and another one at the rear. Whenever possible we remained on the secondary roads, which were covered in red dust. As I always travelled in the second car I arrived at our destination looking like a Red Indian, so after the first trip I transferred to the first car. I tried to explain in Spanish that it was because of vanity and not bravery but I don't think it convinced them.

These six Spaniards became devoted to me and I never had any worries when I was with them, even though at times we were obliged to use the National Routes. If we stopped at a village for a meal and anyone dared to look sideways at me they would stand there looking fierce with their Sten guns at the ready. They would inspect the kitchens and one day they forced two men to show their identity cards simply because they were staring at me during lunch. They were experienced fighters, having gone through the Spanish Civil War. I must have covered thousands of kilometres with my bodyguard. To me it was all very theatrical but the Spaniards took it seriously. I often wondered what the people thought of our little convoy as we passed through the villages.

In the latter part of July and during August I was travelling continuously.

Every night hundreds of containers filled with weapons and explosives were being parachuted on to our fields in anticipation of the Allied landings, which ultimately took place in the south of France on 15 August.

The arrival of the Americans—especially as they were officers wearing such splendid uniforms—had boosted the morale of the Maquisards in the area to such an extent that we had intended to hold a banquet in their honour. The battle the morning after their arrival and several subsequent mishaps had forced us to abandon all major social activities. However, as Tardivat pointed out, we now had two important events to celebrate: firstly, the arrival of our American instructors and secondly, my lucky escape. We chose a night when the moon was low as we would be unlikely to receive an air-drop.

Tardivat was in charge of all the catering arrangements. He conferred with a chef in a nearby town who prepared most of the food in his hotel. The morning of the banquet he was "kidnapped" at gun-point and taken to our forest. The alleged kidnapping was to protect him in case he was interrogated by the Germans or the Milicians at a later date.

Denden, assisted by several experts, installed an elaborate row of lights overhead which could be turned off immediately if our sentries warned us of enemy planes approaching. Our tables consisted of long logs covered by white sheets borrowed from friendly villagers. The chef served a magnificent eight-course meal, accompanied by some superb French wines. He hovered around looking impressive wearing his snow-white chef's hat and apron, assisted by several volunteers from our group, suitably dressed for the occasion.

It was a banquet I will never forget, and most certainly one that could never be repeated. Several hundred men attended and every single one had been spending hours trying to make his clothes look as smart as possible. The lighting system was a huge success—our part of the forest looked like a fairyland. Tardivat greeted the guests with typical French formality and the foreign guests responded with great dignity! We toasted everyone and everything. We swore our eternal allegiance and love to France, Great Britain and the United States of America. When we couldn't think of anything else to toast we swayed to our feet and toasted the Germans and the Allied Forces for not having interrupted our gala dinner.

Half-way through this extraordinary banquet a serious French Maquisard was escorted to my table by a sentry. He was delivering a message from his leader. Naturally we invited him to join our party. He looked at all the food on the tables and the piles of empty bottles on the ground and the full ones in the process of being consumed, and asked me if this was the style in which we dined every night. We managed to keep a serious face and everyone who had heard his question replied, "Yes, of course, don't you?"

In the early hours of the morning a violent thunder and lightning storm forced us to scurry back to our respective camps in a disorderly fashion. The bright and almost continuous flashes of lightning made it easy for me to find my way to my bus, but the ground had become like a bog and I was soaking wet and covered with mud by the time I reached it. Furthermore, I was feeling sorry for myself and for the unceremonious manner in which our banquet had been terminated.

Soon after installing ourselves in the forest we had bought a horse, especially for Roger as sometimes he got bored, although Schley exercised it if he had the time. As I was trying to clean my clothes I heard the horse neighing. I looked through the window and there he was in the pouring rain making a terrible noise. Immediately I stopped feeling sorry for myself and proceeded to lavish all my love and sympathy on the poor unfortunate horse. We had a galvanised iron lean-to attached to my bus which we used as a makeshift bathroom and where we kept our toilet necessities. I dragged the horse in, talking to him all the time, telling him not to worry about the storm as I would look after him. Then I fell asleep.

I woke up several hours later. The horse and the galvanised-iron roof had disappeared. Actually he was foolish to run away as, with the meat shortage, he could not have gone far before ending up in some hungry person's saucepan. We found the roof some distance away. The contents of our bathroom were ruined as they were all mixed up with horse manure. Alsop had been sleeping under a yellow parachute. The rain had soaked through it, so he appeared looking as if he had jaundice. Denden took one look at him and went back to bed. That night our personal message to the BBC was "Andrée had a horse in the bathroom."

Thank goodness the Germans did not attack that night.

Without doubt, Tardivat was the man I most admired then. He was intelligent, disciplined, reliable, honest and very brave. He also had a fantastic sense of fun, which I appreciated. When I was not on the road he would invite me to take part in some of his escapades. We carried out several ambushes together and blew up a few small bridges. If any German convoys were foolish enough to pass through his area he always managed to do some damage to their vehicles. In suitable terrain we loved using what we called a "trip wire." It was attached to a tree on each side of the road and the first vehicle in the convoy would blow up. We liked to be concealed on a nearby hill so we could watch the confusion before withdrawing to a safer spot.

The most exciting sortie I ever made with Tardivat was an attack on the German headquarters in Montluçon. He and his men organised this raid from beginning to end. All the weapons and explosives used were hidden in a house near the headquarters, ready to be picked up just after noon when the Germans would be enjoying their pre-lunch drinks. Each one of us had received specific orders. I entered the building by the back door, raced up the stairs, opened the first door along the passageway and threw in my grenades, closed the door and ran like hell back to my car which was ready to make a quick getaway. The headquarters was completely wrecked inside the building, and several dozen Germans did not lunch that day, nor any other day for that matter. The hardest part of the raid was to convince the nearby residents that the Allies had not landed and that they should return immediately to their homes and remain indoors.

In the early hours of the morning of 15 August, the long-awaited invasion of the south of France became a reality. Nearly 300,000 troops, comprised of Americans, British, Canadians and French, disembarked between Toulon and Cannes. The Resistance movements all over France had been anxiously awaiting the landings, as it would mean the beginning of the end for the Germans.

The numerous Maquis groups in the Allier set about destroying the targets they had been assigned for the second D-day. I'd brought the plans for these raids from England in that handbag—the bridges, roads, cable lines, railways, factories—anything that could be of use to the Germans. They destroyed them all except one which was a synthetic petrol plant at Saint-Hilaire. Tardivat, who had seized the entire output of fuel two months previously, said it would be a shame to destroy the plant as another supply of fuel would soon be available. London gave us permission to leave the plant intact as long as we could be certain the fuel would not fall into German hands.

Tardivat, plus the Anglo-American team, backed by several of our most bloodthirsty-looking Maquisards, called to see the plant manager at his home. He was not a bit co-operative when we informed him we were going to ruin his plant for the Allies. However, he was taken by force to the distillery and then to the boardroom, where he was interrogated by the male members of our team. He was warned that his failure to comply with their orders would have drastic consequences and that as he had traded with the enemy he would be put under arrest and placed under the charge of the Maquis.

He was white in the face and trembling by this time and assured us he would reserve the total output of fuel for the Maquis, mentioning the amount we could expect. I had not been included in this particular conversation, I was just standing by, armed to the teeth and trying to look as fierce as possible. Nevertheless, I did not want to be left out of the proceedings so I piped up and said that according to the figures I had, the amount of fuel he promised was not the entire output. To everyone's surprise, including my own, he agreed that perhaps it could be a little more. Tardivat left several men to protect our interests and keep an eye on the manager, but he was so scared of the Maquis he did not put a foot wrong after that day. Now we were all oil kings we made for the nearest bistro to celebrate our success.

All our operations were not as comical as our Saint-Hilaire one had been, but as the weeks sped by and the Germans were on the run, both from the Allied Forces and the French Resistance, it was often possible to enjoy a little light relief as we carried on with our duties.

At long last the Germans were paying a high price for the suffering they had inflicted on the French people. They knew the Resistance was lurking everywhere, just waiting to pounce. Too often the enemy had behaved like savages and now they were afraid for their own lives.

We trooped over to Cosne-d'Allier, the little village where Hubert and I had stayed when we first arrived. As we had been introduced to the entire village, they all came out of their houses when they saw me and followed us around when we laid our charges on the bridges and road junctions. It was the most enthusiastic audience we had ever seen or heard. They jumped up and down as each was detonated, and clapped and cheered as we withdrew. The difficult part of the operation had been to keep the villagers at a safe distance.

Tardivat decided, after his success with the German headquarters, I that he would like to attack their garrison at Montluçon, where the force had been reduced to about 3,000. He set off with about 300 men and Alsop, Schley and Hubert. All the leaders were armed with bazookas—a popular weapon during World War II and especially suitable for the Maquis. Alsop and Schley led their groups while Hubert returned to our camp with a message from Tardivat inviting me to join in the fun. I had just finished coding my signals for London so I grabbed a bazooka, my carbine and several grenades, and set off for Montluçon in Hubert's car. When we reached the town and made enquiries as to Tardivat's position, we were informed that he had captured half the garrison and we would have to cross a certain bridge in order to reach him. The only trouble was that as we began crossing the bridge someone opened fire with machine-guns. I got out of the car and started waving to Tardivat up in the garrison. It wasn't Tardivat, it was a German, and we were on the wrong bridge. We did a quick about-turn but the others teased us for days.

The fort was held for several days but the Germans sent over strong reinforcements from the east and the Maquis withdrew back to the forest. However, the whole town and the temporary victors could not conceal the satisfaction the event had given them.

It had rained for days, and the forest was like a quagmire. We were soaked to the skin and thoroughly miserable. Now that the Germans had troubles of their own they no longer presented a great threat to the Maquis and we determined to find more comfortable quarters. We were told of Fragne, an empty château a few kilometres from Montluçon. The owner had inherited it from an aunt but as he had not been able to install electricity and running water it had never attracted the attention of the Germans. Hubert and I talked to the caretaker, and through her the owner gave us permission to occupy the château for as long as we wished.

It was a huge place with spacious rooms. We slept on mattresses or in sleeping-bags and it was absolute bliss to be out of the rain. There was a lovely old clock-tower and a deep well at the rear of the château where we fetched our water for washing purposes, but for cooking the caretaker allowed us to fill our buckets from her kitchen tap. We moved in about one week before my birthday, which was on 30 August. As the men were all walking around looking secretive I guessed they were planning some kind of celebration.

We were occupied day and night. Alsop and Schley were instructing men on the use of the weapons and explosives we were receiving; Hubert was conferring with the other leaders; and I was receiving air-drops every night of the moon period. I had about twenty fields scattered all over the area but I decided that in future we would use the grounds of the château for any air-drops intended for our own use.

The men laughed when I announced this but realising I was serious they immediately volunteered to assist me to try to make the plan functional. They prepared an elaborate lighting system, using every available battery, and after a trial run we were convinced we could retire to our beds if the planes were delayed or cancelled. Should we hear them coming while we were in bed, we could switch on the lights which were already in position, hop out of bed and be on the field in time for the reception. London was informed immediately of our latest dropping zone.

At the headquarters of the Special Operations Executive, a Canadian ready to be parachuted on our new field found the château was marked on the Michelin map and wanted to know what idiot was using it. They informed him. Apparently all he said was, "Oh, Nancy." He was the chap who blew up the condom at Beaulieu. He and his travelling companions dropped quite safely on our field. We ushered them into our château with great pride and extended our usual hospitality.

Paris was liberated on 25 August 1944, and the whole country rejoiced; it would be hard to describe the excitement in the air. After defeat and years of humiliation their beautiful capital was free. The aggressors were now the hunted. The Germans were on the run and the French people were overcome with joy. My men were organizing a surprise for my birthday and at the same time we were going to celebrate the Liberation of Paris.

It was a wonderful party, which happily the Germans did not interrupt. All our colleagues were invited and so was our landlord. If anyone was unable to attend the luncheon, they came along afterwards. Everyone we knew helped us obtain the food and wine. It was amazing to see how many bottles of wine and champagne some farmers had been able to bury in their fields. Madame Renard and her daughter were guests. We supplied the ingredients for the marvellous dessert tarts and cakes she made for our party.

When all the guests had arrived we were escorted to the steps of the terrace leading into the rear entrance of the château. It was a secluded spot and could not be seen from the main road, which the Germans were still using. I was presented with a magnificent bouquet of flowers and told at the same time to be ready to take the salute. That was the surprise they had been planning. I was amazed to see we had so many smart, well-trained men. There were hundreds and hundreds of them. Then suddenly I recognised a man I had already seen marching by. The penny dropped. Once they had marched past our steps they ran like the devil right around the château and rejoined the men ahead. Without doubt they were the finest and fittest body of fighters I have ever had the honour and privilege to salute.

We gathered in the immense hall where rows of makeshift tables had been erected. Beautiful floral decorations surrounded the tables so that the emptiness of the vast room was not noticed. The speeches were endless and became more and more sentimental as we consumed bottle after bottle of the best wines and champagne France could offer.

There was only one sad note. Madame Renard's daughter announced at the table that Alex, Denden's boyfriend, had been killed. She had not known of the relationship between the two. We had to console him the best way we could but I'm afraid we were all too busy to be able to sympathise with appropriate dignity.

Everyone brought me some little gift. They must have been searching in the village for ages as at that time everything was in short supply. My Spaniards, who had absolutely no money, had gathered all the wildflowers they could find in the forest and wrapped them in a Spanish flag, and one of the bodyguard had written me a poem. It was all very touching. The party continued until the early hours of the morning. It was a great success and the talk of the Allier for some time.

When the Germans evacuated Montluçon, we were lucky. The château had been empty for so long and still, from the outside, looked deserted. The whole German convoy passed by without disturbing our Allied team hiding inside.

In September 1944 the Germans evacuated Vichy. Gaspard and Hubert had prearranged to join forces and enter the town at the same time. But Gaspard had stolen a march on us and gone on ahead. We gathered our team together and hurried after him. Vichy represented everything we had been fighting against, and we were determined to be a part of its liberation.

The collaborators seemed to have vanished into thin air and the crowds in the street went wild with joy. All through the night we were fêted wherever we went.

A ceremony was organised the following morning at the Cenotaph. All the assembled groups were to lay wreaths. I was nominated by our Allied team to represent them. When the mayor had finished his address, a woman emerged from the crowds and came towards me. She had been a receptionist at the Hôtel du Louvre et Paix in Marseille. Quite abruptly she informed me that Henri was dead. I was stunned. I do not know whether I had decided it was unreasonable to let the nightmare I had had in London influence my feelings; perhaps I had subconsciously put the dream at the back of my mind and determined to carry on as if it had not happened. But I do know that ever since my return to France I had been taking it for granted that Henri was alive. I burst into tears. Denis took me away.

I wanted to go straight to Marseille to find out what had happened. Laurent, who was a magician where vehicles were concerned, put our car into perfect running order and the five of us raced down to Marseille—Hubert, Denden, John Alsop, our doctor friend Pierre Vellat and myself. It was a chaotic journey. The Allied Air Force had destroyed all the major bridges and the Resistance had sabotaged the targets they had been given for the landing in the south of France. We were the only ones going in the opposite direction. Finally, we arrived in Marseille.

I went straight to my butcher's shop, which was closed, so I went around to the back entrance and tapped on the kitchen window. They recognised me and I could see the look of alarm that passed between them as they wondered whether I was aware of the bad news. I put them at ease at once, then asked about Picon. The Ficetoles had taken him when Henri had been arrested, but their home had been destroyed in one of the air raids and no one knew if they were dead or alive.

After spending hours searching for them we were directed to a little place outside Marseille. There was no answer when I knocked on the door but Picon was inside and started howling. After twenty months he had recognised my voice. He was so excited when he was let out after the Ficetoles returned that our doctor, Pierre, had to give him tranquillisers.

Henri had been arrested by the Gestapo in May 1943. He had been imprisoned until his death on 16 October, five months later. It was in the middle of October that I had had that nightmare in London.

We returned to the chateau. Picon, who would not let me out of his sight, came too. We found dozens of invitations waiting there for us from all the towns and villages where we had been known.

I think that somehow I'd been subconsciously mourning Henri since the dream in London nearly a year before. Nothing was going to bring him back, and in spite of my grief I could not be unhappy knowing I'd contributed to the Liberation of France.

Our group of men at the château was preparing to go home. The Americans returned to London. We left the château in good order, thanked the landlord and caretaker for their kindness, and the three of us dawdled back to Paris. All along the route the French were celebrating the Liberation and it seemed to be one glorious party after another. We thought we might be the last ones to report back to Paris, where SOE had opened a branch, but a few more stragglers were still enjoying French hospitality.

Paris had been liberated in August 1944, but it would be another nine months of fighting across France before the German surrender in May 1945. After Paris was freed, Tardivat joined the army and kept fighting. Tragically, after all his adventures as a Maquis leader, he lost a leg in the fighting at Belfort Gap.

As there was a long waiting list for seats on an Allied Transport plane, we proceeded to enjoy ourselves in Paris. Denden spent a whole day at the hairdresser and came out looking ten years younger. Hubert disappeared for days. It transpired he had been looking after his future and organised himself an interesting position in a government department. I tried to trace old friends. Some were dead—some, including Stephanie, had disappeared and others had not returned from the country areas where they had taken refuge.

The Invaders
(from *The Moon is Down*)

John Steinbeck

Tonder sat down on his chair and put his hands to his temples and he said brokenly, "I want a girl. I want to go home. I want a girl. There's a girl in this town, a pretty girl, I see her all the time. She has blonde hair. She lives beside the old-iron stove. I want that girl."

Prackle said, "Watch yourself. Watch your nerves."

At that moment the lights went out again and the room was in darkness. Hunter spoke while the matches were being struck and an attempt was being made to light the lanterns; he said, "I thought I had all of them. I must have missed one. But I can't be running down there all the time. I've got good men down there."

Tonder lighted the first lantern and then he lighted the other, and Hunter spoke sternly to Tonder. "Lieutenant, do your talking to us if you have to talk. Don't let the enemy hear you talk this way. There's nothing these people would like better than to know your nerves are getting thin. Don't let the enemy hear you."

Tonder sat down again. The light was sharp on his face and the hissing filled the room. He said, "That's it! The enemy's everywhere! Every man, every woman, even children! The enemy's everywhere. Their faces look out of doorways. The white faces behind the curtains, listening. We have beaten them, we have won everywhere, and they wait and obey, and they wait. Half the world is ours. Is it the same in other places, Major?"

And Hunter said, "I don't know."

"That's it," Tonder said. "We don't know. The reports—everything in hand. Conquered countries cheer our soldiers, cheer the new order." His voice changed and grew soft and still softer. "What do the reports say about us? Do they say we are cheered, loved, flowers in our paths? Oh, these horrible people waiting in the snow!"

And Hunter said, "Now that's off your chest, do you feel better?"

Prackle had been beating the table softly with his good fist, and he said, "He shouldn't talk that way. He should keep things to himself. He's a soldier, isn't he? Then let him be a soldier."

The door opened quietly and Captain Loft came in, and there was snow on his helmet and snow on his shoulders. His nose was pinched and red and his overcoat collar was high about his ears. He took off his helmet and the snow fell on to the floor and he brushed his shoulders. "What a job!" he said.

"More trouble?" Hunter asked.

"Always trouble. I see they've got your dynamo again. Well, I think I fixed the mine for a while."

"What's your trouble?" Hunter asked.

"Oh, the usual thing with me—the slow-down and a wrecked dump car. I saw the wrecker, though. I shot him. I think I have a cure for it, Major, now. I just thought it up. I'll make each man take out a certain amount of coal. I can't starve the men or they can't work, but I've really got the answer. If the coal doesn't come out, no food for the families. We'll have the men eat at the mine, so there's no dividing at home. That ought to cure it. They work or their kids don't eat. I told them just now."

"What did they say?"

Loft's eyes narrowed fiercely. "Say? What do they ever say? Nothing! Nothing at all! But we'll see whether the coal comes out now." He took off his coat and shook it, and his eyes fell on the entrance door and he saw that it was open a crack. He moved silently to the door, jerked it open, then closed it. "I thought I had closed that door tight," he said.

"You did," said Hunter.

Prackle still turned the pages of his illustrated paper. His voice was normal again. "Those are monster guns we're using in the east. I never saw one of them. Did you, Captain?"

"Oh, yes," said Captain Loft. "I've seen them fired. They're wonderful. Nothing can stand up against them."

Tonder said, "Captain, do you get much news from home?"

"A certain amount," said Loft.

"Is everything well there?"

"Wonderful!" said Loft. "The armies move ahead everywhere."

"The British aren't defeated yet?"

"They are defeated in every engagement."

"But they fight on?"

"A few air-raids, no more."

"And the Russians?"

"It's all over."

Tonder said insistently. "But they fight on?"

"A little skirmishing, no more."

"Then we have just about won, haven't we, Captain?" Tonder asked

"Yes, we have."

Tonder looked closely at him and said, "You believe this, don't you, Captain?"

Prackle broke in, "Don't let him start that again!"

Loft scowled at Tonder. "I don't know what you mean."

Tonder said, "I mean this: we'll be going home before long, won't we?"

"Well, the reorganization will take some time," Hunter said. "The new order can't be put into effect in a day, can it?"

Tonder said, "All our lives, perhaps?"

And Prackle said, "Don't let him start it again!"

Loft came very close to Tonder and he said, "Lieutenant, I don't like the tone of your questions. I don't like the tone of doubt."

Hunter looked up and said, "Don't be hard on him, Loft. He's tired. We're all tired."

"Well, I'm tired, too," said Loft, "but I don't let treasonable doubts get in."

Hunter said, "Don't bedevil him, I tell you! Where's the colonel, do you know?"

"He's making out his report. He's asking for reinforcements," said Loft. "It's a bigger job than we thought."

Prackle asked excitedly, "Will he get them—the reinforcements?"

"How would I know?"

Tonder smiled. "Reinforcements!" he said softly. "Or maybe replacements. Maybe we could go home for a while." And he said, smiling, "Maybe I could walk down the street and people would say 'Hello,' and they'd say, 'There goes a soldier,' and they'd be glad for me and they'd be glad of me. And there'd be friends about, and I could turn my back to a man without being afraid."

Prackle said, "Don't start that again! Don't let him get out of hand again!"

And Loft said disgustedly, "We have enough trouble now without having the staff go crazy."

But Tonder went on, "You really think replacements will come, Captain?"

"I didn't say so."

"But you said they might."

"I said I didn't know. Look, Lieutenant, we've conquered half the world. We must police it for a while. You know that."

"But the other half?" Tonder asked.

"They will fight on hopelessly for a while," said Loft.

"Then we must spread out all over."

"For a while," said Loft.

Prackle said nervously, "I wish you'd make him shut up. I wish you would shut him up. Make him stop it."

Tonder got out his handkerchief and blew his nose, and he spoke a little like a man out of his head. He laughed embarrassedly. He said, "I had a funny dream. I guess it was a dream. Maybe it was a thought. Maybe a thought or a dream."

Prackle said, "Make him stop it, Captain!"

Tonder said, "Captain, is this place conquered?"

"Of course," said Loft.

A little note of hysteria crept into Tonder's laughter. He said, "Conquered and we're afraid; conquered and we're surrounded." His laughter grew shrill. "I had a dream—or a thought—out in the snow with the black shadows and the faces in the doorways, the cold faces behind curtains. I had a thought or a dream."

Prackle said, "Make him stop!"

Tonder said, "I dreamed the Leader was crazy."

And Loft and Hunter laughed together, and Loft said, "The enemy have found out how crazy. I'll have to write that one home. The papers would print that one. The enemy have learned how crazy the Leader is."

And Tonder went on laughing. "Conquest after conquest, deeper and deeper into molasses." His laughter choked him and he coughed into his handkerchief.

"Maybe the Leader is crazy. Flies conquer the flypaper! Flies captured two hundred miles of new flypaper!" His laughter was growing more hysterical now.

Prackle leaned over and shook him with his good hand. "Stop it! You stop it! You have no right!" And gradually Loft recognized that the laughter was hysterical and he stepped closer to Tonder and slapped him in the face. He said, "Lieutenant, stop it!"

Tonder's laughter went on and Loft slapped him again in the face and he said, "Stop it, Lieutenant! Do you hear me!"

Suddenly Tonder's laughter stopped and the room was quiet except for the hissing of the lanterns. Tonder looked in amazement at his hand and he felt his bruised face with his hand and he looked at his hand again and his head sank down towards the table. "I want to go home," he said.

There was a little street not far from the town square where small peaked roofs and little shops were mixed up together. The snow was beaten down on the walks and in the streets, but it piled up on the fences and it puffed on the roof peaks. It drifted against the shuttered windows of the little houses. And into the yards paths were shovelled. The night was dark and cold and no light showed from the windows to attract the bombers. And no one walked in the streets, for the curfew was strict. The houses were dark lumps against the snow. Every little while the patrol of six men walked down the street, peering about, and each man carried a long flashlight. The hushed tramp of their feet sounded in the street, the squeaks of their boots on the packed snow. They were muffled figures deep in thick coats; under their helmets were knitted caps which came down over their ears and covered their chins and mouths. A little snow fell, only a little, like rice.

The patrol talked as they walked, and they talked of things that they longed for—of meat and of hot soup and of the richness of butter, of the prettiness of girls and of their smiles and of their lips and their eyes. They talked of these things and sometimes they talked of their hatred of what they were doing and of their loneliness.

A small, peak-roofed house beside the iron shops was shaped like the others and wore its snow cap like the others. No light came from its shuttered windows and its storm doors were tightly closed. But inside a lamp burned in the small living-room and the door to the bedroom was open and the door to the kitchen was open. An iron stove was against the back wall with a little coal fire burning in it. It was a warm, poor, comfortable room, the floor covered with worn carpet, the walls papered in warm brown with an old-fashioned *fleur-de-lis* figure in gold. And on the back wall were two pictures, one of fish lying dead on a plate of ferns and the other of grouse lying dead on a fir bough. On the right wall there was a picture of Christ walking on the waves towards the despairing fishmen. Two straight chairs were in the room and a couch covered with a bright blanket. There was a little round table in the middle of the room, on which stood a kerosene lamp with a round flowered shade on it, and the light in the room was warm and soft.

The inner door, which led to the passage, which in turn led to the storm door, was beside the stove.

In a cushioned old rocking-chair beside the table Molly Morden sat alone. She was unravelling the wool from an old blue sweater and winding the yarn on a ball. She had quite a large ball of it. And on the table beside her was her knitting with the needles sticking in it, and a large pair of scissors. Her glasses lay on the table beside her, for she did not need them for knitting. She was pretty and young and neat. Her golden hair was done up on the top of her head and a blue bow was in her hair. Her hands worked quickly with the ravelling. As she worked, she glanced now and then at the door to the passage. The wind whistled in the chimney softly, but it was a quiet night, muffled with snow.

Suddenly she stopped her work. Her hands were still. She looked towards the door and listened. The tramping feet of the patrol went by in the street and the sound of their voices could be heard faintly. The sound faded away. Molly ripped out new yarn and wound it on the ball. And again she stopped. There was a rustle at the door and then three short knocks. Molly put down her work and went to the door.

"Yes?" she called.

She unlocked the door and opened it and a heavily cloaked figure came in. It was Annie, the cook, red-eyed and wrapped in mufflers. She slipped in quickly, as though practised at getting speedily through doors and getting them closed again behind her. She stood there red-nosed, sniffling and glancing quickly around the room.

Molly said, "Good evening, Annie. I didn't expect you tonight. Take your things off and get warm. It's cold out."

Annie said, "The soldiers brought winter early. My father always said a war brought bad weather, or bad weather brought a war. I don't remember which."

"Take off your things and come to the stove."

"I can't," said Annie importantly. "They're coming."

"Who are coming?" Molly said.

"His Excellency," said Annie, "and the doctor and the two Anders Boys."

"Here?" Molly asked. "What for?"

Annie held out her hand and there was a little package in it. "Take it," she said. "I stole it from the colonel's plate. It's meat."

And Molly unwrapped the little cake of meat and put it in her mouth and she spoke around her chewing. "Did you get some?"

Annie said, "I cook it, don't I? I always get some."

"When are they coming?"

Annie sniffed. "The Anders boys are sailing for England. They've got to go. They're hiding now."

"Are they?" Molly asked. "What for?"

"Well, it was their brother Jack, was shot today for wrecking that little car. The soldiers are looking for the rest of the family. You know how they do."

"Yes," Molly said, "I know how they do. Sit down, Annie."

"No time," said Annie. "I've got to get back and tell His Excellency it's all right here."

Molly said, "Did anybody see you come?"

Annie smiled proudly. "No, I'm awful good at sneaking."

"How will the Mayor get out?"

Annie laughed, "Joseph is going to be in his bed in case they look in, right in his night-shirt, right next to Madame!" And she laughed again. She said, "Joseph better lie pretty quiet."

Molly said, "It's an awful night to be sailing."

"It's better than being shot."

"Yes, so it is. Why is the Mayor coming here?"

"I don't know. He wants to talk to the Anders boys. I've got to go now, but I came to tell you."

Molly said, "How soon are they coming?"

"Oh, maybe half, maybe three-quarters of an hour," Annie said. "I'll come in first. Nobody bothers with old cooks." She started for the door and she turned midway, and as though accusing Molly of saying the last words she said truculently, "I'm not so old!" And she slipped out of the door and closed it behind her.

Molly went on knitting for a moment and then she got up and went to the stove and lifted the lid. The glow of the fire lighted her face. She stirred the fire and added a few lumps of coal and closed the stove again. Before she could get to her chair, there was a knocking on the outer door. She crossed the room and said to herself, "I wonder what she forgot." She went into the passage and she said, "What do you want?"

A man's voice answered her. She opened the door and a man's voice said, "I don't mean any harm. I don't mean any harm."

Molly backed into the room and Lieutenant Tonder followed her in. Molly said, "Who are you? What do you want? You can't come in here. What do you want?"

Lieutenant Tonder was dressed in his great grey overcoat. He entered the room and took off his helmet and he spoke pleadingly. "I don't mean any harm. Please let me come in."

Molly said, "What do you want?"

She shut the door behind him and he said, "Miss, I only want to talk, that's all. I want to hear you talk. That's all I want."

"Are you forcing yourself on me?" Molly asked.

"No, Miss, just let me stay a little while and then I'll go."

"What is it you want?"

Tonder tried to explain. "Can you understand this—can you believe this? Just for a little while, can't we forget this war? Just for a little while. Just for a little while, can't we talk together like people together?"

Molly looked at him for a long time and then a smile came to her lips. "You don't know who I am, do you?"

Tonder said, "I've seen you in the town. I know you're lovely. I know I want to talk to you."

And Molly still smiled. She said softly, "You don't know who I am." She sat in her chair and Tonder stood like a child, looking very clumsy. Molly continued, speaking quietly: "Why, you're lonely. It's as simple as that, isn't it?"

Tonder licked his lips and he spoke eagerly. "That's it," he said. "You understand. I knew you would. I knew you'd have to." His words came tumbling out. "I'm lonely to the point of illness. I'm lonely in the quiet and the hatred." And he said pleadingly, "Can't we talk, just a little bit?"

Molly picked up her knitting. She looked quickly at the front door. "You can stay not more than fifteen minutes. Sit down a little, Lieutenant."

She looked at the door again. The house creaked. Tonder became tense and he said, "Is someone here?"

"No, the snow is heavy on the roof. I have no man any more to push it down."

Tonder said gently, "Who did it? Was it something we did?"

And Molly nodded, looking far off. "Yes."

He sat down. "I'm sorry." After a moment he said, "I wish I could do something. I'll have the snow pushed off the roof."

"No," said Molly, "no."

"Why not?"

"Because the people would think I had joined with you. They would expel me. I don't want to be expelled."

Tonder said, "Yes, I see how that would be. You all hate us. But I'll take care of you if you'll let me."

Now Molly knew she was in control, and her eyes narrowed a little cruelly and she said, "Why do you ask? You are the conqueror. Your men don't have to ask. They take what they want."

"That's not what I want," Tonder said. "That's not the way I want it."

And Molly laughed, still a little cruelly. "You want me to like you, don't you, Lieutenant?"

He said simply, "Yes," and he raised his head and he said, "You are so beautiful, so warm. Your hair is bright. Oh, I've seen no kindness in a woman's face for so long!"

"Do you see any in mine?" she asked.

He looked closely at her. "I want to."

She dropped her eyes at last. "You're making love to me, aren't you, Lieutenant?"

He said clumsily, "I want you to like me. Surely I want you to like me. Surely I want to see that in your eyes. I have seen you in the streets. I have watched you pass by. I've given orders that you mustn't be molested. Have you been molested?"

And Molly said quietly, "Thank you; no, I've not been molested."

His words rushed on. "Why, I've even written a poem for you. Would you like to see my poem?"

And she said sardonically, "Is it a long poem? You have to go very soon."

He said, "No, it's a little tiny poem. It's a little bit of a poem." He reached inside his tunic and brought out a folded paper and handed it to her. She leaned close to the lamp and put on her glasses and she read quietly:

> Your eyes in their deep heavens
> Possess me and will not depart;

A sea of blue thoughts rushing
And pouring over my heart.

She folded the paper and put it in her lap. "Did you write this, Lieutenant?"
"Yes."
She said a little tauntingly, "To me?"
And Tonder answered uneasily, "Yes."
She looked at him steadily, smiling. "You didn't write it, Lieutenant, did you?"
He smiled back like a child caught in a lie. "No."
Molly asked him, "Do you know who did?"
Tonder said, "Yes, Heine wrote it. It's '*Mit deinen blauen Augen.*' I've always loved it." He laughed embarrassedly and Molly laughed with him, and suddenly they were laughing together. He stopped laughing just as suddenly and a bleakness came into his eyes. "I haven't laughed like this since forever." He said, "They told us the people would like us, would admire us. They do not. They only hate us." And then he changed the subject as though he worked against time. "You are so beautiful. You are as beautiful as the laughter."

Molly said, "You're beginning to make love to me, Lieutenant. You must go in a moment."

And Tonder said, "Maybe I want to make love to you. A man needs love. A man dies without love. His insides shrivel and his chest feels like a dry chip. I'm lonely."

Molly got up from her chair. She looked nervously at the door and she walked to the stove and, coming back, her face grew hard and her eyes grew punishing and she said, "Do you want to go to bed with me, Lieutenant?"

"I didn't say that! Why do you talk that way?"

Molly said cruelly, "Maybe I'm trying to disgust you. I was married once. My husband is dead now. You see, I'm not a virgin." Her voice was bitter.

Tonder said, "I only want you to like me."

And Molly said, "I know. You are a civilised man. You know that love-making is more full and whole and delightful if there is liking, too."

Tonder said, "Don't talk that way! Please don't talk that way!"

Molly glanced quickly at the door. She said, "We are conquered people, Lieutenant. You have taken the food away. I'm hungry. I'll like you better if you feed me."

Tonder said, "What are you saying?"

"Do I disgust you, Lieutenant? Maybe I'm trying to. My price is two sausages."

Tonder said, "You can't talk this way!"

"What about your own girls, Lieutenant, after the last war? A man could choose among your girls for an egg or a slice of bread. Do you want me for nothing, Lieutenant? Is the price too high?"

He said, "You fooled me for a moment. But you hate me, too, don't you? I thought maybe you wouldn't."

"No, I don't hate you," she said. "I'm hungry and—I hate you!"

Tonder said, "I'll give you anything you need, but—"

And she interrupted him. "You want to call it something else? You don't want a whore. Is that what you mean?"

Tonder said, "I don't know what I mean. You make it sound full of hatred."

Molly laughed. She said, "It's not nice to be hungry. Two sausages, two fine, fat sausages can be the most precious things in the world."

"Don't say those things," he said. "Please don't!"

"Why not? They're true."

"They aren't true! This can't be true!"

She looked at him for a moment and then she sat down and her eyes fell to her lap and she said, "No, it's not true. I don't hate you. I'm lonely too. And the snow is heavy on the roof."

Tonder got up and moved near to her. He took one of her hands in both of his and he said softly, "Please don't hate me. I'm only a lieutenant. I didn't ask to come here. You didn't ask to be my enemy. I'm only a man, not a conquering man."

Molly's fingers encircled his hands for a moment and she said softly, "I know; yes, I know."

And Tonder said, "We have some right to life in all this death."

She put her hand to his cheek for a moment and she said, "Yes."

"I'll take care of you," he said. "We have some right to life in all the killing." His hand rested on her shoulder. Suddenly she grew rigid and her eyes were wide and staring as though she saw a vision. His hand released her and he asked, "What's the matter? What is it?" Her eyes stared straight ahead and he repeated, "What is it?"

Molly spoke in a haunted voice. "I dressed him like a little boy for his first day in school. And he was afraid. I buttoned his shirt and tried to comfort him, but he was beyond comfort. And he was afraid."

Tonder said, "What are you saying?"

And Molly seemed to see what she described. "I don't know why they let him come home. He was confused. He didn't know what was happening. He didn't even kiss me when he went away. He was afraid, and very brave, like a little boy on his first day of school."

Tonder stood up. "That was your husband."

Molly said, "Yes, my husband. I went to the Mayor, but he was helpless. And then he marched away—not very well, not steadily—and you took him out and you shot him. It was more strange than terrible then. I didn't quite believe it then."

Tonder said, "Your husband!"

"Yes; and now, in the quiet house, I believe it. Now, with the heavy snow on the roof, I believe it. And in the loneliness before daybreak, in the half-warmed bed, I know it then."

Tonder stood in front of her. His face was full of misery. "Good night," he said. "God keep you. May I come back?"

And Molly looked at the wall and at the memory; "I don't know," she said.

"I'll come back."

"I don't know."

He looked at her and then he quietly went out of the door, and Molly still stared at the wall. "God keep me." She stayed for a moment staring at the wall. The door opened silently and Annie came in. Molly did not even see her.

Annie said disapprovingly, "The door was open."

Molly looked slowly towards her, her eyes will wide open. "Yes, oh yes, Annie."

"The door was open. There was a man came out. I saw him. He looked like a soldier."

And Molly said, "Yes, Annie."

"Was it a soldier here?"

"Yes, it was a soldier."

And Annie asked suspiciously, "What was he doing here?"

"He came to make love to me."

Annie said, "Miss, what are you doing? You haven't joined them, have you? You aren't with them, like that Corell?"

"No, I'm not with them, Annie."

Annie said, "If the Mayor's here and they come back, it'll be your fault if anything happens; it'll be your fault!"

"He won't come back. I won't let him come back."

But the suspicion stayed with Annie. She said, "Shall I tell them to come in now? Do you say it's safe?"

"Yes, it's safe. Where are they?"

"They're out behind the fence," said Annie. "Tell them to come in."

And while Annie went out, Molly got up and smoothed her hair and she shook her head, trying to be alive again. There was a little sound in the passage. Two tall, blond young men entered. They were dressed in pea-jackets and dark turtle-neck sweaters. They wore stocking caps perched on their heads. They were wind-burned and strong and they looked almost like twins, Will Anders and Tom Anders, the fishermen.

"Good evening, Molly. You've heard?"

"Annie told me. It's a bad night to go."

Tom said, "It's better than a clear night. The planes see you on a clear night. What's the Mayor want, Molly?"

"I don't know. I heard about your brother. I'm sorry."

The two were silent and they looked embarrassed. Tom said, "You know how it is, better than most."

"Yes; I know."

Annie came in the door again and she said in a hoarse whisper, "They're here!" And Mayor Orden and Doctor Winter came in. They took off their coats and caps and laid them on the couch. Orden went to Molly and kissed her on the forehead.

"Good evening, dear." He turned to Annie. "Stand in the passage, Annie. Give us one knock for the patrol, one when it's gone, and two for danger. You can leave the outer door open a crack so that you can hear if anyone comes."

Annie said, "Yes, sir." She went into the passage and shut the door behind her.

Doctor Winter was at the stove, warming his hands. "We got word you boys were going tonight."

"We've got to go," Tom said.

Orden nodded. "Yes, I know. We heard you were going to take Mr Corell with you."

Tom laughed bitterly. "We thought it would be only right. We're taking his boat. We can't leave him around. It isn't good to see him in the streets."

Orden said sadly, "I wish he had gone away. It's just a danger to you, taking him."

"It isn't good to see him in the streets." Will echoed his brother. "It isn't good for the people to see him here."

Winter asked, "Can you take him? Isn't he cautious at all?"

"Oh, yes, he's cautious, in a way. At twelve o'clock, though, he walks to his house usually. We'll be behind the wall. I think we can get him through his lower garden to the water. His boat's tied up there. We were on her today getting her ready."

Orden repeated, "I wish you didn't have to. It's just an added danger. If he makes a noise, the patrol might come."

Tom said, "He won't make a noise, and it's better if he disappears at sea. Some of the town people might get him and then there would be too much killing. No, it's better if he goes to sea."

Molly took up her knitting again. She said, "Will you throw him overboard?"

Will blushed. "He'll go to sea, ma'am." He turned to the Mayor. "You wanted to see us, sir?"

"Why, yes, I want to talk to you. Doctor Winter and I have tried to think— there's so much talk about justice, injustice, conquest. Our people are invaded, but I don't think they're conquered."

There was a sharp knock on the door and the room was silent. Molly's needles stopped, and the Mayor's outstretched hand remained in the air. Tom, scratching his ear, left his hand there and stopped scratching. Everyone in the room was motionless. Every eye was turned towards the door. Then, first faintly and then growing louder, there came the tramp of the patrol, the squeak of their boots in the snow, and the sound of their talking as they went by. They passed the door and their footsteps disappeared in the distance. There was a second tap on the door. And in the room the people relaxed.

Orden said, "It must be cold out there for Annie." He took up his coat from the couch and opened the inner door and handed his coat through. "Put this around your shoulders, Annie," he said and closed the door.

"I don't know what I'd do without her," he said. "She gets everywhere, she sees and hears everything."

Tom said, "We should be going pretty soon, sir."

And Winter said, "I wish you'd forget about Mr Corell."

"We can't. It isn't good to see him in the streets." He looked inquiringly at Mayor Orden.

Orden began slowly. "I want to speak simply. This is a little town. justice and injustice are in terms of little things. Your brother's shot and Alex Morden's shot. Revenge against a traitor. The people are angry and they have no way to fight back. But it's all in little terms. It's people against people, not idea against idea."

Winter said, "It's funny for a doctor to think of destruction, but I think all invaded people want to resist. We are disarmed; our spirits and bodies aren't enough. The spirit of a disarmed man sinks."

Will Anders asked, "What's all this for, sir? What do you want of us?"

"We want to fight them and we can't," Orden said. "They're using hunger on the people now. Hunger brings weakness. You boys are sailing for England. Maybe nobody will listen to you, but tell them from us—from a small town—to give us weapons." Tom asked, "You want guns?"

Again there was a quick knock on the door and the people froze where they were, and from outside there came the sound of the patrol, but a double step, running. Will moved quickly towards the door. The running steps came abreast with the house. There were muffled orders and the patrol ran by, and there was a second tap at the door.

Molly said, "They must be after somebody. I wonder who, this time."

"We should be going," Tom said uneasily. "Do you want guns, sir? Shall we ask for guns?"

"No, tell them how it is. We are watched. Any move we make calls for reprisals. If we could have simple, secret weapons, weapons of stealth, explosives, dynamite to blow up rails, grenades, if possible, even poison." He spoke angrily. "There is no honourable war. This is a war of treachery and murder. Let us use the methods that have been used on us! Let the British bombers drop their big bombs on the works, but let them also drop us little bombs to use, to hide, to slip under the rails, under tanks. Then we will be armed, secretly armed. Then the invader will never know which of us is armed. Let the bombers bring us simple weapons. We will know how to use them!"

Winter broke in. "They'll never know where it will strike. The soldiers, the patrol, will never know which of us is armed."

Tom wiped his forehead. "If we get through, we'll tell them, sir, but—well, I've heard it said that in England there are still men in power who do not care to put weapons in the hands of common people."

Orden stared at him. "Oh! I hadn't thought of that. Well, we can only see. If such people still govern England and America, the world is lost, anyway. Tell them what we say, if they will listen. We must have help, but if we get it"—his face grew very hard—"if we get it, we will help ourselves."

Winter said, "If they will even give us dynamite to hide, to bury in the ground to be ready against need, then the invader can never rest again, never! We will blow up his supplies."

The room grew excited. Molly said fiercely, "Yes, we could fight his rest, then. We could fight his sleep. We could fight his nerves and his certainties."

Will asked quietly, "Is that all, sir?"

"Yes," Orden nodded. "That's the core of it."

"What if they won't listen?"

"You can only try, as you are trying the sea tonight."

"Is that all, sir?"

The door opened and Annie came quietly in. Orden went on, "That's all. If you have to go now, let me send Annie out to see that the way is clear." He looked up and saw that Annie had come in. Annie said, "There's a soldier coming up the path. He looks like the soldier that was here before. There was a soldier here with Molly before."

The others looked at Molly. Annie said, "I locked the door."

"What does he want?" Molly asked. "Why does he come back?"

There was a gentle knocking at the outside door. Orden went to Molly. "What is this, Molly? Are you in trouble?"

"No," she said, "no! Go out the back way. You can get out through the back. Hurry, hurry out!"

The knocking continued on the front door. A man's voice called softly. Molly opened the door to the kitchen. She said, "Hurry, hurry!"

The Mayor stood in front of her. "Are you in trouble, Molly? You haven't done anything?"

Annie said coldly, "It looks like the same soldier. There was a soldier here before."

"Yes," Molly said to the Mayor. "Yes, there was a soldier here before."

The Mayor said, "What did he want?"

"He wanted to make love to me."

"But he didn't?" Orden said.

"No," she said, "he didn't. Go now, and I'll take care."

Orden said, "Molly, if you're in trouble, let us help you."

"The trouble I'm in no one can help me with," she said. "Go now," and she pushed them out of the door.

Annie remained behind. She looked at Molly. "Miss, what does this soldier want?"

"I don't know what he wants."

"Are you going to tell him anything?"

"No." Wonderingly, Molly repeated, "No." And then sharply she said, "No, Annie, I'm not!"

Annie scowled at her. "Miss, you'd better not tell him anything!" And she went out and closed the door behind her.

The tapping continued on the front door and a man's voice could be heard through the door.

Molly went to the centre lamp, and her burden was heavy on her.

She looked down at the lamp. She looked at the table, and she saw the big scissors lying beside her knitting. She picked them up wonderingly by the blades. The blades slipped through her fingers until she held the long shears and she was holding them like a knife, and her eyes were horrified. She looked down into the lamp and the light flooded up in her face. Slowly she raised the shears and placed them inside her dress.

The tapping continued on the door. She heard the voice calling to her. She leaned over the lamp for a moment and then suddenly she blew out the light. The room was dark except for a spot of red that came from the coal stove. She opened the door. Her voice was strained and sweet. She called, "I'm coming, Lieutenant. I'm coming!"

The Blooding of the *Compass Rose*
(from *The Cruel Sea*)

Nicholas Monsarrat

Dunkirk, as it was bound to, made a great difference to the balance of things in the Atlantic: the operation itself drew off many ships, destroyers and corvettes alike, from regular convoy-escort, and some of them were lost, others damaged, and still others had to remain in home waters when it was over, to be on hand in case of invasion. The shortage of escorts at this stage was ludicrous: even with the arrival of fifty obsolescent destroyers which America had now made available to the Allies, convoys sailed out into the Atlantic with only a thin token screen between them and the growing force of U-boats. When, after Dunkirk, the Royal Navy turned its attention to the major battle again, it was to find control of the battlefield threatened by a ruthless assault, which quickened and grew with every month that passed.

There was another factor in the altered account. The map now showed them a melancholy and menacing picture: with Norway gone, France gone, Ireland a dubious quantity on their doorstep, and Spain an equivocal neutral, nearly the whole European coast-line, from Narvik, to Bordeaux, was available to U-boats and, more important still, as air-bases for long-range aircraft. Aircraft could now trail a convoy far out into the Atlantic, calling up U-boats to the attack as they circled out of range: the liaison quickly showed a profit disastrous to the Allies. In the three months that followed Dunkirk, over two hundred ships were sent to the bottom by these two weapons in combination, and the losses continued at something like fifty ships a month till the end of the year. Help was on the way - new weapons, more escorts, more aircraft: but help did not come in time, for many ships and men, and for many convoys that made port with great gaps in their ranks.

It was on one of these bad convoys, homeward bound near Iceland, that *Compass Rose* was blooded.

* * *

When the alarm bell went, just before midnight, Ferraby left the bridge where he had been keeping the first watch with Baker, and made his way aft towards his depth-charges. It was he who had rung the bell, as soon as the noise of aircraft and a burst of tracer bullets from the far side of the convoy indicated an attack; but though he had been prepared for the violent clanging and the drumming of feet that followed it, he could not control a feeling of sick surprise at the urgency which now possessed the ship, in its first alarm for action. The night was calm, with a bright three-quarter moon which bathed the upper deck in a cold glow, and showed them the nearest ships of the convoy in hard revealing outline; it was a perfect night for what he *knew* was coming, and to hurry down the length of *Compass Rose* was like going swiftly to the scaffold. He knew that if he spoke now there would be a tremble in his voice, he knew that full daylight would have shown his face pale and his lips shaking; he knew that he was not really ready for this moment, in spite of the months of training and the gradually sharpening tension. But the moment was here, and somehow it had to be faced.

Wainwright, the young torpedo-man, was already on the quarter-deck, clearing away the release-gear on the depth-charges, and as soon as Wainwright spoke—even though it was only the three words "Closed up, sir,"—Ferraby knew that he also was consumed by nervousness…He found the fact heartening, in a way he had not expected: if his own fear of action were the common lot, and not just a personal and shameful weakness, it might be easier to cure in company. He took a grip of his voice, said: "Get the first pattern ready to drop," and then, as he turned to check up on the depth-charge crews, his eye was caught by a brilliant firework display on their beam.

The attacking aircraft was now flying low over the centre of the convoy, pursued and harried by gun-fire from scores of ships at once. The plane could not be seen, but her swift progress could be followed by the glowing arcs of tracer-bullets which swept like a huge fan across the top of the convoy. The uproar was prodigious—the plane screaming through the darkness, hundreds of guns going at once, one or two ships sounding the alarm on their sirens: the centre of the convoy, with everyone blazing away at the low-flying plane and not worrying about what else was in the line of fire, must have been an inferno. Standing in their groups aft, close to the hurrying water, they watched and waited, wondering which way the plane would turn at the end of her run: on the platform above them the two-pounder gun's-crew, motionless and helmeted against the night sky, were keyed ready for their chance to fire. But the chance never came, the waiting belts of ammunition remained idle: something else forestalled them.

It was as if the monstrous noise from the convoy must have a climax, and the climax could only be violent. At the top of the centre column, near the end of her run, the aircraft dropped two bombs: one of them fell wide, raising a huge pluming spout of water which glittered in the moonlight, and the other found its mark. It dropped with an iron clang on some ship which they could not see— and they knew that now they would never see her: for after the first explosion there was a second one, a huge orange flash which lit the whole convoy and the whole sky at one ghastly stroke. The ship—whatever size she was—must have disintegrated on the instant; they were left with the evidence—the sickening succession of splashes as the torn pieces of the ship fell back into the sea, covering and fouling a mile-wide circle, and the noise of the aircraft disappearing into the darkness, a receding tail of sound to underline this fearful destruction.

"Must have been ammunition," said someone in the darkness, breaking the awed and compassionate silence. "Poor bastards."

"Didn't know much about it. Best way to die."

You fool, thought Ferraby, trembling uncontrollably: you fool, you fool, no one wants to die…

From the higher vantage-point of the bridge, Ericson had watched everything; he had seen the ship hit, the shower of sparks where the bomb fell, and then, a moment afterwards, the huge explosion that blew her into pieces. In the shocked silence that followed, his voice giving a routine helm-order was cool and normal: no one could have guessed the sadness and the anger that filled him, to see a whole crew of men like himself wiped out at one stroke. There was nothing to be done: the aircraft was gone, with its frightful credit, and if there were any men left alive—which was hardly conceivable—*Sorrel*, the stern escort, would do her best for them. It was so quick, it was so brutal…He might have thought more about it, he might have mourned a little longer, if a second strike had not followed swiftly; but even as he raised his binoculars to look at the convoy again, the ship they were stationed on, a hundred yards away, rocked to a sudden explosion and then, on the instant, heeled over at a desperate angle.

This time, a torpedo…Ericson heard it: and even as he jumped to the voice-pipe to increase their speed and start zig-zagging, he thought: if that one came from outside the convoy, it must have missed us by a few feet. Inside the Asdic-hut, Lockhard heard it, and started hunting on the danger-side, without further orders: that was a routine, and even at this moment of surprise and crisis, the routine still ruled them all. Morell, on the fo'c'sle, heard it, and closed up his gun's-crew again and loaded with star-shell: down in the wheel-house, Tallow heard it, and gripped the wheel tighter and called out to his quartermasters: "Watch that telegraph, now!" and waited for the swift orders that might follow. Right aft, by the depth-charges, Ferraby heard it, and shivered: he glanced downwards at the black water rushing past them, and then at the stricken ship which he could see quite clearly, and he longed for some action in which he could lose himself and his fear. Deep down in the engine-room, Chief E. R. A. Watts heard it best of all: it came like a hammer-blow, hitting the ship's side a great splitting crack, and when, a few seconds afterwards, the telegraph rang for an increase of speed, his hand was on the steam-valve already. He knew what had happened, he knew what might happen next. But it was better not to think of what was going on outside: down here, encased below the water-line, they must wait, and hope, and keep their nerve.

Ericson took *Compass Rose* in a wide half-circle to starboard, away from the convoy, hunting for the U-boat down what he presumed had been the track of the torpedo; but they found nothing that looked like a contact, and presently he circled back again, towards the ship that had been hit. She had fallen out of line, like one winged bird in a flight of duck, letting the rest of the convoy go by: she was sinking fast, and already her screws were out of water and she was poised for the long plunge. The cries of men in fear came from her, and a thick smell of oil: at one moment, when they had her outlined against the moon, they could see a mass of men packed high in the towering stern, waving and shouting as they felt the ship under them begin to slide down to her grave. Ericson, trying for a cool decision in this moment of pity, was faced with a dilemma: if he stopped to pick up survivors, he would become a sitting target himself, and he would also lose all chance of hunting for the U-boat: if he went on with the hunt, he would, with *Sorrel* busy elsewhere, be leaving these men to their death. He decided on a compromise, a not-too-dangerous compromise: they would drop a boat, and leave it to collect what survivors it could while *Compass Rose* took another cast away to starboard. But it must be done quickly.

Ferraby, summoned to the quarter-deck voice-pipe, put every effort he knew into controlling his voice.

"Ferraby, sir."

"We're going to drop a boat, Sub. Who's your leading hand?"

"Leading-Seaman Tonbridge, sir."

"Tell him to pick a small crew—not more than four—and row over towards the ship. Tell him to keep well clear until she goes down. They may be able to get some boats away themselves, but if not, he'll have to do the best he can. We'll come back for him when we've had another look for the submarine."

"Right, sir."

"Quick as you can, Sub. I don't want to stop too long."

Ferraby threw himself into the job with an energy which was a drug for all other feeling: the boat was lowered so swiftly that when *Compass Rose* drew away from it and left it to its critical errand the torpedoed ship was still afloat. But she was only just afloat, balanced between sea and sky before her last dive; and as Tonbridge took the tiller and glanced in her direction to get his bearings, there was a rending sound which carried clearly over the water, and she started to go down. Tonbridge watched, in awe and fear: he had never seen anything like this, and never had a job of this sort before, and it was an effort to meet it properly. It had been bad enough to be lowered into the darkness from *Compass Rose*, and to watch her fade away and be left alone in a small boat under the stars, with the convoy also fading and a vast unfriendly sea all round them; but now, with the torpedoed ship disappearing before their eyes, and the men shouting and crying as they splashed about in the water, and the smell of oil coming across to them thick and choking, it was more like a nightmare than anything else. Tonbridge was twenty-three years of age, a product of the London slums conditioned by seven years' Naval training; faced by this ordeal, the fact that he did not run away from it, the fact that he remained effective, was beyond all normal credit.

They did what they could: rowing about in the darkness, guided by the shouting, appalled by the choking cries of men who drowned before they could be reached, they tried their utmost to rescue and to succour. They collected fourteen men: one was dead, one was dying, eight were wounded, and the rest were shocked and prostrated to a pitiful degree. It was very nearly fifteen men: Tonbridge actually had hold of the fifteenth, who was gasping in the last stages of terror and exhaustion, but the film of oil on his naked body made him impossible to grasp, and he slipped away and sank before a rope could be got round him. When there were no more shadows on the water, and no more cries to follow, they rested on their oars, and waited; alone on the enormous black waste of the Atlantic, alone with the settled wreckage and the reek of oil; and so, presently, *Compass Rose* found them.

Ferraby, standing in the waist of the ship as the boat was hooked on, wondered what he would see when the survivors came over the side: he was not prepared for the pity and horror of the appearance. First came the ones who could climb aboard themselves—half a dozen shivering, black-faced men, dressed in the filthy oil-soaked clothes which they had snatched up when the ship was struck: one of them with his scalp streaming with blood, another nursing an arm flayed from wrist to shoulder by scalding steam. They looked about them in wonder, dazed by the swiftness of disaster, by their rescue, by the solid deck beneath their feet. Then, while they were led to the warmth of the messdeck, a sling was rigged for the seriously wounded, and they were lifted over the side on stretchers: some silent, some moaning, some coughing up the fuel oil which was burning and poisoning their intestines: laid side by side in the waist, they made a carpet of pain and distress so naked in suffering that it seemed cruel to watch them. And then, with the boat still bumping alongside in the eerie darkness, came Tonbridge's voice: "Go easy—there's a dead man down here." Ferraby had never seen a dead man before, and he had to force himself to look at this pitiful relic of the sea—stone-cold, stiffening already, its grey head jerking as it was bundled over the side: an old sailor, unseamanlike and disgusting in death. He wanted to run away, he wanted to be sick: he watched with shocked amazement the two ratings who were carrying the corpse: how can you bear what you are doing, he thought, how can you touch it…? Behind him he heard Lockhart's voice saying: "Bring the whole lot into the fo'c'sle—I can't see anything here," and then he turned away and busied himself with the hoisting of the boat, not looking behind him as the procession of wrecked and brutalized men was borne off. When the boat was inboard, and secure, he turned back again, glad to have escaped some part of the horror. There was nothing left now but the acrid smell of oil, and the patches of blood and water on the deck: nothing, he saw with a gasp of fear and revulsion, but the dead man lying lashed against the rail, a yard from him, rolling as the ship rolled, waiting for daylight and burial. He turned and ran towards the stern, pursued by terror.

In the big seamen's messdeck, under the shaded lamps, Lockhart was doing things he had never imagined possible. Now and again he recalled, with a spark of pleasure, his previous doubts: there was plenty of blood here to faint at, but that wasn't the way things were working out…He had stitched up a gash in a man's head, from the nose to the line of the hair—as he took the catgut from its envelope he had thought: I wish they'd include some directions with this stuff.

He had set a broken leg, using part of a bench as a splint. He bound up other cuts and gashes, he did what he could for the man with the burnt arm, who was now insensible with pain: he watched, doing nothing with a curious hurt detachment, as a man who had drenched his intestines and perhaps his lungs with fuel oil slowly died. Some of *Compass Rose's* crew made a ring round him, looking at him, helping him when he asked for help: the two stewards brought tea for the cold and shocked survivors, other men offered dry clothing, and Tallow, after an hour or two, came down and gave him the largest tot of rum he had ever seen. It was not too large…Once, from outside, there was the sound of an explosion, and he looked up: by chance, across the smoky fo'c'sle, the bandaged rows of wounded, the other men still shivering, the twisted corpse, the whole squalid confusion of the night, he met the eye of Leading-Seaman Phillips. Involuntarily, both of them smiled, to mark a thought which could only be smiled at: if a torpedo hit them now, there would be little chance for any of them and all this bandaging would be wasted.

Then he bent down again, and went on probing a wound for the splinter of steel which must still be there, if the scream of pain which the movement produced was anything to go by. This was a moment to think only of the essentials, and they were all here with him, and in his care.

It was nearly daylight before he finished; and he went up to the bridge to report what he had done at a slow dragging walk, completely played out. He met Ericson at the top of the ladder: they had both been working throughout the night, and the two exhausted men looked at each other in silence, unable to put any expression into their stiff drawn faces, yet somehow acknowledging each other's competence. There was blood on Lockhart's hands, and on the sleeves of his duffle-coat: in the cold light it had a curious metallic sheen, and Ericson looked at it for some time before he realized what it was.

"You must have been busy, Number One," he said quietly. "What's the score down there?"

"Two dead, sir," answered Lockhart. His voice was very hoarse, and he cleared his throat. "One more to go, I think—he's been swimming and walking about with a badly-burned arm, and the shock is too much. Eleven others. They ought to be all right."

"Fourteen…The crew was thirty-six altogether."

Lockhart shrugged. There was no answer to that one, and if there had been he could not have found it in his present mood: the past few hours, spent watching and touching pain, seemed to have deadened all normal feeling. He looked round at the ships on their beam, just emerging as the light grew.

"How about things up here?" he asked.

"We lost another ship, over the other side of the convoy. That made three."

"More than one submarine?"

"I shouldn't think so. She probably crossed over."

"Good night's work." Lockhart still could not express more than a formal regret. "Do you want to turn in, sir? I can finish this watch."

"No—you get some sleep. I'll wait for Ferraby and Baker."

"Tonbridge did well."

"Yes…So did you, Number One."

Lockhart shook his head. "It was pretty rough, most of it. I must get a little book on wounds. It's going to come in handy, if this sort of thing goes on."

"There's no reason why it shouldn't," said Ericson. "No reason at all, that I can see. Three ships in three hours: probably a hundred men all told. Easy."

"Yes," said Lockhart, nodding. "A very promising start. After the war, we must ask them how they do it."

"After the war," said Ericson levelly, "I hope they'll be asking us."

Hiroshima—The Fire
(from *Hiroshima*)

John Hersey

Immediately after the explosion, the Reverend Mr Kiyoshi Tanimoto, having run wildly out of the Matsui estate and having looked in wonderment at the bloody soldiers at the mouth of the dugout they had been digging, attached himself sympathetically to an old lady who was walking along in a daze, holding her head with her left hand, supporting a small boy of three or four on her back with her right, and crying, "I'm hurt! I'm hurt! I'm hurt!" Mr Tanimoto transferred the child to his own back and led the woman by the hand down the street, which was darkened by what seemed to be a local column of dust. He took the woman to a grammar school not far away that had previously been designated for use as a temporary hospital in case of emergency. By this solicitous behavior, Mr Tanimoto at once got rid of his terror. At the school, he was much surprised to see glass all over the floor and fifty or sixty injured people already waiting to be treated. He reflected that, although the all-clear had sounded and he had heard no planes, several bombs must have been dropped. He thought of a hillock in the rayon man's garden from which he would get a view of the whole of Koi—of the whole of Hiroshima, for that matter—and he ran back up to the estate.

From the mound, Mr Tanimoto saw an astonishing panorama. Not just a patch of Koi, as he had expected, but as much of Hiroshima as he could see through the clouded air was giving off a thick, dreadful miasma. Clumps of smoke, near and far, had begun to push up through the general dust. He wondered how such extensive damage could have been dealt out of a silent sky; even a few planes, far up, would have been audible. Houses nearby were burning, and when huge drops of water the size of marbles began to fall, he half thought that they must be coming from the hoses of firemen fighting the blazes. (They were actually drops of condensed moisture falling from the turbulent tower of dust, heat, and fission fragments that had already risen miles into the sky above Hiroshima.)

Mr Tanimoto turned away from the sight when he heard Mr Matsuo call out to ask whether he was all right. Mr Matsuo had been safely cushioned within the falling house by the bedding stored in the front hall and had worked his way out. Mr Tanimoto scarcely answered. He had thought of his wife and baby, his church, his home, his parishioners, all of them down in that awful murk. Once more he began to run in fear—toward the city.

Mrs Hatsuyo Nakamura, the tailor's widow, having struggled up from under the ruins of her house after the explosion, and seeing Myeko, the youngest of her three children, buried breast-deep and unable to move, crawled across the debris, hauled at timbers, and flung tiles aside, in a hurried effort to free the child. Then, from what seemed to be caverns far below, she heard two small voices crying, "*Tasukete! Tasukete!* Help! Help!"

She called the names of her ten-year-old son and eight-year-old daughter: "Toshia! Yaeko!"

The voices from below answered.

Mrs Nakamura abandoned Myeko, who at least could breathe, and in a frenzy made the wreckage fly above the crying voices. The children had been sleeping nearly ten feet apart, but now their voices seemed to come from the same place. Toshio, the boy, apparently had some freedom to move, because she could feel him undermining the pile of wood and tiles as she worked from above. At last she saw his head, and she hastily pulled him out by it. A mosquito net was wound intricately, as if it had been carefully wrapped, around his feet. He said he had been blown right across the room and had been on top of his sister Yaeko under the wreckage. She now said, from underneath, that she could not move, because there was something on her legs. With a bit more digging, Mrs Nakamura cleared a hole above the child and began to pull her arm. "*Itai* It hurts!" Yaeko cried. Mrs Nakamura shouted, "There's no time now to say whether it hurts or not," and yanked her whimpering daughter up. Then she freed Myeko. The children were filthy and bruised, but none of them had a single cut or scratch.

Mrs Nakamura took the children out into the street. They had nothing on but underpants, and although the day was very hot, she worried rather confusedly about their being cold, so she went back into the wreckage and burrowed underneath and found a bundle of clothes she had packed for an emergency, and she dressed them in pants, blouses, shoes, padded-cotton air-raid helmets called *bokuzuki*, and even, irrationally, overcoats. The children were silent, except for the five-year-old, Myeko, who kept asking questions: "Why is it night already? Why did our house fall down? What happened?" Mrs Nakamura, who did not know what had happened (had not the allclear sounded?), looked around and saw through the darkness that all the houses in her neighborhood had collapsed. The house next door, which its owner had been tearing down to make way for a fire lane, was not very thoroughly, if crudely, torn down; its owner, who had been sacrificing his home for the community's safety, lay dead. Mrs Nakamoto, wife of the head of the local air-raid defense Neighborhood Association, came across the street with her head all bloody, and said that her baby was badly cut; did Mrs Nakamura have any bandage? Mrs Nakamura did not, but she crawled into the remains of her house again and pulled out some white cloth that she had been using in her work as a seamstress; ripped it into strips, and gave it to Mrs Nakamoto. While fetching the cloth, she noticed her sewing machine; she went back in for it and dragged it out. Obviously, she could not carry it with her, so she unthinkingly plunged her symbol of livelihood into the receptacle which for weeks had been her symbol of safety—the cement tank of water in front of her house, of the type every household had been ordered to construct against a possible fire raid.

A nervous neighbor, Mrs Hataya, called to Mrs Nakamura to run away with her to the woods in Asano Park—an estate, by the Kyo River not far off, belonging to the wealthy Asano family, who once owned the Toyo Kisen Kaisha steamship line. The park had been designated as an evacuation area for their neighborhood. Seeing fire breaking out in a nearby ruin (except at the very center, where the bomb itself ignited some fires, most of Hiroshima's citywide conflagration was caused by inflammable wreckage falling on cook-stoves and live wires), Mrs Nakamura suggested going over to fight it. Mrs Hataya said, "Don't be foolish. What if planes come and drop more bombs?" So Mrs Nakamura started out for Asano Park with her children and Mrs Hataya, and she carried her rucksack of emergency clothing, a blanket, an umbrella, and a suitcase of things she had cached in her air-raid shelter. Under many ruins, as they hurried along, they heard mulled screams for help. The only building they saw standing on their way to Asano Park was the Jesuit mission house, alongside the Catholic kindergarten to which Mrs Nakamura had sent Myeko for a time. As they passed it, she saw Father Kleinsorge, in bloody underwear, running out of the house with a small suitcase in his hand.

Right after the explosion, while Father Wilhelm Kleinsorge, S.J., was wandering around in his underwear in the vegetable garden, Father Superior LaSalle came around the corner of the building in the darkness. His body, especially his back, was bloody; the flash had made him twist away from his window, and tiny pieces of glass had flown at him. Father Kleinsorge, still bewildered, managed to ask, "Where are the rest?" Just then, the two other priests living in the mission house appeared—Father Cieslik, unhurt, supporting Father Schiffer, who was covered with blood that spurted from a cut above his left ear and who was very pale. Father Cieslik was rather pleased with himself, for after the flash he had dived into a doorway, which he had previously reckoned to be the safest place inside the building, and when the blast came, he was not injured. Father LaSalle told Father Cieslik to take Father Schiffer to a doctor before he bled to death, and suggested either Dr Kanda, who lived on the next corner, or Dr Fujii, about six blocks away. The two men went out of the compound and up the street.

The daughter of Mr Hoshijima, the mission catechist, ran up to Father Kleinsorge and said that her mother and sister were buried under the ruins of their house, which was at the back of the Jesuit compound, and at the same time the priests noticed that the house of the Catholic-kindergarten teacher at the front of the compound had collapsed on her. While Father LaSalle and Mrs Murata, the mission housekeeper, dug the teacher out, Father Kleinsorge went to the catechist's fallen house and began lifting things off the top of the pile. There was not a sound underneath; he was sure the Hoshijima women had been killed. At last, under what had been a corner of the kitchen, he saw Mrs Hoshijima's head. Believing her dead, he began to haul her out by the hair, but suddenly she screamed, "*Itai! Itai!* It hurts! It hurts!" He dug some more and lifted her out. He managed, too, to find her daughter in the rubble and free her. Neither was badly hurt.

A public bath next door to the mission house had caught fire, but since there the wind was southerly, the priests thought their house would be spared. Nevertheless, as a precaution, Father Kleinsorge went inside to fetch some things he wanted to save. He found his room in a state of weird and illogical confusion. A first-aid kit was hanging undisturbed on a hook on the wall, but his clothes, which had been on other hooks nearby, were nowhere to be seen. His desk was in splinters all over the room, but a mere papier-mâché suitcase, which he had hidden under the desk, stood handle-side up, without a scratch on it, in the doorway of the room, where he could not miss it. Father Kleinsorge later came to regard this as a bit of Providential interference, inasmuch as the suitcase contained his breviary, the account books for the whole diocese, and a considerable amount of paper money belonging to the mission, for which he was responsible. He ran out of the house and deposited the suitcase in the mission air-raid shelter.

At about this time, Father Cieslik and Father Schiffer, who was still spurting blood, came back and said that Dr Kanda's house was ruined and that fire blocked them from getting out of what they supposed to be the local circle of destruction to Dr Fujii's private hospital, on the bank of the Kyo River.

Dr Masakazu Fukii's hospital was no longer on the bank of the Kyo River; it was in the river. After the overturn, Dr Fujii was so stupefied and so tightly squeezed by the beams gripping his chest that he was unable to move at first, and he hung there about twenty minutes in the darkened morning. Then a thought which came to him—that soon the tide would be running in through the estuaries and his head would be submerged—inspired him to fearful activity; he wriggled and turned and exerted what strength he could (though his left arm, because of the pain in his shoulder, was useless), and before long he had freed himself from the vise. After a few moments' rest, he climbed onto the pile of timbers and, finding a long one that slanted up to the riverbank, he painfully shinnied up it.

Dr Fujii, who was in his underwear, was now soaking and dirty. His undershirt was torn and blood ran down it from bad cuts on his chin and back. In this disarray, he walked out onto Kyo Bridge, beside which his hospital had stood. The bridge had not collapsed. He could see only fuzzily without his glasses, but he could see enough to be amazed at the number of houses that were down all around. On the bridge, he encountered a friend, a doctor named Machii, and asked in bewilderment, "What do you think it was?"

Dr Machii said, "It must have been a *Molotoffano hanakago*"—a Molotov flower basket, the delicate Japanese name for the "bread basket," or self-scattering cluster of bombs.

At first, Dr Fujii could see only two fires, one across the river from his hospital site and one quite far to the south. But at the same time, he and his friend observed something that puzzled them, and which, as doctors, they discussed: although there were as yet very few fires, wounded people were hurrying across the bridge in an endless parade of misery, and many of them exhibited terrible burns on their faces and arms. "Why do you suppose it is?" Dr Fujii asked. Even a theory was comforting that day, and Dr Machii stuck to his. "Perhaps because it was a Molotov flower basket," he said.

There had been no breeze earlier in the morning when Dr Fujii had walked to the railway station to see his friend off, but now brisk winds were blowing every which way; here on the bridge the wind was easterly. New fires were leaping up, and they spread quickly, and in a very short time terrible blasts of hot air and showers of cinders made it impossible to stand on the bridge any more. Dr Machii ran to the far side of the river and along a still unkindled street. Dr Fujii went down into the water under the bridge, where a score of people had already taken refuge, among them his servants, who had extricated themselves from the wreckage. From there, Dr Fujii saw a nurse hanging in the timbers of his hospital by her legs, and then another painfully pinned across the breast. He enlisted the help of some of the others under the bridge and freed both of them. He thought he heard the voice of his niece for a moment, but he could not find her; he never saw her again. Four of his nurses and the two patients in the hospital died, too. Dr Fujii went back into the water of the river and waited for the fire to subside.

*   *   *

The lot of Drs Fujii, Kanda, and Machii right after the explosion—and, as these three were typical, that of the majority of the physicians and surgeons of Hiroshima—with their offices and hospitals destroyed, their equipment scattered, their own bodies incapacitated in varying degrees, explained why so many citizens who were hurt went untended and why so many who might have lived died. Of a hundred and fifty doctors in the city, sixty-five were already dead and most of the rest were wounded. Of 1,780 nurses, 1,654 were dead or too badly hurt to work. In the biggest hospital, that of the Red Cross, only six doctors out of thirty were able to function, and only ten nurses out of more than two hundred. The sole uninjured doctor on the Red Cross Hospital staff was Dr Sasaki. After the explosion, he hurried to a storeroom to fetch bandages. This room, like everything he had seen as he ran through the hospital, was chaotic— bottles of medicines thrown off shelves and broken, salves spattered on the walls, instruments strewn everywhere. He grabbed up some bandages and an unbroken bottle of Mercurochrome, hurried back to the chief surgeon, and bandaged his cuts. Then he went out into the corridor and began patching up the wounded patients and the doctors and nurses there. He blundered so without his glasses that he took a pair off the face of a wounded nurse, and although they only approximately compensated for the errors of his vision, they were better than nothing. (He was to depend on them for more than a month.)

Dr Sasaki worked without method, taking those who were nearest him first, and he noticed soon that the corridor seemed to be getting more and more crowded. Mixed in with the abrasions and lacerations which most people in the hospital had suffered, he began to find dreadful burns. He realized then that casualties were pouring in from outdoors. There were so many that he began to pass up the lightly wounded; he decided that all he could hope to do was to stop people from bleeding to death. Before long, patients lay and crouched on the floors of the wards and the laboratories and all the other rooms, and in the corridors, and on the stairs, and in the front hall, and under the portecochère, and on the stone front steps, and in the driveway and courtyard, and for blocks each way in the streets outside. Wounded people supported maimed people; disfigured families leaned together. Many people were vomiting. A tremendous number of schoolgirls—some of those who had been taken from their classrooms to work outdoors, clearing fire lanes—crept into the hospital. In a city of two hundred and forty-five thousand, nearly a hundred thousand people had been killed or doomed at one blow; a hundred thousand more were hurt. At least ten thousand of the wounded made their way to the best hospital in town, which was altogether unequal to such a trampling, since it had only six hundred beds, and they had all been occupied. The people in the suffocating crowd inside the hospital wept and cried, for Dr Sasaki to hear,

"*Sensei!* Doctor!," and the less seriously wounded came and pulled at his sleeve and begged him to go to the aid of the worse wounded. Tugged here and there in his stockinged feet, bewildered by the numbers, staggered by so much raw flesh, Dr Sasaki lost all sense of profession and stopped working as a skillful surgeon and a sympathetic man; he became an automaton, mechanically wiping, daubing, winding, wiping, daubing, winding.

Some of the wounded in Hiroshima were unable to enjoy the questionable luxury of hospitalization. In what had been the personnel office of the East Asia Tin Works, Miss Sasaki lay doubled over, unconscious, under the tremendous pile of books and plaster and wood and corrugated iron. She was wholly unconscious (she later estimated) for about three hours. Her first sensation was of dreadful pain in her left leg. It was so black under the books and debris that the borderline between awareness and unconsciousness was fine; she apparently crossed it several times, for the pain seemed to come and go. At the moments when it was sharpest, she felt that her leg had been cut off somewhere below the knee. Later, she heard someone walking on top of the wreckage above her, and anguished voices spoke up, evidently from within the mess around her: "Please help! Get us out!"

Father Kleinsorge stemmed Father Schiffer's spurting cut as well as he could with some bandages that Dr Fujii had given the priests a few days before. When he finished, he ran into the mission house again and found the jacket of his military uniform and an old pair of gray trousers. He put them on and went outside. A woman from next door ran up to him and shouted that her husband was buried under her house and the house was on fire; Father Kleinsorge must come and save him.

Father Kleinsorge, already growing apathetic and dazed in the presence of the cumulative distress, said, "We haven't much time." Houses all around were burning, and the wind was now blowing hard. "Do you know exactly which part of the house he is under?" he asked.

"Yes, yes," she said. "Come quickly."

They went around to the house, the remains of which blazed violently, but when they got there, it turned out that the woman had no idea where her husband was. Father Kleinsorge shouted several times, "Is anyone there?" There was no answer. Father Kleinsorge said to the woman, "We must get away or we will all die." He went back to the Catholic compound and told the Father Superior that the fire was coming closer on the wind, which had swung around and was now from the north; it was time for everybody to go.

Just then, the kindergarten teacher pointed out to the priests Mr Fukai, the secretary of the diocese, who was standing in his window on the second floor of the mission house, facing in the direction of the explosion, weeping. Father Cieslik, because he thought the stairs unusable, ran around to the back of the mission house to look for a ladder. There he heard people crying for help under a nearby fallen roof. He called to passers-by running away in the street to help him lift it, but nobody paid any attention, and he had to leave the buried ones to die. Father Kleinsorge ran inside the mission house and scrambled up the stairs, which were awry and piled with plaster and lathing, and called to Mr Fukai from the doorway of his room.

Mr Fukai, a very short man of about fifty, turned around slowly, with a queer look, and said, "Leave me here."

Father Kleinsorge went into the room and took Mr Fukai by the collar of his coat and said, "Come with me or you'll die."

Mr Fukai said, "Leave me here to die."

Father Kleinsorge began to shove and haul Mr Fukai out of the· room. Then the theological student came up and grabbed Mr Fukai's feet, and Father Kleinsorge took his shoulders, and together they carried him downstairs and outdoors. "I can't walk!" Mr Fukai cried. "Leave me here!" Father Kleinsorge got his paper suitcase with the money in it and took Mr Fukai up pickaback, and the party started for the East Parade Ground, their district's "safe area." As they went out of the gate, Mr Fukai, quite childlike now, beat on Father Kleinsorge's shoulders and said, "I won't leave. I won't leave." Irrelevantly, Father Kleinsorge turned to Father LaSalle and said, "We have lost all our possessions but not our sense of humor."

The street was cluttered with parts of houses that had slid into it, and with fallen telephone poles and wires. From every second or third house came the voices of people buried and abandoned, who invariably screamed, with formal politeness, "*Tasukete kure!* Help, if you please!" The priests recognized several ruins from which these cries came as the homes of friends, but because of the fire it was too late to help. All the way, Mr Fukai whimpered, "Let me stay." The party turned right when they came to a block of fallen houses that was one flame. At Sakai Bridge, which would take them across to the East Parade Ground, they saw that the whole community on the opposite side of the river was a sheet of fire; they dared not cross and decided to take refuge in Asano Park, off to their left. Father Kleinsorge, who had been weakened for a couple of days by his bad case of diarrhea, began to stagger under his protesting burden, and as he tried to climb up over the wreckage of several houses that blocked their way to the park, he stumbled, dropped Mr Fukai, and plunged down, head over heels, to the edge of the river. When he picked himself up, he saw Mr Fukai running away. Father Kleinsorge shouted to a dozen soldiers, who were standing by the bridge, to stop him. As Father Kleinsorge started back to get Mr Fukai, Father LaSalle called out, "Hurry! Don't waste time!" So Father Kleinsorge just requested the soldiers to take care of Mr Fukai. They said they would, but the little, broken man got away from them, and the last the priests could see of him, he was running back toward the fire.

Mr Tanimoto, fearful for his family and church, at first ran toward them by the shortest route, along Koi Highway. He was the only person making his way into the city; he met hundreds and hundreds who were fleeing, and every one of them seemed to be hurt in some way. The eyebrows of some were burned off and skin hung from their faces and hands. Others, because of pain, held their arms up as if carrying something in both hands. Some were vomiting as they walked . Many were naked or in shreds of clothing. On some undressed bodies, the burns had made patterns—of undershirt straps and suspenders and, on the skin of some women (since white repelled the heat from the bomb and dark clothes absorbed it and conducted it to their skin), the shapes of flowers they had had on their kimonos. Many, although injured themselves, supported relatives who were worse off. Almost all had their heads bowed, looked straight ahead, were silent, and showed no expression whatever.

After crossing Koi Bridge and Kannan Bridge, having run the whole way, Mr Tanimoto saw, as he approached the center, that all the houses had been crushed and many were afire. Here the trees were bare and their trunks were charred. He tried at several points to penetrate the ruins, but the flames always stopped him. Under many houses, people screamed for help, but no one helped; in general, survivors that day assisted only their relatives or immediate neighbors, for they could not comprehend or tolerate a wider circle of misery. The wounded limped past the screams, and Mr Tanimoto ran past them. As a Christian he was filled with compassion for those who were trapped, and as a Japanese he was overwhelmed by the shame of being unhurt, and he prayed as he ran, "God help them and take them out of the fire."

He thought he would skirt the fire, to the left. He ran back to Kannan Bridge and followed for a distance one of the rivers. He tried several cross streets, but all were blocked, so he turned far left and ran out to Yokogawa, a station on a railroad line that detoured the city in a wide semicircle, and he followed the rails until he came to a burning train. So impressed was he by this time by the extent of the damage that he ran north two miles to Gion, a suburb in the foothills. All the way, he overtook dreadfully burned and lacerated people, and in his guilt he turned to right and left as he hurried and said to some of them, "Excuse me for having no burden like yours." Near Gion, he began to meet country people going toward the city to help, and when they saw him, several exclaimed, "Look! There is one who is not wounded." At Gion, he bore toward the right bank of the main river, the Ota, and ran down it until he reached fire again. There was no fire on the other side of the river, so he threw off his shirt and shoes and plunged into it. In midstream, where the current was fairly strong, exhaustion and fear finally caught up with him—he had run nearly seven miles—and he became limp and drifted in the water. He prayed, "Please, God, help me to cross. It would be nonsense for me to be drowned when I am the only uninjured one." He managed a few more strokes and fetched up on a spit downstream.

Mr Tanimoto climbed up the bank and ran along it until, near a large Shinto shrine, he came to more fire, and as he turned left to get around it, he met, by incredible luck, his wife. She was carrying their infant daughter. Mr Tanimoto was now so emotionally worn out that nothing could surprise him. He did not embrace his wife; he simply said, "Oh, you are safe." She told him that she had got home from her night in Ushida just in time for the explosion; she had been buried under the parsonage with the baby in her arms. She told how the wreckage had pressed down on her, how the baby had cried. She saw a chink of light, and by reaching up with a hand, she worked the hole bigger, bit by bit. After about half an hour, she heard the crackling noise of wood burning. At last the opening was big enough for her to push the baby out, and afterward she crawled out herself. She said she was now going out to Ushida again. Mr Tanimoto said he wanted to see his church and take care of the people of his Neighborhood Association. They parted as casually—as bewildered—as when they had met.

Mr Tanimoto's way around the fire took him across the East Parade Ground, which, being an evacuation area, was now the scene of a gruesome review: rank on rank of the burned and bleeding. Those who were burned moaned, "*Mizu, mizu!* Water, water!" Mr Tanimoto found a basin in a nearby street and located a water tap that still worked in the crushed shell of a house, and he began carrying water to the suffering strangers. When he had given drink to about thirty of them, he realized he was taking too much time. "Excuse me," he said loudly to those nearby who were reaching out their hands to him and crying their thirst. "I have many people to take care of." Then he ran away. He went to the river again, the basin in his hand, and jumped down onto a sandpit. There he saw hundreds of people so badly wounded that they could not get up to go farther from the burning city. When they saw a man erect and unhurt, the chant began again: "*Mizu, mizu, mizu.*" Mr Tanimoto could not resist them; he carried them water from the river—a mistake, since it was tidal and brackish. Two or three small boats were ferrying hurt people across the river from Asano Park, and when one touched the spit, Mr Tanimoto again made his loud, apologetic speech and jumped into the boat. It took him across to the park. There, in the underbrush, he found some of his charges of the Neighborhood Association, who had come there by his previous instructions, and saw many acquaintances, among them Father Kleinsorge and the other Catholics. But he missed Fukai, who had been a close friend. "Where is Fukai-san?" he asked.

"He didn't want to come with us," Father Kleinsorge said. "He ran back."

When Miss Sasaki heard the voices of the people caught along with her in the dilapidation at the tin factory, she began speaking to them. Her nearest neighbor, she discovered, was a high-school girl who had been drafted for factory work, and who said her back was broken. Miss Sasaki replied, "I am lying here and I can't move. My left leg is cut off."

Some time later, she again heard somebody walk overhead and then move off to one side, and whoever it was began burrowing. The digger released several people, and when he had uncovered the high-school girl, she found that her back was not broken, after all, and she crawled out. Miss Sasaki spoke to the rescuer, and he worked toward her. He pulled away a great number of books, until he had made a tunnel to her. She could see his perspiring face as he said, "Come out, Miss." She tried. "I can't move," she said. The man excavated some more and told her to try with all her strength to get out. But books were heavy on her hips, and the man finally saw that a bookcase was leaning on the books and that a heavy beam pressed down on the bookcase. "Wait," he said. "I'll get a crowbar."

The man was gone a long time, and when he came back, he was ill-tempered, as if her plight were all her fault. "We have no men to help you!" he shouted in through the tunnel. "You'll have to get out by yourself."

"That's impossible," she said. "My left leg…" The man went away.

Much later, several men came and dragged Miss Sasaki out. Her left leg was not severed, but it was badly broken and cut and it hung askew below the knee. They took her out into a courtyard. It was raining. She sat on the ground in the rain. When the downpour increased, someone directed all the wounded people to take cover in the factory's air-raid shelters. "Come along," a torn-up woman said to her. "You can hop." But Miss Sasaki could not move, and she just waited in the rain. Then a man propped up a large sheet of corrugated iron as a kind of lean-to, and took her in his arms and carried her to it. She was grateful until he brought two horribly wounded people—a woman with a whole breast sheared off and a man whose face was all raw from a burn—to share the simple shed with her. No one came back. The rain cleared and the cloudy afternoon was hot; before nightfall the three grotesques under the slanting piece of twisted iron began to smell quite bad.

The former head of the Nobori-cho Neighborhood Association to which the Catholic priests belonged was an energetic man named Yoshida. He had boasted, when he was in charge of the district air-raid defenses, that fire might eat away all of Hiroshima but it would never come to Nobori-cho. The bomb blew down his house, and a joist pinned him by the legs, in full view of the Jesuit mission house across the way and of the people hurrying along the street. In their confusion as they hurried past, Mrs Nakamura, with her children, and Father Kleinsorge, with Mr Fukai on his back, hardly saw him; he was just part of the general blur of misery through which they moved. His cries for help brought no response from them; there were so many people shouting for help that they could not hear him separately. They and all the others went along. Nobori-cho became absolutely deserted, and the fire swept through it. Mr Yoshida saw the wooden mission house—the only erect building in the area—go up in a lick of flame, and the heat was terrific on his face. Then flames came along his side of the street and entered his house. In a paroxysm of terrified strength, he freed himself and ran down the alleys of Nobori-cho, hemmed in by the fire he had said would never come. He began at once to behave like an old man; two months later his hair was white.

As Dr Fujii stood in the river up to his neck to avoid the heat of the fire, the wind blew stronger and stronger, and soon, even though the expanse of water was small, the waves grew so high that the people under the bridge could no longer keep their footing. Dr Fujii went close to the shore, crouched down, and embraced a large stone with his usable arm. Later it became possible to wade along the very edge of the river, and Dr Fujii and his two surviving nurses moved about two hundred yards upstream, to a sandpit near Asano Park. Many wounded were lying on the sand. Dr Machii was there with his family; his daughter, who had been outdoors when the bomb burst, was badly burned on her hands and legs but fortunately not on her face. Although Dr Fujii's shoulder was by now terribly painful, he examined the girl's burns curiously. Then he lay down. In spite of the misery all around, he was ashamed of his appearance, and he remarked to Dr Machii that he looked like a beggar, dressed as he was in nothing but torn and bloody underwear. Later in the afternoon, when the fire began to subside, he decided to go to his parental house, in the suburb of Nagatsuka. He asked Dr Machii to join him, but the Doctor answered that he and his family were going to spend the night on the spit, because of his daughter's injuries. Dr Fujii, together with his nurses, walked first to Ushida, where, in the partially damaged house of some relatives, he found first-aid materials he had stored there. The two nurses bandaged him and he them. They went on. Now not many people walked in the street, but a great number sat and lay on the pavement, vomited, waited for death, and died. The number of corpses on the way to Nagatsuka was more and more puzzling. The Doctor wondered: Could a Molotov flower basket have done all this?

Dr Fujii reached his family's house in the evening. It was five miles from the center of town, but its roof had fallen in and the windows were all broken.

All day, people poured into Asano Park. This private estate was far enough away from the explosion so that its bamboos, pines, laurel, and maples were still alive, and the green place invited refugees—partly because they believed that if the Americans came back, they would bomb only buildings; partly because the foliage seemed a center of coolness and life, and the estate's exquisitely precise rock gardens, with their quiet pools and arching bridges, were very Japanese, normal, secure; and also partly (according to some who were there) because of an irresistible, atavistic urge to hide under leaves. Mrs Nakamura and her children were among the first to arrive, and they settled in the bamboo grove near the river. They all felt terribly thirsty, and they drank from the river. At once they were nauseated and began vomiting, and they retched the whole day. Others were also nauseated; they all thought (probably because of the strong odor of ionization, an "electric smell" given off by the bomb's fission) that they were sick from a gas the Americans had dropped. When Father Kleinsorge and the other priests came into the park, nodding to their friends as they passed, the Nakamuras were all sick and prostrate. A woman named Iwasaki, who lived in the neighborhood of the mission and who was sitting near the Nakamuras, got up and asked the priests if she should stay where she was or go with them. Father Kleinsorge said,

"I hardly know where the safest place is." She stayed there, and later in the day, though she had no visible wounds or burns, she died. The priests went farther along the river and settled down in some underbrush. Father LaSalle lay down and went right to sleep. The theological student, who was wearing slippers, had carried with him a bundle of clothes, in which he had packed two pairs of leather shoes. When he sat down with the others, he found that the bundle had broken open and a couple of shoes had fallen out and now he had only two lefts. He retraced his steps and found one right. When he rejoined the priests, he said, "It's funny, but things don' t matter any more. Yesterday, my shoes were my most important possessions. Today, I don't care. One pair is enough."

Father Cieslik said, "I know. I started to bring my books along, and then I thought, 'This is no time for books.'"

When Mr Tanimoto, with his basin still in his hand, reached the park, it was very crowded, and to distinguish the living from the dead was not easy, for most of the people lay still, with their eyes open. To Father Kleinsorge, an Occidental, the silence in the grove by the river, where hundreds of gruesomely wounded suffered together, was one of the most dreadful and awesome phenomena of his whole experience. The hurt ones were quiet; no one wept, much less screamed in pain; no one complained; none of the many who died did so noisily; not even the children cried; very few people even spoke. And when Father Kleinsorge gave water to some whose faces had been almost blotted out by flash burns, they took their share and then raised themselves a little and bowed to him, in thanks.

Mr Tanimoto greeted the priests and then looked around for other friends. He saw Mrs Matsumoto, wife of the director of the Methodist School, and asked her if she was thirsty. She was, so he went to one of the pools in the Asano rock gardens and got water for her in his basin. Then he decided to try to get back to his church. He went into Nobori-cho by the way the priests had taken as they escaped, but he did not get far; the fire along the streets was so fierce that he had to turn back. He walked to the riverbank and began to look for a boat in which he might carry some of the most severely injured across the river from Asano Park and away from the spreading fire. Soon he found a good-sized pleasure punt drawn up on the bank, but in and around it was an awful tableau—five dead men, nearly naked, badly burned, who must have expired more or less all at once, for they were in attitudes which suggested that they had been working together to push the boat down into the river. Mr Tanimoto lifted them away from the boat, and as he did so, he experienced such horror at disturbing the dead—preventing them, he momentarily felt, from launching their craft and going on their ghostly way—that he said out loud, "Please forgive me for taking this boat. I must use it for others, who are alive." The punt was heavy, but he managed to slide it into the water. There were no oars, and all he could find for propulsion was a thick bamboo pole. He worked the boat upstream to the most crowded part of the park and began to ferry the wounded. He could pack ten or twelve into the boat for each crossing, but as the river was too deep in the center to pole his way across, he had to paddle with the bamboo, and consequently each trip took a very long time. He worked several hours that way.

Early in the afternoon, the fire swept into the woods of Asano Park. The first Mr Tanimoto knew of it was when, returning in his boat, he saw that a great number of people had moved toward the riverside. On touching the bank, he went up to investigate, and when he saw the fire, he shouted, "All the young men who are not badly hurt come with me!" Father Kleinsorge moved Father Schiffer and Father LaSalle close to the edge of the river and asked people there to get them across if the fire came too near, and then joined Tanimoto's volunteers. Mr Tanimoto sent some to look for buckets and basins and told others to beat the burning underbrush with their clothes; when utensils were at hand, he formed a bucket chain from one of the pools in the rock garden. The team fought the fire for more than two hours, and gradually defeated the flames. As Mr Tanimoto's men worked, the frightened people in the park pressed closer and closer to the river, and finally the mob began to force some of the unfortunates who were on the very bank into the water. Among those driven into the river and drowned were Mrs Matsumoto, of the Methodist School, and her daughter.

When Father Kleinsorge got back after fighting the fire, he found Father Schiffer still bleeding and terribly pale. Some Japanese stood around and stared at him, and Father Schiffer whispered, with a weak smile, "It is as if I were already dead." "Not yet," Father Kleinsorge said. He had brought Dr Fujii's first-aid kit with him, and he had noticed Dr Kanda in the crowd, so he sought him out and asked him if he would dress Father Schiffer's bad cuts. Dr Kanda had seen his wife and daughter dead in the ruins of his hospital; he sat now with his head in his hands. "I can't do anything," he said. Father Kleinsorge bound more bandage around Father Schiffer's head, moved him to a steep place, and settled him so that his head was high, and soon the bleeding diminished.

The roar of approaching planes was heard about this time. Someone in the crowd near the Nakamura family shouted, "It's some Grummans coming to strafe us!" A baker named Nakashima stood up and commanded, "Everyone who is wearing anything white, take it off." Mrs Nakamura took the blouses off her children, and opened her umbrella and made them get under it. A great number of people, even badly burned ones, crawled under bushes and stayed there until the hum, evidently of a reconnaissance or weather run, died away.

It began to rain. Mrs Nakamura kept her children under the umbrella. The drops grew abnormally large, and someone shouted, "The Americans are dropping gasoline. They're going to set fire to us!" (This alarm stemmed from one of the theories being passed through the park as to why so much of Hiroshima had burned: it was that a single plane had sprayed gasoline on the city and then somehow set fire to it in one flashing moment.) But the drops were palpably water, and as they fell, the wind grew stronger and stronger, and suddenly—probably because of the tremendous convection set up by the blazing city—a whirlwind ripped through the park. Huge trees crashed down; small ones were uprooted and flew into the air. Higher, a wild array of flat things revolved in the twisting funnel—pieces of iron roofing, papers, doors, strips of matting. Father Kleinsorge put a piece of cloth over Father Schiffer's eyes, so that the feeble man would not think he was going crazy. The gale blew Mrs Murata, the mission housekeeper, who was sitting close by the river, down the embankment at a shallow, rocky place, and she came out with her bare feet bloody. The vortex moved out onto the river, where it sucked up a waterspout and eventually spent itself.

After the storm, Mr Tanimoto began ferrying people again, and Father Kleinsorge asked the theological student to go across and make his way out to the Jesuit Novitiate at Nagatsuka, about three miles from the center of town, and to request the priests there to come with help for Fathers Schiffer and LaSalle. The student got into Mr Tanimoto's boat and went off with him. Father Kleinsorge asked Mrs Nakamura if she would like to go out to Nagatsuka with the priests when they came. She said she had some luggage and her children were sick— they were still vomiting from time to time, and so, for that matter, was she— and therefore she feared she could not. He said he thought the fathers from the Novitiate could come back the next day with a pushcart to get her.

Later in the afternoon, when he went ashore for a while, Mr Tanimoto, upon whose energy and initiative many had come to depend, heard people begging for food. He consulted Father Kleinsorge, and they decided to go back into town to get some rice from Mr Tanimoto's Neighborhood Association shelter and from the mission shelter. Father Cieslik and two or three others went with them. At first, when they got among the row of prostrate houses, they did not know where they were; the change was too sudden, from a busy city of two hundred and forty-five thousand that morning to a mere pattern of residue in the afternoon. The asphalt of the streets was still so soft and hot from the fires that walking was uncomfortable. They encountered only one person, a woman, who said to them as they passed, "My husband is in those ashes." At the mission, where Mr Tanimoto left the party, Father Kleinsorge was dismayed to see the building razed. In the garden, on the way to the shelter. He noticed a pumpkin roasted on the vine. He and Father Cieslik tasted it and it was good. They were surprised at their hunger, and they ate quite a bit. They got out several bags of rice and gathered up several other cooked pumpkins and dug up some potatoes that were nicely baked under the ground, and started back. Mr Tanimoto rejoined them on the way. One of the people with him had some cooking utensils. In the park, Mr Tanimoto organized the lightly wounded women of his neighborhood to cook. Father Kleinsorge offered the Nakamura family some pumpkin, and they tried it, but they could not keep it in their stomachs. Altogether, the rice was enough to feed nearly a hundred people.

Just before dark, Mr Tanimoto came across a twenty-year-old girl, Mrs Kamai, the Tanimoto's next-door neighbor. She was ·crouching on the ground with the body of her infant daughter in her arms. The baby had evidently been dead all day. Mrs Kamai jumped up when she saw Mr Tanimoto and said, "Would you please try to locate my husband?"

Mr Tanimoto knew that her husband had been inducted into the Army just the day before; he and Mrs Tanimoto had entertained Mrs Kamai in the afternoon, to make her forget. Kamai had reported to the Chugoku Regional Army Headquarters—near the ancient castle in the middle of town—where some four thousand troops were stationed. Judging by the many maimed soldiers Mr

Tanimoto had seen during the day, he surmised that the barracks had been badly damaged by whatever it was that had hit Hiroshima. He knew he hadn't a chance of finding Mrs Kamai's husband, even if he searched, but he wanted to humor her. "I'll try," he said.

"You've got to find him," she said. "He loved our baby so much. I want him to see her once more."

Acknowledgements

The Publishers wish to thank the following for their permission to use the material below:

Irwin Shaw, Jonathan Cape Ltd and John Farquharson Ltd for Chapter 21 of *The Young Lions*; J. G. Ballard, Victor Gollancz Ltd and Simon & Schuster, Inc. for Chapters 20-22 of *Empire of the Sun* © 1984 by JG. Ballard; Dell for Chapter 20 of *From Here to Eternity* by James Jones; James A. Michener, William Collins, Sons & Co. Ltd and Macmillan Inc. for *The Landing on Kuralei* from *Tales of the South Pacific*; Macmillan Publishers Ltd and Mr J. Lovat Dickinson for Chapter 6 of *The Last Enemy* by Richard Hillary; Kurt Vonnegut, Jonathan Cape Ltd and Donald G. Farber for Chapter 2 of *Slaughterhouse-Five*; The Peters, Fraser & Dunlop Group Ltd and Little, Brown and Company for an extract from *Officers and Gentlemen* by Evelyn Waugh, Copyright© 1955 by Evelyn Waugh; Chapter 2 of *The Naked and the Dead* by Norman Mailer. Reprinted by permission of the author and the author's agents Scott Meredith Literary Agency, Inc., 845 Third Avenue, New York, New York 10022; Michael Joseph Ltd for Chapter 18 of *Enemy Coast Ahead* by Guy Gibson, VC; Joseph Heller, Jonathan Cape Ltd and Simon & Schuster Inc. for Chapter 9 of *Catch-22*. Copyright© 1955, 61 by Joseph Heller; Raymond Paull and the Octopus Publishing Group, Australia for *The Invasion of Papua* from *Retreat from Kokoda*; Mrs Ronald Seth for Chapters 5 and 6 of *Stalingrad: Point of Return* by Ronald Seth; Nancy Wake, Curtis Brown (Australia) Pty Ltd and Macmillan, Australia for Chapter 9 of *The White Mouse* published by the Macmillan Company of Australia Pty Ltd, Melbourne 1985; The Estate of John Steinbeck, William Heinemann Ltd and Viking Penguin, Inc. for an extract from *The Moon Is Down*; Cassell and Alfred A. Knopf, Inc. for an extract of *The Cruel Sea* by Nicholas Monsarrat; John Hersey and Alfred A. Knopf, Inc. for Chapter 2 of *Hiroshima*. Copyright© 1946, 1985 by John Hersey. Copyright renewed 1973 by John Hersey.

Every effort has been made to clear the copyright material in this book. The Publishers trust that their apologies will be accepted for any errors or omissions.

For the endpapers image:
Dated Event Invasion Map of Fortress Europe, 7th edition, 1944. Map by C C Petersen Publishing and Advertising, Toronto, Canada. Published by Allyn & Bacon, Boston, USA.

DATED EVENTS
INVASION MAP
OF FORTRESS EUROPE

NAVAL BASES — Anglo-American	Russian	Neutral
Anglo-American battlefields + raids	Russian victims 1943-44 advance	
German advance bases	Fortified lines	
Railways	Roads	Canals	Oil pipe lines
PRE-WAR BOUNDARIES	Land depression	Beaches

Shore line protected by cliffs or hills
German aircraft production centers

HOW TO FOLLOW THE INVASION

With this invasion map you will be able to follow the progress of the Allied troops on their way
to smash Germany. On this map are shown the maze of highway communications, these are the
RED lines except in Allied territory where they are shown in WHITE. Railroads are shown
covering the entire continent, these are the BLACK lines.

The plains and valleys are indicated in YELLOW color of the higher
ground. Beaches, depth of water and character of coast line is carried all around the Continent.
Rivers stand out in BLUE, while the tremendously important mountain ranges appear in GREEN.
Note the heavily fortified lines and bombs coming down in bombed areas — these in BLACK.
It will be well for you to remember that major battles are seldom fought on the tops of mountains. For centuries the battles have taken place on the plains, in the valleys, on the beaches
and for communication lines.